Soul of Tyrants

Jonathan Moeller

ISBN: 1484990994
ISBN-13: 978-1484990995

EPIGRAPH

"God, whose law is that he who learns must suffer. And even in our sleep pain that cannot forget, falls drop by drop upon the heart, and in our own despite, against our will, comes wisdom to us by the awful graces of God."

-Aeschylus

OTHER BOOKS BY THE AUTHOR

Child of the Ghosts

Ghost in the Flames

Ghost in the Blood

Ghost in the Storm

Ghost in the Stone

Ghost in the Forge

Demonsouled

Soul of Tyrants

Soul of Serpents

Soul of Dragons

Soul of Sorcery

Soul of Skulls

Soul of Swords

CHAPTER 1
WOLVES AMONG SHEEP

Lord Mazael Cravenlock left the camp and watched the sun rise over the Grim Marches, as he did every morning. The dawn seemed to paint the winter-brown plains the color of blood.

Mazael scowled, his bearded jaw clenching.

The blood might prove real, soon enough.

"My lord?"

A stern-faced boy of about fifteen years stepped to Mazael's side, carrying a pile of armor.

Mazael nodded. "Adalar. I am ready."

Adalar Greatheart grunted. "Hold out your arms, my lord."

Mazael complied. The dawn's bloody rays slanted into the camp, throwing long black shadows. Squires hastened back and forth, bearing arms and armor, polishing shields and sharpening swords. Bacon sizzled over the campfires, and horses neighed and grunted.

Despite his rise to the lordship of Castle Cravenlock, Mazael still wore the battered armor from his days as a wandering, landless knight; a mail shirt, scarred steel cuirass, leather gauntlets, and a helmet. A black surcoat with the House of Cravenlock's three crossed swords was his sole mark of rank.

Around his waist went a worn leather belt with a battered scabbard. In the scabbard rested a magnificent longsword with a golden pommel shaped like a lion's head.

"Send Sir Gerald to me," said Mazael, "and get yourself something to eat before we set out."

"My lord," said Adalar.

"And I mean it," said Mazael, pointing. "Eat something. The other

1

squires can manage themselves long enough for you to eat."

Adalar flashed a rare grin. The boy was sterner than his father, sometimes. "My lord."

Mazael shook his head, crossed his arms, and watched the camp. He had forty knights and their attendant squires with him. More than enough for what he had in mind.

Or so he hoped.

Armor clanked, and Mazael looked over his shoulder. A young, gold-haired man in polished plate and a fine blue surcoat emblazoned with a stylized greathelm walked towards Mazael, followed by a dour, pimpled squire of about thirteen.

"Gerald," said Mazael to his armsmaster. "Are we ready?"

"Soon enough," said Gerald. He scratched a mustache trimmed with razor precision. "We'll be ready to ride soon. Mayhap these ruffians will see reason."

Mazael snorted. "And maybe we'll all sit down for a feast afterwards."

Gerald shrugged. "It does seem unlikely. Wesson! Fetch some breakfast, please."

The pimpled squire grunted and hastened to the cook fires.

"No, it'll come down to steel," said Mazael. "We've dealt with these bands before. Lord Richard killed most of Mitor's damned mercenaries, but the survivors have failed to appreciate the lesson."

"Slow fellows," said Gerald. "A pity your brother didn't think to hire smarter mercenaries."

"Mitor never thought of anything," said Mazael, scowling at the mention of his dead brother, the previous Lord of Castle Cravenlock. "And if he had hired smarter mercenaries, he might still be alive."

"No loss, that," said Gerald. Wesson returned, bearing some bread and bacon. "Perhaps we can talk some sense into this band."

"Not likely."

Gerald shook his head. "You always take such a bleak view," he said, around a mouthful of bacon.

"And I'm usually right," said Mazael. He raised his voice. "Break camp and mount up! Move! I want to be at White Rock before midday!"

The squires began rolling up tents and rounding up the horses. Mazael took a piece of Gerald's bacon and watched the camp vanish. Soon the toiling squires loaded the pack animals, the knights mounted their horses, and they were ready.

A thin knight with a pinched face and a scraggly mustache rode towards Mazael. In his left hand he carried a tall lance crowned with the black-and-silver Cravenlock banner.

"Sir Aulus?" said Mazael.

"My lord," said Sir Aulus Hirdan, his deep voice incongruous against his wasted appearance. "We are ready."

"Good," said Mazael. Adalar returned, leading a large, ill-tempered destrier. The horse looked like it wanted to bite someone. Mazael stepped to the beast's side, running his hand along its neck. The big horse stamped and snorted, throwing its mane.

"Well, Chariot," said Mazael to his war horse. "Once again. You'll kill someone before the day's done."

Chariot almost looked pleased.

Mazael sprang up into the saddle. The squires mounted their palfreys, leading the pack horses, and rode to the side of their knights.

"We ought to say a prayer before we ride out," said Gerald.

"Steel will settle this, not the gods," said Mazael.

"The gods watch over all mortal affairs," said Gerald

"Aye," said Mazael, closing his eyes. He knew that very well, knew it far better than Gerald. "Ride out!"

They rode away to the south.

A few hours later they came to the village of White Rock, near the silent, looming trees of the Great Southern Forest. The village itself huddled within a stout palisade of sharpened logs. White Rock had survived Lord Richard Mandragon's conquest of the Grim Marches, Lord Mitor's failed rebellion, and a small army of corpses animated by necromantic arts.

Compared to that, a band of sixty ragged mercenaries seemed a small threat. And Mazael was determined that no harm would befall White Rock. The village had sworn him loyalty, and Mazael had promised protection.

He drew his knights in a line facing both White Rock and the mercenary camp. White Rock had proven inhospitable to the mercenaries, to judge from the arrow-ridden corpses near the palisade's gate.

"Rabble," said Mazael. He rarely became angry, not since Romaria's death, but faint flicker of anger burned in his chest. These scum dared to prey upon his lands, his people?

"Perhaps they'll be wise enough to stand down," said Gerald, reining in at Mazael's side.

Mazael snorted. "Perhaps. Aulus!"

Sir Aulus spurred his horse forward, the Cravenlock banner flapping, his right hand raised in parley. The ragged mercenaries turned and faced him, muttering with interest.

"Hear ye all!" Aulus called, his stentorian voice booming over the plains. "Mazael, Lord of Castle Cravenlock, commands you to lay down your arms and depart peacefully from his lands at once. Amnesty shall be offered to those who surrender!"

JONATHAN MOELLER

A chorus of jeers and ragged laughs went up. The largest of the mercenaries, a hulking brute in rusty mail, whirled and dropped his trousers.

"Disgraceful," said Gerald. Aulus turned and galloped back to Mazael's line.

"I told you," said Mazael. He reached down and drew his longsword. Lion's blade gleamed like blue ice in the dull winter sunlight.

"They've no respect for you," said Gerald, shaking his head.

"Of course not," said Mazael. "I'm Mitor's younger brother. Mitor was fat and weak and stupid. Why should I be any different?"

Of course, Mazael was only Mitor's half-brother. But Gerald didn't know that, and neither did the mercenaries.

If they had known Mazael's true father, they might have regarded him differently.

With outright terror, most likely.

Gerald grinned, drawing his own blade. "Shall we teach them otherwise?"

"I suppose so," said Mazael.

In his younger days, he had felt a raging joy at the prospect of battle, a ferocious and delighted bloodlust. Since Romaria had died, he had felt nothing of the sort. Now he felt only disgust and a vague weariness. This was necessary, and nothing more.

But if he had to fight, he would fight well.

He adjusted his helm, pointed Lion at the mercenaries, and kicked Chariot to a gallop. The big horse snorted and rumbled forward. A half-second later Mazael's knights surged after him, swords and lances gleaming.

The mercenaries gaped at them for a moment, then lunged for their weapons in a scrambled panic. They managed to form into a ragged line, but too late to stop the knights. Mazael beat aside a spear, reversed Lion, and took off a mercenary's head in a sweeping backhand. Chariot ran down another, pummeling the man to bloody pulp.

The knights tore through the line of mercenaries. Nearly half had been cut down, without loss to Mazael's men, while the rest fled in all directions.

"Reform!" yelled Mazael, wheeling Chariot around. "Another charge!"

"Stand, lads!" roared the big mercenary in the rusty mail shirt, brandishing a ridged mace. "Stand and fight, if you don't want to die!"

Some of the mercenaries kept running. Others turned, gripped their weapons, and set themselves. Mazael guided Chariot towards the mercenary leader, raising Lion for an overhand slash.

The mercenary snarled and flung his mace at the last minute, jumping out of Chariot's path. The mace's head crashed into Mazael's breastplate with a shriek of tortured metal. Mazael hissed in pain, heard something crack within his chest. He reeled in the saddle, Lion dangling from his grasp. The mercenary yanked a dagger free and sprang, howling, and Mazael

4

thrust out. The mercenary impaled himself and died twitching.

Mazael kicked the dying man free and found that the battle had ended. Most of the mercenaries lay dead and dying, the brown grasses stained with red blood. The few survivors stood in a ring of scowling knights. Mazael grunted in pain and trotted Chariot towards the ring. He knew the pain well; he had broken ribs more than once.

The pain lessened as he rode, an odd tingling spreading through his chest.

"Mazael!" Gerald rode towards him, blood dripping from the length of his longsword. "Are you well? I saw that mace hit you…"

"I'll be fine," said Mazael.

"Perhaps you should…"

"I said I'll be fine," said Mazael, trying not to growl. "Any losses?"

"None," said Gerald. Wesson rode up and set to work cleaning Gerald's sword. "I think you were the only one wounded."

"Embarrassing," said Mazael. He jerked his head at the captured mercenaries. "How many prisoners?"

"Seven," said Gerald. Adalar joined them, cast a concerned look at Mazael.

"Seven," repeated Mazael. "Good enough. Question them."

"Why?" said Gerald.

"We've taken a half-dozen of these mercenary bands in the last three months," said Mazael. "Mercenaries love easy plunder, not armed opposition. They should have fled long ago." He took a long, painful breath. "I think someone's hiring them."

Gerald looked stunned. "Who would do such a thing?"

"I don't know," said Mazael. "Not all my vassals were pleased to see me replace Mitor." He shrugged. "Lord Richard, maybe. Or Toraine Mandragon. Or perhaps even your father."

"My father would not do something so underhanded!" said Gerald.

Mazael shrugged again. "Perhaps not. But I doubt he was pleased to hear of me becoming Lord of Castle Cravenlock. Sir Aulus!" Mazael's herald rode over. "Question them. If I am pleased with their answers, they might yet leave the Grim Marches alive." He considered this for a moment. "Possibly."

Aulus nodded and went about his work.

Mazael sat in the saddle and waited.

A fierce itching filled his chest, as if the broken rib was knitting itself back together.

###

"Sir Roger Gravesend," said Gerald, disgusted.

The surviving mercenaries trudged away, relieved of their weapons, armor, coin, and cloaks.

"I should have known," said Mazael, shaking his head. "He was not happy when Mitor was killed."

"And rumor held that he followed the San-keth way," said Gerald. "Is he at Castle Cravenlock?"

"As it happens, yes," said Mazael, turning Chariot around. "Perhaps we'll have a long talk with him."

"How is your chest?" said Gerald.

Mazael frowned. "What?"

Gerald pointed. "That mace. It looked like a fierce blow."

"That?" said Mazael. He had forgotten. "It's fine. The armor turned the worst of it."

Gerald gave the dent in Mazael's breastplate a dubious look.

Mazael forced a smile. "I'm well. Enough talk. Let's go home."

Gerald nodded. "I would enjoy spending a night under a proper roof." He rode for the squires and knights, herding them into the line.

Mazael sighed in relief. Gerald had not noticed. It would take weeks for a normal man to recover from a badly broken rib.

Mazael's injury had healed in a matter of minutes.

No one knew the truth. Romaria had known, but she was dead at the hands of the Old Demon.

Mazael was Demonsouled, the Old Demon's son, and the blood of the Great Demon flowed through his veins.

CHAPTER 2
THE LORD OF CASTLE CRAVENLOCK

Two days' ride took them home.

Castle Cravenlock squatted atop a craggy hill, a massive pile of dark stone, grim towers, and arched windows. The Cravenlock banner flapped from the highest tower, while the banners of Mazael's knights and vassals flew from the lower battlements. It was an ugly castle. Romaria had said it looked like the lair of an evil wizard from a children's tale, and Mazael agreed with her.

Still, it was home.

Mazael and his knights rode past flocks of sheep, heavy with winter wool, and through the castle's town, an overgrown village of four thousand people. They clattered up the road and to the castle's barbican. The watchmen bowed and stepped aside. Mazael reined up before the keep's gates, dirty snow and frozen earth churning beneath Chariot's hooves. Servants hurried to and fro, intent on their various tasks. Chickens waddled through the yard, pecking for dropped corn.

Adalar took Chariot's reins as Mazael swung out of the saddle. A small army of squires and pages hastened out of the keep, assisting their knights. Every now and again Adalar cast them fierce glares, and Mazael grinned. If the castle's squires feared Adalar, then the pages held him in naked terror.

"Sir Gerald!" called Mazael, pulling off his leather gauntlets. "See to things here!"

Gerald nodded and let Adalar and Wesson drive the squires.

Mazael crossed the courtyard, entered the keep, and strode into the castle's cavernous great hall. Stale smoke drifted beneath the vaulted stone arches. Perhaps twenty men lay wrapped in blankets on the floor, snoring, weapons and armor piled besides their bedrolls. Mazael was lord of over four hundred knights and a few dozen minor lords. From forty to eighty loitered about his hall at any given time. Some came to fulfill their obligations of armed service. Some came because they had nothing better to do. Sir Aulus Hirdan served as herald year-round to escape his nagging wife.

And one, Sir Roger Gravesend, had come to kill Mazael.

Mazael spotted Sir Roger sleeping near one of the fireplaces. In his younger days, Mazael might have simply walked over and killed the man. But Mazael had rejected his Demonsouled heritage, renounced it at great cost, and would not murder Sir Roger out of hand.

Besides, he had better ways to deal with Sir Roger.

Mazael made his way unnoticed to the dais at the far end of the hall and climbed the lord's private stair. It led to what had once been the lord and lady's apartments. The apartments also contained one of the concealed entrances to the catacombs and San-keth temple beneath the castle. Mazael had no wish to ever set foot in that accursed temple again. So he had ordered the rooms walled up. Now only a narrow corridor remained, leading to the chapel's balcony.

He entered the balcony and looked into the chapel. Incense hung heavy in the air, wisps of smoke curling beneath the domed ceiling. A half-dozen priests moved about the altar, droning prayers in the ancient tongue of Tristafel, beseeching Amatheon and Amater and Joraviar for protection.

The balcony was deserted but for a slender woman with dark hair and a green gown, her head bowed, lips moving soundlessly. The priests concluded their ceremony, and Mazael crossed the balcony and sat beside the woman.

She looked up in surprise, sad green eyes widening, and smiled. "Mazael!"

"Rachel," he said.

His sister leaned over and kissed his cheek.

Of course, she was only his half-sister. But Mazael didn't care. She was his sister, by blood or not. They had been through too much together. They had outlived their ruthless and cruel mother, had endured Lord Adalon's defeat, and had survived Lord Mitor's doomed rebellion and San-keth worship. Mazael had almost killed Rachel, succumbed to the Old Demon's hideous taunts and taken her life.

He was glad he hadn't.

"You're back early," said Rachel. She hesitated. "Did things go well?"

"Well enough," said Mazael. "Another band of Mitor's mercenaries decided to indulge in a little looting and raping before they left. We persuaded them otherwise."

Rachel's lip twitched. "I'm sure. Is...Gerald all right?"

"Untouched," said Mazael.

"A letter came from Lord Malden while you were gone," said Rachel.

"It did?" said Mazael, thinking of Gerald's father. "What did it say?"

"Nothing," said Rachel. "At least nothing of importance. Only that he was sending his son Sir Tobias Roland here to negotiate the terms of the marriage." She hesitated. "Do...you think he will say yes?"

"I don't know," said Mazael. Lord Malden Roland was a proud and masterful man, and revealed little of his mind even to trusted servants.

Lord Malden might not approve of Mazael becoming Lord of Castle Cravenlock.

And he might not approve of his youngest son marrying Mazael's sister.

"I don't know," repeated Mazael, feeling a twinge of guilt. He had spent fifteen years as a landless knight, fighting and drinking and whoring his way across the High King's lands. Rachel had spent those same years trapped at Castle Cravenlock, dominated by Mitor, twisted bit by bit to the worship of the San-keth.

She gave him a brittle smile. "You think there might not be a wedding?"

Mazael sighed. "Lord Richard gave his approval, but grudgingly, and he might change his mind."

Rachel scoffed. "What does Richard Mandragon's will mean to us?" Rachel had never quite gotten over her hatred of the man who had defeated her father.

"He is the liege lord of the Grim Marches, our liege lord, like it or not," said Mazael, "and could crush us, if he chose. But he won't. It's Gerald's father that worries me."

"Lord Malden."

Mazael nodded. "He may not agree to this marriage."

"Why not?"

"He hates Lord Richard," said Mazael. "He's never forgiven him for Belifane's death." Mazael looked at the chapel's windows, remembering the bloody sunrise. "He's wanted revenge for fifteen years. If he has to cover the Grim Marches in a sea of blood to kill Lord Richard, he'll do it." Mazael sighed again. "And he might want to kill me."

"You? Why?"

"I was a knight in his court," said Mazael. "Since I've become Lord of Castle Cravenlock, he'll expect me to side with him against Lord Richard."

"And you won't."

"No. No more wars. I've seen enough of it. I will fight if I must, but only if I must." Mazael remembered the Old Demon's gloating boasts and shuddered. The Old Demon had arranged Lord Mitor's rebellion, manipulated everything, for the sole purpose of releasing Mazael's Demonsouled nature. What might the Old Demon do with a war between Lord Richard and Lord Malden?

And the Old Demon had other children. Romaria had saved him from his Demonsouled nature, but Mazael doubted his Demonsouled half-brothers and half-sisters had been so fortunate. What might they do in such a war?

"Mazael?"

Mazael shook himself out of the reverie.

"You looked so grim," said Rachel, looking at him with a hint of fear.

"I will not slaughter men to slake Lord Malden's pride," said Mazael. "If that ruins the marriage, I am sorry."

"I love Gerald, Mazael," said Rachel.

"What has love to do with marriage?" said Mazael.

"Nothing, usually," said Rachel. "Our mother and father hated each other. Mitor and his wife loathed each other." She shrugged. "I always expected Mitor to marry me to someone I would hate. Some lord or knight or even a bandit chief he needed. Then you betrothed me to Gerald. I thought you did that…to keep me from falling into my old ways, the San-keth worship."

"I did," said Mazael.

"I know," said Rachel. "But he's different than I thought he would be. He's not like Mitor. He's…helped me so much, he's kind and thoughtful. I love him, Mazael. I want to marry him."

Mazael squeezed her hand. "If I can make it happen, I will. If you're married to Gerald, Lord Malden can't move against Lord Richard without my aid, and I won't help him war against Lord Richard."

"And if I marry Gerald, I'll be happy," said Rachel.

"That as well," said Mazael. "Though if Lord Malden goes to war against Lord Richard, I doubt you, or anyone else, will be happy." He thought again of the Old Demon's boasts.

"Are you sure you are well?" said Rachel. "You looked a bit pale."

"I need to ask you something. How well do you know Sir Roger Gravesend?"

"Sir Roger?" said Rachel, frowning. "Better than I would like. He supported Mitor from the beginning, encouraged him to rebel," she hesitated, "and went right along with him when Skhath encouraged the San-keth worship."

"So he worshipped the snake-god with Mitor," said Mazael, avoiding Rachel's own participation in the foul rites.

"He did," said Rachel. "Mitor trusted him as much as he trusted anyone, except maybe Simonian." Mazael winced at the mention of the necromancer's name, the disguise the Old Demon had assumed. "Mitor would probably have wound up giving me to him, except…"

"Except he pledged you to Skhath," said Mazael. Rachel would have become the bride of the San-keth priest, given birth to changelings of mixed San-keth and human blood.

Rachel closed her eyes. "Don't remind me. I don't like to think of those days."

"I'm sorry."

Rachel shook her head. "Don't be. Why did you ask?"

"Sir Roger is hiring those mercenary bands," said Mazael.

"Why would he do that?"

Mazael shrugged. "I don't know. Revenge, perhaps. Or maybe he's trying to kill me. I doubt he appreciates my lordship."

"If he's trying to kill you, why not hang him at once?" said Rachel.

"No proof," said Mazael.

"He's trying to kill you!" said Rachel, a hint of hysteria entering her voice. "You're the only hope Castle Cravenlock has. If you die…I don't know what we'd do…"

"Rachel," said Mazael, taking her shoulders. "After surviving Mitor, Skhath, and Simonian, I think it will take more than a petty knight to kill me."

"If you say so," said Rachel.

"I do," said Mazael. "Go. Gerald's probably wondering where you."

Rachel smiled. "He would be." She rose, adjusting her skirts.

"Wait." Mazael caught her wrist. "Do you know where Sir Nathan and Timothy are?"

"The north wall, I think," she said, brushing back a stray lock of hair.

"Thank you," said Mazael. "I'll see you at dinner, then."

She smiled, kissed him again, and vanished through the door.

Mazael stared at the altar, watching the last of the smoke dissipate. He wanted Rachel's marriage to Gerald, wanted it as a lever to keep Lord Richard and Lord Malden from each other's throats. He had expected Gerald to treat Rachel gallantly, Rachel to serve as a dutiful wife.

He had not expected the two of them to fall in love.

Mazael had failed Rachel before. Wars or no wars, he did not want to fail her again. He glanced at the stairs before the altar, his vision blurring a bit. Romaria had fallen there, slain at the hands of the Old Demon. Mazael would have married her, as Gerald was now going to marry Rachel…

He could brood later. Right now he had work to do. He gathered his cloak about him, exited the keep, and climbed the stairs to the castle's curtain wall. The wind was warmer than it had been earlier in the day.

Three men stood in a loose circle on the northern wall, arguing with each other. The first looked as old and tough as an ancient oak, the hilt of a greatsword rising over his shoulder. The second wore all black, and had a nervous, twitchy look. The third man was red-faced, balding, and paused every now and again to wipe his brow.

"The castle is still here," said Mazael, "so I will assume you have done well."

As one the men turned to look at him.

"Lord Mazael," said the old man, handing him a rolled sheet of vellum.

"Thank you, Sir Nathan," said Mazael, taking the scroll and opening it. At the bottom of the page glimmered the silver greathelm sigil of the Rolands. "From Lord Malden, I presume?"

"How did you know?" said the nervous, black-clad man.

"Rachel mentioned it," Mazael told Timothy deBlanc, his court wizard. Timothy looked like a frightened farmer, but had stayed at Mazael's side through some very dangerous times. "Sir Tobias will be here any day, I see."

"Aye," said the fat man, wiping his brow again. "Lord Malden must have sent the letter only a few days before Sir Tobias left Knightcastle. We should have ample food to lodge Sir Tobias and his men." He hesitated, biting his lip. "Though I hope Sir Tobias doesn't wish to stay overlong."

"Knowing Sir Tobias, Master Cramton, I doubt it," said Mazael. Cramton served as Mazael's seneschal. The man had the courage of a mouse, but could smell graft and embezzlement from fifty miles away. "See to the preparations."

"My lord." Cramton hastened away.

"Was my son's service satisfactory, my lord?" said Sir Nathan.

"Quite," said Mazael. "You always ask the same question, and I always give you the same answer. Sir Gerald is in the courtyard, and could use your help, probably."

"He is the armsmaster," said Sir Nathan, "not I." Sir Nathan had been Castle Cravenlock's armsmaster for decades, until Mitor had stripped him of the post. Mazael had tried to give it back to Nathan, more than once, but the old knight always refused.

"Go help him anyway."

A ghost of a smile touched Nathan's weathered face. "My lord." He left, leaving Mazael alone with Timothy.

"How goes the work?" said Mazael.

"Well enough," said Timothy, scratching his chin. He coughed and squinted at the wall. "Lucan and I have almost finished the ward-spell against the undead. No San-keth clerics will enter the castle without our knowledge."

"Good," said Mazael. "I have had enough of the San-keth to last a lifetime."

Timothy offered a vigorous nod. "As have I."

"What of the catacombs?" The hidden San-keth temple had lain beneath Castle Cravenlock for centuries, forgotten and secret. Mazael would have collapsed it, if doing so would have not brought most of the castle crashing down.

"Mostly sealed, I'm pleased to say," said Timothy. "The images have been smashed, the bas-reliefs destroyed. I'll have the peasants fill the entrances with as much rubble as possible. With any luck, no eyes will ever see that place again. The destruction of the temple's library is the most difficult remaining task."

Mazael snorted. "How hard can it be to destroy a pile of scrolls and books? Just toss the damned things into the fire and have done with it."

"They won't burn, I'm afraid," said Timothy. "Most of them are warded by powerful spells. A few of the books have protections that are, ah, dangerous, and will blast a man's mind if he opens the cover. Lucan and I must go through them one by one, pierce the warding spells, and destroy the books."

Mazael thought for a moment. "Is Lucan's help useful?"

"Invaluable, my lord," said Timothy. He seemed to brace himself. "In all honesty, I must say that he is a far more skilled than I. He would make a better court wizard."

"No," said Mazael. "Lucan is…not a man others trust. Or even like."

"No," agreed Timothy. "He…is moody, certainly. But he has never done anything to alarm me. I don't understand why he's so feared."

"You wouldn't," said Mazael. Lucan was a more powerful wizard than Timothy. But Timothy was loyal and plainspoken. And folk, noble and common alike, feared and loathed wizards. Timothy rarely inspired such fear.

Besides, Mazael trusted Timothy.

He did not trust Lucan Mandragon.

"I will finish the wards as soon as possible," said Timothy. He hesitated. "The San-keth will come again, someday. For revenge."

"Oh, they will," said Mazael. "But we'll be ready."

Timothy nodded, though he did not look very confident.

"And your other duties?" said Mazael.

"I've finished the ward-spells around the granaries," said Timothy. He shrugged. "I think I did them right. With any luck, rats won't be a problem this year. Though I'll have to rework them next season."

"Good enough," said Mazael, clapping the wizard's shoulder. Timothy smiled, bowed, and hastened away. Mazael stood on the wall for a moment, watching the castle, his castle, bustle with activity. The place had lost much of the pall that had hung over it during Mitor's rule. The Grim Marches were half-desolate, had never quite recovered from Lord Adalon's defeat. More ruined villages than prosperous ones filled the plains. Mazael meant to change that. He wanted his people to be prosperous and fat and happy, safe from bandits and cruel lords.

He looked up.

A dark-cloaked shape stood atop the highest tower of the keep, gazing to the west.

That dark figure might hold the key to the Grim Marches's prosperity or destruction.

It was no use putting it off. Mazael descended into the courtyard and circled around the back of the keep, past the kitchens. Chickens destined for the table picked at the barren earth, while the sheep huddled together in their pen. A half-dozen servants burst from the kitchen doors, carrying buckets. A young woman in a rough skirt and a white peasant blouse stalked after them, waving a wooden spoon and shouting orders.

"And see that you fill the buckets to the brim this time! When I tell you I want six buckets of water, I want six buckets of water, by all the gods." She slapped the spoon against her hand. "Run!" She turned, saw Mazael, and offered him a brilliant, albeit gap-toothed, smile.

"My lord Mazael," she said, gripping her skirt and doing a deep curtsy.

He saw right down the front of her blouse.

"Madame Bethy," said Mazael, smiling, despite himself. "All's well in the kitchens?"

"Well enough, my lord," she said, her smile widening, "though we don't see nearly enough of you."

Bethy was mistress of the kitchens, and ruled them with a firm hand that made Adalar and his father look downright mild.

Mazael suspected she also wanted to become his mistress.

"Do the new servants give you much trouble?" said Mazael.

"No end of it," said Bethy, snorting. "Not a one of them knows which end of a spoon is which." She stepped forward, lowering her voice, and her scent, smoke mixed with sweat, flooded into Mazael's nostrils. He stifled an urge to smell her hair. "But none of them are snake-kissers. I'd know."

"Good," said Mazael. The folk of Mazael's lands had abandoned the San-keth faith, or so they claimed. Mazael did not doubt that more than a few holdouts remained, praying to Sepharivaim in hidden cellars and abandoned barns. "Keep a close eye on them."

"I will," said Bethy. "If I find any, I'll tell you at once." Her expression softened, became playful, and she stepped so close to Mazael that she almost touched him. "In private, perhaps, when my lord is alone?"

Mazael stared at her. The heat from the kitchens' fires had made her sweat, given her face a slight sheen. Her hair rested in an untidy bun atop her head, but it only exposed the curve of her neck.

"So mighty a lord," she murmured, "ought not to be alone."

Mazael had not lain with a woman for over a year. The Old Demon had taken Romaria from him before they ever had the chance. But Romaria was dead and Mazael was not, and Bethy was here and willing. But Mazael dared not sleep with her, nor with any other woman.

Mazael was Demonsouled, son of the Old Demon.

His tainted blood, his curse of murder and rage, would pass on to his children.

And he had not led a chaste life before learning the truth of his heritage. Suppose he had fathered a Demonsouled child on some merchant's widow, on a long-forgotten whore? Suppose he had fathered more than one?

Mazael dared not take that risk, no matter how much a woman made his blood boil.

"If you find any snake-kissers," said Mazael, his voice a bit hoarse, "let me know at once."

Bethy looked disappointed, but smiled again. "Of course, my lord." She did another curtsy, letting Mazael see down her blouse again, and vanished into the kitchens.

"Damn her," Mazael muttered.

The guards at the keep's gates bowed to him and pulled open the doors at his approach. Mazael would never get used to that. He nodded to the guards, took to the stairs, and climbed to the top of the keep.

He stepped onto the highest turret, the wind tugging at his hair and cloak.

The Grim Marches stretched away in all directions, flat and brown. Gray clouds covered the sky, slashed with red light from the rising sun. Spirals of smoke rose from the chimneys in the town below.

A man stood at the battlements, wrapped in a voluminous black cloak.

"So you've returned," said the man, not turning. His voice, as always, held a sardonic edge, as if amused at a private, cruel joke.

"So I have," said Mazael, his hand twitching to Lion's hilt. "Surprised? Or disappointed?"

"Neither. You have, Lord Mazael, proven remarkably difficult to kill." The voice's dark amusement grew. "To your late brother's great dismay, no doubt."

"I'm sure," said Mazael, walking to the cloaked man's side.

The top of the black cowl came to Mazael's bearded jaw.

"Another glorious morning in the Grim Marches," said the man. He had a pale, gaunt face, and eyes like glittering disks of obsidian. Many men named him the Dragon's Shadow in a mixture of scornful mockery and sheer terror.

They had good reason to fear him. Lucan Mandragon, son of Richard Mandragon, was the most powerful wizard in the Grim Marches.

He could not have been older than twenty.

"The mercenaries proved foolish enough to fight?" said Lucan.

"As always."

"Ah," said Lucan. His cruel smile seemed out of place on such a young man. "The bloody sunrises of the Grim Marches. Appropriate, really. Given that the Grim Marches themselves may soon drown in blood."

"Not if I can do anything about it," said Mazael.

"Can you?" said Lucan. "I have never met Lord Malden, but he does not seem a man to forgive the death of a son."

"Sir Belifane's death was his own fault," said Mazael, "not your father's."

"I doubt Lord Malden views matters with such equanimity."

"Lord Malden can't fight Lord Richard without my aid," said Mazael. "And if Rachel marries Gerald Roland, Lord Malden won't get my help."

"My father will consider such a marriage a threat to his power. And my noble lord father," Lucan's sneer intensified, "is not a man to suffer challenges."

"He doesn't want war, either," said Mazael. "He told me so himself."

Lucan scoffed. "He doesn't want war because he doesn't believe he can win. If my father ever has the chance to rid himself of Malden Roland, he will do so ruthlessly and without hesitation."

"And he cannot do so without my aid," said Mazael, "and so, we will have no war."

The younger man stared at him. Mazael met the black gaze without flinching. Lucan had stayed at Castle Cravenlock for over a year, at Lord Richard's express wish, yet Mazael had never been able to determine just what Lucan wanted. The Dragon's Shadow had a black reputation, yet Mazael had seen no reason for it, save for Lucan's constant foul humor.

Lucan smiled without rancor. He rarely did so, yet the black mood seemed to fall from his face, and for a moment he seemed an entirely different man. "A noble goal, Lord Mazael. Certainly noble." His face hardened, the mask returning. "Now let us see if you can achieve it."

"I will," said Mazael.

"And likely you'll fail," said Lucan. "Strive for peace all you wish. But it will come to war. Blood and terror in the end." He waved his hand over the expanses of the Grim Marches. "It always does."

Mazael thought of the Old Demon standing on the altar in Castle Cravenlock's chapel, his mocking, hideous boasts. "No. It need not."

But Mitor and his wife had died there, as had the San-keth priest Skhath.

As had Romaria.

"We will not come to war if I can avoid it," said Mazael.

Lucan inclined his head, yielding nothing.

"Now. Tell me. What do you know of Sir Roger Gravesend?" said Mazael.

"A braying ass. A man without wisdom, subtlety, or any trace of wit. Though a competent enough swordsman."

"He has been hiring the mercenary bands," said Mazael.

A dark eyebrow rose. "Has he? It seems a wasted effort."

"I wonder where he obtained the gold," said Mazael. "From your father, perhaps?"

"My father?" Lucan looked amused. "I am hardly one to sing of the praises of Lord Richard, the great and mighty Dragonslayer, but he is not one to throw his gold down a black hole."

"He approves only grudgingly of Rachel's betrothal to Gerald," said Mazael. "He might use a man like Sir Roger to show his disapproval."

Lucan laughed aloud. "If my father were unhappy with you, he'd come here himself, with his armies, raze this ugly pile of a castle to the ground, and mount your head on a pike." He laughed again, the sound ugly. "Or he'd just have me kill you."

Mazael dropped his hand to Lion's hilt. "You might try."

They glared at each other for a moment, the wind snapping their cloaks.

Lucan sighed. "A futile gesture, since my father has not ordered me to kill you. In fact, he's quite pleased with you." He shrugged. "You're certainly an improvement over that toadstool Mitor, at least."

"High praise," said Mazael. "Where do you think Sir Roger's getting his gold?"

"The San-keth, probably."

"The San-keth? Why?" said Mazael.

Again Lucan's eyebrow rose. "Why not? They have every reason to wish you and Lady Rachel dead. You killed a San-keth priest. And your sister betrayed them. In their eyes she is now an apostate." Lucan smirked. "And no faith has ever been tolerant of apostates."

"A clumsy way to go about it," said Mazael.

"It is," agreed Lucan, "quite clumsy. I have seen better. The San-keth have thrice tried to murder my father. Fortunately, my father had my aid," his lip twitched, "however unappreciated."

"I will find out the truth tomorrow, at court," said Mazael.

"And just how shall you accomplish this feat?"

"A peasant has come to the castle, bringing accusations against Sir Roger," said Mazael. "I'll need your help."

Lucan smirked. "In what fashion?"

"You will tell me if Sir Roger speaks the truth or not," said Mazael.

"Ah," breathed Lucan. "So I see. Well." His black eyes glittered like glass knives. "This ought to be interesting. I'll look forward to it."

Mazael nodded. Timothy claimed not to understand why so many feared Lucan Mandragon.

But Mazael understood, understood quite well.

He turned and left.

###

Mazael hated holding court.

He recognized the necessity, of course. If he wanted his lands to become prosperous and safe, he needed to rule them. Without a strong lord in Castle Cravenlock, marauders and bandits of all sorts would descend on the southern Grim Marches like flies to a corpse.

But, by all the gods, court irritated him. He suffered a never-ending stream of landless knights, petty lordlings, and lords seeking a husband for their daughters. They all wanted money, or lands, or for Mazael to fight their enemies.

Mazael hated to sit in one place for long. Lord Mitor had held court in the Great Hall, issuing his judgments from his throne-like chair. Mazael preferred to stalk the Great Hall as he listened and spoke. Sometimes he wandered into the courtyard. His court had no choice to follow him, like prostitutes trailing an army. It drove the clerks mad, but that didn't trouble Mazael.

It did not help that Lord Richard had banished the Justiciar Order from his lands. The Justiciar Knights had supported Lord Mitor's rebellion and paid the price. Lord Richard stripped them of their lands and expelled them from the Grim Marches, with the threat of death should they ever return. Richard Mandragon had taken the lion's share of the seized lands for himself, of course. But he had given a goodly portion of them to Mazael.

Lord Malden must have been enraged. The Justiciar Order was one of his closet allies.

Ever since, landless knights and petty lords had besieged Mazael, offering eternal fidelity and service in exchange for land. He had refused most and forcefully evicted the rest.

Now Mazael paced the great hall, fingers drumming on Lion's pommel, listening to the speech of a would-be vassal, yet another landless knight with more ambition than sense.

"My lord Mazael," said the knight, a thick-bearded, red-nosed man with battle-scarred armor, "this manor, from the western bank of the Northwater to the village of Gray Barrow, belongs to my bloodline by right."

"Oh?" said Mazael. He had not heard this argument before. "Why is that?"

"Because," said the knight, "I am Sir Jarron Dracarone, last of that line, and my house was one of the original founders of Dracaryl. We were among the first to swear fealty to the first Lord of Castle Cravenlock, twelve hundred years ago, and served him loyally since."

"You are, are you?" said Mazael. "I've been Lord of this castle for nearly a year, yet I seem to have missed your loyal service."

"My house was banished, centuries ago," said Sir Jarron, "and only now have I returned to claim my ancestral lands."

"What a stirring tale," said Mazael. "Worthy of a high ballad. Lady Rachel?"

Rachel stirred. She sat on the dais, at the high table, besides Gerald. "Lord brother?"

"You're more familiar with the lore of the Grim Marches than I," said Mazael. "Tell me, when was the House of Cravenlock founded?"

"A thousand years ago," said Rachel.

"Really?" said Mazael, glancing sidelong at Sir Jarron. "Not twelve hundred? And, pray, just what happened to the last son of House Dracarone?"

"He died five hundred years ago, along with both his brothers," said Rachel, "at the Battle of Markast Bridge, when the High King overthrew the last king of Dracaryl."

"So," said Mazael, staring at Sir Jarron, who had begun sweating, "you're either the long-lost scion of a noble house five centuries extinct, or you're a particularly incompetent liar. Which one, I wonder?"

"My lord," croaked Sir Jarron, "I…"

"Sir Gerald!" said Mazael. "Please have Sir Jarron shown out." Gerald pointed. Two armsmen stepped to Sir Jarron's side.

"You dare!" said Sir Jarron, scowling. "These are my rightful lands! I will not be denied."

"You may go to Swordgrim and press your suit before Lord Richard, if you like," said Mazael. "But I am far more tolerant of fools than Lord Richard. I am merely banishing you from my lands. Lord Richard would mount your head above his gates as a warning to other charlatans. Safe journeys, sir knight."

Sir Jarron got redder.

The armsmen led him away.

A shadow swirled on one of the balconies. Mazael glanced up. Lucan Mandragon stood at the rail, wrapped in his dark cloak, and titled his head. He stood amongst a gaggle of knights' wives, yet none seemed to notice him. Lucan possessed the ability, spell-granted or otherwise, to move unnoticed among people. He could stand among a crowd and remain utterly unobserved.

Mazael wondered if Lucan had ever used that power on him.

He pushed the disquieting thought away and glanced aside. Sir Roger Gravesend sat on a bench near the high table, his cloak thrown back, his black hair and beard glinting. He spoke in low tones to one of Rachel's maids, making the girl giggle and blush.

He didn't seem like a follower of the San-keth way. But, then, neither had Mitor.

Nor had Rachel, for that matter.

"Sir Aulus!"

"My lord!" said Mazael's herald, straightening from his post by the doors.

"Send in Wat of Bloody Ridge," said Mazael.

Sir Roger's head turned at the mention of the smallest village in his manor.

"The freeman Wat!" said Sir Aulus, his sonorous voice booming through the hall, "freeholder in the village of Bloody Ridge!"

A short, sun-browned man shuffled through the doors, clutching a battered hat in his hands. He wore rough, but clean, homespun, his shoes scraping against the stone floor. A bloodstained bandage wrapped his forehead.

Sir Roger's eyes narrowed, the maid forgotten.

"My lord," said Wat, bowing, "I'm honored to be here...I am, truly..."

"Yes, yes," said Mazael. "Why are you here?"

"My lord," said Wat, bowing again, "I'll..."

"Stand up!" said Mazael. "I can't hear if you talk to the floor."

"My lord." The peasant straightened. "My family's held their land in Bloody Ridge since the time of the old kings. We always paid a third to our lords, as tradition says, no more, no less." He swallowed, eyes darting to Sir Roger. "Then after old Lord Mitor was...ah, died, Sir Roger said..."

"Lies!" said Sir Roger, stalking to Mazael's side. "This peasant lies."

"Is he not Wat of Bloody Ridge?" said Mazael.

"He is," said Sir Roger, "but..."

"And is he not a freeholder in your lands?" said Mazael.

"He was," said Sir Roger, "but..."

"He has not lied yet." Mazael gestured to Wat. "Speak."

Wat swallowed, but kept talking. "Sir Roger told us all the land in the manor was his now, his alone, and that all the folk had to give him two-thirds of their crops. We wouldn't stand for it...we thought maybe his bailiff was just dishonest, that Sir Roger didn't know what was happening. So we went and petitioned him. I showed Sir Roger the paper old kings had given my forefathers, the paper saying the land was ours. Sir Roger laughed at me, threw my paper in the fire! Then he sent his men into the village. They took all the crops, everything. My second son tried to stop them. They," Wat's face worked, "they cut my boy down, and they struck me when I tried to stop them." His fingers twitched at the bandage. "I woke up, and I didn't know what to do. But my wife heard you were a just man, my lord, and she said I should go to you. So I did."

20

"A filthy lie!" said Sir Roger, snarling. "It has always been the tradition of Bloody Ridge that the peasants give two parts of their crops to their lord. The peasants revolted against their rightful lord and I put them down."

Mazael glanced up at the balcony.

Lucan shook his head, smirking.

"That, sir knight, is a lie," said Mazael, "and I become wroth when my vassals lie to me."

"You accuse me of lying?" said Sir Roger.

"Were you not listening?" said Mazael. "And I wish to know something else. Why have you been hiring Mitor's old mercenaries to loot and ravage?"

"What is this?" said Sir Roger. "I have done nothing of the sort!"

Lucan shook his head, lip curling.

"You have," said Mazael. "That is why you've been stealing your peasants' crops, I deem. You needed some way to pay the mercenaries. Another thing, Sir Roger. Did you kiss the snake when my brother still ruled?"

Sir Roger paled. "You issued amnesty to all those who worshipped the snake-god, so long as they confessed."

"I did," said Mazael, "but you never confessed to anything."

"I never worshipped that filthy idol!" said Sir Roger.

Lucan laughed. No one but Mazael heard him.

"A day for lofty tales, it seems," said Mazael. "A lost son of House Dracarone returns to claim his lands, and poor Roger Gravesend has to defend himself from rebellious peasants. Of course, Sir Jarron was a fraud, and you are as well, sir knight. I suspect you kissed the snake, have been displeased with my rule, and now hire mercenaries to show your displeasure. Have I neared the mark?"

Sir Roger's face twisted. "I will not be called a liar!" He began to draw his sword.

Mazael was faster. He stepped forward, seized Sir Roger's wrist, and twisted. Sir Roger hissed, the sword dropping from his hand, and went white with pain.

"Drawing steel against your lord in his own hall?" said Mazael. Sir Roger tried to wrench away, but Mazael tightened his grip and twisted. "You'd abandon both guest right and your vows to your lord? It's a fortunate thing I stopped you. Otherwise I could cut you down right now and no one would protest."

Sir Roger wheezed and dropped to his knees.

"As your previous bailiff is guilty of murder," said Mazael, "you'll need a new one. Wat!"

The peasant gaped at Sir Roger. "My lord?"

"You'd make a fine bailiff, I believe," said Mazael. "Henceforth, you are the bailiff of Bloody Ridge."

Wat's jaw dropped.

"Appointing the bailiff is my right!" groaned Sir Roger through clenched teeth.

"True," said Mazael. "But, alas, the manor of Bloody Ridge seems insufficient for a knight of your stature." He gestured to Sir Gerald, who barked a command. Two more armsmen hastened forward. "Until we find suitable lands for you, you'll remain here, as my honored guest." He let go.

Sir Roger toppled to the floor with a groan.

"Kindly see Sir Roger to his chambers," said Mazael.

The two armsmen dragged the groaning Sir Roger away.

"As it happens," said Mazael, "I would prefer that my vassals only take a fourth of their peasants' crops."

"My lord is generous," said Wat, bowing, "most generous."

"Sir Gerald," said Mazael, "send Wat back to Bloody Ridge, with an appropriate escort of armsmen. He will have to remove the former bailiff, after all."

Gerald gave the orders. Wat left the hall, half-weeping with gratitude.

Mazael sighed and glanced up at the balcony. Lucan smirked, and moved his hands in mocking applause. Then he turned and vanished in a swirl of black cloak.

"Lord Thomas Malacast," called Sir Aulus, thumping his herald's staff against the stone floor, "of Graywind Hold, seeking the Justiciar manor that bordered upon his estate."

Mazael sighed.

###

Hours later, court concluded, Mazael dropped into Mitor's old throne with a sigh, looping his leg over the carved arm. "By all the gods, Adalar, get me some wine."

Adalar glanced at a page, who dashed from the hall.

"Thirsty?" said Gerald, Rachel on his arm. His squire Wesson followed after, still carrying Gerald's shield.

"I could drink a damned river," said Mazael. "Preferably of wine."

The pages returned, bearing a flagon and a goblet of wine. Mazael took the goblet, drained it, and gestured for the page to refill it.

"What are you going to do with Sir Roger?" said Gerald.

"I haven't decided yet," said Mazael. "I could banish him, but he'd only raise a band of brigands and make trouble. I could keep him imprisoned indefinitely." He shrugged, took another drink of wine. "Or perhaps I'll hand him over to Lord Richard."

"Maybe..." Rachel hesitated, looking away, "maybe you should just kill him."

"Rachel!" said Gerald, looking shocked. "A man under Mazael's own roof!"

"He did draw his sword in the hall," said Rachel. "And he's…he's…" She sighed and shook her head, dark hair sliding over her shoulders. "I look at him and fear that he'll bring woe upon us in the future."

"He's powerless enough, locked in the north tower," said Mazael. "He can't harm us from there."

"I know," said Rachel. "It's just…"

"I'll have close watch kept over him," said Mazael. "Perhaps even have Lucan watch him."

"No!" said Rachel.

"Why not?"

"I don't trust Lucan Mandragon," said Rachel. "He's Richard Mandragon's son, for one."

"That's hardly a crime," said Mazael, "and it's only by Lord Richard's sufferance that we still live."

"I know," said Rachel, sighing, "I know. Lucan frightens me, Mazael."

"I agree with my betrothed," said Gerald. "The Dragon's Shadow is not to be trusted."

Mazael glanced at the balconies, but saw no sign of Lucan. "Why not?"

"Rumor has it that he is a powerful necromancer, nearly the equal of Simonian," said Gerald.

"Rumors say many things," said Mazael.

"And…and I see no fear in him," said Rachel. "Of anyone, or anything. Nothing but contempt. I…think he might betray you, one day." She stared at her hands. "Don't you remember? You told me that Lord Richard promised Castle Cravenlock to Lucan, if you died in battle."

Mazael said nothing.

The bas-reliefs had been smashed, the statues broken, the graven images shattered, their rubble used to choke the entrances leading into the temple. Now the corridors, the storerooms, the libraries, the dungeons, and the great temple chamber lay dark and silent. The titanic golden serpent-idol, an image of the snake-god Sepharivaim, had been melted, the gold buried. Only one narrow spiral stairwell led up to the castle.

Once the staircase had been filled with rubble, the San-keth temple would lie buried and forgotten forever.

Or, Lucan Mandragon mused, so Mazael Cravenlock thought.

A boot scraped against stone. Timothy deBlanc came down the stairs, brushing dust from his black coat, a lantern blazing his hand.

"Timothy," said Lucan, inclining his head.

"Lucan," said Timothy. He coughed and waved a hand in front of his face. "I'll be pleased when we're done with this place. I've had quite enough."

"Fear not," said Lucan, taking the lantern and holding it aloft. "Another day's work, and you'll never need to set foot in here again."

Of course, Lucan himself intended to return frequently.

He had long needed a secret place to work without interruption. He had used the vaults under Swordgrim, but his ever-suspicious father knew about it, and Lucan's labors had been hampered to no end. But here, if everyone believed the San-keth temple sealed and forgotten, Lucan could come and go as he pleased.

"Another case of those books and scrolls to destroy," said Timothy, "and we'll be done."

"Or so we think," said Lucan, adjusting his cloak. "I think it would be wise to cast your divinatory spell once again. We may have missed something."

"We were very thorough," said Timothy, frowning.

"Yet we may have missed something," said Lucan, "and it would not reflect well upon us if we left some evil tome to torment future generations."

Timothy nodded, rubbing his goatee. "You're likely right. A moment." He stepped back, pulled a quartz crystal from his pocket, and wrapped it with a length of silver wire. He stepped back, closed his eyes, and began muttering, gesturing with the wire-wrapped crystal. Lucan watched, following the motions of the crystal, feeling the gathering of arcane power as Timothy continued the spell.

The crystal flashed and shimmered. Timothy spoke the last word of the spell and shuddered. The crystal blazed with silver light and went dim. Lucan watched Timothy, ready with a spell of his own.

"Nothing," said Timothy, wiping sweat from his brow. "Rather, nothing else. I sense only the last shelf in the temple's library. Nothing more."

Lucan nodded, hiding a smile of relief.

Timothy had not sensed the cache of books and scrolls Lucan had hidden. The temple's library had proven a marvelous depository of arcane and necromantic lore. Lucan could not let such a treasure trove escape his grasp.

"Good," said Lucan, "good. No reason to become careless, especially before the end."

"A rule applicable to so many situations," said Timothy.

"Quite right," said Lucan, gesturing at the door to the temple's library.

"Shall we?"

They walked down the vaulted corridor and into the temple's library. Ancient bookshelves lined the walls, mantled in shadows and dust. A single shelf held crumbling tomes and bound scrolls. Lucan walked in a circle around the walls, lighting the torches. Timothy gathered up an armful of books and scrolls and dumped them on the long table running the center of the room. Lucan set the lantern on the table, sat down, and they began work.

Lucan muttered the spell to sense magic over a scroll. "A simple warding, no more." He handed it to Timothy. The older man nodded, lit a brass brazier with the lantern, and tossed the scroll into the coals. The scroll snarled with raging green and blue flames for a moment, then crumbled into embers.

Timothy muttered the same spell, tracing a sigil over a closed book. "Ah…a necromantic ward. You'd best do this one, Lucan."

Lucan grunted and examined the book, probing the spell. It was a petty necromantic trick, designed to shrivel the arm of anyone who opened the cover. He shielded himself in a ward and opened the cover. The necromantic enchantment spat green flames, but fizzled against Lucan's protections.

"High Tristafellin," mused Lucan, examining the writing. He shook his head in disgust. "Bastardized. Some pages in San-keth, probably added later." He flipped through the book. It held simple and feeble spells, the sort any idle dilettante might master.

"Perhaps the oft-copied remnants of a work that may have existed in the time of Tristafel," suggested Timothy, tossing a bundle of ragged parchments into the brazier. A glowing snarl of crimson smoke shot upward, lashed against the ceiling, and vanished. "Certainly we've seen other books of that nature."

"Certainly," said Lucan.

Something on the last page caught his eye, a spell written in San-keth.

"Verily," read the spell's description, "many creatures of diverse natures do throng the world, cunning in deception, and servant of Sepharivaim may find himself hard-pressed to tell the True People from the lesser races. Therefore, a skilled adept may perform this ritual, upon a few drops of blood, to learn the true nature of a soul, whether of the True People, mortal men, elder race, and demon-blooded…"

Lucan gazed at the spell with interest.

"Lucan? Is something amiss?"

Lucan looked up. Timothy stared at him with concern, half-rising from his chair.

"I am well," said Lucan. He tipped the book back.

"I feared you had been beguiled by some enchantment."

Lucan laughed. "Certainly not." In one swift motion he tore the page with the spell free, concealed it in his cloak, and tossed the book into the flames. It shuddered with sparks and purple flames, flared with gray light, and then crumbled into glowing dust. "I fail to see how anyone could find value in these scribbled ravings."

"I quite agree," said Timothy, squinting at a tattered scroll. "Lord Mazael was most insistent that they be destroyed. These books are too dangerous."

"Yes," murmured Lucan.

Lord Mazael.

Now there was an enigma. The man mystified him. Mazael Cravenlock had been a landless, rogue knight before becoming a lord. Lucan had dealt with dozens of such men, and they were almost always bloodthirsty and rapacious, eager to expand their wealth and power, whatever the cost.

Yet Mazael wanted peace between Lord Richard and Lord Malden. He could have sided with Lord Malden against Lord Richard. Or he could have broken his old ties with Lord Malden and attacked Knightrealm in Lord Richard's name.

Yet Mazael refused to do either. Such altruistic behavior made Lucan suspicious. What did Lord Mazael really want?

"Once we've finished with this," said Timothy, tearing a scroll into pieces and tossing the shreds into the fire one by one, "we ought to focus further on the wards to sense the undead. Perhaps we should begin with the barbican and gates."

"As you wish," said Lucan, feigning interest. He rather doubted, though, that the San-keth or their minions would bother to come through the gate.

But something besides Lord Mazael's apparent noble character troubled Lucan.

To Lucan's magical senses, Mazael felt unusual, almost blurred, as if his spirit had been scarred by some potent spell.

Or as if two spirits inhabited his flesh.

And he seemed immune to the mindclouding spell Lucan used to move unobserved through the castle. Nor could Lucan read Mazael's thoughts. His spells permitted Lucan to pluck thoughts from the minds of others, usually without much difficulty.

Yet to Lucan's spells, Mazael's mind felt like an impenetrable wall of molten iron.

"I'm grateful for your assistance," said Timothy, "truly. You ought to be the court wizard, not I."

Lucan looked up in surprise, jarred out his musings. "Oh?"

"Your skills far surpass my own," said Timothy.

Lucan laughed. "They do. But what of that? You aren't dreaded and loathed from one end of the Grim Marches to the other. The peasants don't consider you a devil. " A bit of anger rose in Lucan's chest, and to his annoyance, it crept into his voice. He calmed himself and continued. "But it matters not. I would not be Lord Mazael's court wizard, not even if he begged me." He threw a book into the fire with a bit more force than necessary.

"Why is that?" said Timothy.

"Why is what?" said Lucan, watching the book burn.

"Why are you so feared?" said Timothy. He shrugged. "Certainly, you're powerful. And wizards are feared everywhere, though more so in some lands that others."

"I certainly will not be visiting Swordor or Mastaria," said Lucan.

"Nor I," said Timothy. "Neither the Knights Justiciar nor the Knights Dominiar are very favorable to our art. But that is not the point. Why do they fear you so?" He shrugged. "I see no reason for it, after all."

"That is most kind," said Lucan. He stared at the brazier for a moment. "Let us say…I had an unsavory teacher."

One half of his mind laughed and gibbered. The other half recoiled in frightened horror.

"That wasn't your fault," said Timothy.

"No," said Lucan, shaking himself. The dark laughter in his mind faded away. "It was not. But that matters very little." He picked up the next scroll in the diminishing pile. "I wish to speak no more of this."

"Of course," said Timothy. "But if you wish to speak more of it, I will be glad to listen."

Lucan smiled. The expression felt strange, almost alien, on his face. He did not often smile any more. "Thank you. I'll remember that." Of course, he had no intention of ever discussing his past with Timothy, or anyone.

But the thought pleased him, a little bit.

"We should resume work," said Lucan, gesturing at the piled books.

Timothy nodded.

Lucan felt the torn page within his cloak and smiled.

Soon enough, he would solve the riddle of Lord Mazael Cravenlock.

CHAPTER 3
HEIR OF SWORDGRIM

Mazael awoke with a headache and a foul taste in his mouth. He rolled out of bed, walked naked to the table against the wall, and washed out his mouth with a swallow of wine.

He rarely slept well, these days. The Old Demon no longer troubled him with spell-wrought nightmares, but feverish dreams had drifted across his mind like poisoned foam over fouled waters. He had dreamt of Sir Roger, his hands clamped about Rachel's throat, and of giant snakes slithering through the foundations of Castle Cravenlock.

And he saw, over and over again, the killing flare of the Old Demon's spell, saw Romaria topple before the chapel's altar.

Mazael took another swallow of wine. For a moment he wanted to fall back into bed. Today would only bring another succession of scheming vassals and greedy lords. Why even bother? Lucan was right. It would end in blood or death, one way or another.

The thought repulsed him. Mazael growled and pushed the wine away. He had lands to rule and people to lead, and could not do so if he staggered about drunk.

It was still dark, though the sun had just begun to rise, and Adalar and the pages still lay asleep. Mazael saw no reason to wake them and dressed himself. He slipped down the stairs of the King's Tower and into the chilly courtyard.

Gerald and Sir Nathan trained the armsmen and squires just after sunrise. Mazael tapped Lion's pommel and grinned. He had spent too much time dealing with recalcitrant vassals and corrupt knights. A few hours spent thrashing his armsmen and knights would shake off his depression.

He glanced up at the curtain wall and stopped. Gerald and Sir Nathan stood atop the barbican gate, leaning against the battlements. Sir Nathan pointed over the wall, shaking his head. Mazael frowned and joined them.

"Trouble?" said Mazael.

"Possibly," said Gerald. "We were just about to send for you."

Sir Nathan pointed. "Look."

Mazael saw the glimmer of campfires on the horizon. He made out the dark shapes of tents, hazy in the morning gloom.

"How many men?" said Mazael.

"A hundred, possibly," said Sir Nathan. "Maybe one hundred and fifty."

"More mercenaries?" said Gerald.

Sir Nathan shook his head. "The camp is too orderly."

"Then who?" said Gerald.

Mazael shrugged. "We'll just have to wait and see."

The sun crept up, inch by inch, and Mazael saw dozens of tethered horses. Figures moved back and forth through the camp. He saw a banner flapping over the tents, though it was too dark to make out details.

"If they take it into their heads to burn the town, they're close enough to do it," said Sir Nathan.

"Aye," said Mazael. "Gerald. Rouse the squires and the knights. Get them ready. If our visitors ride for the town, we'll sally out and stop them."

Gerald ran from the ramparts.

"He shouldn't run," said Sir Nathan. "He ought to show confidence to his men."

"Well, do you want to be armsmaster?"

"No."

"Then he can run."

Sir Nathan grunted, but said nothing more. The courtyards clattered and echoed as squires led out the horses from the stables, as knights donned armor and helm, picked up sword and shield. In the camp men rolled up tents and mounted horses.

Mazael folded his arms and waited.

The sun brightened, and Mazael saw the black sigil on the red banner. He swore softly.

"We should prepare a welcome," said Sir Nathan.

Mazael saw a black-armored figure emerge from a tent, swing onto a magnificent destrier. "Or maybe we should stay armed."

"Is that not Lord Richard?" said Sir Nathan.

Mazael shook his head. "No. I might have preferred rogue mercenaries. They would have been easier to handle than Toraine Mandragon."

A flicker of surprise went over Sir Nathan's face. "What would Toraine want here?"

"I don't know," said Mazael. Why had Lord Richard's eldest son come here? Toraine's party began riding for the castle, the Mandragon banner flapping overhead. "Let's go find out."

He descended to the courtyard, Sir Nathan at his side. Gerald emerged from the keep with Rachel on his arm. Mitor had considered marrying Rachel to Toraine, and Lord Richard had done likewise. Mazael hoped Gerald didn't do anything rash.

Gerald gave orders, and armsmen moved into an honor guard around the gate. A few moments later a band of horsemen thundered into the courtyard, the Mandragon banner billowing overhead. A dozen knights in gleaming plate followed. In their midst rode a tall man in a strange combination of black chain and dull black plate, riding the most expensive destrier Mazael had ever seen. The rider reined up, pulled off his helmet, and vaulted from the saddle in a single fluid movement. He had piercing black eyes, red hair, and a trimmed beard like a spike of flame.

He looked a lot like Lucan Mandragon, except taller, stronger, and more striking. And where Lucan's expression seemed contemptuous, Toraine's resembled that of a rabid wolf.

Men often said that Toraine was not Demonsouled, but ought to be.

"Lord Heir," said Mazael, inclining his head, using the title Toraine Mandragon insisted upon.

"Lord Mazael," said Toraine, a cold glint in his eye. "My father's favorite vassal. I thought you'd look fatter after a year ruling this," he gestured at the castle's tower, "ugly heap. But you look wasted away. Pity." He thrust out his helmet. A squire in Mandragon livery took it. "Pity indeed. You know, if fat Mitor had managed to kill you instead of the other way around..."

"I didn't kill Mitor," said Mazael.

"Oh, of course," said Toraine. His smirk resembled Lucan's. "If Mitor had killed you, then my father would have killed Mitor." He gestured at the castle again. "Then my father would have given Castle Cravenlock to me. Though I would have torn this wreck down and begun from scratch."

Mazael returned Toraine's smirk. "But as it happened, Skhath killed Mitor, I survived, and Castle Cravenlock is mine, not yours."

Mazael saw Rachel's knuckles whiten as she gripped Gerald's hand.

Toraine scowled. "You're not frightened of me, are you?"

"No," said Mazael. Toraine's squires flinched. "Should I be? You're my liege lord's eldest son. Assuming we both live long enough, you'll be my liege lord, one day. We ought to be the closest of friends."

"Even my closest friends are frightened of me, and rightly," said Toraine, sounding thoughtful. "You should be too."

"Whatever for?" said a scornful voice. "I see no reason to be frightened. Amused, perhaps, but not frightened."

Lucan stepped past Rachel and Gerald, adjusting his black cloak.

Anger flashed across Toraine's face, vanishing behind his smirk. "Why, brother. It has been too long."

"It has been a year," said Lucan, "and not at all long enough."

"Not long enough?" said Toraine. "I had thought you would want to return to Swordgrim and end your banishment."

"It was not banishment, as you well know," said Lucan. "I am weary of Swordgrim and weary of you, my dear brother. Or had you forgotten that? Just as you seem to have forgotten that our lord father promised Castle Cravenlock to me if Lord Mazael fell, not to you."

Toraine laughed, his eyes narrowed. "Then you ought to count yourself lucky, Lord Mazael. Those Lucan finds inconvenient tend to die most mysteriously."

"I find you inconvenient, not mention dull and tiresome," said Lucan, his glower a dark mirror of Toraine's, "and yet you still live."

Toraine's hand dropped to the hilt of the curved blade at his belt. "A threat against your future liege lord, brother? I ought to strike you dead for that."

"You are not my liege lord yet," said Lucan. "You have to outlive our lord father first. A doubtful proposition, that." His voice hardened. "And I remember what I promised you, after Tymaen's wedding. Raise a hand against me and I'll wither the flesh on your bones."

Toraine snarled, drew his sword, and took a step forward. Lucan sneered and raised his hand, muttering under his breath. Things might have gone very bad, but Mazael stepped between them, grabbed Lucan's wrist, and seized Toraine's sword arm.

The two brothers glared at Mazael.

"Enough of this!" said Mazael.

"You dare lay a hand on the Heir of Swordgrim!" spat Toraine, eyes blazing with fury.

"I don't give a damn if you're the High King and Lucan's the Patriarch of the Amathavian Church!" said Mazael. "I am the Lord of Castle Cravenlock, not you, not him, and I will not have blood spilled in my courtyard! Do you understand? Raise a hand against each other, and I'll kill both of you and deal with Lord Richard later."

Both sons of Richard Mandragon gaped at Mazael as if he'd gone mad.

Then Lucan laughed and shook free of Mazael's grip. "I believe you're serious, Lord Mazael." He laughed again. "It would almost be amusing to watch."

Toraine just stared at Mazael, eyes furious. Mazael realized that he had made an enemy.

It didn't trouble him. Toraine had never been friendly, anyway.

Toraine turned and bowed to Rachel. "My fair lady," he said. "You look as radiant as I remember." He took her hand and kissed it.

Gerald's eyes narrowed.

"Thank you, Lord Heir," said Rachel. Her voice only trembled a bit.

Toraine glanced at Gerald, smirked. "Lord Malden's youngest son, eh?"

"I am Sir Gerald Roland."

Toraine ignored him and kept speaking to Rachel. "Youngest sons are never important." He glared at Lucan. "No doubt Sir Gerald will become lord of some rock on Knightrealm's coast. You can sit at his side as he rules over dead fish and seagulls. And you could have been the lady of the Grim Marches." He shook his head and stepped back.

"I'm quite happy, my lord Heir," said Rachel.

"And what concern is that of mine?" snapped Toraine. He turned to Mazael. "I will lodge here for three or four days, I think. Long enough to meet this emissary Lord Malden dispatched. Sir Tobias, yes?"

Mazael tried not to wince. The thought of Toraine Mandragon and Sir Tobias Roland in the same room was alarming. "I believe so."

"Excellent," said Toraine. He gestured, and the rest of his party filed through the gate. Mazael saw thirty knights, a number of armsmen, some ragged merchants, and a large band of whores. "Walk with me, Lord Mazael. Alone. We have things to discuss."

"As you wish," said Mazael. Gerald and Master Cramton hurried forward, directing the knights to the stables.

Toraine wandered across the courtyard, leaving Mazael with no choice but to follow. They climbed to the battlements, Toraine's red cloak, emblazoned with a black dragon, flaring out behind him. Toraine reached the ramparts and strolled with a proprietary air, running his hand along the cold stone battlements.

"You seem to have attracted quite a few followers," said Mazael, looking at the merchants and whores in Toraine's party.

Toraine laughed. "They have their uses. The common folk are drawn to our power, like maggots to meat. When I am finished with them, I will discard them and take new ones."

Mazael's lips thinned. "No doubt."

"I assume you're wondering why I've come," said Toraine, "as I have far better things to do than to loiter about backwater castles."

"I assume Lord Richard commanded you," said Mazael.

Toraine's obsidian eyes narrowed. "My father does not command me in all matters."

"Yes, but in most matters," said Mazael, "he keeps you on a short leash. Else you'd have razed most of the neighboring lands, alienated your father's vassals, and gotten yourself killed or assassinated."

Toraine whirled and glared, face inches from Mazael's "You ought to speak with more respect."

"I speak forthrightly," said Mazael, "as I do with Lord Richard. Shall I do any less with you? Though Lord Richard does accept counsel more calmly than you."

Toraine stepped back, but his glare did not waver. Mazael felt a wave of disgusted disquiet. Lord Richard was a vigorous man in his mid-forties, likely to rule for at least another score of years. Yet disease and mishap were all too common. Suppose Lord Richard died and Toraine became the new lord of the Grim Marches? Or suppose Toraine had Lord Richard assassinated and seized the lordship?

One day Mazael might find himself fighting this young madman.

For a brief moment Mazael considered shoving Toraine from the rampart. Better to kill him here and now, before Toraine had the chance to lead thousands of others to death. Mazael could claim it was an accident. Lord Richard would believe the lie…

His hands had tightened into fists before he stopped in horror. Random, sudden murder was the way of his Demonsouled blood. He would not give in to it. Romaria had died to free him from its curse, and by all the gods, he would not make her sacrifice meaningless.

"Ill, Lord Mazael?" said Toraine, watching him with an expression of guarded caution. Perhaps he had divined something of Mazael's thoughts. "Or distracted?" He smiled. "Some of my whores are most skilled…"

"Enough," growled Mazael, shaking his head. "We argue all day, and as you've said, I have better things to do. Why did Lord Richard send you here?"

Toraine looked at Rachel and Gerald, who stood speaking with Toraine's knights. "Your sister's marriage to this Roland."

"What of it?" said Mazael. "Lord Richard gave his assent, if grudgingly."

"Yes," said Toraine. "Why do you plan to wed your sister to a son of my father's mortal enemy?"

"Simply because your father and Gerald's are mortal enemies, and their strength is evenly matched" said Mazael. "Castle Cravenlock is the second strongest lordship in the Grim Marches, after Swordgrim. Without my help, Lord Richard cannot fight Knightrealm. And unless I aid Lord Malden, he cannot fight the Grim Marches."

"Yes," said Toraine, his smirk returning. "Unless you aid Lord Malden, unless you betray the Mandragons, they will be no war."

"And I won't," said Mazael, "so there will be no war."

"Unless you betray us," said Toraine.

"I gave Lord Richard my sworn word," said Mazael, voice hardening.

Toraine laughed. "And what worth has sworn word? Your brother swore to my father, as well." He laughed again. "And he joined the snake-kissers, and would have sought Knightcastle's aid, if Lord Malden hadn't been too wise to support such a fool." He grinned. "You want to know why I'm here, Lord Mazael?"

Mazael said nothing.

"If you betray my father, then you will have to contend with me."

Mazael still said nothing.

"They call me the Black Dragon for good reason. If you betray us, I'll fall on your lands like a storm. I will burn your crops, raze your villages, slaughter your peasants like sheep. I'll take this castle for my own. Then I'll hunt you down. I'll take your sister, rape her bloody, and throw her to my men when I'm finished with her. And then I'll kill you."

Now Mazael glared into Toraine's eyes. "I won't betray Lord Richard. I don't want war between Knightrealm and the Grim Marches. And by all the gods, I swear that if you do any of that...if you raise a finger against my sister...if you even so much as give her a threatening glance, then I will kill you."

Toraine looked away first. "Twice you've threatened to kill me today."

"Not threatened," said Mazael, "but promised. And only if you threaten me first." He gestured at the castle. "No doubt you're weary from the journey. I'll have a page see you to your chambers."

"I am not weary," said Toraine, "and feel the need to stretch my muscles. Your armsmaster trains the men in the morning, no? Perhaps I shall train with them."

Mazael gritted his teeth. "As you wish."

Sir Roger Gravesend paced his tower cell, scowling.

Of course, it wasn't really a cell. It had rich carpets, ornate tapestries, comfortable chairs, and large bed. He had as much wine as he wished, and in fact spent most of his time drunk.

But it was a cell, just the same.

Sir Roger filled his goblet again and drained it in a swift gulp.

"It wasn't supposed to happen like this," he mumbled. "They promised me." The room began to spin. He refilled his goblet, wine splashing across his tunic, and staggered to a chair. "They betrayed me."

The door opened. A serving girl in rough homespun entered, curtsied, and laid a platter of meat, bread, and dried fruit on the table.

"They said it was just the beginning," mumbled Sir Roger, oblivious to the serving girl, "they'd help me." He took a long drink of wine and slammed the goblet against the arm of the chair. "They betrayed me!"

"Perhaps they haven't, sir knight," murmured the serving girl.

Sir Roger looked up. "What? What did you say?"

"Maybe they haven't abandoned you," she said, looking at him.

Sir Roger smiled. The girl looked about fifteen or sixteen. "You're a comely wench." He beckoned. "Why don't you come over here, eh? We'll have ourselves a good time."

She gave him a shy smile, swayed across the room, and settled on his lap. A wide, unsteady grin spread across his face.

"We'll have ourselves a good time tonight, we surely will," whispered the girl. "And they didn't betray you, sir knight."

Sir Roger blinked. "What?"

"Why don't you open the front of my dress?" cooed the girl, nipping at his ear. She leaned back and smiled.

Sir Roger grinned back and fumbled for the leather ties at her throat. The front of her dress fell open. Sir Roger licked his lips, and reached for her breast.

His hand froze a few inches from the pale skin, his jaw dropping open in sudden alarm.

Above her left breast, over her heart, rested the small mark of a coiled serpent.

Sir Roger looked at the girl's face.

Her eyes flashed yellow and he caught a glimpse of pointed, dripping fangs.

"Oh, gods!" shrieked Sir Roger, rocking back into the chair. "Get off me. Get off me!" He tried to push her away, but the girl's hands locked about his wrists like iron bands, slamming his arms against the chair.

She leaned forward, face against his, and ran the pointed tips of her fangs down his cheek.

"You need a shave, sir knight," purred the girl.

"Don't kill me," said Sir Roger, sweating. "I didn't betray our master," her fangs pressed deeper, "don't kill me, please, don't…"

"Sir Roger," said the girl, leaning back, "we know you didn't betray us." She pulled her dress open wider. On her shoulder rested a small black mark, the sigil of a serpent wrapped about a cloak-black fang.

"You…you serve the holy one Blackfang?" said Sir Roger, awed. "He is coming himself?"

"He is," said the girl, closing her dress. "The time has come, faithful Roger Gravesend. The enemies of our faith will pay tonight. Lord Mazael Cravenlock shall die for the murder of holy Skhath. Rachel Cravenlock shall die for her apostasy. And both Lucan and Toraine Mandragon shall die, for their father's crimes against the priests of great Sepharivaim."

"Toraine Mandragon is here?" said Sir Roger.

"He is," said the girl, "come to threaten Mazael."

"But…but Lucan Mandragon is a powerful wizard. Extremely dangerous. All folk hold him in fear…"

The girl scoffed. "Do you think his puny arts can threaten a servant of great Sepharivaim?"

"No, no, of course not," said Sir Roger.

"They will die tonight," said the girl, "and you, faithful Roger, shall have your freedom, and great reward for your loyalty to the servants of mighty Sepharivaim." She smiled, eyes glinting yellow. "Perhaps we will arrange for you to become the new Lord of Castle Cravenlock." She slid off him. "Wait for us. Be ready."

She vanished through the door in a swirl of skirts.

Sir Roger stared after her, and took another swallow of wine.

Wood clacked against wood.

Men crowded the courtyard before the castle's barracks. In one corner the armsmen drilled with halberds and spears, under the scowling gaze of grizzled sergeants. Archery butts had been lined against the curtain wall, and crossbowmen sent bolts thudding into the straw. Before the steps of the barracks the squires and pages stood in pairs, crossing wooden practice swords. Sir Gerald and Sir Nathan stood on the stairs, overseeing everything.

Mazael walked towards the barracks, Toraine Mandragon at his side. Toraine strolled unconcerned through the various melees. Rumor had it that the dull black plates of his armor were the scales of a black dragon, a black dragon slain upon Toraine's blade, the scales capable of deflecting almost anything.

"How orderly," said Toraine, observing the crossbowmen.

"The Land Heir approves, then," said Mazael.

Toraine gave a thin smile. "Such effort. I might think you were training an army for rebellion. But I have your protestations of loyalty, of course."

Mazael almost wished he had let Lucan and Toraine come to blows.

"Do you ever participate?" said Toraine. "Such a mighty lord as yourself. You must be able to defeat any man in this castle."

"Sometimes," said Mazael, "when the mood takes me. Usually I spar with some of my most trusted knights."

"Prudent, perhaps," said Toraine, "for you never know when a man will take the opportunity to shove steel down your gullet. But mayhap it is foolish. Your skills will have gone to rust."

"Is that your concern?" said Mazael. "It's not as if we will ever war against each other, of course."

"Of course," said Toraine, smirking. "But, come, I feel the need for exercise. Let us train against each other."

Some of the squires and armsmen stopped to stare at them.

"My lord Heir?" said Mazael.

"It has been a while since you faced a proper challenge, I think," said Toraine, snapping his fingers. Two of his squires removed his cloak. "Let us see the mettle of Castle Cravenlock's lord."

"As you wish," said Mazael. "Adalar!" Adalar broke free from the squires and ran to Mazael's side. "My armor. And two practice swords."

"Practice swords?" scoffed Toraine. "Are we boys, to play with sticks? Proper steel, I think." He thumped the pommel of his sword.

Adalar and two pages returned with Mazael's mail hauberk, cuirass, and gauntlets. "I've no wish hurt you by mischance, lord Heir."

Toraine smiled. "You won't."

"And shall we just gut each other, then?" said Mazael. "Or fight until first blood?"

"I doubt my father would appreciate it if I spilled Cravenlock blood here," said Toraine. He tapped his chest. "No, a simple tap to the breastplate will suffice." He watched as Adalar carried over Mazael's armor. "Assuming that can block a sword thrust, of course."

More silence fell over the courtyard as the squires and armsmen drifted over to watch. Mazael gritted his teeth and wished Sir Nathan would order them back to work. It reminded him too much of his fight with Skhath, when the San-keth priest had still cloaked himself in the illusion of a human knight.

Mazael pulled on his armor, aided by Adalar. Toraine stepped back and drew his sword, settling into a guard position. His squires hastened forward and undid his sword belt, lest his scabbard entangle his legs. Toraine held a long sword with curved blade, the light, fast saber favored by the nomads of the south. Mazael drew Lion, the blade glimmering with a cold blue sheen.

Toraine stepped forward, sword held in both hands, the blade before his face. "Ready, Lord Mazael?"

Mazael dropped into a light crouch, body sideways, Lion out before him. "If you are!"

Toraine moved in a blur of black armor and red hair, chopping at Mazael's face. Mazael sidestepped, parried, and thrust for Toraine's throat. Toraine pushed Lion down, spun, and brought his saber down for an overhead chop. The swords clanged and rang with the effort of the battle.

Toraine stepped back, saber point tracing figure-eights. "Fast, for an old man."

"I'm but ten years your senior," said Mazael, circling Toraine. Toraine began circling him in return, neither his eyes nor his blade wavering. "Boy."

Toraine sprang forward, feinted for Mazael's head, and dropped his strike low. Mazael kicked the flat of the blade aside and stabbed. Toraine twisted away, sword flailing.

"Poor form," growled Toraine, "using your boot in such a manner."

"In battle," said Mazael, feinting for Toraine's arm, Toraine stepping aside, "form matters less than who still's standing when it's all over. You've killed enough people. I thought you'd know that."

Toraine growled, his eyes blazing, and flung himself at Mazael. His saber flashed high, low, whirling in steel spirals. Mazael blocked and ducked and parried, Lion clanging in his hands. Toraine's momentum played out, and Mazael spun and threw a two-handed chop that Toraine's saber barely turned.

They reeled back and forth in the ragged circle, Toraine's saber flashing and stabbing against Lion's blade. Mazael's blood pumped through his arms, his breath deep and strong. Despite himself, he began to enjoy the swordplay. Toraine moved his blade with masterful skill, perhaps better than almost anyone in Castle Cravenlock. It had been a long time since Mazael had faced a serious challenge. Even the battles against the scattered mercenaries had been little more than organized slaughter.

Bit by bit, Mazael probed the edge of Toraine's defenses, Lion's blade flashing. Toraine had skill, but lacked Mazael's experience. He did not vary his defensive moves. Mazael thrust and swung, following Toraine's defenses, preparing his winning blow.

Then something slammed hard into his back.

Mazael stumbled, pain bursting through his shoulders. He dropped to one knee, even as Toraine's thrust screamed past and tore a ragged furrow across Mazael's left bicep. Toraine overbalanced, surprise and triumph and alarm mingled on his face. Agony spread through Mazael's arm.

Rage exploded within him, turned his blood to howling flame.

Mazael leapt back to his feet with a roar and a surge of speed, backhanding Toraine across the face, and the younger man fell back with a groan of pain. Lion gleamed, and Mazael raised it high, ready to ram it through Toraine's eye, ready to watch blood and brains splash across the courtyard earth...

"Mazael!"

He blinked.

Rachel gripped his arm, staring at him with a worried expression. Gerald was at her side, sword half drawn.

"Rachel?" said Mazael. He scarce recognized his own voice. Blood dripped from the cut on his arm, soaking into the ground. Toraine stared up at him, breathing hard, hands raised in guard. He looked terrified.

"For gods' sake, don't kill him," said Rachel, pleading. "It was just a cut. Just a little blood. It'll heal."

"Blood," croaked Mazael, looking down at Toraine. He watched his dripping blood spatter on the ground.

His blood…

With a surge of horror, Mazael realized that his Demonsouled blood had almost taken hold of him once more, had almost driven him to murder in a blind rage.

It had almost made Romaria's sacrifice worthless.

Disgusted and ashamed, he stepped back, picking up Toraine's saber.

Toraine climbed to his feet, rubbing his jaw. "Well." His voice had a slight tremor. "So this is the famous rage of Mazael Cravenlock. Quite impressive."

Mazael reversed the blade and handed the hilt to Toraine. "My apologies. I did not mean to frighten you."

"You didn't," said Toraine. "I…suppose it was my fault. I shouldn't have thrust when you stumbled."

A fresh flicker of rage awoke in Mazael's mind. "Someone pushed me."

"Who would dare? You lost your balance, surely," said Toraine, still rubbing his jaw.

"Someone pushed me," said Mazael, "I'm sure."

"It doesn't matter," said Rachel. "We'd best get your arm bandaged. Adalar!" Mazael's squire hurried to her side. "Get Timothy at once!"

"My lady." Adalar dashed away.

"I think perhaps I will retire to those guest chambers now," said Toraine. "Getting knocked to the ground does rather knock the wind from a man."

"Of course." Mazael ordered a page to show Toraine to the guest chambers in the southwestern tower. Timothy appeared, face furrowed with concern, and began clucking over the cut in Mazael's arm. Mazael endured the ministrations, brooding. Timothy cleaned the wound and wound bandages about it.

He cursed his folly. What hope of peace might the Grim Marches have if he cut down Lord Richard's son in a blind fury? Lord Richard would seek vengeance, and Mazael would have no choice but to seek Lord Malden's aid, and then the Grim Marches would drown in blood and war.

And how would the Old Demon exploit such a bloodletting?

Mazael sighed.

"You look pale. I hope the wound doesn't fester," said Rachel, still frowning.

"It won't," said Mazael.

"Your confidence flatters me, my lord," said Timothy.

Mazael had the utmost confidence in Timothy, but that didn't matter.

The power in his Demonsouled blood healed even the most grievous wounds.

And even as Timothy finished, the wound closed beneath the bandage, the skin knitting together of its own accord.

"Let us have some breakfast," said Rachel, touching his arm.

"You look thirsty, after all," said Gerald, trying to smile.

Mazael nodded and let Rachel lead him to the great hall.

Some time later, Lucan Mandragon strolled through the deserted courtyard, wrapped in his mindclouding spell and his dark cloak.

It had been a risk, though a slight one, to strike Mazael with the spell from behind. Lucan's mindclouding permitted him to stand ignored in the crowd of spectators, but Mazael had always been able to see through it. Fortunately, Mazael's attention had always been focused on Toraine.

Of course, Mazael might have killed Toraine in his wrath.

Lucan laughed. That had would have been less of risk and more of a pleasant surprise. But, still, Lucan wanted peace as much as Mazael, and Toraine's death would hardly help.

He stopped where Toraine and Mazael had fought. A few drops of dried blood stained the earth. Lucan's cold smile widened as he knelt. He produced a dagger and scraped the bloodstained dirt into a pouch.

"Now, my lord Mazael," said Lucan, rising, "we'll find things out, will we not?"

He remembered Mazael's furious rage, the murderous light in his eyes, and Lucan's smile vanished in a sudden chill.

He had never encountered such fury before, though he had read of it, and suspected its source.

"Yes, Lord Mazael," he murmured, flexing his fingers, fingers that could conjure a storm of lethal spells, "we'll find out, will we not?"

CHAPTER 4
THE WRAITH OF SEPHARIVAIM

Mazael rubbed his aching head. "That didn't go well."

He stood alone with Gerald and Rachel in the courtyard. Night had fallen, and most of the castle's residents had retired.

Rachel shrugged. "At least Toraine didn't kill anyone."

The Lord Heir had loitered about the great hall during court, glaring at Mazael over dinner. He had insulted several of Mazael's knights, and made vigorous efforts to seduce their wives. Mazael hoped he had been unsuccessful. If a vengeful husband gutted Toraine in a duel, Lord Richard would be wroth.

"I have a pair of armsmen at his door," said Gerald, "as an honor guard. They'll let us know if he tries anything…troublesome."

"Good," said Mazael, clapping Gerald's shoulder, "good. No wonder Lucan hates him so. Quite a pair, aren't they? Lucan may be a black wizard, but at least he has a civil tongue in his head."

"Speaking of Lucan," said Gerald, "where is he? I haven't seen him since this morning."

Mazael shrugged. "Nor have I."

Rachel scowled. "He's up to something, I'm sure."

"Maybe," said Mazael. "Or perhaps he's afraid he can't control himself around Toraine." He grimaced. "Like me."

"That was an accident…" Gerald and Rachel began in unison.

"I know, I know," said Mazael, waving his hand. "Go to bed. I'm weary enough, and I've no doubt you are also. Go."

Gerald gave Rachel a chaste kiss on the cheek, and she turned and joined her waiting maids. Mazael turned and stalked towards his bedchamber. He barred the door behind him and threw himself on the bed, not bothering to undress.

But he could not sleep, and stared at the ceiling. For a moment he considered summoning Bethy, but shoved the notion aside. Bad enough he had succumbed to his Demonsouled nature once today. No need to risk passing his curse on to an unwitting child.

Lucan crossed to the far wall of his chamber, a small cell wedged beneath the chambers of the court wizard. To most eyes, the wall looked blank, a featureless stretch of worn gray stone.

Only Lucan's eyes saw the complex sigil painted onto the stone, an ornate combination of summoning and conjuration symbols. Of course, a wizard of sufficient skill would have noticed the mark, but Lucan doubted another wizard in the Grim Marches possessed such mastery.

He stepped forward, ran his fingers along the sigil's lines, and muttered a quick incantation. Gray mist welled from the sigil, wrapping him in its chilly embrace.

When it cleared, Lucan stood in the vaulted central corridor of the sealed San-keth temple. He smiled in satisfaction. The sigil had worked, snatching him from the material world, through the spiritual world, and depositing him into the temple corridor.

He adjusted the pouch holding the bloodstained dirt and made his way to the cathedral-like temple chamber itself. A towering golden image of Sepharivaim, god of the San-keth, had once loomed over the altar. Reliefs on the walls and columns had displayed images of the San-keth torturing helpless humans. Mazael had ordered the idol destroyed, the statues smashed.

The temple had quite a different look now.

Sagging bookshelves lined the walls of the balconies, laden Lucan's books and scrolls. Long tables on the temple's main floor held alchemical equipment, vast collections of bottles, and a variety of arcane machinery that would have baffled poor Timothy. Lucan descended to the temple floor, looking about in satisfaction. He had wanted a secret haven for years, a place to carry on his work away from his father's eyes.

Lucan laughed aloud, his mirth echoing off the silent stones. Ironic. His father's own orders had given Lucan the opportunity to claim the temple for his own. He strolled past the tables, glancing over his collection of magical tools.

He stopped before an intricate double circle painted on the floor. A bewildering array of intricate runes lay between the two circles, like a ring of crawling spiders. Lucan crossed to a bookstand and a small table on the far side of the circle. On the bookstand rested the page torn from the San-keth spell book.

Lucan set the pouch of dirt on the table, focused his will, and began to chant.

He chanted for a long time. Soon, gray mist roiled and writhed within the circle. Lucan lit a small bronze censer and waved it in complex patterns. With his free hand he seized handfuls of various powders and flung them into the mist. Magical force trembled and shuddered in the air.

Lucan clapped his hands and shouted the final word of the spell.

A shrieking, tearing sound filled the temple. The circle blazed with blue light for an instant, the mist transmuting into a curtain of blue flame.

And then a hulking shape reared within the circle.

Lucan looked away at once. The spell had described no danger, but Lucan had dealt with conjured spirits often enough to know that staring at it might prove perilous, even fatal.

A hissing voice snarled out of the circle, making both Lucan's bones and the stone floor vibrate.

"You are not of the San-keth race! What do you want of me, mortal dog?"

"One simple service, nothing more," said Lucan, resisting the urge to gaze at the spirit creature.

"I am obligated to do nothing!"

"Of course not. But, then, you are quite imprisoned within the circle, and you cannot return to your world until I release you. So. You may perform this simple, insignificant service for me, or you will remain within that circle for the rest of time. It matters very little to me."

Actually, Lucan would have found it inconvenient. He had no wish to move his workroom yet again. But the thing in the circle needn't know that.

"Wretched mortal! I shall rend your soul from your flesh."

The air shuddered with a scream of fury, the circle sparking with sapphire light. Lucan waited. The shudders and sparks intensified, growing louder and brighter. The display went on for some minutes, then fell silent.

"You'll find," said Lucan, "that the circle is quite impregnable. A greater spirit could have broken it, but you're scarcely a lesser spirit. Perform a service for me, or sit there until the world crumbles into dust."

A long silence followed. Lucan smirked.

"Very well, mortal man." The awful voice sounded resigned. "What do you wish?"

"A simple favor, nothing more," said Lucan. He undid the drawstring on the pouch. "Tell me what manner of mortal creature shed this blood."

Something like a chuckle escaped the circle. "An enemy?"

"Perhaps. I don't yet know." Lucan scowled. "But it is no concern of yours. Do as I say!"

He flung the bloodstained earth into the circle.

The mist roiled and snarled, and for a brief moment blazed with black flames.

The chuckle came again. "Ah, mortal man! You have mighty enemies!"

"Do I?" said Lucan.

"This blood is of he who mortals called the Great Demon, long ago."

"Ah." Many things became clear to Lucan.

Mazael's uncanny speed and strength, his rage, the way his eyes blazed on the rare occasions when he lost his temper. For that matter, how else could Mazael have survived both a San-keth priest and the notorious necromancer Simonian of Briault?

Mazael, Lord of Castle Cravenlock, was Demonsouled.

Lucan contemplated what to do next.

"The spirit of demonkind blazes within this blood like a black star," hissed the creature. "This blood...ah, such might, such potency! This blood came from the Great Demon's own line."

Lucan's eyes widened.

Had the Old Demon himself fathered Mazael? Lucan had always believed the Old Demon a myth, a creature of peasant fable. But if the last son of the Great Demon still walked the earth after three thousand years...

"I prophesy, mortal. The Demonsouled shall destroy you," cackled the creature, "and I shall laugh..."

"Be silent and be gone," snarled Lucan, muttering a spell.

A thunderclap rang out, the floor trembling, a flash of light throwing dark shadows against the wall. Lucan lifted his head and gazed into the circle.

It was empty but for a scattering of bloodstained dirt.

"So," whispered Lucan.

He didn't know quite what to do. But best to deal with Mazael now, immediately, when Lucan could catch him off guard.

He left the temple workroom behind, making for Mazael's chambers.

###

Sir Roger Gravesend sat up in bed, drenched in sweat.

The serving girl stood by the window, moonlight illuming her pale skin, her eyes glinting gold and back.

"It's time, loyal Sir Roger," she whispered.

"How did you get in here?" he croaked.

"Get dressed," she said, pointing.

"But the guards..."

Her lips pulled back, fangs glinting. "The guards were lonely, and couldn't resist a kiss from a pretty girl. Get dressed."Roger obeyed and followed the girl into the hall.

The guards lay dead on the ground, lips black and eyes bulging. Sir Roger noticed the twin puncture wounds on their cheeks and shuddered.

"Take his sword," said the girl, "you'll need it."

Roger scooped up a dead man's sword, his sweaty fingers curling around the hilt. "What now?"

"Why, we will kill Mazael and Rachel Cravenlock, and then Lucan and Toraine Mandragon," said the girl. "Weren't you listening before?" She smiled at him. "But first we'll kill the guards keeping watch at the gate, you and I."

"But why?" said Roger, rubbing his free hand on his trouser legs. "Shouldn't we kill Lord Mazael first?"

"That honor is reserved for holy Blackfang," said the girl.

Roger almost dropped the sword. "He's...he's coming here. Himself?"

"You fail to listen, again," said the girl. "Now you will see a holy one of Sepharivaim. Now you will see the power of Sepharivaim unleashed." Her fangs pressed against her lower lips. "But first, one final test of loyalty. You will betray Mazael and kill the guards at the barbican gate."

Roger stared at her cold face, her reptilian eyes. "But...but..." He had gone too far to quail now. "All right. But...what is your name?"

Her tongue flicked across her lips. It was forked. "You...may call me Calibah. Now come. We have unbelievers to kill."

Sir Roger shrugged and followed her through the darkened corridors.

###

Mazael's eyes shot open. He had not spent fifteen years as a landless, wandering knight without sleeping lightly. He rolled out of bed, snatched up Lion, and came into a crouch, sword ready.

Lucan Mandragon stood in the doorway, his face a pale blur beneath his black cowl.

"Lucan?" said Mazael, lowering his sword. "What the hell are you doing here?"

Lucan said nothing, but walked into the room, cloak whispering against the floor.

"How did you get past the guards?" said Mazael.

"Please," said Lucan. He walked to the table, waved his hand, and muttered something. The candles lit themselves, throwing their glow over the room. "You may have observed me moving through the castle unnoticed, ignored by everyone."

"I have," said Mazael. Something in Lucan's tone made him raise Lion once more.

Lucan settled in a cushioned chair, adjusting his cloak. "I possess a mindclouding spell that permits me to walk unseen, so long as I do nothing to draw attention to myself. A spell that leaves you curiously unaffected."

"What do you want?" said Mazael.

"I have observed you for over a year now," said Lucan, "and from the moment I first saw you walk...or swagger, really...into my father's tent, I suspected something amiss."

Mazael said nothing, Rachel's warnings racing through his mind.

"Your strength, your speed, are clearly unnatural," said Lucan. "Consider your rage. Knights are, as a rule, violent men. But there is anger, and then there is...something more."

"I have reasons enough to rage," said Mazael. "Such as this intrusion, for instance."

"And most interesting of all, your strange ability to heal," said Lucan. "Oh, you hide it well, I'll grant. But I have seen you recover in hours from wounds that should have taken weeks to heal."

"Perhaps I'm simply vigorous," said Mazael.

"Quite vigorous," said Lucan, gesturing. "That cut on your arm. It has vanished entirely."

"I'll ask one more time," said Mazael, "What do you want?"

"Merely to talk," said Lucan, his smirk reappearing. "You see, Lord Mazael, you've hidden your secret quite well. But I can look deeper and harder than most men." His black eyes glittered. "You are Demonsouled."

Mazael moved so fast that he scarce registered the movement himself. One moment he stood by the bed. The next he stood before the chair, his blade held to Lucan's throat.

"You speak madness," growled Mazael.

"Do I?" said Lucan, showing no fear at all. "I think Lord Adalon Cravenlock was not your father. I think, in fact, that your mother so loathed him that she lay with the Old Demon himself. Hence, you."

Mazael pressed Lion closer.

"Don't deny it," said Lucan.

"I should kill you," said Mazael.

"You could try," said Lucan. "But even though your sword rests at my throat, you may find my death harder to work than you think. Do you think I came to speak with a child of the Old Demon without first preparing ample protections? And why would you want to kill me, in any case?"

"Because if your father finds out he'll kill me," said Mazael. "If Gerald, Rachel, Sir Nathan, Timothy ever found out...they'd turn against me. Every hand would be raised against me, to kill me before I became a monster." His voice hardened. "And have you come to kill me, Dragon's Shadow?"

"And why," said Lucan, "would I do that?" A single bead of sweat slithered down his forehead.

"Don't play riddling games with me," said Mazael. "You know I'm Demonsouled. Why wouldn't you try to kill me?" A dark thought came to him. "Unless you're Demonsouled yourself."

Lucan laughed. "Please. My soul is black enough, or at least half-black, but not Demonsouled. No, Lord Mazael, I don't want to kill you." He paused. "Perhaps I want to help you."

"Help me?" said Mazael. "And how would you help me?"

"Take the sword away and we'll speak."

Mazael said nothing, his pulse hammering in his temples. Perhaps it was a trick. Perhaps Lucan would spell-blast him the minute Mazael lifted Lion. His fingers tightened about the hilt. Mazael had almost killed Toraine today. No sense in sparing one of Lord Richard's sons and killing the other.

He stepped back, keeping Lion raised.

Lucan stood, rubbing his throat. "So. Tell me, if you will. When did your abilities first manifest?"

"Only a year ago," said Mazael, "when I first returned to Castle Cravenlock."

"You do realize your father was the Old Demon, do you not?" said Lucan.

"I do," said Mazael, watching Lucan. "How did you find out?"

"Your blood," said Lucan, "burns with the power. There are degrees of Demonsouled blood. Some stronger, some weaker. Yours is the strongest I have ever seen." He lifted an eyebrow. "How did you learn the truth?"

"The Old Demon told me."

"Himself?" said Lucan. "You stay in communication with him?"

"No," said Mazael, growling. "You might have met him. He disguised himself as Simonian of Briault."

For the first time a flicker of surprise crossed Lucan's face. Mazael took a perverse pleasure in it. "Simonian?"

"Yes, Simonian," said Mazael. "You seem to know everything. Didn't you know that?" Lucan said nothing. Mazael paced, snarling. "You want to know the truth, Lucan? Here it is. The Old Demon was the puppeteer, and we were his puppets. He fathered me on Lady Arissa. He brought Skhath to the Grim Marches, had him create the serpent-cult. He disguised himself as Simonian, convinced Mitor to rise against Lord Richard. Do you know why?" Lucan shook his head. "Me. He arranged Mitor's rebellion to unleash my Demonsouled blood, to force my true nature to manifest."

"Why?" said Lucan.

"He wanted me to become something called the Destroyer," said Mazael.

"Destroyer," repeated Lucan.

"You know of it?"

"An ancient Tristafellin legend," said Lucan. "It was written that of the Great Demon's blood, one mighty scion would rise to enslave the nations of the earth and take the Great Demon's throne for himself." He shrugged. "Or herself, possibly." Lucan glanced out the window, frowning. "Though it does seem odd. I rather imagine the Old Demon would want to claim the Great Demon's throne for himself."

"He does," Mazael said, shuddering as he remembered the terrible glee and rage in the Old Demon's burning gaze. "When…when I refused him, when I denied him, he…told me that all his children rebel, sooner or later. Then he devours them."

Lucan lifted his eyebrow. "Raising them as cattle, I imagine. Harvesting them like a crop, absorbing their essence, their power. I suspect when he finds a Demonsouled mighty enough to become the Destroyer, he'll murder the child and claim that power as his own."

"Most likely," muttered Mazael, remembering the Old Demon's gaping jaws, the stench rising from his jagged fangs.

"I am curious, though," said Lucan. "The Old Demon is at least three thousand years old. I can only imagine how powerful his arcane art has become, with centuries of practice, with his Demonsouled essence fueling his spells. How did you escape him?"

Mazael closed his eyes. "I…didn't, not really. I would have fallen, become like him. But Romaria… stopped me. He killed her for it. That stopped me. I rejected him, called on the gods. Their power repelled him."

"The gods?" said Lucan, dubious. "Of course." A strange note entered his voice. "I am sorry to hear of Romaria's end, though. You told us Simonian killed her. I suppose he did, at that. But I am still sorry. I understand that pain."

Mazael opened his eyes, glared. "You understand nothing."

"Don't I?" said Lucan, voice cooling. "I understand quite well."

"Do you?" said Mazael. "Then tell me."

Lucan scowled.

"I've told you my secrets," said Mazael. "Or, rather, you have forced them from me. What of the Dragon's Shadow, eh? What of your secrets?"

Lucan opened his mouth. "Does not rumor tell you…"

His eyes widened, and he stepped back, lifting his hand.

"What?" said Mazael, raising Lion. "What is it?"

"The ward against undead!" hissed Lucan. "I feel it! An undead has entered the castle!"

Mazael didn't have time to respond. His door shuddered, an axe blade bursting between the boards. An instant later the door splintered into fragments and collapsed to the stone floor.

"What is this?" yelled Mazael. "Who the devil are you?"

A half-dozen men and women skidded to a stop. Mazael recognized them from the merchants and whores that had traveled with Toraine. The biggest man carried an axe.

"What in blazes?" snarled Mazael.

They had black-slit yellow eyes, like a serpent's, and ivory fangs curling over their lips.

"He was supposed to be asleep!" shrilled one of the serpent-eyed women.

"It matters not!" roared the man, brandishing his axe. "Die, Mazael, die for your crimes against the great god Sepharivaim! Kill him!"

As one the serpent-eyed men and women rushed at Mazael, fangs bared.

Mazael sprang to meet them. He dodged an axe blow, swung, and Lion rammed halfway through the axeman's neck. He kicked the corpse off his blade, sending another of the assassins tumbling. One of the whores lunged at Mazael, snapping and biting. Drops of liquid fell from her fangs, drops that sizzled and smoked against the floor. Mazael dodged the poisoned bite and slammed his fist into the whore's gut. She doubled over with a shriek, and Mazael shoved her into another of the assassins.

He sprang backwards onto his bed, kicking one man in the jaw. The leather of his boot sizzled beneath the poisoned fangs, and the man dropped. The four still on their feet stepped back, eyeing him. The whore Mazael had struck writhed on the floor.

"Lucan!" yelled Mazael. For a brief instant Mazael wondered if Lucan had fled, or, worse, if he had invited these snake-worshippers...

A ringing chant echoed through the room, and a pool of gray mist swirled across the floor. The assassins froze, frowning. Lucan surged out of the shadows, cloak billowing, and pointed.

A pair of enormous, wraithlike wolves sprang out of the mist, shimmering with pale blue light, and sprang on the assassins. Their ghostly claws and fangs had no trouble tearing skin and shredding flesh. The assassins shrieked and stumbled back, trying to ward off the ethereal beasts. Mazael sprang from the bed, Lion raised high, but to no avail. The wolves ripped the last assassin to shreds and vanished in a swirl of mist.

"Are you injured?" said Lucan.

"No," said Mazael. "Who the devil are they?"

"Calibah," muttered Lucan, toeing a bloody corpse. "Changelings. The spawn of a union between a human woman and a San-keth male." Lucan smirked. "The San-keth claim to be a master race, but lack limbs, so they must sire changelings to perform their dirty work. The sort of creatures Skhath would have fathered on your sister, I imagine, had you not killed him."

"Rachel!" said Mazael. "Gods! They're here to kill her!" He jumped over the corpses and sprinted into the corridor, Lucan at his heels.

###

"Wake up, my lady."

Rachel blinked open her eyes. "Is it morning already? I…"

Sir Roger Gravesend stood in her doorway, a cold-faced serving girl at his side.

"Good-bye, my lady," said Sir Roger, laughing. "You ought to have wed me when you had the chance."

"What?" said Rachel, flinching. "Get out! Mazael will have your head for this! Get…"

She fell silent in terror.

The serving girl had the eyes and fangs of a serpent, of a San-keth. She was a changeling, the sort of monstrous half-breed Skhath would have planted in Rachel's womb, if Mazael had not rescued her from the dreadful cult. Rachel sat up, trying to tear free of the blankets.

Something moved, a green glow flooding the darkness.

A headless human skeleton stood at the foot of her bed, green fire writhing in its joints.

Rachel screamed in remembered terror.

The coils of an enormous, black-scaled serpent clung tight around the skeleton's spine, the wedge-shaped head rearing up in place of the skull. Cold, reptilian eyes cored into Rachel, the forked tongue caressing the air. From one skeletal hand dangled a corroded brass urn, swinging from a rusted chain.

"Lady Rachel," hissed the San-keth cleric, its voice rasping. "I am Blackfang, servant of great Sepharivaim. It pleases me to taste your scent at last."

"Get away from me," said Rachel, "get away from me!"

"You are an apostate to the faith, a traitor," said Blackfang. "Did you think to escape punishment? You were pledged to Skhath, one of great Sepharivaim's most faithful servants, and you betrayed him! The vengeance of the San-keth has found you. Take her!"

Four more changelings rushed through the door. She scrambled for the dagger Mazael insisted she keep under her pillow. Her fingers closed about the hilt just as the changelings seized her shoulders. She yelled and slashed out, tearing a gash in a changeling's arm. The man snarled and struck her across the face, the dagger tumbling from her stunned fingers.

The changelings yanked her upright and ripped away her nightgown, leaving her naked. They forced her to her knees before Blackfang, her arms pinned behind her back. The stone floor felt very cold against her knees and legs.

"You met yet recant and return to the true faith," said Blackfang. The witch-light of his skeletal carrier dazzled Rachel's eyes. "Renounce the false gods of men, and pledge your soul and body to Sepharivaim, and you will live."

"No," said Rachel, her voice shaking. "No. I…I want nothing to do with you…"

"So be it," said Blackfang.

One of the changelings seized Rachel's hair and yanked her head back. She knew how San-keth clerics executed apostates. After pronouncing the rite of condemnation, Blackfang would plunge his poisoned fangs into her eyes, leaving her to die blinded and in agony. She screamed and fought, but the changelings' hands held her ankles and arms like iron shackles.

"You have betrayed great Sepharivaim and the San-keth people," intoned Blackfang.

Rachel could see nothing but the ceiling, illuminated in the ghostly glow from Blackfang's carrier.

"I name you anathema and accursed to the San-keth, outcast and wretched," said Blackfang. "In the name of Sepharivaim, I condemn you. Perish!"

Rachel screamed.

###

Two of the damned changelings blocked the corridor, lunging with their poisoned fangs. Mazael was in no mood for delay. He killed them both, blood splashing against the walls, and kept running.

"Can you summon those ghost-wolves of yours again?" said Mazael, racing down the tower steps.

"No," said Lucan. "Under the laws of the binding compact, I cannot call them again until the full moon as passed. But I am not without other…"

A dark shape came up the stairs.

"My lord!" It was Timothy. "The ward against undead! It…" His eyes widened at the blood on Lion's blade.

"I know, they came for me," said Mazael. "Move, man! Rouse the castle! Take as many armsmen as you can find and get to Toraine's quarters. The changelings were men from his party. He might have gone over to the San-keth himself…"

"Toraine?" scoffed Lucan. "Not likely. He hasn't the wit to entertain faiths other than his own, which is only in himself. He was duped, most likely."

"Go, damn it!" said Mazael, pushing Timothy. "We can debate later. Run!"

Mazael dashed into the castle's courtyard. Two of his watchmen lay dead on the cold ground, faces locked in terrible grins, fang wounds on their necks. Mazael spat a furious oath and ran to the great hall. The night guard lay dead, and the doors hung ajar. He kicked them open and raced for the stairs, his heart hammering with rage and alarm.

A hideous vision of Rachel lying dead on the floor, her face twisted in that agonized grin, played through his mind.

"Wake, you fools!" shouted Lucan to the knights sleeping on the floor. "Wake! We are attacked! San-keth changelings! Arm yourselves!"

Rachel's chambers lay in the keep's western tower. Mazael sprinted up the steps. If they lived through this, he would move her into the rooms besides his...

A pair of changelings stood guard at the top of the steps, and attacked him in one smooth motion. Mazael threw himself aside and the changelings crashed into each other. He rolled to one knee and hamstrung the nearest man, Lion's blade shearing through skin and muscle. The changeling toppled with an agonized scream. Mazael punched out, and Lion's pommel smashed the second changeling's nose. The snake-eyed man stumbled back, poison bubbling from his fangs. Lion ripped through the changeling's neck, and Mazael's boot crushed the first changeling's throat.

A woman's faint scream rang out, fanning Mazael's alarmed fury to new heights. He kicked free of the dead changelings and ran down the corridor.

In the back of his mind he felt his Demonsouled rage stirring, threatening to break free and transform him into a whirlwind of death. Lion jolted in his hand, and Mazael felt a wave of warmth from the sword. The edges of the blade shimmered with azure light.

Dark magic was nearby.

He turned the corner and sprang into Rachel's room, sword leading.

A dozen changelings crowded his sister's bedchamber. Rachel knelt naked on the floor, held by a trio of changelings, her head pulled back, the cords bulging in her neck. Sir Roger Gravesend stood by the door, watching Rachel with a mixture of lust and glee.

A black-scaled San-keth cleric stood over Rachel, riding the usual undead human skeleton. An ancient bronze urn dangled from one bony hand.

Lion jolted in Mazael's hand once more, almost eagerly. The enspelled weapon had been forged in the last days of Tristafel, created to destroy undead and San-keth and Demonsouled.

Sometimes Mazael wondered why the sword hadn't destroyed him.

Lion burst into raging blue fires, drowning out the necromantic glow from the San-keth's skeleton.

The San-keth's head snapped around, fangs bared. "Him! Kill him now!"

"Oh, gods!" shouted Sir Roger.

"Mazael!" shrieked Rachel, sobbing, "run, run, go before they kill you too…"

"We are yours, holy Blackfang!" howled the changelings, flinging themselves at Mazael.

Mazael roared, took his blazing sword in both hands, and sprang to meet them. He beheaded one changeling, smashed another in the face with Lion's pommel, lopped off the hand of a third. Sir Roger lunged at Mazael, stabbing with a longsword. Mazael blocked the blow and backhanded Sir Roger across the face with his free hand. The traitor knight went down, spitting blood. A changeling struck Mazael across the chest with a club, while another raked a dagger across his leg. He bellowed and beheaded the changeling holding Rachel's legs. She scrambled free and backed towards Mazael, trying to cover herself with her arms.

"Run!" he roared, killing another changeling.

"They'll kill you!" Rachel half-sobbed, half-screamed.

Sir Roger seized her ankle and yanked. Rachel toppled with a yell, landing hard on her stomach. Mazael pivoted and kicked Roger in the face, and the traitor rolled away with a yell of pain. A changeling took the opening to stab Mazael in the side, fangs brushing his ear. He howled, jerked free of the blade, and gutted the changeling.

The San-keth cleric called Blackfang laughed, backing towards the window. "The apostate and the enemy of our faith shall die together! Perhaps the bards of your wretched race shall make a song of it! Perish!" The skeletal fingers opened the urn and sprinkled a few flecks of charred bone across the floor. Blackfang's hissing voice droned in a necromantic spell, green fire blazing to around his fingers.

A hooded, ghostly form materialized between Mazael and Blackfang. The San-keth pointed, and the skeletal wraith plunged at Mazael, wrapping itself about him. Mazael gagged, a hideous chill spreading through him, his head spinning with vertigo.

"This enslaved spirit shall drain away your life," said Blackfang. "Perhaps I'll raise your carcass to serve as my new carrier…"

Mazael snarled and took a staggering step towards Blackfang, but the changelings closed around him.

A rushing wind filled the chamber, and some unseen force seized Blackfang and slammed him against the far wall, bones clattering. The wraith holding Mazael vanished, and warmth flooded into him once more. He spun and killed another changeling.

Lucan stood in the doorway, hand raised.

"The Dragon's Shadow," spat Blackfang, coils slithering against the skeleton's spine. "I fail to see why you are held in such dread."

A changeling sprang at Mazael, jaws yawning, fangs glistening. Mazael rammed Lion into the changeling's mouth. Black-slit eyes bulged, and the changeling fell back, its mouth a splintered ruin.

"Do you, now?" said Lucan, stepping into the chamber. "A failure of perception on your part." He laughed, hard and mocking. "You were sent to contend with the likes of me?" He laughed again. "Your superiors must wish you to die, and to die horribly."

Mazael took another changeling, trying to cut his way to Blackfang.

"Fool!" snarled Blackfang. "You shall see the wrath of mighty Sepharivaim." The carrier skeleton thrust its hands at Lucan, the San-keth leaning forward.

Lucan was faster. His hand moved in a dark blur. Again the strange rushing sound filled the room, and Blackfang rammed into the stone wall. Blackfang regained his balance, hissing and snarling, skeletal hands blurring in a spell. Mazael whirled, ducked, and gutted another changeling. The floor grew slippery with spilled blood.

Lucan thrust out both his hands, and a thunderclap shook the walls. Blackfang tumbled backwards out the window, falling to the courtyard with an enraged snarl. Mazael killed the last changeling and stepped back, panting.

"Are you all right?" said Mazael. Rachel stood in the corner, arms wrapped over her chest.

"I'm...I'm fine," she managed, shivering. "A bit cold..."

Mazael snatched a blanket from the bed and swirled it around her shoulders. Lucan shoved past him and glared out the window.

"He yet lives," said Lucan. "Surprising. Perhaps his arcane art is more potent than I had thought."

Mazael frowned. "Where's Sir Roger?" In the fury of battle, he had forgotten about the traitor.

"I don't know," said Lucan.

"He slipped out, during the fight," said Rachel, "and ran."

The sound of fighting rose from the courtyard. A flare of green light illuminated the night, accompanied by the sizzling crackle of an arcane spell.

"Let's go," said Mazael. "Rachel, stay with us. Gods know what will happen if we leave you alone."

Rachel gave him a tight nod, clutching the blanket close.

Mazael hurried back into the courtyard. Armed chaos greeted him. His knights and armsmen struggled against the San-keth changelings. Blood and bodies stained the ground. A changeling saw Rachel, shrieked in delight, and lunged for her. Mazael caught the changeling on Lion's point, and kicked the corpse off his blade.

Gerald and Sir Nathan fought nearby, yelling commands to the armsmen. Mazael joined the fight, Lion rising and falling. Bit by bit they herded the changelings into a corner of the courtyard and cut them down without mercy. The changelings themselves fought with desperate courage, biting, stabbing, and grappling with their bare hands.

The last changeling fell dead. Mazael stepped back, breathing hard. The azure fires on Lion's blade had not yet gone out. He looked about, trying to find either Sir Roger or Blackfang. Rachel stood on the steps to the keep, sobbing into Gerald's shoulder.

"Perish!"

Blackfang stood atop the curtain wall, brandishing the bronze urn. Again the shadowy wraith sprang forth and plunged into the chest of one of Mazael's knights. The man groaned and collapsed. The wraith burst from the fallen man and shrieked towards Rachel.

"No!" shouted Mazael, reaching for her.

Lucan whirled, cat-quick, fingers blurring. The wraith shuddered, moaned, and flew back to the urn.

"Faithless interloper!" screamed Blackfang, fangs snapping. "You have meddled with us for the last time."

Lucan worked a spell in answer. A roar echoed through the courtyard and Blackfang reeled back, the witch-fires of his carrier flickering. No human expression crossed Blackfang's reptilian face, but it seemed as if the great serpent reared back in fear.

The courtyard fell silent as all watched the confrontation between the San-keth cleric and the Dragon's Shadow.

"Come, holy one!" called Lucan, his voice brimming with amusement. "Use your great arts! Strike me down! Surely a man of lesser race cannot stand against a servant of great Sepharivaim!"

Blackfang waved the urn in a complex pattern, green fires writhing in the metal. "Perish, dog!" The wraith burst from the urn and shrieked towards Lucan.

Lucan raised his hand, fingers crackling with magical force. The wraith struck his hand and vanished in a swirl of smoke. The urn exploded in Blackfang's skeletal hand, knocking the San-keth back.

"Is that mightiest spell at your command?" said Lucan, grinning. "Have you nothing better?" He spread his arms, his laughter redoubling. "I stand right here, holy one. Why do you not strike me down?" .

The knights and armsmen stared at him in terror.

"You might slay me," said Blackfang, "but you can never prevail against the children of Sepharivaim!"

"Oh, no doubt," said Lucan, flexing his fingers, "but I weary of your prattle."

He thrust out his hand, his fingers blazing again.

Blackfang's skeleton blasted apart in a spray of bone shards. The San-keth fell screeching into the courtyard and tried to slither away. Lucan strode towards the fallen cleric, black cloak swirling behind him. Blackfang whirled and reared up, fangs bared.

"Please," said Lucan. "I cannot decide whether to be amused or contemptuous. You've no hands to wield weapons, nor legs to run. Your miserable people lost them long ago. You're naught but an overlarge worm."

Lucan lifted his hand. Blackfang floated into the air, writhing and snapping. Lucan laughed and waved his hand in a circle. Blackfang began to spin, slowly at first, but faster and faster, like some giant sling. The Sanketh's curses of rage degenerated into one long shriek of terror, mingling with Lucan's maddened laughter.

Lucan thrust out his hand one last time. Blackfang's head crashed into the wall at incredible speed.

The sound of shattering bone was quite loud.

Blackfang's limp coils collapsed to the ground.

"Fool," said Lucan, still chuckling, his face twisted with glee. For a moment his face resembled that of an ancient, depraved old man. Then he shook himself and pulled his dark hood close.

Silence fell over the courtyard.

Sir Roger's mouth felt as if he had swallowed a coal.

Every few feet he stumbled, spitting out yet another tooth.

"Keep up!" snapped Calibah, glaring. "Mazael will send out horsemen once he's realized you've escaped, and if they find you, it'll be our heads."

"If Blackfang doesn't kill him first," wheezed Roger, glancing back at Castle Cravenlock.

Calibah scoffed. "Do you seriously believe that? Blackfang has proven…unworthy."

"This is your fault," said Roger, staggering towards her. He fumbled for the stolen sword dangling from his belt. "You made me do this, it's your…"

Calibah seized his tunic and pressed her mouth against his throat. Sir Roger went rigid, the tips of her fangs pricking against his skin.

"You should have died there," she murmured, her lips moving up his neck to his ear. "Mazael would have killed you, if I hadn't pulled you out of his sister's bedchamber. Do you know why I didn't let you die?"

Roger shook his head, barely.

"Because my master believes you may yet prove useful," said Calibah.

"Blackfang's dead by now, most likely," said Sir Roger, sweat and blood dripping down his face. "You saw it. His spells couldn't do anything against Lord Richard's brat." He remembered Lucan Mandragon's cold laughter and shuddered. "At least, Blackfang probably wishes he was dead."

"Blackfang was sent to die," purred Calibah.

"What?" said Roger. She let him go.

Calibah smiled at him. "If Blackfang had succeeded, well and good. But my master had wearied of him. His death is no loss. And why did I save you? My master may yet have use for you."

"Who," said Sir Roger, licking his swollen lips, "who is your master?"

"I will show you." She gave him a scornful look. "If you can keep up. My master thinks you might be useful. But if I leave you to die here, he will think it no great loss."

"The village of Greenhaven lies a few miles east," said Roger. "If we make for there, we can steal horses and cover more ground."

Calibah smiled, cold eyes glinting. "That's better."

CHAPTER 5
THE NECROMANCER

Pyres burned below Castle Cravenlock's walls.

The dead changelings had been thrown atop the pyres, doused with oil, and set afire. Five of Mazael's knights and nineteen of his armsmen had been killed, either poisoned or cut down in the fighting. The bodies of the knights had been sent back to their heirs and lands, while the armsmen went to the town's church for burial.

Mazael stood by the pyres with Master Cramton and Bethy, watching the changelings burn.

Or watching their bodies burn. Their heads sat on spears over Castle Cravenlock's gate. Blackfang's head rested among them, mouth open in his final scream.

A warning to the others.

"That's the last of them," said Master Cramton, mopping his brow. "Forty-nine, all told." He shook his head in dismay. "Quite a lot of wood, too."

"Winter's almost over, anyway," said Mazael.

"A bloody business, my lord," said Bethy, hair blowing across her face. "The servants are terrified."

"At least it wasn't any of our people," said Mazael. "Besides Sir Roger. By all the gods, he had best hope I never lay eyes on him again. But the changelings hid themselves among Toraine's party, not my people."

"Aye," said Bethy, scowling. "It's not my place to say so, my lord, but…"

"Say whatever you will," said Mazael.

Her scowl deepened. "It's all Lord Toraine's fault, I say. He kissed the snake, I'll wager, and came here to kill you and Lady Rachel."

"The changelings tried to kill him," said Mazael. Six of them had burst in on Toraine, who had been lying with one of his whores. Fortunately, Toraine had held them off until Timothy had arrived with a half-dozen armsmen.

"Bah, it's but a cover," said Bethy. "They were just pretending to kill him, I say."

Mazael smiled. Bethy's fierce loyalty cheered him. She smiled back at him, and Mazael felt a wave of heat.

"Ah…Sir Gerald and Lord Toraine are coming," said Cramton.

Gerald and Toraine strode down from the castle, Wesson stomping afterwards. Cramton and Bethy bowed and withdrew. Bethy avoided looking at Toraine, and Mazael hid another smile.

"How's Rachel?" said Mazael.

"As well as can be expected," said Gerald. "I think she'll be better in a few days. She's still upset."

"You'd best go to her, I think."

"But my duties…"

"Sir Nathan can handle them for the day," said Mazael. "Go."

Gerald bowed and walked away, leaving Mazael alone with Toraine.

Toraine scowled, his teeth grinding.

"Just get it over with," said Mazael.

"I am sorry," spat Toraine. "I did not realize the snake-kissers had hidden themselves among my party."

"You ought to observe your camp followers carefully," said Mazael. "Though I suppose even you can't sleep with all the whores at once."

Toraine growled.

"Some even think you swore to Sepharivaim and came here to kill me," said Mazael.

"Who says that?" said Toraine, eyes flashing. "I'll kill anyone who says that!"

"Then I most definitely will not tell you," snapped Mazael. "Is it true or not?"

Toraine almost looked shocked. "It is not! Do you question my word?"

"If not for Lucan, my sister and I both would have been killed," said Mazael.

"Lucan!" spat Toraine. "Why not question him? The San-keth have tried to kill both my father and myself in the past. Maybe Lucan invited them. Have you thought of that?"

"I did." Lucan's display of raw power had alarmed Mazael. Timothy, fifteen years Lucan's senior, had no such magic. Even Master Othar, Castle Cravenlock's old court wizard, couldn't have worked such spells. Yet Lucan was just twenty years old.

Where had he gained such power?

"But as it happens, I believe you," said Mazael. "The Mandragons are foes of the San-keth, as are the Cravenlocks. Blackfang did his very best to kill us both, and failed miserably. We will speak of this no more."

"Let us hope Tobias Roland arrives soon," said Toraine. "I am eager to leave this place."

With that, he stalked away.

Mazael sighed. He had mollified one of Lord Richard's sons, if not made peace.

Now what to do about the other?

Mazael had not seen him since Blackfang's grisly demise. He knew the truth about Mazael's demon heritage. What had Lucan decided to do? Would he say nothing?

Or did he plan Mazael's demise even now?

Mazael decided to settle this without delay. He walked back to the castle, hand drumming on Lion's hilt.

Adalar awaited him at the gate. "My lord. Do you require anything?" He had a bandage around his forearm.

Mazael waved his hand. "No. I'm fine." He paused. "You fought well last night, I hear." Adalar had rallied the squires, helping to drive the maddened changelings into the courtyard.

Adalar gave one of his rare smiles. "My lord. Thank you."

"Go," said Mazael. "Just don't train too hard. You'll reopen that cut."

Adalar bowed and jogged away. Mazael smiled after him. The boy had indeed done well. Mazael only wished he had dozen more like him. He looked up at the keep and his smile faded. Adalar's valor could not help him against Lucan.

Mazael entered the keep, climbed the wizards' tower, and knocked at Lucan's door. No one answered. Mazael pushed the door, and it swung open. He stepped into the room and looked around.

It was little more than a monk's cell, bare and cold. The window, little more than an arrow loop, looked down into the courtyard fifty feet below. It surprised Mazael that Lucan had been content with such humble lodgings. Toraine had demanded the finest chambers in the castle. At the very least, Mazael would have expected Lucan to require a workroom for his arcane efforts. He walked to the window, scowling at the courtyard.

But where had Lucan gone? Had he ridden for Swordgrim, intending to warn his father about the Demonsouled Lord of Castle Cravenlock?

"Lord Mazael?"

Mazael whirled, hand flying to his sword hilt. Lucan stood against the far wall, arms folded. There had been nowhere for Lucan to hide within the small chamber. Nor had Mazael heard him come through the door.

"Where the devil have you been?" said Mazael.

"Verifying a few matters," said Lucan, unperturbed. "No changelings remain in the castle."

"And how do you know that?" said Mazael.

"I have my methods." Lucan glanced out the window. "You wished to speak, I suppose?"

"I did," said Mazael. "We never finished our conversation last night."

"Ah," said Lucan. He closed the door. "That. I know you are Demonsouled. But I did not say, however, what I intend to do about it."

"And what, then, will you do?" said Mazael, his hand curling around Lion's hilt.

Lucan's lips twitched. "Nothing."

"Nothing?"

"Correct." Lucan sat on his cot with a sigh. "You spoke to me of peace. I told you I thought it a noble goal, albeit unattainable." He shrugged. "But with you, I believe, it has a better chance than with anyone else."

"But I'm Demonsouled," said Mazael, "spawn of the Old Demon."

"True," said Lucan, wrapping his cloak about him. "But it doesn't seem to have driven you mad, as with most Demonsouled, or have corrupted your heart. Besides," his lips twitched again, "there are advantages to working at Castle Cravenlock, advantages I might lose if you were killed. I have no wish to lose them."

"A place away from your brother?" said Mazael.

Lucan shrugged again. "You may look at it that way, if you wish."

"I don't," said Mazael.

Lucan blinked.

"That explanation is not good enough," said Mazael.

Lucan arched an eyebrow. "An explanation for what? I am not the man with something to hide."

"I think you are," said Mazael.

Lucan said nothing.

"You crushed that San-keth cleric last night," said Mazael.

Lucan laughed, eyes flickering. "The San-keth are not so formidable as rumor makes them."

"Timothy could not have used the spells you worked," said Mazael, "nor could old Master Othar."

"What is your point?" said Lucan.

"You are but a score of years old," said Mazael. "How did you gain such power?"

"Perhaps I'm simply talented."

"Or perhaps not."

A flicker of irritation passed over Lucan's cold face. "I have no wish to discuss it."

"Oh? You were so keen to drag out my secrets. Now I'm returning the favor. How did you gain such power? Master Othar wielded arcane arts for four decades, and I never saw him do anything like what you did last night."

"You know nothing," said Lucan, stepping towards the door.

Mazael blocked him. Lucan's eyes flashed with rage, and perhaps something like fear. "You're right. I know nothing, but I suspect. Toraine thought you consorted with the San-keth yourself."

"The San-keth are of no use to me."

"Then where did you gain your powers?" said Mazael. "I doubt you discovered them on your own. Someone taught you. Who, I wonder? The San-keth? The Old Demon?"

"Absurd," said Lucan. "I thought the Old Demon a legend until last night."

"Then where," said Mazael, "did you gain such power?"

For a moment they glared at each other, standing not three feet apart. Lucan's hands trembled, the fingers flexing. Mazael wondered if he could draw Lion before Lucan struck with some killing spell.

Then Lucan laughed and spun away. "Why not? I know your black secret, after all. Why should you not know mine? No one knows, at least no one living." For a moment the bitterness fell from his face, and he looked young and weary.

Mazael waited. Lucan paced the tiny room, his face working.

"When I was a squire, just eleven," said Lucan finally, "I began showing signs of magical talent. I tried to conceal it as first, for I feared to be burnt as a warlock. But my father discovered anyway, as he always discovers everything." He smirked, the bitter sneer returning. "Most boys displaying magical potential are sent to the school of wizards at Alborg, usually, unless they are first burnt. Women are almost always burnt before Alborg can find them. But my wise father did not trust the wizards of Alborg, has never trusted them. He feared they might gain some hold over me," his smirked hardened, "and therefore break his own hold over me. So after my first term of study at Alborg, he recalled me to the Grim Marches. He had decided to hire a tutor to finish my magical education, and settled upon a man named Marstan, a wizard from Travia. A wizard," Lucan shook his head, "as I later learned, who had once been an apprentice of Simonian of Briault."

"The Old Demon," said Mazael.

"Not necessarily," said Lucan. "Simonian of Briault was a real, and much feared, necromancer. The Old Demon, I suspect, simply masqueraded as him from time to time. Whether the real Simonian still lives I don't know. He was, according to rumor, already three hundred years old when he disappeared. But that is unimportant. Marstan was a powerful necromancer, and none of us realized it at the time."

"What happened?" said Mazael.

"Marstan taught me the basics of arcane sciences," said Lucan. "His purpose was not to impart learning, but to…prepare me. Marstan was old. His body was failing. So he desired a new one." He smirked. "Mine."

"You mean…"

"His spell would have displaced my soul, and he would have claimed my body as his own," said Lucan. "It was not the first time he had done it. He was a least a century and a half old when he came to Swordgrim."

"He failed, then?" said Mazael.

"Not…entirely."

Mazael's hand twitched back toward his sword.

Lucan laughed without humor. "I'm not completely sure what went wrong. My father discovered Marstan's crimes, and sent knights to kill him. So Marstan was in haste, and hasty men make mistakes. Plus he had trained me a bit too well. I was able to fend him off. And…I had something to fight for, at least back then. Marstan failed, and his spirit went to whatever torments awaited it. But…" His cold, bitter smirk returned. "But it almost worked. I have all his memories, Lord Mazael. All of his knowledge, his secret lore, his necromantic secrets. And most of his powers came to me as well."

Mazael stared at him.

Lucan's mouth twisted. "The wraith Blackfang conjured? It was but a minor spirit trapped within the ashes of a cremated body. I could create one with ease, if I chose. I know so many black secrets, necromantic incantations the archpriests of the San-keth would kill to learn." He loosed his mirthless laugh again. "Like you, my secret could be my death. The Church, the Knights Dominiar and Justiciar, the Cirstarcian Order, the wizards of Alborg, all would try to kill me if they knew what spells echo inside my head."

"Does Lord Richard know?"

"Have you not been listening? No one knew." Lucan shook his head. "But my father suspected something. I had…changed. Marstan's expressions, his mannerisms, his way of speaking…much of that came to me. My father thought I had become Marstan's apprentice in truth, that I had willingly taken up black arts. It cost me everything." Lucan's voice cracked. He closed his eyes and kept talking. "I was betrothed. To a woman named Tymaen. I loved her more than anyone, more than anything. After…after, she was horrified by my change. She wished to break off the betrothal. My father agreed. She married Lord Robert Highgate instead. So you see, Lord Mazael, when you told me of Romaria, I did indeed understand. At least she did not renounce you."

Lucan looked away, sunk in his black cloak. For a moment they said nothing.

"If it's any consolation," said Mazael, "I broke Robert Highgate's leg when we were squires together."

Lucan snorted. "Did you?"

"Sir Nathan kept telling him to watch his legs," said Mazael. "Swordplay is as much footwork as anything else. I could have ridden a horse through the holes in his guard." He shrugged. "Instead, I took a leaded practice sword and broke his leg."

"I find that cheering," said Lucan. "Utterly useless, but still cheering." He leaned back against the wall, sighing. "I could have killed Robert, you know. In any number of ways. From afar, and no one would ever have known. It would have looked like a mishap. Or I could have simply blasted the flesh from his bones." He stared into nothing. "Or, if I chose, I could have twisted Tymaen's mind and forced her to come to me."

"Why didn't you?" said Mazael, chilled at the recitation.

"I don't know," murmured Lucan. "Marstan would have, I know."

"And you are not Marstan," said Mazael.

"Am I not? Perhaps I am, and only masquerade as Lucan Mandragon."

"I think not," said Mazael. "After all, if you were truly Marstan, you would have exterminated your brother and your father, and seized the lordship of the Grim Marches yourself."

"And how do you know I'm not planning that as we speak?"

"Because then your father and brother would already be dead," said Mazael. "Believe me, I know what it is to hate a brother. But I didn't kill him." He scowled, remembering the whispers. "Despite what people say."

Lucan inclined his head.

"So," said Mazael. "You don't want to kill Sir Philip, and you don't want to kill your family. Then what do you want?"

Lucan was silent for a moment. Then he said, "I want to find enough power…find a way to keep what happened to me from ever happening again. No one else will have their life ruined by black arts."

Mazael thought of Skhath, of the hidden San-keth cultists, of the Old Demon. "Not likely, I fear."

"Is peace any more likely?" said Lucan.

"No," said Mazael. "But no less a noble goal, as you said."

Lucan nodded again.

Neither man said anything for a while.

Lucan cleared his throat. "If you truly desire peace…the way might lie in an advantageous marriage."

"No," said Mazael.

"It might seem a betrayal of Romaria, I know," said Lucan, "but it is likely your best hope for lasting peace. Lord Malden has unwed daughters."

"Lord Malden's not likely to wed one of his daughters to me," said

Mazael. "Most likely he wants me dead, for swearing to your father. But that's still not the danger…"

"The Lord of Cadlyn has unwed daughters," said Lucan, "as does the Lord of the Green Plain. Either would make a strong enough alliance to keep my father and Lord Malden from warring…"

"You don't understand," said Mazael. "I'm Demonsouled."

"So?" said Lucan.

"So?" repeated Mazael. "I'm the son of the Old Demon. Any child of mine will be Demonsouled as well."

"That's not necessarily a problem," said Lucan. "There are numerous barren, unwed noblewomen. No doubt they would be delighted to wed a Lord of Castle Cravenlock," his cold smirk flickered, "assuming you can stomach bedding an old cow, of course."

"I still dare not take that risk," said Mazael. "Until a woman's moon blood stops, can you say for certain if she is barren or not? Suppose I wed a woman and she became pregnant? The child…sooner or later the demon blood would manifest…"

"Then you will spend your life celibate?" said Lucan. "That is no way for a man to live. You're no monk."

"I dare not risk it," said Mazael.

"You may not have to." Lucan reached into his cloak and produced a tarnished brass ring. "Wear this."

"What is it?"

"A ring," said Lucan.

Mazael scowled. "I can see that."

"It is enspelled. Wear it while you lie with a woman, and you cannot impregnate her."

Mazael gave the ring a dubious look.

Lucan rolled his eyes. "On your hand, lord. I wrought several of them at my father's request, for Toraine." He sneered. "My father doesn't wish a crop of little Mandragon bastards running about, upsetting his orderly domain."

Mazael shrugged and took the ring. It felt quite warm. "I'll consider it."

"Of course you will," said Lucan, the sardonic edge reentering his voice. "Now. You want peace, yes? Sir Tobias will arrive any day. Lord Malden probably wants to kill you. Have you decided what you're going to do?"

"No," said Mazael, turning towards the door.

"Toraine will probably try to ruin things."

"I know."

Lucan stood, adjusting his cloak. "I can…hinder him, if you wish."

Mazael thought about it, almost said yes. "Best not."

"If you wish."

###

That night, Mazael paced his bedchamber, scowling at the candles. Lucan's bronze ring rested on the third finger of his right hand. It still felt quite warm. Every now and again he rubbed it.

Bethy came into the room, the candlelight glinting off her hair.

"My lord," she said, doing a deep curtsy. Mazael could never tell if she let him see down the front of her blouse on purpose or not. "You wished to speak with me?"

"I did," said Mazael. "How are the servants?"

"Frightened, my lord, but better," said Bethy, stepping closer. "You defeated the changelings, after all."

"And you're sure none of our people kissed the snake?"

"Positive." Bethy smiled. "But you asked me that already. Did you want to talk about anything else, my lord?"

"I…"

She looked at him. "I'm cold, my lord. I'm sure you are too." She pulled back the blankets on his bed, slipped out of her clothes, and lay down, candlelight shining off her white skin and auburn hair. "Why doesn't my lord come and warm me?"

Mazael did.

She smiled her gap-toothed grin, and levered up on her elbows to meet him.

###

"You should have done this long ago," murmured Bethy into his chest.

"Um?" said Mazael, opening one eye. He lay on his back, Bethy wrapped about him like a living blanket.

She pushed her hair out of her face and smiled. "You looked so cold and alone. No lord ought to be that way. No man either, for that matter."

"It…" said Mazael, voice hoarse. What could he tell her? That he was Demonsouled, that he had only now found a way to keep from impregnating her with a demon-blooded child?

"It was Lady Romaria, wasn't it?" said Bethy.

"I suppose so," said Mazael, closing his eyes.

"It's not a betrayal," said Bethy, laying her head back on his chest. "Lady Romaria was fearless. We all wish she were still here, all of us in the kitchen."

"So do I." Mazael wanted that more than anything.

"But she's gone," said Bethy, "and you're not. You can't go on alone. Besides," her voice took a playful tone again, "a lord ought to have a mistress. It's only proper. A lord ought to have many mistresses."

"Proper." He laughed, coughed, and cleared his throat. "Not everyone would think so. I can only imagine what Sir Gerald would say."

She laughed, her whole body shaking against him. "Oh, Sir Gerald's a good man, but...well, a woman looks at him, and his tongue ties up in knots."

"And these other mistresses?" said Mazael, opening his eyes. "Won't you get jealous? Put poison in my wine? You do cook my food, after all."

Bethy clucked her tongue. "Whatever for? I'm your mistress, not your wife. I can choose your other mistresses, though. Make certain they're right for you." She rose up on one elbow and gave him a level look. "Though speaking of a wife, when are you going to get married?"

Mazael coughed. "You're lying in my bed, and you're asking me to take a wife?"

She remained unperturbed. "Of course. You're Lord of Castle Cravenlock! You'll have to marry some silly-headed noble wench sooner or later. Someone with lands and knights, a big dowry. Doesn't matter if she's stupid or ugly or wishes she were a nun." She wriggled against him, hooking her hands around the back of his neck. "You can get her with child and come back to us."

"Us?" said Mazael.

"The other mistresses I will pick for you, of course," said Bethy. Her eyes sparkled and she kissed him.

"Of course," said Mazael, kissing her back.

Mazael awoke to sunlight streaming into his eyes.

He had slept late, since he hadn't gotten very much sleep last night.

He had a vague memory of Bethy slipping away to start breakfast. Mazael yawned, rolled out of bed, and poured himself a goblet of wine. Sleeping with her would cause problems, he supposed. Still, almost every lord had mistresses.

And he felt better than he had in months.

Mazael drained his wine, dressed himself, and walked into the corridor.

Adalar waited outside his door, holding his cloak. He did not look happy. "My lord."

Mazael took the cloak and wrapped it around his shoulders. "I'm sorry to have kept you waiting."

"I suppose you were busy last night, after all."

Mazael lifted an eyebrow. "And what the devil is that supposed to mean?"

Adalar said nothing, a jaw in his muscle working.

"Out with it, boy. I'll not have you glaring daggers at my back all day."

"A true knight sleeps only with his wife," said Adalar.

Mazael burst out laughing. "Is that it? I don't even have a wife."

"A true knight is faithful only to his wife," said Adalar.

"Aye, but I've no wife," said Mazael, "and a chaste life is fine for monks and priests, but I'm neither a monk nor a priest."

Adalar's scowl did not abate.

"She was willing, as was I," said Mazael, "so what harm in it?"

Adalar still said nothing.

"I'm your lord," said Mazael, irritated, "and I've no need to defend myself to you." He set off for the stairs, Adalar trailing. "If you want a life of chastity and arms, join the Justiciar Knights." He shook his head. "Though your father would have a fit."

Adalar scoffed and shook his head. "He never did approve of the Justiciars."

"Because they tend towards the fanatic," said Mazael, "and kill folk for drinking overmuch and looking crosswise at a woman. I'd rather have a wise libertine for a lord than a pious fool." He shook his head. "Though perhaps I'm a foolish libertine, at that. I'll hear no more of this, Adalar. Understand?"

Adalar scowled, but nodded. "My lord."

"I hear you had a busy night," said Rachel, shaking her head.

Mazael speared a bit of meat on his dagger and glanced at her. "Not you, too."

"It is impious," said Rachel.

Mazael took a bite. "I'm sure the gods have other things on their minds."

"Suppose you father a bastard?" said Rachel. "We could have another rebellion in twenty years."

Mazael rubbed the bronze ring on his left hand. "I've taken precautions."

"What man and woman do when they lie together is wrong," said Rachel, "and is only sanctified when a child is born."

"You would have become a nun," said Mazael, "if not for Gerald, so don't lecture me on the matter."

Next time he vowed to bring Bethy to his rooms in secret, if only for the sake of peace and quiet.

CHAPTER 6
EMBASSY

The next day, twenty horsemen flying the banner of the Rolands rode for Castle Cravenlock's gates. At their head galloped a knight in his thirties who looked like a shorter, more muscular version of Sir Gerald.

"Here they come," muttered Mazael, striding across the courtyard. He wore his finest tunic, boots, and cloak, and Lion rode in a scabbard of polished wood and leather. His whole court had gathered in the yard, Gerald and Rachel, Timothy and Sir Nathan and Master Cramton and the others.

Even Lucan stood in the courtyard, his black cloak stark against the finery of the knights and minor lords, though Mazael doubted the others could see him.

"Is not Sir Tobias your friend?" said Adalar.

"He is. Or at least he was," said Mazael.

Mazael squared his shoulders as the horsemen clattered through the gate. In the next five minutes he would learn if Lord Malden had become an enemy or not. In the next five minutes Mazael would learn if his lands would know peace or the ravages of war.

Sir Aulus cleared his throat and began to declaim. "Sir Tobias Roland, son of Lord Malden of Knightcastle!"

Mazael walked to the lead rider. The stocky knight sprang out of the saddle with ease. He carried a long, crescent-bladed axe over his shoulder in lieu of a sword.

"Sir Tobias," said Mazael. "Welcome to Castle Cravenlock."

"Mazael, you dog!" roared Sir Tobias, grinning. "Lord of Castle Cravenlock! Ha! I never thought you'd do half as well." He seized Mazael in a rough embrace. "Always though you'd wind up in a shallow grave!"

"And you'd be dead with a pox caught from some whore," said Mazael.

Sir Tobias laughed again. He had a broad, ruddy face suited for both laughter and rage. "Not yet, but I'm working on it." He turned, his grin widening. "Gerald, boy!"

"Tobias!" Gerald stepped forward, Rachel trailing behind him, and caught Tobias in a hug. "You're looking well."

"And you, brother," said Tobias. Rachel caught his eye. "So this is the fair and noble lady who has captured my brother's heart, eh?" He took her hand and kissed it, sweeping his blue cloak in a flourishing bow.

"My lord," said Rachel, a touching of color entering her cheeks. "Gerald has always spoken most highly of you."

"He has, has he?" said Tobias, snickering. "And I'm not lord of anything yet. Though I'm working on that. Sooner or later Father will let me carve a domain of my own out of the Dominiar lands, like old Mandor almost did."

Lucan snorted. No one noticed. Mazael glanced at him, and Lucan gave a slow nod. None of Sir Tobias's party were San-keth changelings.

Tobias began to regale Rachel with a tale of Mazael's exploits during the Dominiar war. He said nothing of Gerald's marriage or Lord Malden's will. Mazael wondered why Lord Malden had sent Tobias to negotiate a marriage. Tobias was bold and fearless, but not particularly subtle.

"Aye, it was a sight," said Tobias, gesturing. "We charged them outside the gates of Tumblestone. Sir Mazael…"

"Lord Mazael," said Rachel and Gerald in unison.

"Lord Mazael in the front, and the Dominiar footmen broke and ran, and we rode into Tumblestone without trouble," said Tobias. "We ought to have kept going, drove them into the sea. I could be lord of Castle Dominus even now."

"Or you could be dead," said a weary voice. "Our strength was spent, as you might recall."

A man in a brown robe rode through the gate, his thinning brown hair shot with gray, his face lined and tired. Mazael felt an enormous wave of relief. Great difficulties and bitter negotiations might lie ahead.

But Lord Malden would not oppose the marriage.

"Brother Trocend," said Mazael, inclining his head.

Trocend slid from the saddle with pained precision and bowed. "Lord Mazael."

Trocend Castleson, known to the world as Brother Trocend, served as Lord Malden's seneschal, right-hand man, advisor, and master of spies. Not many men knew that Trocend had once been an Amatavian monk, but had later left the order for reasons Mazael never learned. And very few people knew that Trocend was a wizard of considerable skill. Mazael suspected if it had something to do with the man's departure from the Amatavian Order.

Or perhaps it was the utter ruthlessness Trocend displayed on occasion.

"Are you well?" said Mazael.

Trocend had a kindly smile, the sort of smile that inspired trust. "As well as can be expected. Old joints do not travel well."

"And Lord Malden," said Mazael, "how is he?"

Trocend's smile turned crooked. "That is what I have come to discuss." He glanced up at the walls. "Let us walk together. We have much to talk about, I think."

"As do I," said Mazael. "Sir Gerald!"

"My lord?" said Gerald.

"See to it that Sir Tobias is entertained." He caught Gerald by the arm and lowered his voice. "And keep him away from Toraine."

Gerald bowed, Rachel on his arm, and led Tobias away.

"Shall we?" said Trocend.

"Of course," said Mazael.

Yet to Mazael's surprise, Trocend walked away from the walls, his pale eyes on Lucan. Lucan stared back, then after a moment, walked towards them.

"So," said Lucan, "my father always suspected Lord Malden kept a wizard, despite his law against magic. Disguised as a monk? Clever."

Trocend gave him a thin smile. "And you are Lucan Mandragon, the Dragon's Shadow? I thought you'd be older."

The two wizards watched each other.

"If you're going to unleash battle-magic on each other, do it outside my walls," said Mazael.

"Direct, as ever, Lord Mazael," said Trocend. "No, I am in fact quite glad to see Lucan. I wished to speak with one of Lord Richard's emissaries."

"The Lord Heir," said Lucan, "has condescended to visit us. Why not speak with him?"

"All men agree that Toraine Mandragon is bold and fierce," said Trocend, "but lacks in…subtlety, perhaps."

Lucan smirked. "I find myself liking you already."

"How splendid," said Trocend. "My old joints feel in need of a walk. Shall we?"

They climbed the ramparts and walked along the curtain wall. A brisk wind blew over the Grim Marches, driving steel-gray clouds across the pale sky. The wind ruffled Trocend's hair, tugged at his robe.

"A fine view from these walls," said Trocend at last. "Not quite so fine as the view from the parapets of Knightcastle, of course, nor from the heights of Swordgrim, but grand nonetheless." He laughed to himself. "Yet it seems that neither Lord Malden nor Lord Richard can see what you will do next."

"Spare me the rhetoric," said Mazael. "This isn't the court of Knightcastle. There's no need to hide your meaning in flowery phrases."

Trocend's laugh remained dry. "Are all you Marcher folk so direct?"

Lucan lifted an eyebrow. "And are all the folk of Lord Malden's court so duplicitous?"

"Come, come," said Trocend. "No one here is a stranger to duplicity, I am sure." Mazael said nothing. "But this is the Grim Marches, after all, and I will follow the custom of the country. So, Lord Mazael. You want your sister to wed Sir Gerald?"

"I do."

Trocend came to a stop. "Why?"

"Because I have a tie to Lord Richard," said Mazael, "since I have become his liegeman. Yet I was a knight in Lord Malden's court for years, and he and Lord Richard are mortal enemies. I therefore want a tie to Lord Malden as well. If I am between them, they will not go to war."

"Or so you think," added Lucan.

"You want peace," said Trocend. "How peculiar. I have never known a lord to refuse war. War is the way of lordship, after all. For with war comes spoils, lands, wealth, and glory. Everything the heart of a knight desires."

"And war also brings misery and suffering and plague," said Mazael. "Will I slaughter thousands to slake my pride? The lords make war and the common folk suffer for it."

Trocend shrugged. "What of that? That is as it always has been. It is what the common folk are there for, after all."

"No," said Mazael, with some heat. "No. A lord's purpose is to be a guardian to his people, not to drive them to the slaughter, nor to hide in his castle as they suffer."

"A novel sentiment," said Trocend.

"I will not have war between Lord Richard and Lord Malden," said Mazael.

Lucan and Trocend laughed in unison.

"Do you really believe you can stop them?" said Trocend.

Mazael said nothing.

Trocend shrugged. "But, as it happens, Lord Malden agrees with you."

Mazael frowned in surprise. "He does? I cannot see him ever forgiving Lord Richard for Sir Belifane's death."

"Has your master come to unexpected reason, then?" said Lucan.

Trocend's thin smile returned. "Lord Malden remains determined to avenge valiant Sir Belifane's cruel death. But...he feels that the time is not yet right." He turned from his contemplation of the countryside. "Besides, other urgent matters occupy his attention."

"Other matters?" said Mazael.

Trocend nodded. "Lord Malden contemplates war against the Dominiar Knights."

It took a few moments for Mazael to grasp this.

"But that's madness," he said. "We defeated the Dominiars once before, but barely. And that was four years ago. They must have rebuilt their strength by now."

"The Old Kingdoms revolted against the Dominiar Order after you defeated them at Tumblestone," said Trocend. "Grand Master Malleus no doubt has his hands full with rebellion."

"What of that?" said Mazael. "That was four years ago. Malleus has either crushed the Old Kingdoms by now, or abandoned them and rebuilt his armies. The Dominiars will be strong again. Why does Lord Malden even want to fight them?"

"Because they want Tumblestone back," said Trocend.

"Why?" said Mazael.

"The Dominiars never quite accepted that you took Tumblestone," said Trocend. "It was, after all, their key harbor." His mask-like smile returned. "For all the Dominiars' devotion to the ideals of piety and crusading zeal, most of Mastaria's foreign trade went through that one city."

"Crusading armies do not pay for themselves, after all," said Lucan.

"Quite right," said Trocend. "For that matter, it is hard to send crusading armies to ravage heathen lands without a port."

"Lord Malden wishes to defend his lands, then," said Mazael.

"Not quite," said Trocend. "Lord Malden desires more land." He craned his neck. "Where, pray, are the Justiciar Knights?"

"They aren't here," said Mazael. "Lord Richard expelled them from the Grim Marches for siding with Mitor."

"Whereupon they all returned to Swordor," said Trocend.

"The stronghold of the Justiciar Knights, the Dominiars' sworn enemies," said Lucan, "and Lord Malden's closest allies."

Trocend inclined his head. "And the Justiciars are most desirous of war against the Dominiars. They are in dire need of land. Those expelled knights need supporting, after all."

"So both the Dominiars and Lord Malden are eager for war," said Lucan, glancing sidelong at Mazael. "Difficult to avert, if a man desires peace."

"And why are you telling me this?" said Mazael.

Trocend smiled. "Lord Malden is eager for Gerald to wed. And your sister seems an appropriate match for Sir Gerald, fair and pious and courteous, despite her somewhat questionable past. But...well," he smiled, "if your sister marries a Roland, then you must be a friend to the house of

Roland, no? Lord Richard is your liege lord, and Lord Malden would not ask you to become an oathbreaker for his sake…"

"But if Rachel is to marry Gerald," said Mazael, "then Lord Malden may ask for my help against the Dominiars."

Trocend studied him. "Exactly."

Mazael sighed and stared over the battlements. He did want to go to war with anyone. Yet Lucan was right. War would come, sooner and later. And if it did, would it not be better to fight in a distant land, to spare his people from its horrors?

But how would the Old Demon use such a war? The thought made Mazael's gut clench. Yet it seemed he had no other choice.

He shivered. And it had seemed he had no other choice, too, when Mitor rose against Lord Richard, no choice at all until the Old Demon offered to make him king of the world…

Trocend and Lucan stood in silence, watching him. "I would have to speak to Lord Malden before I make any decision."

"Of course," said Trocend. "You can speak with Lord Malden when you come to Knightcastle."

Mazael frowned. "Come to Knightcastle?"

"Lord Malden wishes the wedding to take place at Knightcastle, in the Hall of Triumphs," said Trocend. "After all, Lord Malden cannot come to the Grim Marches himself."

Lucan smirked. "Wise of him."

"Lord Malden will offer several manors in southeastern Knightrealm to Gerald as a wedding gift," said Trocend. "Fine estates. Superb for grapes. Of course, Lord Malden also expects Sir Gerald to have…appropriate means of support within the Grim Marches."

"I have numerous manors without a lord," said Mazael. "Bloody Ridge, for instance." He thought of Roger Gravesend and ground his teeth. "I had planned to combine several manors and make Gerald a lesser lord anyway."

"Good, good," said Trocend. "Now, as to the lesser details…"

Mazael nodded. He had, no doubt, several days of polite dickering in his future. But the heart of the matter had settled. Rachel would marry Gerald, and Lord Malden would not go to war against Lord Richard.

But Mazael thought of war against the Dominiars, of the Old Demon, and wondered what this might cost.

The next week went quickly.

During the day Mazael discussed details with Trocend, about wines, taxes, tolls, vassals, and wedding costs. It made his head ache. That Trocend found such subjects endlessly fascinating only made it worse. Trocend could lecture on tolls and taxes for hours without end.

Every day Gerald took Sir Tobias out hunting. Sir Nathan took it on himself to keep Toraine entertained, to Mazael's boundless relief and gratitude. Everyone agreed that keeping hot-headed Sir Tobias and brutal Toraine apart was a good idea, and neither man seemed eager to meet the other.

And at night Bethy came to his rooms, and they lay together with enthusiasm. Two nights Bethany had to prepare food for the guests, so in her place she sent one of the new servants, a girl named Anne. Anne was about twenty, had blue hair, brown eyes, freckles in unusual places, and remarkable vigor.

One night both Bethy and Anne came to his chamber. During the next day's negotiations, Trocend commented on Mazael's unusually languid manner.

Adalar's scowls got ever wider. Mazael, preoccupied with affairs of state, did not notice.

He and Trocend concluded their negotiations. Mazael would take Rachel and Gerald to Knightcastle himself, accompanied by thirty of his knights, with Sir Tobias and his knights acting as a guard of honor. Mazael planned to bring Timothy, and Sir Aulus Hirdan, who would no doubt appreciate escaping from his wife for a few more months.

He appointed Sir Nathan to act as castellan in his absence. Sir Nathan refused. Mazael refused the refusal, and Sir Nathan acquiesced, though with little pleasure.

That left one man to convince.

Mazael pushed open the door to Lucan's chamber. The room looked bare and empty, and a thin layer of dust covered the ragged cot. Mazael stared at in some confusion. Where did Lucan sleep, if not here?

"Lord Mazael."

Lucan had appeared from nowhere, again.

"How the devil do you do that?" said Mazael.

"Do what?" said Lucan, running his hand against the wall.

"Disappear like that," said Mazael.

Lucan lifted his eyebrow. "Do I? Perhaps I walk quietly."

"No doubt," said Mazael.

Lucan smirked. "How can I be of service?"

"Trocend Castleson saw through your mindclouding spell," said Mazael.

"He did."

75

"Will he always be able to see you?"

Lucan laughed. "Trocend is quite skilled, but not nearly as clever as he believes. There is more than one way to work a mindclouding. I could stand before his face and he would never notice me."

"Are you sure?"

"I stood over his shoulder and watched him write a secret letter to Lord Malden," said Lucan.

"And?"

Lucan turned, stepped to the narrow window. "It seems he doesn't believe that you truly wish peace. Trocend believes that you will play Lord Malden and Lord Richard against each other, and plan to ally with whomever offers you greater rewards."

"But I told him I want peace!" said Mazael.

"That's right, you did. And lying lords are so rare."

Mazael sighed through gritted teeth. In the end, it didn't matter what Trocend believed. Mazael had to convince Lord Malden, not his lackeys. "All right. I am leaving for Knightcastle tomorrow, and will likely not return until autumn."

"I know."

"I want you to come with me," said Mazael.

Lucan frowned. "No."

"Why not?" said Mazael.

"Because I'm not a fool," said Lucan. "I can conceal myself, but Trocend might discover me, and Lord Malden could have other wizards lurking about Knightcastle. If Lord Malden finds me he will do his utmost to kill me. A son for a son, after all."

"You didn't seem the sort to fear death," said Mazael

"Don't be trite," said Lucan. "If Lord Malden tries to kill me, I might be forced to kill several important people, possibly Lord Malden's surviving sons, or even the old man himself." His lip curled. "You'd then find peace rather unattainable, I expect."

"I expect," said Mazael. He sighed again, wishing he had room to pace. He hated standing still. "I need your help."

Lucan said nothing.

"You were right," said Mazael. "The San-keth will not stop at anything to kill Rachel. I don't...I couldn't have stopped Blackfang myself. I can't protect Rachel by myself. Not against black magic."

"And what is your sister's life to me?" said Lucan.

Mazael glared in a sudden flash of rage. How dare he say such a thing? Mazael throttled back his fury and forced himself to speak.

"Because," he grated, "don't you want to defend others against the dark powers that took you? This is your chance. You heard what Trocend said about the Dominiars. War is coming, I fear."

"I told you as much," said Lucan.

"This is the sort of war the Old Demon will manipulate," said Mazael. "Or the San-keth. You saw it yourself, when Mitor rose against your father. He was a puppet on the Old Demon's strings." He hesitated. "So was I."

"Men often make war, with or without demonic prompting," said Lucan. "Demons walk the earth, but that does not mean they lurk in every shadow."

"Yet suppose they lurk in the shadows of this war," said Mazael, staring at Lucan, "and you could have stopped them, but you did not."

Lucan drew in a deep breath, folded his arms, and lowered his head. For a long moment he stared at the ground. Mazael watched him. A distant part of his mind realized that Lucan was but five years older than Adalar, and yet his face looked so old, so grim.

"Why not?" said Lucan. "It would startle my lord father. That alone would make the journey worth it." He did a mocking little bow. "I will travel with you, Lord Mazael."

"Good," said Mazael, thinking of what it might mean if Lord Malden discovered a son of Lord Richard Mandragon in his court. This, like the marriage, might too have its price. "Very good."

###

They left Castle Cravenlock the next day, in a spring morning that still had winter's bite.

A line of a hundred riders wound its down from the castle. Sir Aulus rode in the front, carrying the Cravenlock banner with its three crossed swords on the black background. Mazael rode behind him, glancing to the north. He saw another band of horsemen riding in that direction, the Mandragon banner flapping in the wind. Toraine had departed for Swordgrim, no doubt to deliver a lengthy report to his lord father.

Toraine's departure filled Mazael with vast relief. The gods alone only knew what kind of havoc the man could have wreaked during Mazael's absence.

He took his horse, a sturdy gray palfrey named Mantle, and rode down the line. Gerald and Tobias were towards the front, Tobias bellowing a dirty ballad, and laughing every time Gerald scowled. Adalar and Wesson rode behind them, Adalar leading Chariot. The big horse suffered himself to be led, albeit grudgingly.

Rachel was in the middle of the column, surrounded by her maids and the wives of various knights and lords. Mazael beckoned to her, and she steered her mare to his side.

She rode better than Mazael would have thought.

"You look nervous," said Mazael. In fact, she looked haunted, a look that had not left since Blackfang's attempt on her life.

She gave him a wan smile. "I am well, I suppose." She looked at the broad plains and shuddered. "It's just…"

"The San-keth?" said Mazael.

"That?" said Rachel, frowning. "I haven't thought about it much. If I do…I'll get upset. You understand." Mazael nodded. "I've…never left the Grim Marches before, Mazael." She waved her hand at the sky. "I've never been farther west than that inn at the Northwater."

"You're pointing southeast," said Mazael, following her hand.

Her expression turned arch. "And which way is west, lord brother?"

Mazael smiled and pointed.

Rachel pointed west. "Then I've never been further west than the inn." She dropped her hand, staring. "I've always wondered what other lands are like."

Mazael smiled again. "Then I will be glad to show you."

Rachel smiled back, and they rode to the front of the line.

CHAPTER 7
DUSTFOOT

They crossed over the Northwater and rode west.

The western reaches of the Grim Marches bordered on the northeastern corner of Knightrealm and the eastern edge of the High Plain. Most travelers to Knightrealm took the road through the High Plain, and then south to Knightcastle itself, or chartered a river barge to take them up the Riversteel, one of Knightrealm's two great rivers.

Mazael did neither, instead leading his party southwest into Knightrealm. The Lord of the High Plain was not on friendly terms with Lord Richard. And the road southwest was not well-traveled. Mazael wished to avoid chance meetings.

Who knew when they might encounter more San-keth changelings, disguised as normal men?

The road wound southwest, through the wild lands between the Great Southern Forest and Knightrealm's low mountains. Rachel stared at everything with wondering eyes. Mazael realized that she had never seen mountains before. She even seemed enchanted by the mud of the road.

Timothy rode at the rear, clutching small crystal wrapped with copper wire. Every now and again the crystal flashed. With luck, Timothy's divinatory magic could sense any enemies before they attacked.

Besides Timothy rode a slight figure wrapped in a black cloak.

No one had noticed Lucan. That still raised the hairs on the back of Mazael's neck. Even Trocend had failed to notice Lucan, or, at least, pretended not to.

###

Four days later, Mazael decided to talk with Gerald.

On their left loomed the silent, towering trunks of the Great Southern Forest, filled with shadows. No one dared lumber within the forest, fearing the predations of the wood devils. Mazael had met the Elderborn of the wood, and had found them no devils, though ruthless in defending their homes.

To the right rose the worn, green-mantled slopes of Knightrealm's mountains. A few rose high enough to have crowns of snow, but most had jagged peaks of bare stone and tree-cloaked flanks. The mountains looked stately, but often held many bandits. Every few years the local lords sent armsmen and knights to sweep out the bandits. Mazael himself had done so at Lord Malden's bidding, years past.

He shook aside stray memories and came to Gerald's side. Gerald rode with his brother, and together they told Rachel stories from Knightrealm's past. Every damned rock in Knightrealm, it seemed, had legends attached to it. At this village a knight had made a valiant last stand. Or beneath that tree two lords had fought each other to the death over the love of a fair lady, slaying each other, while the lady killed herself in grief. Mazael wondered how much was true, and how much puffed-up twaddle.

"It's said that King Lancefar Roland, the fourth of his name, took this road eight hundred years past to wage war against the kings of the High Plain and Dracaryl," said Gerald. "Along the road he met and killed the bandit-king Black Ricard in single combat."

"Did he?" said Rachel. Rachel ate it up. She had always loved songs and tales. Maybe, Mazael mused, that was how the San-keth had ensnared her. Perhaps they had told her a better tale.

"Aye," said Tobias, grinning. "And then as he rode back from war, though yon hills," he waved his hand at the worn mountains, "he came upon a meadow where seven lonely shepherdesses dwelt, yearning for a manly embrace to ease…"

"Tobias!" said Gerald. "That is hardly an appropriate tale for a lady's ear."

"What isn't?" said Mazael. "There's not a jongleur's song in the world that doesn't have some fool beheaded ere it's done, or some maiden lass who's no longer maiden by the end. Gerald! I need to speak with you. If you can trust Tobias alone with your betrothed, of course."

"My lord!" said Gerald. "He is my brother."

Tobias guffawed. "Fear not. You seem the sort of man to be most jealous of his sister's honor."

"Keep that well in mind," said Mazael.

He and Gerald rode to the back of the line. Lucan lifted a dark eyebrow as they passed, and Gerald failed to notice him. Mazael suppressed a shudder. Despite Lucan's pledge, his powers still made Mazael uneasy.

"What's amiss?" said Gerald.

"A question. From here," said Mazael, "if a man wished to go to Knightcastle, what road would he take?"

Gerald blinked. "Well…we'd take the road through Krago Town, cross the Black River, then head north to Knightcastle. A bit out of the way, to be sure, but most folk traveling from the Grim Marches to Knightcastle go through the High Plain."

"We're not going through Krago," said Mazael. "We'll head west through Stillwater, instead, take the road to Knightcastle from there."

"Stillwater?" said Gerald, frowning. He glanced at his squire. "I suppose Wesson would be glad to see his father." Wesson's father, Lord Tancred, was Lord of Stillwater. His prodigious capacity for ale had earned him the nickname Tancred the Tankard. "But that would be farther out of our way. We'll have to cross both the Black River and the Riversteel, then approach Knightcastle from the north."

"We will," said Mazael. "But I'm not riding through Krago Town."

"Why not?" said Gerald. "The place has an unpleasant reputation, but I've never been there." He shrugged. "Though I did meet Krago's lord once. Rather uncouth fellow, really. Krago Town's ill name may just rise from him."

"Or it may not," said Mazael. He closed his eyes, letting his horse follow the road. "Skhath. The San-keth priest, when he still masqueraded as a man. Where did he claim to have been born?"

Gerald nodded. "Krago Town."

"And Skhath told me he had come from Karag Tormeth in truth," said Mazael.

"The San-keth high temple," said Gerald. "The heart of their cult."

"Nobody knows where it is," said Mazael, "but I'd wager it's not far from Krago Town."

"In Knightrealm?" Gerald shook his head. "I can't believe that such a place would remain hidden for so long. And Skhath most likely just lied. Mayhap he picked Krago Town for its obscurity, knowing that no one from Castle Cravenlock had ever been there."

"And maybe not," said Mazael. "But it's possible there's a hidden snake-cult at Krago Town, as there was at Castle Cravenlock." He looked at Rachel, laughing at Tobias's stories. "But if there is…then it's not someplace we should take Rachel."

"Agreed," said Gerald, face grim. "Stillwater it is, then."

They rode in amiable silence for a moment.

"At least," said Gerald, "if we do encounter a San-keth cleric, you've got that magic sword of yours."

"I wonder about that," said Mazael.

"About Lion?" Gerald's eyes flicked to the longsword dangling from Mazael's belt. "Of course it is enspelled. I've seen it with my own eyes, and you have too."

"We have," said Mazael. "But where did it come from?"

Gerald frowned. "Don't you remember? Sir Commander Aeternis of the Dominiars gave it to you in surrender, after we took Tumblestone."

"And where did Aeternis get it from?" said Mazael. Gerald shrugged. "This thing is a relic of old Tristafel." He patted Lionel's pommel. "It's at least three thousand years old. I wonder where Aeternis found it."

"Maybe you'll have the chance to ask…"

"Lord Mazael!" Timothy's shout cut off Gerald's conversation.

Mazael booted Mantle to a trot and hastened to Timothy's side. "What is it?"

Timothy's eyelids fluttered, his hand tightening around the crystal. "There's…ah, people. Ahead. Over the next hill." He jerked his chin at a craggy hill. The road wound its way around the base. "About four or five dozen. And…I think one group's trying to kill the other group."

"Gerald," said Mazael, "get the knights ready. This isn't our concern, but fights have a way of pulling in bystanders. And for gods' sake, have some men stay with the women." Gerald nodded and galloped ahead, giving orders, and took his shield from Wesson.

"Lord Mazael!" said Trocend, steering his horse towards Mazael. "Is something amiss?"

"I don't know yet," said Mazael. "Ready yourself, just in case. Sir Tobias!" Tobias looked up from telling another bawdy story. "There might be bandits ahead." Or, of course, a battle between minor lordlings. "Get your men ready!"

Tobias grinned. "Ha!" He pulled his long axe free. The crescent blade looked scarred and very sharp. "A boring journey, so far. A little excitement would be welcome!"

Mazael rode to Adalar and dismounted Mantle. Adalar took Mantle's reins, and Mazael climbed up into Chariot's saddle. The big horse snorted and tossed his head as Mazael took the reins, pawing at the ground.

"You're as eager as Tobias," muttered Mazael. His destrier looked ready for blood and mayhem, which was the horse's usual mood. Mazael wondered if horses could become Demonsouled, shook aside the ridiculous thought, and rode to the head of the column. Sir Tobias and Gerald settled on either side of him.

They rode around the rocky hill, into a broad valley between two of the low mountains. A small river, little more than a creek, ran down the center of the valley. A dozen heavy wagons stood on the road running alongside the creek, the oxen snorting in fright.

Close to seventy ragged men ran in circles around the wagons, shouting and brandishing crude weapons. A dozen men in studded leather jerkins stood atop the wagons, wielding short swords, fighting for their lives. Even as Mazael as watched, one of the men fell with a scream, pierced with a javelin, and fell into the creek.

"Bandits," muttered Mazael. He yanked Lion free and stood up in his stirrups. "Charge! At them, at them!"

Tobias whirled his axe over his head and whooped.

Mazael kicked Chariot to a gallop. The horse sprang forward with an eager whinny, hooves tearing at the turf. Behind him the knights shouted and surged forward. Mazael wished there had been time to don his armor, and then he had no thought for anything but sword play.

The bandits did not even have time to turn around. Chariot crashed into a ragged man, running him down, even as Mazael struck the head from another. The knights thundered into the bandits, blades flashing, hooves stamping. Mazael galloped through the bandits, his arm rising and falling, leaving dead men in his wake. He caught a glimpse of a tall, lean man in a dusty brown cloak atop the lead wagon, staring at him beneath bushy gray eyebrows.

The knights tore past the wagons, wheeling their mounts around. Most of the bandits lay dead, their blood staining the brown grass. About a dozen survivors fled in all directions, throwing down their weapons. The knights broke into small bands and set after the fleeing bandits. Mazael cursed and wheeled Chariot around. Trying to keep his knights in disciplined formation after a charge had proven almost impossible.

He rode to the lead wagon. "Which of you is the master of this caravan?"

"That would be me, sir knight," said the man in the dusty cloak, his voice polite and smooth. He set his short sword on the wagon's seat and sprang down. Everything about the man looked dusty. His boots were dusty. Even his bushy gray eyebrows and gray hair looked like they had been colored with dust. He gripped the edge of his cloak and did grand bow. "Harune Dustfoot, a humble merchant of Tumblestone, at your service."

Mazael snorted. "Dustfoot? Appropriate enough."

"Well, I do quite a lot of traveling, after all," said Harune. "There's very little profit in standing still." He cocked his head to the side. "I presume I have the honor of speaking with Lord Mazael of Castle Cravenlock?"

"You do," said Mazael, frowning. "How the devil did you know that?" Sir Aulus rode past, sword in one hand and Cravenlock banner in the other. "Of course, the banner."

"Actually," said Harune, "my youngest brother was long a merchant in Knightport, before he left for distant shores to pursue his fortune. He told me of a formidable, though landless, knight named Sir Mazael Cravenlock who used to guard his caravans."

"That was years ago," said Mazael. "I've come up a bit in the world since then." He missed those days. He had had no responsibilities, no bonds, and the freedom to go wherever he chose.

And he had known nothing of his Demonsouled blood.

"I thank my lord for saving my humble caravan," said Harune, bowing again. "Bandits are always thick in the mountains after the winter, though I have never seen quite so large a band."

"Where are you bound?" said Mazael.

"Knightcastle," said Harune, "as I am carrying cheeses from Cadlyn and sausages from Farsifel. Lord Malden's youngest son is getting married, rumor says, and rumor claims that he'll throw a grand feast for the folk of Castle Town." Harune shrugged. "He'll need to buy food."

"You mean," said Sir Tobias, who had ridden up to Mazael's side, "those bandits tried to kill you over a cartload of damned cheeses?"

Harune shrugged. "They're fine cheeses."

"As it happens, the rumors speak true," said Mazael. "Sir Gerald is marrying Lady Rachel Cravenlock." He waved his hand at them. "My sister. No doubt your brother told you that as well."

"My second cousin passed along the rumor, actually," said Harune.

"We're heading for Knightcastle ourselves," said Mazael, "since we have the bride and groom with us, and it would be hard to hold the wedding without them."

"Or without fine cheeses," agreed Harune.

Mazael snorted. "Undoubtedly. So, ride with us. We'll take no reward."

"But…" said Tobias.

"He can't pay your lord father's tax if he can't get to Castle Town in one piece," said Mazael.

Tobias sighed. "True enough."

"Gerald!" said Mazael. The younger man rode over, Wesson trailing behind, wiping down Gerald's sword. "Dispose of the corpses, and get our men in line. Have them stay around Harune's wagons…we wouldn't want you to get married without cheese, after all."

Gerald gave him an odd look, but rode off, shouting commands.

Mazael watched his knights and Tobias's for a moment, then rode past them. Lucan sat on his horse, wrapped in his dark cloak, ignored and unnoticed.

"Well?" said Mazael.

"No changelings," murmured Lucan, shaking his head. "Common bandits, nothing more." He frowned. "Though there is something odd about this Harune fellow…"

"What?" said Mazael. "A changeling?"

"No," said Lucan, shaking his head. "I...think he has some sort of enspelled bauble on his person."

"Dangerous?"

Lucan shook his head again. "Hardly. You have one, after all." He pointed at the bronze ring on Mazael's hand. "And you use it quite frequently, as I understand. Best get back to your men, before they wonder why you're sitting here talking to yourself."

"Keep an eye on Harune," said Mazael, "just in case."

"Your whim is ever my command, lord," said Lucan, doing a mocking little bow.

Mazael sighed and rode back to the line.

A few hours later they rode away, leaving behind a massive, crackling pyre, the bandits' heads mounted atop spears as a warning to others.

CHAPTER 8
STRAGANIS

Another week took them to the Black River and the ford of Tristgard.

Lord Tancred had not been at Stillwater, having already left for Knightcastle. They stayed one night at Stillwater Keep, wined and dined by Lord Tancred's seneschal, a dour man with neither humor nor wit. Mazael had left the next day, with some relief, and pushed on to the Black River and Tristgard.

It seemed that village of Tristgard, like every other castle, village, and ruin in Knightrealm, had its legends.

"It was at this ford that King Tristifane stood against the Malrag hordes," Gerald told Rachel, warming to the tale, "with only eight hundred loyal knights, against a hundred thousand."

"The numbers inflated with every retelling, no doubt," said Mazael. "It was most likely twelve knights and sixty Malrags."

Both Gerald and Tobias gave him reproachful looks. Mazael rolled his eyes and fell silent.

"Old King Tristifane won against the horde," said Tobias, "though he fell in the battle, and two-thirds of his loyal knights perished. His son raised this statue to commemorate the battle." Tobias pointed. "You can see it up ahead, here. It's worn down a bit, over the centuries."

A massive monolith sat at the base of a hill, crusted with generations of lichen. It might have once been a statue, though it looked more like a random boulder fallen from the hill.

"It's also said that if enemies ever cross the Black River, old King Tristifane's ghost will rise up to drive them out," said Gerald.

"And here's the Black River," said Mazael. "Perhaps we'll see if Lord Malden think us enemies or not, eh?"

The Black River stretched before them, winding its way through the craggy hills. Its name came from the chunks of black stone that littered the riverbed, lending the water a dark color. Tristgard held the only safe ford through the river. There were bridges over the river to the north and south, but both charged higher tolls.

The village stood on the far side of the river, built of weatherworn gray stone and red shingles. Wisps of smoke curled from the chimneys. A cluster of tents and wagons stood outside the village's walls. Because of its location, Tristifane played host to a near-perpetual merchants' fair.

Yet the tents looked deserted, and the wagons empty.

Gerald frowned. "It's usually more crowded than this."

"Merchants, bravos for hire," said Tobias. "Whores." He looked disappointed.

"Harune!" said Mazael. The merchant's wagon rolled up. "Have you passed through Tristgard recently?"

"I did, my lord," said Harune, staring at the village with fixed intensity. "On my way to Cadlyn. Though that was a year past."

"My knights and I rode through two months ago," said Tobias, "and the village seemed more normal then."

"Timothy?" said Mazael.

Timothy joined them, clutching his quartz crystal, his eyelids fluttering. "There are…people in the village. Nine hundred or so." He frowned. "Nobody in the merchants' tents, though. Peculiar."

"Perhaps the villagers have plague," said Rachel, frowning.

"There's no plague marks on the gate," said Timothy

Trocend gazed at the wall with his cool eyes. "They may have been too stricken to make the effort."

Something about Tristgard did not sit right with Mazael. He had passed through the village several times over the last fifteen years, and the place had always seemed boisterous. Never before had it seemed to quiet.

Lucan rode up, ignored by the others. Mazael risked a glance at him. Lucan shrugged.

"Then let's go see what's wrong with Tristgard," said Mazael.

He urged Mantle into the ford.

###

Calibah, Roger Gravesend discovered, had stripes of pale scales on her thighs and breasts.

She had more or less ordered him into bed once they had taken control of Tristgard. Roger had obeyed, mostly out of terror. The minute Calibah no longer found him useful, she would give him a kiss with her fangs, and he would die in agony. Besides, she was shapely enough, if a man disregarded her more serpentine attributes.

After they finished, she walked naked across their room on the top floor of Tristgard's inn, and glared out the window.

"Get dressed," she ordered.

"Eh?" said Roger, lifting his sweaty head from the pillow.

Calibah glared at him, baring her fangs. "I said to get dressed!"

Roger all but fell from the bed in his haste. He cursed the way his hands shook as he buckled his belt and laced his boots. A few months ago he had lived in comfort in his own hall, master over his peasants. Now he was little more than a slave to this half-mad, half-human woman. How had he ever come to this?

"Bring me my clothes," said Calibah.

Roger scooped up her skirt and blouse and boots, his face burning with anger and shame, and walked to her side. The sunlight glistened off her skin and pale scales. She took the clothes from his arms and dressed.

As she bent over to pull on her boots, Roger contemplated plunging his sword into her back. One quick thrust and he could be free of her. But could he get out of Tristgard alive? All the other calibah, the changelings, held her in awe. She seemed to be their chief. The other changelings all had names, but she was only Calibah.

Calibah pulled on her blouse, smiling, and something her cold eyes made Roger very glad he had not drawn his sword.

"What's happening?" said Roger.

"They're here," said Calibah.

"Lord Mazael?" said Roger, his hands tightening into fists. This was all Mazael Cravenlock's fault. If not for him, Roger would never have been reduced to his current misery.

"He is," said Calibah. "And Rachel Cravenlock and two of Lord Malden's three surviving sons…and, ah, the Dragon's Shadow as well. My master is pleased."

Sir Roger licked dry lips. "The Dragon's Shadow slaughtered Blackfang. Your master should be wary."

"Blackfang was a child," murmured Calibah. "Skhath was a child. Both were fools who displeased my master. He is one of the great holy ones, an archpriest of Karag Tormeth. You thought Blackfang wielded the power of great Sepharivaim? Now you will see true power." She titled her head to the side. "Ah. My master wishes to meet you. Come." She beckoned, moving to the door. "He awaits us in the common room."

Roger swallowed and followed Calibah through the inn's hallways. None of the rooms were empty. Most held terrified villagers, lying bound and gagged on the floor. A few held the corpses of villagers who had proven troublesome.

Calibah swept into the common room, Roger at her heels. A dozen changelings stood in a cluster near the door, around a hunched figure wrapped in a filthy black cloak. Roger gagged as the stench from the cloaked shape struck him. The changelings stepped back, fear on their faces. The hunched shape turned towards Sir Roger.

"Master," said Calibah, falling on her face before the cloaked figure.

"Sir Roger Gravesend." The voice was slow, creaking, and quite hideous. "So we meet at last."

Roger saw the creature beneath the cloak, and stifled a scream.

"Have the women stay by the riverbank," said Mazael. "Behind Harune's wagons, if possible. They'll make for cover." Harune nodded and shouted instructions to his drivers. "Adalar. Get Chariot."

Gerald frowned. "You really expect trouble? We're not a week from Knightcastle!"

"I don't know," said Mazael, scowling. Adalar took Mantle's reins, and Mazael climbed off the palfrey's back and swung into Chariot's saddle. He did know that he felt better equipped to face trouble atop his black-tempered warhorse. "Timothy, Sir Aulus, Sir Gerald, Sir Tobias, Brother Trocend; with me." He cast a quick glance at Lucan, who nodded and rode up.

The seven of them rode over the ford, through the abandoned caravansary, and to the open gates of Tristgard. Within Mazael saw a cobblestone street, well-tended stone houses, and a fountain bubbling within a market square.

Yet he saw no people.

"Damned strange," he muttered. "Sir Aulus."

Sir Aulus nodded and stood up in his stirrups, the black Cravenlock banner flapping over his head. "Folk of Tristgard!" His voice boomed over the stone walls. "Lord Mazael Cravenlock wishes to purchase provisions of you, and means you no harm! He bids you to send out an emissary for parley!"

Nothing moved within the silent village.

"Timothy?" said Mazael.

Timothy's fingers clenched over the quartz crystal. "It's...I'm sure there's hundreds of people within, my lord. But... only a few of them are moving. And I'm sure some of them are watching us."

"Plague, then," said Trocend. "That's the only reason so many would lie abed this time of day. We must make all haste to Knightcastle and warn Lord Malden."

"No," said Mazael. "Plague...no, that's not right. Something else is wrong..."

The door to the village's inn burst open.

"They're not coming into the village," whispered Roger, staring at Lord Mazael and his band through the inn's window. They sat unmoving on their horses a few yards from the gate. "They know something's wrong." He wiped sweating palms on his cloak.

Calibah glared at him. "Do you question the master?"

"No," said Roger, "it's just...I..."

"Come," croaked the cloaked, stinking shape. "Let us go and meet our guests." A hissing approximation of laughter came from the black cowl. "We do not want to be discourteous, no? Calibah, Gravesend. Follow."

"But he'll kill me," said Roger.

"Your presence will drive him to rage," said the cloaked form, "overruling his reason, and then I shall exterminate him."

Roger, as usual, had no choice but to follow.

A hunched shape in a ragged black cloak stumbled from the village's inn.

Mazael watched in growing alarm. The figure moved with a strange lurching, almost skittering gait, filthy cloak dragging against the cobbles. Had a plague indeed taken Tristgard? Mazael's Demonsouled blood could resist plague, but what of those around him?

Then he saw the man and the woman behind the cloaked form, and Mazael's fists clenched in sudden fury.

The lean, pretty woman, in the rough dress of a serving girl, was a changeling. The man was Sir Roger Gravesend.

"You traitor dog," said Mazael, yanking Lion free. "You should have run to the ends of the earth if you wanted to live."

The cloaked figure stopped, and a pair of enormous, fish-pale hands reached up and opened the filthy cloak.

Trocend jerked back in the saddle, his cool mask shattering. "By all the gods!"

Mazael's breath hissed through clenched teeth.

A San-keth cleric stood beneath the cloak. Most San-keth clerics, Skhath and Blackfang included, used undead human skeletons to carry their limbless bodies.

This one seemed to have preferred a living body. Of sorts.

A vaguely human-like torso, knotted with muscle, squatted atop an armored carapace and eight spider-like legs, each one hard and sharp. A scorpion's stinger reared over one shoulder, shimmering with greenish slime. By some black sorcery the San-keth's serpentine body had been grafted into the pale flesh of the torso. Mazael saw knots of muscles and nerves interwoven with the faded red scales. The San-keth's eyes were ancient and cloudy with centuries of cruelty.

The entire freakish assemblage of mismatched meat stank like carrion.

"Gods," said Trocend, still shaken. "What sort of black alchemy is this?"

"Gods?" croaked the San-keth cleric. "Your cursed gods stripped us of our limbs, for they feared our great might." It spread its human arms. "The lesser servants of great Sepharivaim use the undead corpses of the inferior races for their carriers. We greater servants may manufacture our own limbs."

"Greater?" said Mazael.

Lucan cursed, very softly.

"I am Straganis, archpriest of Karag Tormeth, master of the seventh circle," hissed the San-keth. "You are Lord Mazael Cravenlock, who murdered Skhath, servant of great Sepharivaim. You are sister to Rachel Cravenlock, apostate and betrayer. You both shall perish for your crimes." His hands began working patterns, fingers crackling with green flames.

Mazael hefted Lion. The sword began to shimmer with an azure glow. "I think not."

Straganis cackled, hands thrusting out. Emerald flame blazed, and a black shadow flew at Mazael. A chill stabbed into his chest, and he tried to raise his crackling sword to block the shadow...

Lucan sprang from the saddle and threw out his hand. The shadows scattered in a snarl. Straganis whirled, hissing. Lucan surged towards the San-keth archpriest, a spell glowing around his fingertips.

"So!" laughed Straganis. "The troublesome dilettante. I'll slay you myself. Kill them all!" Straganis made a twisting motion with his hands.

Mist swirled, and both he and Lucan vanished.

Mazael blinked in astonishment, and looked up to see dozen crossbow-armed changelings standing atop the village's walls.

"Get back!" he yelled, waving Lion. "Back, damn you, back!"

The others turned their horses.

Mazael just had time to curse himself for not donning his armor.

A crossbow quarrel slammed into Mazael's left shoulder, another into his leg, still another into his gut.

He thought he heard Rachel scream his name.

He reeled, trying to keep his saddle and his sword, as Sir Roger and a swarm of changelings charged at him.

###

Lucan caught his balance and looked around.

He stood in a mist-choked forest of gnarled, twisted trees. The fog swirled around his boots and cloak. Hulking shapes lumbered through the trunks, menacing and shadowy.

Before him he saw the translucent, ghostly walls of Tristgard, watched a horde of wraith-like changelings charge a shimmering Mazael.

"Do you know where you are, foolish boy?"

Straganis emerged from the misty trees, spider legs tearing up the mossy ground, tongue flicking at the air.

"The spirit realm, of course," said Lucan, circling the San-keth. "The parallel world to the realm of mortals." He flicked a hand at the ghostly, transparent walls of Tristgard. "Material objects cast their shadows to his realm." He paused, watching Straganis's forked tongue flick at the air. "An impressive trick, bringing me here, but a futile gesture. Did you think to impress me with your power?"

"The thoughts of the lesser races mean nothing to me, Dragon's Shadow," said Straganis. "You have long been an irritant to the servants of great Sepharivaim. You have crossed our paths, and meddled in our business, for the final time. My power is strengthened here." Straganis's knotted, pale hands rose, and worked a summoning spell.

A dozen shimmering, hazy tigers loped from gloom, eyes glowing, claws leaving gashes in the damp earth. They were creatures of the spirit world, similar to the ones Lucan could summon in the material world.

Here, of course, they were much stronger.

But Lucan had resources of his own.

His fingers flew through the arcane gestures, his lips mouthing the spell. The mist swirled, and a dozen horse-sized, glowing wolves burst from the gloomy trees. They streaked forward and crashed into the tigers, snarling and snapping, sparks of fire bursting from their claws. Lucan gritted his teeth, trying to keep his balance. Creatures of the spirit realm were stronger here, and took that much more effort to control. If his grip wavered, they would turn on him in a heartbeat…

Straganis began another spell, his words echoing with arcane force. Lucan felt a moment's astonishment. Straganis had strength to spare for another spell?

Lucan began a spell of his own to meet Straganis's attack, even as he tried to keep his will focused on the wraith-wolves.

Timothy saved Mazael's life.

Mazael slumped in the saddle, blood flowing from his wounds. The quarrels' steel heads grated against the bones of his shoulder and leg, Lion dangling from his pain-wracked hand. He had to lift his arm, had to defend himself against the charging changelings, but he could not move…

Timothy dropped to one knee before Chariot, hand pawing inside his coat. He yanked free a slender copper tube, about a foot long, capped on one end with a cork. Timothy yanked the cork free, held the tube out before him, and began shouting a spell,.

Even through his pain, Mazael felt a surge of alarm. He had seen Timothy use that spell before.

One of the changelings raised an axe, his face a few feet from the copper tube, when Timothy finished the spell.

A blast of flame exploded from the tube and howled into the lines of the changelings. The heat struck Mazael like a burning blanket. A dozen changelings fell dead, charred beyond recognition. Another dozen fell, screaming, flames chewing into their flesh. The rest skidded to a halt, gaping. Mazael caught a glimpse of Roger Gravesend, jaw hanging open.

Timothy coughed, sweat sheeting down his face, and fell to one knee, panting. The surviving changelings charged forward, eager for blood.

But Mazael had gotten his breath back.

He roared and spurred Chariot forward, brandishing Lion. Chariot, less dazed than his master, leapt into motion. The big horse galloped past Timothy and trampled a changeling. Mazael screamed and brought Lion crashing down again and again, changeling blood splashing against him and mingling with his own. Their weapons raked at his legs and chest, but Mazael ignored the wounds.

The pain failed to penetrate the wall of his rage.

"To Mazael!" Gerald sounded half-panicked. "For the gods' sake, after him!" Mazael glimpsed Gerald crashing into the lines of the changelings, his gleaming sword rising. Tobias and Sir Aulus and the rest of the knights thundered after him. Mazael even saw Harune Dustfoot fighting with a sturdy short sword.

Mazael had just enough time to wonder where the devil Lucan had gotten to, and then battle rage drowned all thought.

###

The misty air snarled with arcane energies.

Straganis summoned more spirit-creatures, nightmarish shapes that looked like the bastard offspring of a spider and a rabid rat. Lucan countered with another calling spell, conjuring more of the spirit-creatures he had bound to his service. Things like winged jackals dropped from the sky, falling upon Straganis's minions.

Lucan's lips peeled back from his teeth. Power thrummed through his limbs, his head aching with the strain. Every spark of his magical strength strained, yet he still needed more.

Straganis's power was greater than his. For the first time in a long while, perhaps for the first time ever, Lucan found himself overmatched.

Straganis hissed yet another spell, tongue slithering past his yellowed fangs, and raised a hand. The earth trembled.

One of the trees uprooted itself, rising into the air, roots dangling like filthy hair. It hovered for a moment, then Straganis pointed.

The hovering tree hurtled at Lucan.

Lucan thrust out his own will, straining his power to the utmost. The trunk shattered in the middle, shards of wood spraying in all directions. The effort of the spell sent agony through Lucan's forehead, and for a moment it felt like his brain had begun to flow out his ears and nose.

"Is that the limit of your power?" said Straganis, laughing. "Can you do no better? You cannot stop me from crushing your life."

"Gloat as you will," snarled Lucan, trying not to gasp. "I am still unbeaten."

But he while had the strength to stop Straganis's spells, he did not have enough power left to strike back. Sooner or later, Straganis would wear down his defenses and cast a killing spell…

Straganis threw out both of his hands, the full force of his will hammering into Lucan.

Lucan flew backwards, smashed into a tree, and slumped to the ground, his concentration scattered.

Chaos thundered through Tristgard's gate. The rage in Mazael's blood filled him, making him stronger, faster, tougher. A changeling lunged at him with a spear, and Mazael blocked it, his blade beating aside the iron blade. Another changeling sprang at him with a long dagger. Mazael yanked the crossbow quarrel from his shoulder and rammed it into the changeling's eye.

It hurt, but that didn't concern Mazael just then.

The changelings broke and ran. The charge of the knights had forced them back through the village's gate. Sir Tobias and Sir Aulus galloped onto the ramparts, cutting down the crossbowmen. The surviving changelings threw down their weapons and ran. Mazael grinned, wiping sweat and blood from his eyes. These changelings were deadly enough when they struck from the shadows with poisoned fang and blade.

But they could not stand in a fair fight.

"Kill them!" yelled Mazael, standing up in his stirrups, sweeping Lion over his head. "Cut them all down. No mercy!"

The knights rode down the street and into the square, where the changelings had gathered for a last stand. It was over quickly.

Calibah snarled in the hissing San-keth tongue. "It is time to go."

Roger didn't answer. They stood on the roof of the inn, watching the slaughter. Sir Roger had seen Mazael fight before, of course, had even seen the man angry.

But Roger had never seen Lord Mazael Cravenlock in such a furious rage. He looked more like a devil than man. And the way he grinned! It chilled Roger to his toes. To think that he once though to go blade to blade with that madman!

Calibah grabbed his shoulder. "We must go, fool."

Roger found the courage to scowl at her. "It seems your great master has failed."

Poisoned fangs snapped an inch before his nose. Roger managed not to scream, but only just. "We cannot serve Sepharivaim if we are dead. Unless you'd prefer your skeleton to be raised as a cleric's carrier?"

"I'd rather not," said Roger.

A chorus of screams rose from the square as the knights cut down the last changelings.

"Then we run," said Calibah. She shrugged. "I know not why great Straganis chose this attack. Our kind strikes best from the shadows. But we shall kill Lord Mazael and apostate sister yet. Now run!"

She sprinted for the stairs. For an instant Roger considered hiding out, going on his own, escaping from the grasp of the San-keth and Calibah.

He saw Lord Mazael's horse trampling the dead changelings.

Sir Roger sprinted after Calibah as fast as his legs could carry him.

Lucan staggered back to his feet, spitting out blood. Straganis's creatures had driven Lucan's creatures back. Some fled in all directions, their pain and fear breaking through the bonds of Lucan's control.

Straganis hissed, his will striking out again. Lucan just had the strength to turn the spell aside. A nearby tree exploded in a spray of splinters and shredded leaves. Lucan's few surviving spirit-creatures fell back, overwhelmed. He didn't have the strength left to summon any more.

"It is finished, human," said Straganis, creaking forward on his spider-legs. "Lie down and die."

"No," said Lucan. Strewn about the ground lay the ghostly images of slain changelings, dozens of them. "I've heard such empty threats before, old snake." But this threat didn't seem very empty.

He looked again at the flickering images of the dead changelings.

Unless…

He began another spell, a summoning spell in reverse, and chopped his hands.

The air snarled about him, and the bodies of the changelings became substantial, pulled into the spirit-world by his spell.

Lucan reached into his dark half, the part filled with old Marstan's shadowed memories, and began muttering a spell. Green fire blazed to life around his fingertips, throwing back the gloom of the spirit-realm.

"You use the arts of great Sepharivaim against me?" laughed Straganis. "Foolish boy."

Lucan ignored the taunts and sent his will ramming into the corpses. The green fire sprang from his fingers, stabbed into their staring, dead eyes.

The corpses moved.

Lucan raised his hands, gritting his teeth. The corpses shambled up, their movements limp and wooden. Straganis hissed a command in the San-keth tongue and pointed. Three creatures, crab-like things with dozens of eyes, lunged at Lucan, claws clacking.

Lucan focused his strained mind and sent a command to the animated corpses.

The undead shambled into the path of the spirit-creatures, ignored their slashing claws, and tore Straganis's creatures apart. Straganis made a lifting gesture. A tree rose from the earth with a groaning roar and flew at Lucan. One of the animated corpses stepped into the flying tree's path. The blow reduced the corpse of bloody pulp, but the tree fell to the ground.

Straganis struck back. His first spell ripped a corpse to shreds. The second sent an undead hurtling through the air. But the remaining corpses continued their grim, plodding advance. Lucan kept working spells, pulling more corpses into the spirit-realm,. The power of the necromancy thrummed through him, filling his flesh with an icy cold, drowning his pain with numbness. No wonder Marstan had practiced this art for so long!

Death conquered all, but Lucan's arts made him master of the dead.

Dozens of animated corpses shambled towards Straganis. The San-keth cleric backed away, tongue flicking, head waving back and forth.

"Are not the great arts of Sepharivaim enough to stop me?" said Lucan.

"The fool!" snarled Straganis. "I told him this would fail!" His alien eyes met Lucan's. "We will meet again, Dragon's Shadow, in the last moment of your life."

Mist swirled around him, and the San-keth cleric vanished. His last few spirit-creatures turned and fled.

The intact corpses, some two dozen, stopped.

Lucan commanded them to watch over him, and then promptly passed out.

###

The last changeling died screaming, slashing with a short sword. Mazael's blade swooped past the changeling's guard and crashed through its neck.

An exhausted silence fell over the village of Tristgard.

Mazael wheeled Chariot around, the rage hammering through his veins. He had not yet had his fill of killing. He wanted to ride through his knights, striking right and left, leaving a fresh layer of blood on his sword.

Then he remembered Romaria lying on the floor, dead.

The rage drained away, leaving only a sick weariness.

And quite a bit of pain. He had torn out all the crossbow quarrels in his frenzy, but the wounds still gaped, along with a half-dozen cuts taken during the battle.

If he were a normal man, he would have died by now.

"Mazael!" Gerald galloped to his side, trailed by Sir Aulus and Adalar and Wesson, "Mazael, gods, you're hurt…"

"I'm fine," lied Mazael, trying to keep his voice steady. Wounded or not, he was still lord, and had men to lead. "How many men wounded?"

"Five were killed," said Gerald. "Perhaps a dozen wounded, I think."

"Timothy!" Timothy hastened over on wobbling legs, still wiping sweat from his brow. "Check the wounds of the men; make sure none were bitten or poisoned. And I thank you. If not for your timely intervention I might be in a dire state."

"But… you are in a dire state!" said Timothy. "I saw those crossbow bolts plunge into you. I was sure you were dying, or already dead. By all the gods, I amazed that you can speak, let alone still keep your saddle."

"The bolt but grazed me," said Mazael, looking at himself. He did look awful, his clothes soaked with drying blood, his hands bloody and soot-stained. "Much blood, but little hurt."

Timothy shook his head in befuddlement. "I would have sworn on the names of Amatheon, Amater, and Joraviar that I saw a bolt buried in your gut." He managed a feeble smile. "It is a miracle, a blessed miracle."

"No doubt," said Mazael. Timothy, he suspected, would find the truth unpleasant. Mazael did, after all. "Get going. We have men that need tending."

Timothy dashed away.

"Sir Aulus." Mazael looked over the stone houses and the bloodstained street, a grim thought coming to him. "Take some men and search the village. See if you can find what became of the village folk."

Ghastly images of cellars and wells stuffed with corpses played through his head. "I doubt the entire village was peopled with San-keth changelings."

"Lord." Aulus turned, bellowing commands in his sonorous voice.

Mazael tried to wipe the sweat from his forehead. His hand came away bloody. "Gerald. Did you see what happened to…" He almost asked what had become of Lucan and caught himself. "Did you see what happened to that devil Straganis? He flung that spell at me, and vanished."

"I don't know," said Gerald. "I couldn't see clearly. It…something like a black shadow appeared before him. I don't know what it was…but it hurt to look at it. Straganis yelled something and disappeared." Gerald shrugged. "Mayhap his own foul magic turned back upon him."

"Let us hope," said Mazael. What the devil had happened to Lucan? Had he and Straganis destroyed each other?

"My lord," said Adalar, edging his horse past Gerald. "You must see to your wounds at once, lest they fester. I was sure you had been killed."

"I'll be fine," said Mazael. Neither Gerald nor Adalar appeared to believe him. Mazael certainly couldn't tell them the truth. "All right. Just a moment. I'll…"

"Lord Mazael!" Trocend waved at him. "We have found someone."

Mazael kicked Chariot to a trot and hastened down the street. Sir Aulus and a half-dozen other knights helped a group of women and children from a house.

"We found them bound and gagged in a cellar," said Sir Aulus.

"Search the rest of the village," said Mazael. He glanced at Adalar. "I'll have Timothy look at my wounds momentarily."

Adalar scowled, but nodded.

But already the burning pain had begun to lessen, replaced by itching and tingling as his torn flesh knitted itself together of its own accord.

The men, it appeared, had been held prisoner in the village's inn. A brief search discovered the elderly Sir Lindon Tristgard, lord of the village. He did not seem well.

"They came yesterday," he croaked, leaning on his daughter's arm. "Out of the hills. They claimed to be fleeing a flood in the high passes. So I gave them sanctuary and refuge…and…" His daughter offered him a cup of wine, which the old man drained. "They were monsters, San-keth devils. I had always thought the San-keth monsters, nightmares, peasants' prattle. I never thought them real…"

"They came for me," said Mazael. "I am sorry I brought this misfortune upon you." He cursed under his breath. How had Straganis followed his movements? Had he used some sort of far-seeing magic?

"You saved us," said the old knight, clutching at Mazael's knee. "I heard them speak. Once they killed you…they were going to kill us. Sacrifice us all to their foul snake-god." He offered a quavering smile. "But you were stronger! You are our deliverer. Please, just ask, and I will give you whatever you desire."

"A flagon of wine, to begin," said Mazael, "and a quiet place where I can be undisturbed for a short time." Adalar gave him an odd look. "I wish to pray to the gods, to offer thanksgiving for our victory, for it was a very close thing."

"Of course," said Sir Lindon. "The church." The church stood on one side of the village's square, facing the inn. "No one will disturb you there."

Mazael nodded and slid from Chariot's saddle. It hurt, but not as much as he expected. One of the villagers pressed a wooden goblet of wine into his aching fingers. He drained it away, walking to the church with as steadily as possible.

"My lord," said Adalar, trailing after him, "you're hurt, you need assistance."

"I'll be fine," Mazael snapped, "I told you." He thought a moment. "Go and see if Lady Rachel needs any assistance." He thought of going to Rachel himself, and discarded the notion. The sight of his bloody clothing would likely throw her into hysterics. "I need to pray alone. I'll rejoin you and the others shortly."

"But…"

"Go!" said Mazael, growling. "I told you, go."

Adalar bowed and departed.

Mazael opened the church's heavy door and slid inside, pulling it shut behind him. Beams of dusty light sliced through the church's windows, illuminating ancient pews and a high altar adorned with the images of Amatheon and the other gods. Mazael stripped off his blood-wet tunic, tossed it aside, and collapsed onto one of the pews. It felt quite uncomfortable, but he didn't care. He just wanted to lie down for a moment.

His chest, leg, and arm began tingled, the itch digging deep into his skin.

He turned his head and looked at the wound on his shoulder. The torn muscle and shredded flesh began to tie itself together again, the ripped skin closing. The gods only knew what Trocend and Gerald would make of that, if they happened to see it.

His Demonsouled blood continued its work, healing him.

Mazael sighed and lay back. A few more minutes and he could face his men without them noticing anything amiss.

He dozed off.

###

Adalar picked his way through the chaos in the village square, carrying a bundle of clean clothing.

"Go and see to him at once!" Lady Rachel had told him. "I care not what he says, he's hurt! Give him some clean clothes, and make him have Timothy see to his wounds."

"But, lady," Adalar had said, "he doesn't..."

Lady Rachel gave him a look. Most of the time she seemed mild, even timid. Yet in some matters, her will was just as formidable as her lord brother's.

So Adalar pushed open the church's door and slipped inside. The place was quiet, save for the sound of heavy breathing. Adalar did a quick genuflection in the high altar's direction and walked through the pews, seeking for Lord Mazael.

Adalar found him lying on the pew, sleeping. His tunic was gone. Adalar winced at the sight of the garish wounds on Mazael's stomach and shoulder. Gods, they looked bad. If Timothy did not see to that gut wound at once ...

Still, the wounds looked better than Adalar remembered. Maybe he hadn't seen right. What kind of man could take three crossbow bolts and live, let alone ride and fight?

And even as Adalar watched, Lord Mazael's wounds began to vanish.

He blinked, his mind unable to trust his eyes. Bit by bit, the wound on Mazael's shoulder shrank. The torn hole in his stomach contracted. His ragged, heavy breathing became lighter and easier.

Adalar stood rooted with horror, the hair on the back of his neck standing up. What sort of diabolical power had done this? Had Lord Mazael sold himself to some black force?

Adalar turned and fled from the church.

###

Mazael blinked his eyes open.

He must not have been dozing long; the sunlight streaming through the church's windows had not changed. He stood, grunting at the stiff ache in his back and shoulders.

But despite that, he felt fine.

His wounds had vanished, leaving unmarked skin in their place. He pulled on his tunic and strode to the church's door. He hadn't wanted to rest with it on; otherwise the skin might heal over the cloth, and it would hurt like the devil to pull if off.

The door stood just slightly ajar.

Mazael frowned. He had closed it, or so he had thought. Then again, he had been hurt and dazed at the time. He shrugged and stepped back into the village's square.

The gods knew he had far bigger problems to deal with, after all.

CHAPTER 9
KNIGHTCASTLE

The next morning they began the final leg of the journey to Knightcastle, leaving the wounded knights to recover in Sir Lindon's manor house. Old Sir Lindon himself insisted on coming, to praise their valor before Lord Malden. Sturdy Harune Dustfoot and his ox-drawn carts rumbled on behind them.

"You did well, merchant," Mazael had said. "I would not have expected such valor from you."

Harune shrugged. "Well, my lord…if they had defeated you, after all, my fate would have been grim indeed."

"True," said Mazael, "but valor is valor. Come to Castle Cravenlock someday and I will see that you are properly rewarded."

Harune bowed. "I look forward to that."

In fresh tunic, trousers, and cloak, Mazael rode on Mantle. He had seen no sign of Lucan, nor had anyone discovered his body. What had happened to him? Had he and Straganis destroyed each other? Certainly Straganis would have struck again, if he yet lived.

And if Lucan was dead…gods only knew if Lord Richard would be angry or relieved.

###

They crossed the Riversteel, and made their way south.

Traffic thronged the roads. Merchants hauling their carts, pilgrims, landless knights, wandering scholars, and vagrants filled the roads of Knightrealm. Mazael had no qualms about forcing people off the road.

Lordly rank had its privileges, after all.

They passed dozen villages in a day, every inch of land cultivated. Spring had come, and the peasants labored in the fields, preparing for the sowing. Vineyards clung to the rocky slopes, and orchards stood beneath the hill. The lands looked pleasant, peaceful, prosperous.

Mazael wanted the Grim Marches to look that way, one day.

Though he could have done without the Justiciar Knights.

They were everywhere, riding on their horses, scowling at the peasants, their blue cloaks with the silver star flapping. They scowled at the Cravenlock banner, but did not dare make trouble, not with two of Lord Malden's sons.

Every now and again they passed the remnants of a pyre. A sign proclaimed that here a woman had been burned for witchcraft, or a man for being a warlock, under the authority of the Justiciar Knights. Mazael doubted there were more than a half-dozen wizards in all of Knightrealm, and most of them were in Lord Malden's court.

Perhaps it was just as well Lucan had disappeared. Some Justiciar Knights might have come to miserable deaths, otherwise.

They did not have any difficulty finding lodgings. The local lords fell over each other offering room and board to two of Lord Malden's sons. Mazael had not eaten so well since leaving Castle Cravenlock and Bethy's well-ordered kitchens. The spirits of the others rose. Gerald and Tobias ruminated at vast length about the history and lore of Knightcastle to Rachel.

Even Trocend smiled, every now and again.

Still, Mazael brooded over what had happened to Lucan, and what lay ahead. Even if Straganis had been killed, the San-keth would not give up. Without the help of a powerful wizard, Mazael might not be able to protect Rachel. And he dared not confide the secret of his true nature to either Trocend or Timothy.

Adalar seemed troubled, almost shaken. Mazael supposed the boy had been horrified by Straganis. Gods knew the creature had been horrific enough.

###

"We're almost there," said Gerald.

Mazael rode with Trocend, Gerald, Tobias and Rachel. Adalar rode at his side, watching him from the corner of his eye. The boy's vigilance amused Mazael. No doubt Adalar still thought Mazael bore some dire wound.

Their party, now nearly one hundred and sixty strong, traveled along the banks of the Riversteel. The river looked like a ribbon of cold steel, flowing through the green earth. Barges and rafts navigated the river, the boatmen bawling curses. Knightrealm's low mountains rose sharp and rocky against the sky, while the valley bloomed with new greenery. Villages and vineyards and small castles dotted the banks and the hills.

"You've never been to Knightcastle, my lady?" said Trocend, in his dry, lecturing tone.

"No," said Rachel. "I've never even been out of the Grim Marches, ere now."

Tobias laughed. "And what a trip, eh? Bandits and snake-kissers. Another week of this and she'll never want to leave the Grim Marches again."

"Around the next bend in the road," said Gerald, "and you'll see Castle Town, and then Knightcastle itself." He smiled. "It's…quite a sight."

They rode around the next hill, and Knightcastle rose before them like a cloud of stone.

The valley stretched away to the south, following the line of the Riversteel until it came to Mastaria, the land of the Dominiar Knights. On the western bank of the Riversteel sat Castle Town, a prosperous city of ten thousand, stone steeples and steep roofs stark against the sky. A maze of tents and wagons surrounded Castle Town, no doubt drawn by the news of the impending wedding. Away to the northeast went the canal to Knightport, a project that had taken generations of Roland lords to build.

Behind Castle Town, on the sheer hills, stood Knightcastle.

"By the gods," whispered Rachel, her mare slowing to a stop, "it's so huge."

"Best hope she says that on your wedding night, eh?" said Tobias. Gerald gave him a look just short of murderous.

Rachel didn't notice, her eyes fixed on Knightcastle.

The castle was enormous, far bigger than Castle Cravenlock, larger even than Lord Richard's seat of Swordgrim. It had been started three thousand years ago, when the first Rolands built a refuge in the foothills, fleeing the ruin of Tristafel. Every Roland king and lord since had expanded the castle, raised new towers, reared new walls.

Now Knightcastle was the size of a small city, a fantastic jumble of towers and walls and keeps atop a series of high foothills. It had three concentric curtain walls, each higher than the other, encircling rings of towers and bastions. Dozens of banners flew in the breeze coming down from the mountains, one each from the lords under Lord Malden's rule. A Roland banner the size of a small house flew from the Old Keep, the highest tower in the castle, the keep the first King Roland had built, long ago.

"I've never seen anything like it," said Rachel. Tobias snickered.

"Let's not stand about staring," said Mazael. "Lord Malden is waiting, no doubt."

The horsemen spurred forward, starting towards the great pile of Knightcastle. Mazael turned and rode back down the line, until he came to Harune Dustfoot.

"We part ways here, master merchant," said Mazael. "You're for Castle Town, no doubt."

A wide grin spread across Harune's face. He still looked dusty. "That I am, Lord Mazael. Maybe we'll meet again at Lady Rachel's wedding, I think?"

"Maybe," said Mazael. "Bring some of those cheeses."

Harune laughed, bowed from his seat, and steered his wagons towards Castle Town.

Mazael trotted back to Gerald and Tobias, and they rode up the hills towards Knightcastle's mighty barbican. Gerald and Tobias vied with each other telling tales to Rachel, how the first King Roland had turned back a Malrag horde on this road, how the fifth King Roland had defeated his brothers here to claim the throne of Knightcastle, how Knightcastle had been besieged many times, once for nine years, yet had never fallen to an enemy.

They rode through an arched gate large enough to swallow a house, and reined up in a barbican larger than the market squares in many cities. Armsmen in the colors of the Rolands bowed and stepped aside. From the far gate came a dozen armsmen, escorting a red-faced man in noble finery.

"Welcome, my lords," said the man in finery, "to Knightcastle."

He was in his mid-forties, and looked a lot like both Gerald and Tobias, but was short and plump where Gerald was tall and lean. He smiled and bowed from the waist.

Mazael slid from the saddle, boots thumping against the stone paving, and bowed back. "Sir Garain."

"Sir Mazael," said Sir Garain, Lord Malden's oldest son, the heir to Knightcastle. He smiled again. "Lord Mazael, rather. You went out a knight of my father's household, and came back a lord."

"It wasn't my choice," said Mazael.

"I suspected not," said Sir Garain. "You, your highest ambition was always to drink and whore, as I recall."

"Things change," said Mazael.

"Yes…they rather do, don't they?" said Garain, titling his head. Mazael met his pale blue eyes without flinching. "You've…been through a lot, haven't you, since you left? And most of it not good."

"I have," said Mazael.

Tobias might be the strongest of Lord Malden's surviving sons, and Gerald the most pious.

But Garain was the smartest by far.

"We can speak at length later," said Garain. "Father is waiting for you."

"Eagerly, I hope," said Mazael.

Garain sighed. "Not really. He's…ah, in one of his moods."

Mazael shook his head. "You mean he's enraged and wants to kill someone."

"Father does have his moods," said Garain.

Mazael opened his mouth to answer, then Gerald and Tobias barreled past.

"Garain!" bellowed Tobias, catching up the smaller man in a bear hug. Garain coughed and pounded his brother on the back.

"Ah, Brother Trocend!" said Garain. Trocend slid from the saddle with age-stiffened joints. "Good to see you again. I'm glad you got Lord Mazael and kin here safely."

"It was not easy," said Trocend, moving with stiff steps. "Not at all."

"We've much to discuss," said Garain. His tone became formal. "Lord Mazael! My lord father awaits you in the Hall of Triumphs, and bids you, your lady sister, and Sir Gerald to make your way there with all haste."

"We will," said Mazael. Garain moved off with Trocend, both men speaking in low tones. Mazael wished he could overhear them. Trocend was Lord Malden's seneschal, and secret court wizard, and Garain was his chancellor. Both men knew more of Lord Malden's mind than anyone else.

And conducted most of Knightrealm's governance. Lord Malden was getting old, after all.

Rachel squinted up at the Old Keep, the banner of the Rolands flapping seven hundred feet over their heads. "Is it a long walk to the Hall of Triumphs?"

"Walk?" said Mazael, swinging back up into Mantle's saddle.

"But won't we take our horses to the stable?" said Rachel.

"My lady." Gerald took her hand and kissed it. "Let me show you Knightcastle."

Mazael grinned, and they galloped through the lowest courtyard and up the ramp to the second curtain wall. They rode past the Garden of Lady Gwendolyn, where Gwendolyn Roland had wed Lord Randerly, adding Knightport to the Rolands' holdings. Then they rode through the Court of Victors, a vast square filled with hundreds of statues, each of a long-dead Roland. Here, Gerald explained, stood statues of the Rolands that had conquered, yet fallen in battle.

Stone images of two of Lord Malden's sons stood there. Sir Mandor, who had died at the Battle of Deep Creek, slain by the Dominiars. Mazael had taken command of his army and taken Tumblestone. Next to Mandor's statue stood the statue of Sir Belifane, who had died sixteen years ago fighting against Lord Richard.

Lord Malden had not forgiven that when Mazael had left. Mazael doubted the last year had changed his mind.

They climbed to the last barbican and curtain wall, and reined up the High Court. The Old Keep, grim and ancient and scarred, stood over them. On the opposite side stood a hall the size of a small cathedral, towering over the Court. Guards in gleaming mail and Roland tabards stood at the center of the court, around a bronze statue of the first King Roland on horseback.

Mazael took a deep breath. He had come to Knightcastle.

Now he just had to keep Lord Malden from killing him.

CHAPTER 10
LORD MALDEN

An army of squires arrived to take their horses. Knights and lords vied with each other for the honor of sending their sons to Lord Malden's court, and Lord Malden had more squires than most lords had knights. Mazael slid from the saddle and handed Mantle to one of the fresh-faced squires, and warned another about Chariot's foul temper.

"Keep an eye on them, Adalar," said Mazael. "Keep Chariot from biting."

Adalar gave him a distracted nod.

Four men walked from the Hall of Triumph, wearing mail and the Roland colors. The lead man carried a herald's staff and wore a velvet cap with an ornate silver badge. The herald stopped, thumped his staff against the stones, and bowed.

"Lord Mazael. Lord Malden bids you to come before his seat at once, with the Lady Rachel and Sir Gerald. Lodgings have been prepared for your knights and followers."

"Timothy," said Mazael, "Sir Aulus. See to things."

The wizard and the knight went about their tasks. A few Justiciar knights, standing near the wall, cast cold looks at Timothy, but even the Justiciars would not kill a man in Lord Malden's own castle. Or so Mazael hoped.

"Come," said the herald, beckoning.

Mazael looked at Rachel. She gave him a feeble smiled and hooked her arm through Gerald's.

"I'm sure Lord Malden is most eager to see me," said Mazael.

The herald's expression twitched.

They walked in silence across the High Court's stone expanse. The guardsmen threw open the massive double doors, and Mazael, his sister, and his closest friend strode into the Hall of Triumphs.

Slender pillars supported a vaulted roof and a triforium balcony that encircled the hall. The pale marble floor gleamed, so polished that Mazael saw his reflection shimmering beneath him. Sunlight streamed through massive crystal windows behind the dais, revealing a magnificent view of Castle Town and the Riversteel valley. From the ceiling hung dozens of faded banners, dented shields, and ancient weapons. The Lords of Knightcastle had long hung the banners of their vanquished foes in the Hall of Triumphs, trophies to proclaim their might and intimidate their enemies.

An ancient Mandragon banner, no doubt from old King Lancefar's march, hung near the dais.

Hundreds of lords and knights and ladies stood in the hall. The murmur of conversation fell silent as Mazael approached. The lords and knights wore berets adorned with bronze and silver badges, long cloaks, and silk doublets. The ladies wore brocade gowns and hats with proud feathers. Mazael's travel-dusty clothes looked crude by comparison. He didn't much care.

It didn't surprise him to see a large group of Justiciar Knights near Lord Malden's dais, resplendent in their silvered armor and blue cloaks. He was surprised to see a group of black-armored Dominiar Knights not far from the dais. Some of the knights glared at the Justiciars, who glared right back. A few dared to glare at Lord Malden.

And with the Dominiar Knights stood a solid, stocky man, Sir Commander Aeternis, who had surrendered Lion to Mazael after the Battle of Tumblestone. Sir Commander Aeternis gave Mazael a solemn nod, which Mazael returned. Behind Aeternis stood a pale young Dominiar officer in ornate black armor, glaring at Mazael with black eyes. At his side stood a tall woman all in mourning black, her hair the color of blood, a dark veil drawn over her features.

Something about the veiled woman, whether the way the gown covered her hips and bodice, or the sheen of her hair, or the glint of gray eyes beneath the veil, made Mazael's blood stir in a way it had not for a long time. He wrenched his eyes away from the dark woman, promising himself that he would learn more of her later.

Assuming he survived the next few minutes, of course.

The herald moved with a slow, deliberate pace, rapping his staff against the floor with each step. Mazael sighed in annoyance and shoved past the herald, ignoring the gasps. Lord Malden's obsession with ceremony and courtly codes of behavior had always irritated Mazael.

If Lord Malden was going to kill him, best to get it over with right away.

Mazael strode up the long aisle between the crowds of lordly folk, ignoring their hostile stares. He stopped at the foot of the dais and bowed from the waist. "My lord Malden."

Lord Malden Roland, Lord of Knightcastle, liege lord of Knightrealm, scoffed.

He was a lean, thin-faced man of sixty, iron-gray hair just visible beneath his ornate beret with its golden badge. His fine tunic and boots and cloak must have cost a fortune, and his rings and brooch glistened with gemstones. At his side stood a small army of pages, ready to attend to his every whim.

"My lord?" said Lord Malden, voice mocking. "My lord? Yes, Lord Mazael, I was your lord. Did I not take you in when you were landless and friendless? Did I not offer you the comfort of my home and the shield of my protection? Was I not generous to you? And all I asked in return was loyalty." His eyes, bloodshot and blue, narrowed. "And you have cast that away in contempt."

"I have done nothing of the sort," said Mazael.

A surprised rustle went through the court. No one contradicted Lord Malden.

"You have sworn to become the vassal of my worst enemy," said Lord Malden, "a vile usurper, a man who murdered my own beloved son. And then you have the gall, the insouciance, to suggest that your sister marry my youngest son! You have trampled upon my generosity and shown contempt for my good lordship."

"I have not," said Mazael.

Lord Malden's lip curled.

"My brother died without issue, and I became the new Lord of Castle Cravenlock," said Mazael. "Where is the disloyalty in that? If I had been sitting in comfort at your table when Mitor died, I would have still become the new Lord of Castle Cravenlock. Would you accuse me of disloyalty then, my lord?"

Lord Malden leaned forward, eyes flashing. "I accuse you for disloyalty because you have sworn an oath to Richard Mandragon! Such folly is beyond my understanding! That man deposed your father Lord Adalon, made him die a broken man! That accursed Richard Mandragon killed my son."

"He did not," said Mazael.

A muscle in Lord Malden's face twitched. "Do you call me a liar?"

"The archers shot Belifane on the battlefield," said Mazael, "when he was foolish enough to charge Lord Richard's line. Will you find each and every one of those archers and put them to death?"

"The common folk are but tools of their lord's will," said Lord Malden, "and their lord was Richard Mandragon, may the gods blast his name." He leaned back into his throne, glaring. "So Lord Mitor died, as you said, and then you became Lord of Castle Cravenlock. Do you know what you should have done?"

"Enlighten me, my lord," said Mazael. Gerald and Rachel stepped to his side, gazing at him in alarm.

"You should have called for me at once," said Lord Malden. "Together, we could have defeated Richard Mandragon, and annihilated the Mandragons forever. You could have been liege lord of the Grim Marches, as your father was before you. Instead," he waved a hand in disgust, "instead you are nothing more than Richard's lackey."

"No," said Mazael. "A war between you and Lord Richard would have led to nothing but ruination. Both your lands ravaged, your common folk slaughtered. You've already lost two sons to war. Will you lose the other three for Lord Richard's two? You and Lord Richard could both rule over the dead, if you wish."

"Bah!" said Lord Malden. "You concern yourself with Richard Mandragon's spawn? From what I have heard, the older is a murderous madman, and the younger is a black wizard in thrall to dark powers. The earth would be well rid of them."

Lord Malden's description was not far from the mark, but Mazael said, "Blood for blood only leads to more blood." He had a brief vision of the Old Demon standing on the chapel's altar and laughing. "Only ruin."

A rustle of amusement went through the hall.

"Mazael," said Lord Malden. "Come to your senses. I offer you the liege lordship of the Grim Marches. You have only to follow me against a man who ruined your father, a man whose sons will probably plunge the Grim Marches into a bloody civil war one day." He held out his hand. "You were one of my most trusted knights, once. You could have been the Lord Marshal of Knightrealm. Come. Will you not help me?"

"No," said Mazael. "I will not go to war with you against Lord Richard, nor will I go to war with Lord Richard against you."

A vein throbbed in Lord Malden's temple, his breath hissing through his nostrils.

"Lord Mazael and I will walk alone for a moment," said Lord Malden, standing.

The pages surged forward. One replaced Lord Malden's blue cloak with a green walking-cape. Another set a new beret on his head. Still a third pressed a silver-headed walking-stick into his hand.

"Come," said Lord Malden, glaring at Mazael.

He strode from the dais, not bothering to look back. Mazael followed him. After a moment the pages trailed afterwards, along with the rest of the court.

Mazael sighed. This was not going well.

###

A short walk took them from the Hall of Triumphs, across the High Court, and to the Arcade of Sorrows. Its marble columns ran along the top of the innermost wall in lieu of battlements and turrets, since enemies had little chance of ever reaching it. The name came from yet another obscure detail of Knightcastle's history. Four hundred years past the Lady Audea had thrown herself from the wall after hearing a false report that her lover had fallen in battle. He returned, however, found that Audea had killed herself, and flung himself from the Arcade of Sorrows after her. Mazael had always found the story foolish.

But after losing Romaria, he understood it a little better.

Lord Malden strolled along, walking stick tapping against the flagstones. Through the Arcade's arches Mazael had a grand view of the valley, the midday sun glinting off the Riversteel like firelight on a sword blade.

Behind them, it seemed the entire court of Knightcastle stood in the High Court, watching them.

"We're walking alone?" said Mazael.

"After a fashion," said Lord Malden, his voice still angry. "It is a ritual, of sorts. I am Lord of Knightcastle, and they must wait on my will," he waved his hand at the courtiers, "rather than the other way around. A lesson you would do well to learn. So. We are alone…"

"After a fashion."

Lord Malden inclined his head. "Then let us speak candidly. I want your aid, Lord Mazael. I want vengeance on Lord Richard, and you will help me take it."

"No," said Mazael.

The vein in Lord Malden's temple throbbed. "Were you not listening? Did I not tell you that it was better to wait upon my will, rather than to force yours upon me? Richard Mandragon deposed my loyal friend Lord Adalon. He murdered my son…"

"I told you," said Mazael, "Belifane fell in battle. If you hadn't sent him to the Grim Marches, he wouldn't have died. If you wish to blame anyone, perhaps you should start with yourself."

Lord Malden's breath hissed like a drawn sword. "You overstep grievously."

"And so do you," said Mazael, refusing to back down, "by asking me to subject my lands and my people to slaughter, famine, pestilence, and all the other horrors of war, simply so that you can slake your gods-damned pride."

Lord Malden thumped his stick against the ground so hard it almost cracked. "Pride? Is it pride to avenge my son's death?"

"You've lusted for revenge since I've known you," said Mazael, "and that's been ten years. What about Sir Mandor? He fell in Mastaria at the hands of the Dominiars, and you're not screaming for their heads."

"Because the Dominiars already paid," said Lord Malden. "You took Tumblestone from them." His eyes glinted. "You helped me with my revenge against the Dominiars. Why do you blanch now?"

"Because," said Mazael, memories of the grim Mastarian campaign shuffling across his mind. Mandor had been killed by his own incompetence, and his blundering had nearly destroyed his army. Since Gerald had been barely eighteen, it had been up to Mazael to take command. "Because we had no other choice. If we hadn't taken Tumblestone, we would have died in Mastaria, and Malleus would have defeated you and your army. You could lie dead now, or live out your days as a hostage in Castle Dominus." Some long-forgotten anger flared to life. "And you sent us on that fool's quest because of a slight the Dominiars gave to your damned precious Justiciars."

"The Justiciars are my true friends," said Lord Malden, "unlike some." He fixed Mazael with a baleful glare. "Any slight against them is a slight against me. And let us speak of slights against the Justiciars, Lord Mazael, shall we? Richard Mandragon expelled them from the Grim Marches, stealing their lands and usurping their castles."

"He had cause," said Mazael. "They did vow to kill him."

"They vowed to kill a lawless, faithless, murderous usurper," said Lord Malden. "A faithless usurper you saw fit to make your proper liege lord." His voice grated with anger. "Was not my generosity enough for you? You were the best of my knights. You would have received land in my service, eventually, perhaps even marriage to one of my bastard daughters."

"Mitor died," said Mazael. "I didn't have any other choice."

Lord Malden scoffed. "You killed him and took his lands, you mean."

"I did not kill Mitor!" said Mazael, the edges of his temper giving way. "The San-keth cleric murdered him, stabbed him in the back."

"A San-keth, of course!" said Lord Malden. "A convenient excuse. Yes, I'm sure your brother was murdered by a child's tale."

"The San-keth are real enough," said Mazael. "Ask Gerald. He saw Skhath with his own eyes. Ask Tobias. Ask Trocend. Even ask old Sir Lindon Tristgard. They all saw the San-keth cleric at Tristgard."

"I'm sure," said Lord Malden, sneering. "Snake-men skulking about my lands? Perhaps you had Lucan Mandragon conjure up some illusions. No, Lord Mazael, I think you are a black-hearted villain." Mazael's temper frayed a bit more. "You murdered your brother and betrayed me by swearing to Richard Mandragon. Now you throw honeyed words of peace in my face, while plotting with the usurper to kill me and seize my lands. And then, no doubt, once you have no further need of him, you'll kill

Richard Mandragon and make yourself lord over the Grim Marches as well. High King Mazael Cravenlock? That is your real goal, I deem…"

"You old fool!" snarled Mazael, his anger exploding all at once. A shocked gasp escaped from the trailing courtiers, and Lord Malden's face went rigid. "Fine! Take your lands to war! You've lost two sons already. Why not lose the other three? Sir Mandor was a fool, and his death was mostly his fault, but you sent him into Mastaria to die. And Sir Belifane's death was your own damned fault! Yours, lord, and no one else's! And what will you do when all your sons are dead, no one left to carry on your name, your lands ravaged, your people put to the sword? You'll sit in this pile of a castle until you die, brooding over the ruin of your realm, and you will have no one to blame but yourself."

The two men glared at each other for a long moment. Mazael knew he had pushed Lord Malden too hard, too far, but was too angry to care. His hand twitched towards Lion's hilt, wondering if Lord Malden would order him cut down then and there…

Lord Malden began to shudder, his breath rasping. Mazael took an alarmed step towards him, wondering if the old lord's heart had burst from rage.

Then Lord Malden threw back his head and roared with laughter.

Mazael blinked.

"By the gods," wheezed Lord Malden, between burst of laughter, "by the gods. How I've missed that rough speech of yours!"

"Lord?" said Mazael, puzzled.

Still chuckling, Lord Malden waved his hand at the hovering courtiers. "You were the only one who ever had the courage to tell me the truth. The only one! Not a one of those fawning leeches ever has the nerve to disagree with me, even to speak a cross word to my face. Bah!" He thumped his stick against the ground. "I could tell them that flying pigs soar across the full moon, and they'd stand there and nod, and even suggest that winged pork would make a splendid meal."

"But," said Mazael, trying to find his tongue, "but surely Sir Garain and Trocend tell you the truth?"

"Certainly," said Lord Malden. "They'd regret it sorely if they did not. But it's always cloaked in so many fair words, 'if you please, my lord', and 'by your leave, noble lord'. And they'd never dare argue with me. But you!" Lord Malden grinned. "you actually have the courage to disagree with me!" He sighed. "I haven't had a proper argument in months. Maybe even since you left for the Grim Marches. My mistresses try, of course, when I command them, but they can never really work up the proper nerve."

"I…am pleased to be of service, my lord," said Mazael.

"You're not," said Lord Malden, smiling. "And you're still wrong, by the way. Richard Mandragon is a murderer and a usurper, and I will see justice done upon him on day."

"You've mentioned that," said Mazael.

"But," said Lord Malden, "I can see how, in light of certain ill-starred events, becoming the Lord of Castle Cravenlock and swearing to Mandragon might have been, under the circumstances, an…acceptable course of action."

"How terribly gracious of you," said Mazael.

"I know," said Lord Malden with a smug little smile. He raised his voice. "My throat grows parched from all this shouting. Wine!"

Three pages raced forward, bearing a pewter tray with a pair of silver goblets and a pitcher of wine. Lord Malden held out his hand and a page pressed a goblet into his hand. Mazael took the other from the tray.

"Let us resume our walk," said Lord Malden. He took a drink, held out the goblet, and the page carried it for him. "I agree with you on one point. Now is not the time for Knightcastle to wage war against Swordgrim. Lord Richard, damn his name, can match my strength. A war between us would bleed us both dry, leave us vulnerable to the other great lords."

"I'm pleased you see reason," said Mazael. Lord Malden snickered.

The Arcade of Sorrows ended in a large parapet jutting from the corner of Knightcastle's highest wall. A small garden filled most of the parapet. The grass had begun to green, buds showing on the branches of two small trees. Audea's garden, this place was called, where Lady Audea had awaited word of her lover's fate.

Lord Malden moved to one of the marble benches. The pages hastened forward, two lifting the skirts of his cloak while another held his walking stick. Mazael sat on the bench opposite him.

"And as it happens," said Lord Malden, "the strength of Knightcastle must be preserved for a closer, a more…pressing threat."

"The Dominiar Knights," said Mazael.

Lord Malden nodded. "Trocend made my wishes clear, I see."

"The Dominiar Knights were broken after Tumblestone," said Mazael. "I can't believe that Grand Master Malleus would be fool enough to attack Knightrealm."

"Tumblestone was five years ago," said Lord Malden. "Malleus has hardly been idle. He has new commanders, young men vigorous and hungry for glory. They have done a fair job of rebuilding the Dominiar Order's strength." Lord Malden favored him with a mirthless smile. "And now they want the city of Tumblestone back. Peacefully, if possible, but by force, if necessary."

"The Dominiar Knights in your court," said Mazael, "that's why they're here, aren't they? A deputation from Malleus, demanding Tumblestone back."

Lord Malden lifted iron eyebrows. "Oh, they're hardly demanding.

They are far too courteous for that. They make lofty statements about the brotherhood of all men, and the ancient claims of the Dominiar Order on Tumblestone. The demands will come soon. And then come the swords."

"War may not be necessary," said Mazael.

"It is." Lord Malden's voice was hard. "Tumblestone is mine. My son Mandor died to take it. It has been purchased by Roland blood, and I will not give it up. Now, Lord Mazael, let us come to the point of all this argument, delightful though it has been. You want your lady sister to marry Gerald to tie yourself to me, as you are tied to Lord Richard. With you between us, I cannot strike at Lord Richard, nor he at me."

Mazael gave a slow nod.

"I am prepared to grant you that," said Lord Malden. "Rachel may marry Gerald, and I will not make war against Lord Richard. But in return, my lord Mazael, in return, you will help me against the Dominiars."

Mazael took a swallow of the wine. It tasted very fine. "And if I do not?"

"Why, Mazael," said Lord Malden, smiling like an old fox. "You are in my castle, surrounded by hundreds of my knights. Not that I would dream of threatening you, of course." He took a sip of wine, sloshed it around his mouth, swallowed. "But, still. Your poor sister would remain unwed, possibly even for the rest of her days. And, well…there would be nothing to stop me from waging war against the Mandragons. Nothing at all."

Mazael stared hard at the old lord, his mind a thousand miles away. If he refused, Lord Malden would bring fire and sword to the Grim Marches. Yet if he agreed, if he wound up fighting with Lord Malden against the Dominiars…what would happen then? Wars always had dire consequences no one foresaw. How would the Old Demon manipulate such a war? Or the San-keth, for that matter? Even if Lucan had killed Straganis, Mazael doubted that the misshapen creature was the only San-keth archpriest.

Still, Mazael had no other choice. If he refused Lord Malden, war would come to the Grim Marches. But if he offered his help, he might yet have a chance to keep the peace.

"If it comes to war with the Dominiars," said Mazael, "then I will help you."

"Good!" said Lord Malden. "Very good. I knew you would see some degree of reason, if not as much as I might hope." He rose, brushing some dust from the hem of his cape. "Now let us speak of happier matters. My son is getting wed, after all."

Mazael stood. He drained the rest of his wine. "And my sister."

"Tonight, we shall have a great feast," said Lord Malden, "to celebrate the union of our two families." He walked to the edge of the parapet, beckoning Mazael to follow. "And a grand tournament in a week's time, I think." He waved his hand at the ring of tents encircling Castle Town. "A prize of ten thousand crowns for the victor at the knights' tourney. Five thousand for the swordsmen's tourney, and another five thousand for the victor of the squires' melee."

Mazael squinted at the tents. He saw the banners of many lesser noble houses, as well as the ragged leather tents of landless knights and even mercenaries. "You've had this planned well in advance, haven't you?" He looked at the older man. "Did you know I would say yes?"

Lord Malden gave him a sly grin. "And in…a month's time, yes. In a month's time we shall have the ceremony in the Hall of Triumphs, conducted by the Archbishop of Knightrealm himself. We can't have the ceremony at Castle Cravenlock, after all."

There was no archbishop, or even any bishops, in the Grim Marches. Lord Richard was a man to brook any challenges to his authority.

"A month?" said Mazael. "Why not now?"

"Why, we must give the guests time to arrive," said Lord Malden. "Brother Trocend will send messages at once with his, ah, special contacts. But if we want sufficient guests for this joyous occasion, we must give them time."

"As you wish," said Mazael. He wondered if Lord Malden meant to war against the Dominiars immediately after the wedding.

"And now," said Lord Malden, striding back onto the Arcade of Sorrows, "let us meet my son's bride, she who is to be my daughter."

They walked back into the High Court. Gerald and Rachel stood by the great bronze statue of old King Roland, speaking to Tobias and Garain. They fell silent as Lord Malden and Mazael approached.

Gerald bowed from the waist. "My lord father. I am glad to be at home once more."

"And I am glad that you have returned, my son," said Lord Malden, his eyes on Rachel. "So this is the lady who thinks herself worthy to marry a scion of the great King Roland?"

"My lord," said Rachel, dipping into a deep curtsy, the hem of her riding gown sweeping the floor, "it is a great honor to be here."

"Do you think so?" said Lord Malden, tapping his stick against the stones. "I have heard some most dire stories about you, my lady Rachel. Rumors that would positively chill your blood."

"Lord Mazael saved me from all of that," said Rachel. "And it is an honor to be here, truly. I have heard so much of Knightcastle all my life, in songs, in tales…and now that I have seen it, I think it grander than any song. I have never been away from the Grim Marches before. If… nothing else, my lord, if you send us away, I will still be glad I had the chance to see Knightcastle."

"Well," said Lord Malden, his haughty face softening. "Well spoken indeed, my daughter."

Mazael stifled a laugh. Rachel had said exactly the right thing. Lord Malden was proud, arrogant, and often hard and ruthless.

Yet he loved his home, and his sons.

Rachel did another curtsy again, flushing. "Thank you, my lord."

"Come," said Lord Malden, taking her arm. "If you are to wed into the house of the Rolands, then it is only fitting that you know the history of our home. Let us take a walk together, shall we?"

"I would be honored, my lord," said Rachel. They walked off together, Gerald and most of the court trailing behind.

Mazael shook his head and went to find Timothy and Sir Aulus.

Bit by bit, Lucan's mind crawled towards awareness.

He dreamed of killing his father and brother, and striding over their bodies to seize the lordship of the Grim Marches, setting a crown of dragon teeth on his head, proclaiming himself king of the restored kingdom of Dracaryl...

Lucan awoke, coughing and laughing.

Marstan's memories were always strongest when he lay sleeping.

Lucan lay on damp ground, a foul stench filling his nostrils. He groaned and sat up, working moisture into his dry mouth.

Two dozen rotting corpses stood in a ring around him. A dark, misty forest rose around them, pale shafts of light shining through the mist. The memory of Straganis, Tristgard, and the changelings came back to Lucan in a rush.

"Damnation" murmured Lucan. It seemed he had won the duel. He groaned and stood up.

But he had no idea how to return to the material world.

He looked around, rubbing his cold hands. For the matter, he had no idea how Straganis had brought him here in the first place. Lucan hadn't though it possible for a material body to physically enter the spiritual plane. Clearly, it was possible to pull a material object to the spiritual realm from within – the presence of the changelings' corpses proved that – but Lucan didn't know how to reverse the process.

He looked at the animated corpses. They stared back at him with rotting eyes. "Guard me."

The corpses shuffled around him as he moved.

Lucan stared at the flickering, shadowy images of Tristgard and its wall, and glimpsed the villagers going about their business. It seemed Mazael had won the day, despite his wounds. Lucan wasn't terribly surprised, and pushed the matter from his mind. More immediate problems demanded his attention.

He watched flickers of light drifting through the forest, red and green and white. He glimpsed the outlines of men and women and children, some smiling and joyful, others writhing with torment. The souls of the dead passed through this place before moving to their final destination, whether heaven or hell or rebirth. And, of course, the spiritual realm was home to many immortal creatures, some benign, some dangerous, and some downright malevolent.

He considered that for a moment, then began muttering a summoning spell. While such a spell usually pulled a spiritual creature to the material world, it ought to work here. Lucan spoke the name of a spiritual creature, one he had learned from Marstan, and finished the spell. He waited.

Then something stirred in the forest. A short, wizened figure strode out, a shriveled dwarf-shape with an enormous gray beard. It stopped a short distance away, staring at Lucan.

"So," said Lucan, "you have come?"

"Come at thy call, have I" said the creature in a rasping voice, "and a service to thee I will perform, should the price offered be…"

"Spare me," said Lucan. "I know the doggerel."

The dwarf-creature shimmered and disappeared. In its place stood a tow-headed boy of about nine, clad in ragged garments, identical to any orphaned urchin in the great cities.

"But, squire!" said the boy, "I right enjoy the speech, so I do!"

"I'm sure," said Lucan, "but my patience is short. Who are you?"

The boy shimmered and vanished. In his place stood a girl of about seven years, clad in noble garments, and clutching a ridiculous parasol. "Sir!" she said, blue eyes wide, doing a fumbling little curtsy, "but, sir, you called me, unless I am ever so mistaken."

"Your name," repeated Lucan. Best to establish some sort of authority right away.

The creature changed shape again, taking the form of the boy-thief. "Mocker-Of-Hope they call me around here, squire, so they do." He winked at Lucan. "It's cuz I mock their hope, I do, before I eat their souls."

"How fascinating," said Lucan. "I require a service…"

"Nope," said the boy.

Lucan raised an eyebrow. "You refuse me?"

"You look like a bright gent, squire," said Mocker-Of-Hope. "Thought you'd know how this would work. You see, if you call me to the mortal world, why, I have to perform a service for you. But, here…you're in my haunt, squire." The boy's eyes flickered. Something entirely inhuman twitched across his face. "I'd really like to eat your soul."

Lucan lifted his hand. "You could try."

Mocker-Of-Hope again took the girl's form. "But, sir! You wouldn't strike a helpless girl, would you? One who had never done anything in the world to you?"

"So we bargain, then," said Lucan.

Mocker-Of-Hope again became the boy-thief. "Now you've got it, squire." He cleaned his fingernails on his tunic. "I provide all sorts of useful services for the gent in need of…discretion, eh?"

"You will conduct me to a place called Knightcastle, in the mortal realm," said Lucan.

"I will, will I?" said Mocker-Of-Hope. "Why, that's news to me, so it is! Course, I have to be compensated for my efforts."

"Price?" said Lucan.

"Your soul."

Lucan rolled his eyes. "Please."

"Fine, fine," said Mocker-Of-Hope, "I admit maybe that was a little…eh, extravagant? A part of your soul, then. Maybe a third?" He snickered. "Why, your soul's so black, I'd be doing you a favor, taking a part of it off your hands."

"How terribly generous," said Lucan, his eyes wandering over the mist-choked woods. One of the reddish flickers caught his gaze. "Perhaps an entire damned soul, then? Would that prove sufficient payment?"

Mocker-Of-Hope again took the little girl's shape. "But, sir, that's ever so rude. Unless I am terribly mistaken, you refused to part with your soul." She giggled. "Even though it could use a good cleaning."

Lucan pulled a ring from inside his tunic, a golden circle set with a single clear gem, the band marked with a dozen arcane glyphs. He slipped it on his finger, focused on one of the flickering red outlines, and began an incantation. Mocker-Of-Hope watched him, head titled to one side, golden curls sliding. Lucan's necromancy could not touch the souls on their way to paradise, no spells could, and he could not claim one of the souls on their way to rebirth without consent.

But the damned souls…

Lucan finished the spell, gathered his will, and made a clawing motion. One of the reddish outlines flickered, shuddering. Lucan heard a keening scream in the depths of his mind. He closed his fist, and the outline vanished.

The stone on the ring flared with red light, pulsing with the rage and terror of the trapped soul.

"Perhaps," said Lucan, sliding the ring off his finger and laying it on his palm, "this might prove a worthy price?"

An ugly lust came over the girl's face. The edges of her form blurred and shimmered. She reached for the ring with her mouth. Lucan pulled back his hand, and the girl's teeth, suddenly sharp, closed on air.

"Give that to me," said Mocker-Of-Hope, the human veneer of its voice thinning. "Give that to me now."

120

"Why?" said Lucan. "Will you guide me to Knightcastle?"

"I will, I will," said Mocker-Of-Hope. "Now give it to me!"

"Swear it," said Lucan. The spirit-creature's eyes remained fixated on the ring. "Swear by your name that you will guide me, safe from all forms of harm, to Knightcastle."

"I do," said Mocker-Of-Hope, lips peeling back from jagged teeth.

The creature's slow transformation was unnerving, yet Lucan held his ground. "Swear, I said!"

"Fine!" spat Mocker-Of-Hope. "I, Mocker-Of-Hope, swear by my name that I will take you to Knightcastle without harm. Now give me that!"

"As you wish," said Lucan, flipping the ring away.

Mocker-Of-Hope caught it in midair, a terrible expression of glee on a face no longer human. For an instant Lucan glimpsed a creature of nightmare, a thing hideous and near-blasphemous. Then it vanished, and the street urchin returned, an expression of deep satisfaction on his face.

The ring rolled across the ground, its gem clear once more. Lucan scooped it up and tucked it away.

"Right tasty, that was," said the boy, belching. "Right tasty."

"I share your joy," said Lucan. "Now. No further dithering. To Knightcastle."

Mocker-Of-Hope became the noble girl. "So impatient, sir, so terribly impatient. Why, impatience is so dreadfully rude." She gazed off into the distance, brow furrowing with intense concentration.

The mists stirred, writhing in sudden agitation. All at once they parted into two walls, towering up into oblivion, a narrow lane between them.

Mocker-Of-Hope shimmered, the girl disappearing. In her place appeared a large raven. The bird flapped its wings, and settled on Lucan's right shoulder, claws digging into his cloak.

"Forward," croaked the bird, jutting its beak into the lane. "To Knightcastle."

"Very good," said Lucan, striding into the misty lane. "You realize, of course, that if you lead me astray, you will dearly regret it?"

Mocker-Of-Hope cawed with rusty laughter.

Lucan kept walking.

CHAPTER 11
FIRES IN THE BLOOD

Lord Malden held the grand feast in the Court of Challengers.

The Court sat on Knightcastle's second tier, ringed on one side by Oliver's Keep, on the other by Marelle's Chapel. Here, legend held, the Roland kings of old had sat one day a year, and anyone of noble birth could challenge them to single combat.

Now the porters raised long tables and rows of benches. Torches and bonfires blazed, throwing back the dusk. Armies of servants hastened from the kitchens, bearing platters of food and casks of wine. The Court already held Lord Malden's armsmen and household knights as they drank and laughed. From Castle Town below came the distant echoes of revelry as the townsfolk feasted on Lord Malden's largesse.

The lords would later in stately procession, each escorting a noble lady.

This meant Mazael had to wait to eat, which annoyed him to no end. His courtly clothes further aggravated his mood. His fine linen tunic itched damnably, his gleaming boots gripped his feet uncomfortably, and his great black cloak, adorned with the three crossed swords of the Cravenlocks, was too warm.

The lords and ladies milled behind Marelle's chapel, waiting for the heralds to call their names.

"Lord Tancred and Lady Chrisiana, Lord and Lady of Stillwater!"

Wesson's father, who did indeed resemble a tankard, stomped around the chapel, his much younger wife on his arm.

"Damn this," said Mazael, scowling.

Gerald laughed. "Patience, Mazael, patience. You know how my lord father loves his pomp."

"I've nothing against pomp," said Mazael." Unless it keeps me from eating."

Rachel laughed and hooked her arm around Gerald's. "And you will have to wait longer, I fear. We are Lord Malden's honored guests, so the heralds will call us at the very end."

Rachel and Gerald wandered off to speak with Tobias and Garain. Mazael leaned against the stone wall and watched the milling lords and ladies. He saw many blue Justiciar cloaks, but no black Dominiar ones. Lord Malden had seated the Dominiar knights with the armsmen and landless knights, though the officers could sit with the lords. No doubt Lord Malden intended it as an insult. Mazael sighed and rubbed his temples. Lord Malden wanted war with the Dominiars, the Justiciars wanted war with the Dominiars, and Mazael could think of nothing...

"Lord Mazael."

Mazael turned his head and saw a Justiciar knight with a crooked nose. The Justiciar's dark hair had streaks of premature gray, and his eyes looked haunted.

"Sir Commander Galan," said Mazael.

Galan Hawking had once been Lord of Hawk's Reach in the Grim Marches. He had fought against Lord Richard, been stripped of his lands and titles, and sent into the Justiciar Order. Years later he had led the Justiciars of the Grim Marches to war against Lord Richard. For that, the Justiciars had been expelled from the Grim Marches. And Galan himself had been betrayed by Mitor and the San-keth. Mazael had rescued Galan from the San-keth temple under Castle Cravenlock, but the experience had left Galan Hawking a broken man.

"A joyous occasion, this," said Galan, folding his arms. "The union of Cravenlock and Roland."

"And perhaps the beginning of a new war," said Mazael.

"Yes," said Galan, shaking his head. "I am tired, of war, of battle. I have seen far too much. The San-keth...I never though them real."

"Your point?" said Mazael.

"My hopes have long been dashed," said Galan. "Yet it was my folly that led to the Justiciars' expulsion from the Grim Marches. The Justiciar Order has become my home, and I would see that damage undone."

"So war with the Dominiars," said Mazael. "Take their lands to replace your order's lost ones."

"Hardly," said Galan. "The Dominiars can match our strength, and they are just as eager for war. We would have been content to launch a crusade overseas, seize some pagan desert for our own. But the Dominiars want Tumblestone back, and are willing to use force when words fail."

"Why?" said Mazael. "I thought Malleus had accepted his defeat."

"He did," said Galan, "and was occupied with revolt in the Old Kingdoms. But that was before Amalric Galbraith rose to prominence

123

within the Dominiar Order."

"I've never heard of him," said Mazael.

"Not surprising," said Galan. "He's a young man, but six and twenty years old. And he has spent almost all of his service in the Old Kingdoms. After you won at Tumblestone, Malleus made Amalric Galbraith a commander in the Old Kingdoms. Since then he has crushed every revolt, usually by slaughtering all the druids of the old faith, for they often lead the rebellions. During the siege of a rebel city, he impaled five hundred druids and mounted their corpses on stakes around the walls. Once the city surrendered without a fight, he did the same to every tenth citizen, whether man, woman, or child."

"Gods," said Mazael. Both the Justiciars and Dominiars had reputations for brutality, especially to pagans, but that was unusually cruel.

Galan shrugged. "It worked. The Dominiars' subject kingdoms are little more than slave states now, and dare not rebel."

"And this Sir Commander Amalric," said Mazael, "he's the one encouraging Malleus to reclaim Tumblestone."

"Aye," said Galan. "Amalric is now Grand Master Malleus's strong right hand. Malleus would have been content to leave Tumblestone to Lord Malden. But Sir Commander Amalric thinks differently." Galan blew out a long sigh. "This war...this war will be bloody."

"It might not be so bloody," said Mazael. "Tumblestone is well-fortified, well-provisioned. Lord Malden made Rainier Agravain lord of Tumblestone, didn't he? Rainier was never the sort of man to surrender anything. If the Dominiars lay siege to the place, Lord Malden can sweep them away."

"Lord Malden laid siege to Tumblestone," said Galan, "and Malleus defeated him."

"Aye," said Mazael, "but who has Tumblestone now?"

A tired smile spread over Galan's face. "Lord Malden, of course. But that was your doing, not his. If you had not been there, I think a Dominiar banner would fly over Knightcastle now." The herald called Galan's name. The Justiciar knight sighed again. "And you are here again. Maybe things will turn out well for Lord Malden. Perhaps I'll see you at the feast."

Mazael nodded and Galan marched off, blue cloak swirling behind him.

The heralds called more and more of the lords and ladies. The small court behind the chapel emptied. Mazael brooded, for lack of anything better to do. His mind turned over Lucan, Straganis, Lord Malden, and wondered what dire things lay ahead. Did the Old Demon's hand drive this war?

Or maybe Mazael worried too much. Maybe it would all come to nothing in the end.

Gerald and Rachel left, arm in arm, the herald's voice echoing their names over the Court of Challengers. Mazael was the last one left in the little courtyard. Had he missed his name, lost in thought?

"Well, my friend, do you intend to scowl at the wall all night?"

Lord Malden entered, his army of pages and squires trooping behind. On Lord Malden's arm rested his wife Lady Rhea, a lean woman in her mid-fifties, long brown hair streaked with gray. Lady Rhea's expression looked just as haughty as Lord Malden's.

"Perhaps," said Mazael, doing a brief bow. "I presume you intend to eat sooner or later, my lord? Or did you wish to go hungry while keeping your vassals waiting for your august presence?"

Lady Rhea laughed, eyes flashing. "Candid as ever, my lord Mazael. Refreshing to hear frank speech, I daresay."

"Believe me, it soon grows wearisome," said Lord Malden. "But what better way to show our newfound amity and the joining of our two houses? My son and your sister enter together." He shook his head. "A pity you have no wife of your own. I have several suitable candidates in mind, but we can discuss that at a later date."

"Yes," said Mazael, thinking of Romaria. All at once he felt tired and cold. "A pity."

"Lord Mazael!" thundered the herald, "Lord of Castle Cravenlock, and Lord Malden's close friend! Now, all hail the wise and noble Lord of Knightcastle, Malden Roland, and his gracious lady wife, Rhea Roland!"

Lord Malden and Lady Rhea strolled with a slow, lordly gait into the Court of Challengers, Mazael following after. All the guests stood, bowing to the Lord and Lady of Knightcastle. Mazael took his place at the high table, among the Rolands and the Justiciar officers. Lord Malden and Lady Rhea sat, and everyone began to eat.

Mazael ate with some relief, washing down the food with ample quantities of wine. Adalar waited by his chair, ready to serve. Mazael's eyes wandered over the packed Court of Challengers. Jongleurs and dancers moved among the trestle tables, singing and cavorting, jugglers flinging daggers and torches into the air. Against the far-wall stood a table of black-cloaked and black-armored forms, the Dominiar knights.

At their head sat a tall young man with dark hair and eyes, the same man who had scowled at Mazael in the Hall of Triumphs. All the other Dominiars seemed to wait on his words, nodding when he spoke. Mazael supposed this was Sir Commander Amalric Galbraith, Grand Master Malleus's right-hand man, the conqueror of the Old Kingdoms. Romaria had often spoken of the Old Kingdoms, had admired their people and druids.

She would have loathed Amalric Galbraith, and for that reason, Mazael found himself disliking the man.

At Amalric's side sat the blood-haired woman in the black gown. She had pulled back her mourning veil to eat, revealing a pale, cold face, just as haughty as Lady Rhea's, and though she talked, she never seemed to speak to Amalric. In fact, Mazael thought that she hated Amalric, and he hated her. Was she his sister? Or his wife?

"My lord?" said Adalar.

Mazael blinked. "Adalar?"

"Is something amiss?" said Adalar.

"No," said Mazael. "I'm well."

"You looked wroth," said Adalar.

"Just distracted," said Mazael, glancing at the Dominiars.

"My father spoke highly of the Dominiars," said Adalar.

Mazael frowned. "He did?"

Adalar nodded. "Well, at least compared to the Justiciars. He said both Orders were corrupt, hypocritical, greedy, and more concerned with power and wealth than doing the gods' work. But, he said, at least the Dominiars can speak to a woman without burning her."

Mazael laughed. "True enough, I suppose. Of course, the Justiciars call the Dominiars corrupt for that. It's one the reasons why there is a Justiciar Order. They thought the Dominiar commanders had grown too corrupt and split away."

"I know the history," said Adalar.

"Are you all right?" said Mazael. "You've seemed distracted since Tristgard."

"It…" Some of the blood drained from Adalar's face. "It…well, I saw some terrible things there."

"We all did," said Mazael, staring into his wine. "I thought it horrible what the common San keth clerics did, riding on an undead skeleton. But Straganis…gods, a body built out of stolen limbs and a giant spider? If he wasn't mad before, he certainly is now, I'd wager."

Adalar looked about to say something else, but fell silent.

"Go," said Mazael, waving his hand at the squires gathered in the corner of the Court. "Go and enjoy yourself."

"My place is to serve you," said Adalar.

"I'll be fine," said Mazael. He snorted. "I wish I could go. The high lords are hardly enjoyable company."

Adalar still looked dubious, but bowed again. "My lord."

Mazael drank some more and watched the high lords scheme. Lord Malden sat with his favorite mistress, a minor noblewoman named Claretta, and fed her bits of meat off the tip of his dagger. Gerald glared at his father. He had never approved of Lord Malden's many affairs. Lady Rhea appeared not to mind, though, and spent most of her time speaking with a crowd of Lord Malden's young knights. No one ever dared accused of Lady Rhea of infidelity; those who did soon found themselves swinging from the gallows in Castle Town.

The feast ended, the servants pushed the tables to the walls, the jongleurs struck up sprightly tunes, and people began to dance. The armsmen and landless knights joined with the servant girls in a dance that involved much stomping and laughing. The lords and ladies moved in slower, revolving dances. Mazael wished to slip away, but didn't, for fear of further irritating Lord Malden. The old lord loved to dance. Even the Dominiars danced.

The Justiciars did not approve of dancing, or music, but slipped away without protest, lest they offend Lord Malden.

The song ended, and Mazael found himself face to face with Lady Rhea. He had no choice but to bow to her. She bowed back, and he took her hand and hip and led her in the next dance.

"It is so good to see you again, Mazael," she said. "You were always Malden's favorite."

"I am pleased to have his lordship's confidence," said Mazael.

Rhea laughed, and pressed her hand tighter against his neck. "So formal, now that you're a lord? Why don't you come to my rooms after we're done, and see if you can be formal then?" Her other hand came down and brushed Lion's pommel. "You can show me that fine sword at your belt."

Mazael felt himself gape at her.

She laughed again, a wicked smile at her lips. "You never were so hesitant before, or so I hear."

"Things are different now," said Mazael. She was shapely enough, despite her age, and for just a moment Mazael was tempted. "Lord Malden's already annoyed with me. I doubt sleeping with his wife will help." And, gods, what would Gerald say?

"My lord husband and I haven't lain together for years," said Rhea, "not since I had my change, and could no longer bear him sons. He amuses himself with his pretty young ladies, and, well...I can seek out my own entertainments."

"Thank you," said Mazael, "I am honored, but..."

"Ah, well," she said. The dance ended, to Mazael's immense relief. They bowed to each other, and Rhea said, "Still, if you ever change your mind..." She winked and swirled back into the dance with stout Lord Tancred.

"Gods save me," muttered Mazael. He started walking towards Oliver's Keep, determined to escape before he started a war, and stopped.

Sir Commander Aeternis of the Dominiar Order leaned against the Court wall, watching. Aeternis had offered up Lion in surrender after the Dominiar defeat at Tumblestone. Lion was a weapon of magical power, and

Mazael had often wondered how a Dominiar Knight had acquired it.

And perhaps Aeternis might be willing to tell him about Amalric Galbraith.

Aeternis straightened as Mazael approached. A stocky, powerful man, he had a close-cropped black beard and numerous faded battle scars.

"We meet again," said Aeternis, his voice gravelly.

"So we do," said Mazael.

"A lord now, I hear," said Aeternis. "I always thought you'd be dead by now, on some fool errand for Lord Malden."

"And I always thought you'd be dead, too, from Grand Master Malleus's orders," said Mazael.

Aeternis scoffed. "It came close, a few times." He grinned. "I might get another chance at killing you."

"You came close, the last time," said Mazael.

"Hardly," said Aeternis. "You had us. It was only your mercy that kept Lord Malden's men from slaughtering us all."

"Perhaps you'd like to repay that mercy," said Mazael.

Suspicion touched Aeternis's face. "How?"

Mazael turned, showing the scabbard dangling from his left hip. "Remember this?"

"All too well," said Aeternis. "Best sword I ever had. It looks like a showpiece, I know, but by holy Joraviar, I never had a sword so sharp, or so sturdy."

"Where did you find it?" said Mazael.

"Does it matter?" said Aeternis. "Do you want another one?" He laughed. "If I could find another, I would take it for myself."

"Idle curiosity, nothing more," said Mazael.

"Curiosity is never idle for a lord," said Aeternis. He shrugged. "But why not? I bought it from a wandering merchant...oh, five, six years ago. Right before your Lord Malden tried to seize Tumblestone. It was in Cateron, I think, in the Old Kingdoms."

"Do you remember the merchant's name?" said Mazael.

Aeternis thought for a moment. "Tall fellow, polite as a scared maid." He snapped his fingers. "Ah! Harune Dustfoot, that was it."

Mazael felt a chill. "Harune Dustfoot?"

"You know him?" said Aeternis.

"I rescued his caravan from bandits in eastern Knightrealm," said Mazael.

"Did you?" said Aeternis. "Small world. Not surprising. All the trade's dried up in the Old Kingdoms, now that Amalric has killed most of the folk living there."

"You don't approve?" said Mazael.

Aeternis shrugged. "It's not my place to approve or disapprove. I fight who the Grand Master tells me to fight, and that's that." He rubbed his scarred temple. "But when I served in the Old Kingdoms, we tried to leave a peace, or at least a truce, with the folk of the Old Kingdoms. It worked, too, for a while." He shook his head again. "Then Amalric came…and that was the end of any peace."

"What do you think of him?" said Mazael.

"Scouting the enemy, eh?"

"Isn't that what you're doing here?"

Aeternis laughed. "It is, after all." He shrugged. "All right. Amalric has no fear, is deadly with a sword, and can command an army better than almost any other man. And he's as haughty as a lion, hates the other commanders, and only listens to the Grand Master." Aeternis shrugged again. "He'll either become Grand Master of the Dominiars, or he'll get himself killed. But he's old Malleus's favorite these days, and what I think doesn't matter."

"His wife seems to hate him," said Mazael.

Aeternis snorted. "His wife? You mean the woman in widow's black? That's his sister. The lady Morebeth Galbraith. Though you're right that she hates him. Her husband served under Amalric's command in the Old Kingdoms, got killed fighting in the front line. Lady Morebeth never forgave Amalric for that."

Mazael said nothing.

"You were always a worthy foe. It was good speaking to you again," said Aeternis. He held out his hand. "Perhaps we won't have to fight after all."

"Let us hope not," said Mazael. They shook hands, and Aeternis wandered away, black Dominiar cloak swaying behind him.

The music began again, slow and high, a ballad about some long-dead Roland's lost love. The song reminded Mazael of Romaria, made him melancholy. He decided to find Rachel, dance with her, and then go to bed.

A warm hand brushed his arm.

Mazael stopped, something like lightning surging through his blood.

Morebeth Galbraith stood besides him, hair shimmering like flame beneath her hat. She stood only a few inches shorter than him, her gray eyes glinting like sword blades.

Yet Mazael saw something of the fire he felt reflected in her cold eyes.

"Lord Mazael Cravenlock?" she said, voice precise and cold. "Forgive my presumption, but I had heard much of you, and wished to meet you." She stepped back, releasing his arm, and did a deep curtsy. "I am Morebeth Galbraith, of Mastaria."

"My lady," said Mazael. He took her hand, kissed it, and stared back at her. She was not as beautiful as Romaria had been. No woman could ever be, yet she was a close second.

He had not felt such powerful desire in a long time.

"You are famous in Mastaria, among the Dominiars," Morebeth said.

"Infamous, more likely," said Mazael. Something about her voice made his heart race, his blood pulse.

"They are often one and the same," said Morebeth. A smile, like a flower of frost, touched her pale face. "Would my lord consent to dance with a poor widow?"

"He would," said Mazael, taking her hand. "Nothing would please him more."

Mazael glimpsed Sir Commander Amalric glaring at him from across the Court, but did not care. He and Morebeth danced in silence for a long moment, circling around the Court of Challengers. The hems of her black skirts whispered against the stone-paved ground, brushed against his boots. His heart beat ever faster, and he felt the pulse in her wrist quicken.

"My lord dances well."

"As do you."

"I wonder how you learned, with no lady wife on your arm," said Morebeth.

"I have no lady wife."

"Nor I a lord husband." Her voice remained calm, but the muscles near her gray eyes twitched.

"I am sorry," said Mazael. "I…heard what had happened to your husband."

"Thank you, my lord." She hesitated. "I loved him. It does not often happen between nobles, but I loved him."

"I understand," said Mazael. She looked at him sharply. "I…I, too, lost someone…very dear to me. She was not my wife. We never had the chance. But I loved her no less."

"My lord." Morebeth's gloved fingers stroked the back of his neck. "I am sorry. I did not know."

They moved closer together. Mazael felt her heat through his clothes. His hands tightened about her fingers and hip. He watched her gray eyes watching him.

"Come with me," she whispered.

"I dare not," said Mazael. The heat vanished, her cold mask returning. Mazael groped for an excuse, something that could convince her, that could convince him. "If…you become pregnant, then…"

Morebeth leaned against him, her lips brushing his ear. "My shame. My great shame. I cannot bear children." She stepped back from him, her mouth twitching. "What man would have me?"

"I am sorry," said Mazael.

She titled her chin. "Then comfort me."

Mazael kissed her, long and hard, the fire in his blood burning out of all control.

###

They wound up in Mazael's chambers in the Tower of Guard, together in his bed. Mazael supposed that half the court must have seen them, that Knightcastle would crawl with gossip tomorrow, but he did not care, did not care about anything but Morebeth Galbraith's eyes and lips and body.

###

Adalar saw them leave.

He could not put the memory of Mazael's wounds closing out of his mind, could not stop thinking about what that might mean.

CHAPTER 12
SHADOWS IN KNIGHTCASTLE

Afterwards Mazael fell asleep and dreamed:

He stood atop the Old Keep, the highest tower of Knightcastle, gazing down on the Riversteel's valley.

But now the valley was dead, a desolation of blighted ashes, withered trees clawing at the sky. The burned rubble of Castle Town squatted by the riverbank like an open sore. The Riversteel itself had turned the color of blood, corpses floating in the thick waters. Knightcastle was empty and silent, drained of life and energy, a monumental tomb clinging to the hillside like a dying fungus.

The red sun glared down at Mazael from the sooty sky.

Mazael stared in stupefied horror. What catastrophe had befallen Lord Malden's lands?

And then in a surge of rage and terror he remembered the dreams of blood and death that had tormented him before...

"This is a dream!" shouted Mazael at the sky. "I know this is a dream! Show yourself, you damned coward! Show yourself!"

No one answered. His voice echoed off the stony mountains.

And then:

"Such a shame to see a man lose his faith."

Mazael whirled, snarling.

A man walked towards him, a man draped in a simple black robe. He wore the hawk-nosed, gray-eyed face of a wandering jongleur named Mattias Comorian. But the face meant nothing. In dreams he had masqueraded as Lord Adalon Cravenlock. In the waking world he had disguised himself as Simonian of Briault, necromancer and Lord Mitor's advisor.

He was Mazael's father.

He was the Old Demon.

"My prodigal son returns," said the Old Demon, his voice dry. The faintest glimmer of red touched his eyes. "And you have done just as I said. You murdered Mitor, you became Lord of Castle Cravenlock, and now you stand ready to become lord of all the earth."

For the briefest instant Mazael remembered murdering Mitor, remembered striding past his brother's corpse to claim Castle Cravenlock. But that was a lie, a phantasm of the Old Demon's magic. Skhath had killed Mitor, not Mazael. And this monster, this ancient horror, had killed Romaria.

"Skhath killed Mitor, not I," spat Mazael. "And you murdered Romaria, you bastard, you-"

"It was your fault," said the Old Demon, smiling. "A son ought to submit himself to his father. If you had but obeyed me, she would be at your side still..."

"You killed her!" screamed Mazael, stepping towards him.

The red glaze in the Old Demon's eyes darkened. "You've grown stronger, I see."

Mazael said nothing, his fists clenched.

"You've become strong enough to work your will here," said the Old Demon, waving his hand, "at this place which is no place." His lips pulled back, revealing jagged, filthy teeth. "But you still have yet to learn that I am the stronger!"

The Old Demon thrust out his hand, and the world spun around them.

Mazael found himself in the Hall of Triumphs. The great crystal windows had shattered into razor-edged shards. From the arched ceilings hung the gutted corpses of Lord Malden, Lady Rhea, and their children. Rachel dangled naked from a gibbet, turning slowly.

The Old Demon lounged in Lord Malden's throne, black robes like shadow.

"Do you like it?" he said, flicking a finger at the dead. "Your future. And your choices will bring it about."

"You are a liar," said Mazael, "and always have been." He stalked towards the throne. "You murdered Romaria, and I swear that one day I will kill you."

The Old Demon laughed. "Do you know how often I have heard that, my son? How many men and women have sworn vengeance, sworn my destruction? I sit on a throne of their skulls!" His laughter faded into an amused titter. "You thought Lucan Mandragon strong? You think Straganis powerful? Lift your hand against me and I will show you arcane arts that could shatter their minds."

"Theirs, perhaps," said Mazael, "but maybe not mine."

"Fool, fool," said the Old Demon. He rose from the throne and strode towards Mazael, the red haze in his eyes brightening. "You're mine, my son. Deny me as you will, but you are still mine. To think I would have made you king of the world."

"You would have devoured my soul and added my power to yours," said Mazael.

"Then try to strike me down," said the Old Demon. He glanced at the ceiling. "And this is how it will end for those you love, for you."

A bit of Gerald's blood splashed against the floor.

"You will die screaming," said the Old Demon, "and there is nothing you can do to stop it."

"*You lie,*" *said Mazael,* "*as always.*"

"*Your own choices will destroy you,*" *said the Old Demon.* "*You've dared to rebel against me, and you shall pay for it. You chose your mewling sister over my power? You shall see her die…*"

"*No,*" *said Mazael.*

"*You repeat yourself,*" *said the Old Demon.* "*How tedious. It is not a threat, my son. It is not even a promise. It is a certainty.*"

Mazael growled, his hand going to his hip. He had no sword belt, no weapons. He lifted his hand and wished for a sword. The Hall of Triumphs shimmered about him. He stared at his hand, willed for Lion, and it appeared in his grasp.

The sword shone with a clear white flame, hot and pure, illuminating the shadowed hall.

The Old Demon stepped back.

"*I told you,*" *said Mazael,* "*to shut up!*"

"*Then die!*" *snarled the Old Demon, his eyes blazing. His human aspect fell away like a shredded mask, and he sprang at Mazael, hooked claws leading.*

Mazael raised his shining sword and set himself.

The world crumpled around him like a rotten shell…

Mazael awoke with a shuddering gasp, sweat dripping down his face. For a dreadful moment, he could not remember where he was or what had happened to him. Memory flooded back, and Mazael remembered Knightcastle, Lord Malden's ire, and the grand dance…

Morebeth.

He looked over to find her gone. Mazael vaguely remembered that she had left before the sun had risen. He closed his eyes and lay back with a tired groan.

He did not even want to think about what the nightmare meant.

Mazael stared at the ceiling, his mind swirling and twisting. It was past sunrise, and beams of sunlight slashed across the ancient gray stone. Mazael wondered why Adalar hadn't awakened him. No doubt the boy had been too embarrassed.

Mazael sighed, sat up, and blinked in surprise.

The biggest raven he had even seen sat on the windowsill, ruffling its feathers. Beady black eyes stared it him, dark and glistening. Mazael could have sworn it grinned at him.

Someone coughed.

Mazael turned his head. A massive wooden chair stood against the far wall, and in that chair sat Lucan Mandragon.

"I was wondering," said Lucan, "if you would ever notice me."

"You're alive," said Mazael, stunned.

"Obviously," said Lucan. He held a skin of wine in one hand and a joint of beef in the other, eating with apparent relish. "You'll forgive me if I eat as we speak. I haven't eaten anything for three days."

"It's been a week since you vanished," said Mazael.

The raven cawed.

"Really?" said Lucan, around a mouthful. "I had always suspected that time ran at a different pace in the spirit world."

"What the hell happened?" said Mazael. "Is Straganis dead?"

"Regrettably, no." Lucan took a long drink of wine. "Straganis possesses greater power than I. His spell drew us both into the spiritual realm. He came quite close to killing me, in fact, but I," his mouth twisted, "managed to outmaneuver him, and he fled. I spent some time in a stupor, later awoke, and found my way to Knightcastle."

"That's all?" said Mazael. The raven cawed again.

"That's it," agreed Lucan. He glanced at the empty spot in the bed. "I can see why you're confused. You must be exhausted, after all."

"How clever. You should become court jongleur," said Mazael. He scowled. "Were you sitting there the entire time? Damned degenerate."

Lucan laughed. "Hardly. No, I arrived just as your lady was leaving."

"Did she notice you?" said Mazael.

"Of course not," scoffed Lucan. "You scarcely noticed me. Not surprising, given how utterly spent you must be."

"Another word and I'll hand you over to your brother," growled Mazael.

"Such a dire threat," said Lucan. "But you ought to take pride. The lady looked very satisfied as she left, after all. Who is she, anyway?"

"Morebeth Galbraith," said Mazael. He rolled out of bed. "Ah...do you see where my tunic is?"

Lucan pointed at the corner. "Sir Commander Amalric Galbraith's sister?"

"Yes." Mazael gathered his scattered clothes and began dressing. "How did you know his name?"

"In his infinite wisdom, my lord father keeps an eye on the Dominiars," said Lucan, "lest it becomes necessary to use them against Lord Malden. I'm sure Sir Commander Amalric will be thrilled to learn that you bedded his widowed sister." Mazael glared, and Lucan's smirk widened. "How did she leave, by the way?"

Mazael blinked. "What?"

"It was some manner of secret passage. She pressed a stone, part of the wall swung out, and she vanished."

"Oh." Mazael buckled on his sword belt. "The Trysting Ways."

"The what?"

"The Trysting Ways," said Mazael. "It's what they call the secret passages in Knightcastle. Supposedly some old lord or another made them so he could tryst unobserved with his various mistresses."

"Perhaps you should adapt it for Castle Cravenlock," said Lucan.

"I told you, I've heard enough on…"

"So Knightcastle is riddled with secret passages?"

Mazael paused, a boot halfway on. "It is. Miles of them, I suppose. Crypts and catacombs into the hill, as well. Some of them have probably been forgotten for centuries."

"Ah," said Lucan. "That could pose a problem."

"Why?"

"Because," said Lucan, "I'm fairly sure Straganis is here."

"What?"

"I've sensed his spells," said Lucan, "but I can't determine his precise location."

"Why not?"

"I told you," said Lucan. "He's stronger than I am, and somewhat more skilled. I am strong enough to sense him, though," he sighed, "not quite strong enough to find him."

Mazael began to pace, Lion's scabbard tapping against his leg. "What is he doing here?"

Lucan laughed. "That should be obvious. He vowed to kill you and your sister. And he will try to kill me just out of spite, I expect."

"But how?" whispered Mazael, thinking of his dark dream. Was Straganis in league with the Old Demon? Or had the Old Demon manipulated Straganis, as he had manipulated Skhath? Had Mazael himself been tricked by the Old Demon, manipulated into his own destruction?

But he dared not think that way. His doubts and fears could paralyze him.

"You have a thought?" said Lucan, watching him.

"Straganis could disguise himself as anything," said Mazael.

"Most certainly," said Lucan.

"So he could be hiding among Lord Malden's vassals, or the Justiciars, or the Dominiars?"

Lucan nodded.

"If you see him, will you recognize him?" said Mazael.

"Possibly," said Lucan. "Or not. You, too, might be able to recognize him. The…ah, potent nature of your blood might give you strength to see past his illusions. Or it may not." He shrugged. "Divinatory spells are not my strength."

Something occurred to Mazael. "But they are Trocend's."

"Lord Malden's pet wizard?" Lucan sneered. "Certainly he has vast skill at divination. I doubt that you can really trust him."

"He would say the same of you," said Mazael. "And his loyalty is to Lord Malden."

"A fine thing," said Lucan. "Yet I know the truth of you, and your black secret has remained a secret. And our Brother Trocend is very good at finding secrets. Suppose he learns your secret? What do you imagine he will do with it?"

"He would go to Lord Malden," said Mazael, closing his eyes, "and then...yet if Trocend can find Straganis, I can endure the risk."

"If he learns your true nature, you will have no choice but to kill him," said Lucan.

"I...if that happens, I will decide what to do then," said Mazael. "I will speak with him."

Lucan shrugged. "It is your choice, though I think it a foolish one."

"I can endure that," said Mazael. He paused for a moment. "I am glad you survived."

"Because you need my help?"

"Aye, that," said Mazael, "and I'd wish no man dead at the hands of a San-keth cleric." He remembered Skhath plunging a black dagger into Mitor's back. "I'd wish that on no man."

"How splendid. As it happens, I agree with you. I'm quite glad I survived." Lucan's hard eyes glittered. "I told you what I wish. If a dark power of any sort hides within Knightcastle, then I will work with you to crush it utterly."

"Thank you," said Mazael. He looked out the window, past the raven. "I'd best go. Lord Malden probably wants me at breakfast."

"It's late," said Lucan. "You missed breakfast." His smirk returned. "Though you may yet find the Lady Morebeth."

"Straganis may not be the only one to kill you out of annoyance," said Mazael, turning. Lion's scabbard clattered against the stone wall. "Wait. There's something else."

Lucan finished the beef joint and tossed the bone to the raven. The bird cracked it open and began pecking at the marrow. "What is it?"

"I spoke with Sir Commander Aeternis," said Mazael. "Where do you think he found Lion?"

Lucan shrugged. "Weapons of magical power are extraordinarily rare. I assume it was some heirloom from Tristafel, passed down from generation to generation without any understanding of its true worth."

"He bought it," said Mazael. Lucan's eyebrows climbed higher. "From a merchant named Harune Dustfoot."

"Did he?" said Lucan. "The same Harune Dustfoot you rescued?"

"The very same."

Lucan leaned back in the chair. "An astonishing coincidence. In fact, I'd even say it's far too unlikely for a coincidence. This Dustfoot fellow doesn't seem the sort to traffic in weapons of arcane power." He shook his head. "Maybe he simply found it, unaware of its true nature, and sold it for quick profit."

"Yes, but where did he find it?" said Mazael. "Try to find him if at all possible. He ought to be in Castle Town, selling those cheeses of his."

Lucan glanced at the raven, which cawed and flew away. "Then I had best get started, had I not? What will you be doing? Besides entertaining your lady, of course."

Mazael closed his eyes. "I will try to keep Lord Malden from doing anything rash." He thought of Straganis, of how Blackfang had come within a few heartbeats of killing Rachel. "And try to keep Rachel safe."

"I wish you the best of luck," said Lucan. "After all, we shall most certainly need it."

CHAPTER 13
LORDS' WOOD

Mazael spent the next two days alternating between boredom and extreme watchfulness. He argued with Lord Malden over trivial wedding details, the coming tournament, and the feasts, since no one else in Knightcastle had the courage to do so. In the evenings he ate dinner in whichever of Knightcastle's halls happened to catch Lord Malden's fancy. In the mornings he practiced swordplay with the squires and Lord Malden's household knights, many old friends from his days at Knightcastle.

Mazael tried to keep an eye on Rachel, fearing changeling assassins in every shadow. He stared at every servant, every lord, every knight, trying to determine if they were changelings, or even Straganis in disguise.

Mazael's nights were much more pleasant.

Morebeth came to his room, slipping through the Trysting Ways, and left before dawn.

They neither spoke nor slept much.

And on the third day, Lord Malden decided to go hunting.

###

Of course, when Lord Malden went hunting, he took a small army.

His pages and squires rode with him, bearing his weapons. Lord Malden offered knights and lords the honor of hunting with him, and none refused. Mazael received an invitation, and accepted, if only to escape from the boredom.

Even some of the ladies of the court came, clad in riding gowns, bearing bows and hooded falcons. Lady Claretta was a steady hand with a bow, and rode at Lord Malden's side, laughing at his jests.

Mazael suspected Lord Malden wanted a day alone with his mistress, without Gerald's disapproving glares.

And to his surprised delight, Morebeth came as well.

She had asked Lord Malden at dinner the evening before.

"My Lord Malden," she said, sweeping into a deep curtsy. "Is it true you hunt tomorrow?"

Lord Malden smiled and kissed her hand. "It is. Perhaps I'll bring back a stag for the tournament feasts, eh?" He seemed entirely charmed by her presence. Mazael understood.

Morebeth glanced at Mazael, smiled, and turned back at Lord Malden. "Might I ride with you, my lord?"

A stunned silence went over the hall. Lord Malden extended invitations to hunt. No one ever dared ask him.

"Might you?" said Lord Malden, caught between affront and amusement.

A smile spread across Morebeth's lips, and she answered in her cold voice. "Aye, I would, my lord. In Mastaria, we enjoyed hawking, my lord husband and I. He is gone now, and I have not hawked since." She looked him square in the eye. "I would like to begin again, I think."

"I would be honored to have you join us, lady," said Lord Malden. He glanced across the hall, to where a scowling Amalric Galbraith stood, surrounded by his Dominiar Knights. "Assuming your brother doesn't object, of course."

Amalric's scowl deepened, but he gave a sharp nod.

A tiny smirk crossed Morebeth's lips.

An uninvited knight was bold enough to ask to accompany Lord Malden, and received only a frosty glare in answer.

A hundred horsemen stood at the edge of the Lords' Wood.

The Lords' Wood lay a half-day's ride from Knightcastle. While almost all of Knightrealm had been cultivated and farmed for centuries, the Lords' Wood remained still, a remnant of the ancient forests that had once covered the land. First the Kings and later the Lords of Knightcastle had hunted among the looming trees for generations.

Sometimes bandits set up their lairs among the trunks, and the Lords had fine sport driving them out.

Lord Malden and Claretta rode at the party's head, alongside a pack of Lord Malden's prized hounds. Mazael rode in the back, alongside Morebeth. She sat upright in the saddle, her blood-red hair done in an ornate crown of braids, stark against her black gown. A heavy leather glove encased her left hand and forearm. A hooded hawk named Striker rested on the glove, claws digging into the leather.

"Does not your arm grow weary?" said Mazael.

"Not in the least," said Morebeth. She raised her free hand and stroked the hawk's neck. "I am stronger than I look." She turned gray eyes towards him. "As you well know."

They reined up at the edge of the trees.

"My hounds are eager!" called Lord Malden, reining up. "I will ride after them. Sir Tobias will lead those who wish to hunt with the bow." Sir Tobias galloped to his father's side, a short bow resting in his arms. "And Lady Morebeth wishes to hawk. My lord Mazael! I trust you will escort her?"

Someone snickered.

"It would be my honor," said Mazael. Morebeth's eyes glinted.

Lord Malden's party rode off in one direction, as did Sir Tobias's. Mazael sat on Mantle's back, alone with Morebeth and her mare.

"They laugh at us, you know," said Mazael.

"That troubles you? Let them," said Morebeth, still stroking the hawk's neck. "Let them. What are their snickers to us? You are Lord of Castle Cravenlock, and I am a noble lady of Mastaria. We are stronger than they." She gave him one of her rare smiles, a smile with heat behind it. "We may do as we wish."

"And you wish to go hawking?" said Mazael.

"Aye. Very much so." A small, distant smile played over her lips. "Do you know much of falconry, my lord Mazael?"

"Little, I'm afraid," said Mazael. "My lord father devoted most his attentions to my older brothers. And I spent fifteen years wandering as a landless knight. I had little time or wealth for falconry."

"A pity." Morebeth turned her cool eyes back to him. "It is an art, as much as sword work."

"You enjoy it?"

"I do." Morebeth nodded. "Falcons and hawks are solitary birds, you know. Isolated and selfish. They care nothing for others, and Striker here certainly cares nothing for me. Yet if they are trained properly, raised well from the beginning, they are the deadliest of hunters. The training of a hawk…it is something I take great pride in, something I enjoy very much." She paused. "Would you like to see Striker at hunt?"

"Yes," said Mazael. "I would."

They rode into the Lords' Wood. The trees had begun to bud, some even showing leaves. A quiet silence hung over the forest, broken only by the rustling leaves and the creaking branches.

"How will you follow the hawk?" said Mazael. "Won't the leaves block your vision?"

"For a falcon, yes," said Morebeth. "They usually prey on birds, sometimes chase them over long distances. But Striker is a goshawk, and goshawks usually take rabbits, turkeys, sometimes pheasants." She shook her head, a red braid sliding across her black-clad back. "Amalric prefers falcons, but I favor hawks."

"You hate him, don't you?" said Mazael.

Morebeth said nothing.

"I understand it," said Mazael. "My brother…well, he tried to have me killed several times."

Morebeth looked at him. "Clearly he failed. But, yes, I hate Amalric." She sighed. "It wasn't always that way. I loved him once. But he has changed. Yes. I hate him. Your brother. How did you end your conflict?"

"He died," said Mazael. "A San-keth cleric killed him."

Morebeth stared at him.

"Most folk think I killed him," said Mazael.

"I believe you," said Morebeth.

"You do?"

Morebeth nodded. "I cannot see you raising your hand against kin."

Mazael felt an absurd surge of gratitude. Most people believed he had murdered Mitor and seized Castle Cravenlock for himself. But to meet someone who believed him…

Morebeth raised her free hand. "Shh." She pointed.

A small group of pheasants stood at the base of a massive oak, pecking at the ground. Morebeth smiled and undid Striker's hood. The hawk lifted its head, its eyes like amber knives. Morebeth remained still, and Mazael followed suit. Striker did not move. Mazael wondered if the hawk had seen the pheasants. Or smelled them, if that was how hawks hunted…

Striker moved so fast Mazael scarce followed the movement. One moment the hawk sat on Morebeth's gloved fist. The next it stooped over one of the pheasants, claws raking, beak rending. There was an agonized squawk, and the pheasant went still. The others fled in all directions.

"Gods," said Mazael, "that thing is fast."

"Nothing can match the speed of a goshawk over a short distance," said Morebeth, "nothing at all. Come with me, but stay back." She slid from the saddle, skirts rustling, and pulled some shredded meat from one of her saddlebags. Striker kept worrying at the dead pheasant with his beak. Morebeth moved towards the goshawk, then crouched besides the pheasant, black skirts pooling around her, and held out her fist. Striker hopped up onto the leather glove and began eating the meat.

"Why didn't you just pick him up?" said Mazael.

Morebeth laughed. "It is never wise to separate a hunting bird from his food. He would probably have tried to kill me. But he has been trained to eat from my fist, and will abandon a kill for that. Can you take care of the pheasant?" She watched Striker eat. "It's rather hard to do so with one hand."

Mazael laughed. "I imagine." He dressed the pheasant and lashed the bird's legs to Mantle's harness. Striker finished the meat, and Morebeth hooded the bird again, settling him on a little wooden perch attached to her saddle.

"I wonder where Lord Malden and Sir Tobias are," said Mazael.

Morebeth shook her head. "We won't see them again until tonight. Is something amiss?"

"I dislike them being alone," said Mazael.

"Ah," said Morebeth. "The San-keth, I presume."

Mazael frowned. "How did you know about that?"

"I was there when you told Lord Malden about them, remember?" said Morebeth. "They ought to be fine for a few hours."

"We should find them," said Mazael, turning towards Mantle.

"Really? You surprise me," said Morebeth.

"What?" said Mazael.

"We are alone, and you are so eager to find the others?" said Morebeth. She took him in her arms. "Why?"

Mazael found himself speechless.

Morebeth kissed him and laughed into his mouth. "Unless you are afraid, of course?"

He wasn't. It was cool out, the ground strewn with damp leaves, but they lay atop Mazael's cloak and beneath Morebeth's, and warmed each other.

Afterwards Mazael lay in a doze, Morebeth's head resting on his shoulder. The worries and dark thoughts had fled his mind. He felt no particular urge to rise. Morebeth's breathing, slow and steady, lulled him towards sleep.

A dull thud broke his reverie.

Mazael looked up, wondering if Striker had fallen from Morebeth's saddle. Another thud came, then another, and another.

"What's that?" said Morebeth, lifting her head.

"A drum," said Mazael.

"Here?" said Morebeth, frowning. "Lord Malden didn't bring one, did he?"

"Bandits, most likely," said Mazael, scowling in alarm. He had brought Lion, and his old Mastarian war hammer, but no armor and no other weapons. "We'd better get dressed."

Morebeth sighed and stretched against him, sending tingles down his nerves. "Pity, that."

"It is," said Mazael, but he managed to stand anyway. It took him only a short time to dress. Morebeth's more complex garments took longer, and Mazael had to help her.

The drumbeat came louder, harder.

"Damn this frippery," said Morebeth. "I'd wear trousers and a tunic and damn what they think, even my brother. Sometimes I wish I had been born a man."

Mazael grunted. "I'm grateful you weren't, just now."

Her cold stare cracked just long enough to flash him a wicked grin.

They climbed back into the saddle.

"Let's find Lord Malden," said Mazael.

"Why don't we find that noise instead?" said Morebeth.

"You must be kept safe," said Mazael, "and I've only my sword and hammer, and no armor."

Morebeth's cold smile returned. "I'm quite safe, my lord. After all, I am with you, am I not?"

"All right," said Mazael. "We'll look. Maybe it's nothing."

They rode off, following the drumbeat. The land rose, becoming hilly. In places ancient, moss-cloaked boulders jutted from the ground. The drumbeat grew louder, accompanied by a strange, droning noise.

"What the devil is that?" said Mazael.

Morebeth titled her head to the side. "Chanting, I think."

"Chanting?" said Mazael.

Morebeth nodded, pointing at a steep hill. "It's coming from over the next hill."

"Your ears must be better than mine," said Mazael. He dropped from the saddle and drew Lion. "Wait here. I'm going to climb up and take a look."

Morebeth dismounted besides him. "Don't be foolish."

Mazael stared at her, trying to phrase a refusal. She reminded him of Romaria's bravery. He felt a surge of sorrow, and could think of nothing to say.

They climbed the hill together. Morebeth's skirts didn't hinder her, and she made less noise than Mazael. She even seemed to keep her balance better than he could. Mazael wondered at this, and shrugged it off. She was almost ten years younger than he was, after all.

Mazael dropped to his stomach and crawled to the edge. Beyond the hill the land dropped down into a bowl and a small, mirror-bright pond. A crowd of thirty people stood at the edge of the pond, and a black-bearded man and a woman in peasant clothes stood atop a boulder. The woman had the black-slit yellow eyes of a San-keth changeling.

The man was Sir Roger Gravesend.

"Damn," breathed Mazael.

Morebeth crawled to his side and whispered in his ear. "San-keth, aren't they?"

"Aye," hissed Mazael, clenching Lion's hilt. "And the black-bearded fellow? Sir Roger Gravesend, once one of my sworn knights. He tried to kill me and Rachel. Twice. Gods damn it all. I should have killed him when I had the chance."

"A lord can live to regret mercy," said Morebeth. "What are they doing here?" She paused, steely eyes narrowed. "Some of them are human."

"Followers of the San-keth way, no doubt," said Mazael.

The changeling with the drum stopped, and the chanting ended.

"People of great Sepharivaim!" said the woman atop the stone, "hear me!" A frightening madness lit her face. "Our time draws close. Soon the castles of the mighty will fall. Soon the rivers will run red with the blood of the infidels!" The changelings' cheers punctuated her remarks. "And the infidel lords will pay from their crimes against the people of Sepharivaim. Lord Malden Roland will die. Lord Richard Mandragon will beg for mercy before he perishes! The Grand Master of the wretched Dominiars will die screaming! And Lord Mazael and his apostate sister will hang from the highest tower of the castle they stole from us!"

The changelings howled, and Roger grinned.

Morebeth scoffed. "Rabble. I should like to see them try."

"We need to get Lord Malden," said Mazael. "If they catch us here it will be our deaths."

"Why?" said Morebeth.

Mazael beckoned her away from the edge of the hill. "There's thirty of them. I can't take them by myself."

"You need not," said Morebeth. "There's two of us, after all. And we'll be mounted."

Mazael gaped at her. "You?"

Morebeth nodded, a glimmer of amusement in her eyes. "Me."

"You don't have a weapon."

"I'll borrow your hammer."

"Do you even know how to fight from horseback?"

Morebeth shrugged, shoulders rippling beneath black fabric. "You raise the hammer and bring it down on a foe's skull. And I have ridden since I was a small child."

"You must be mad," said Mazael.

"No more than you, my lord," she said.

Mazael met her unwavering eyes for a long moment. "Why not? You, my lady, are at least as fearsome as they. Come." They crept back down the hill, and Mazael pulled the Mastarian war hammer from his saddle. It had a solid head of black steel and an oak handle worn from much use. He handed it to Morebeth, who took it without flinching or staggering. Mazael climbed back up into Mantle's saddle. He wished he had Chariot, but Mantle was sturdy enough.

"Ready?" he said.

Morebeth hefted the hammer easily in her right hand. "I am."

"Then let's go," said Mazael, "and settle my debts with Sir Roger."

Mazael rode around the hill, Morebeth at his side. He heard the changeling woman shrieking, her voice ringing over the hollow. Mazael came around the hill, saw the changelings standing before the stone, and kicked Mantle to a gallop.

The changelings, rapt in their ecstasy, did not see him until Lion came down and ripped through the nearest man's neck. Mantle raced through their ranks, Mazael striking right and left, Lion's blade running with blood. Untrained for war, Mantle did not try to bite and trample as Chariot would have. Nevertheless, the changelings and the snake-kissers reacted with panic, turning to flee.

Roger blanched, almost falling from the stone. Mazael risked a quick glance at Morebeth. She swung the hammer with cool ease, leaving a trail of dead changelings in her wake.

"Kill them!" screamed the changeling woman. "Kill them now!"

Roger jumped from the stone and started running as fast as his legs could carry him. The woman stared after him and snarled . Mazael galloped through the mass of changelings and wheeled around, Lion clenched in his fist. A heartbeat later Morebeth brained a changeling and reined in besides him. A dozen dead changelings marked their path.

The survivors fled in every direction. One made the mistake of dashing past Mantle, and Mazael took off his head. He caught a glimpse of Roger dashing for the trees on the far side of the pond.

"Morebeth!" he yelled. "Stay with me!" He did not wait for an answer, but booted Mantle to a gallop. Roger glanced over his shoulder, cursed, and redoubled his pace. Mazael gritted his teeth, raising. If he could just catch the traitor before he reached the trees...

Sir Roger raced into the forest, and Mazael spurred Mantle after him, ducking low to avoid an overhanging branch. But the wrist of his sword hand slammed hard into the branch, the crack of bone filling his ear, Lion tumbling from his grasp. Mazael hissed in pain, just as his forehead smacked into another branch. He fell backwards off his horse and hit the ground hard.

Mazael spat in furious pain and lurched back to his feet.

Roger was gone, and he saw none of the other changelings. Mazael rubbed his broken wrist, cursing. Already his flesh writhed as the broken bones began to knit themselves together.

"Mazael!" Morebeth reined up besides him and jumped from the saddle. "Are you all right? I was sure you had split your skull."

"I'm fine," said Mazael, releasing his wrist. He did not want to draw Morebeth's attention to his healing ability. "My pride is the worst injury. Gods, but this was foolish. I should have gone back to find Lord Malden."

He scooped up Lion with his left hand.

"You did as you thought best," said Morebeth, still holding the hammer. "And suppose you had gone to find Lord Malden? The changelings would have gone by the time we returned."

"I suppose," said Mazael. "Perhaps we ought to track down Roger Gravesend."

"No," said Morebeth. "You're not a tracker, and neither am I. At best we'll get lost. At worst, the changelings can set up an ambush. We caught them off guard once, but we'll not do so again. The best thing to do is to find Lord Malden."

"You're right," said Mazael He eased his right hand through Mantle's reins, trying not to wince, and led the palfrey back into the hollow. The bodies of the dead changelings lay strewn about the ground. He severed a changeling's head, waited for the blood to drain, and wrapped it in a dropped cloak.

"A trophy?" said Morebeth.

Mazael shook his head. "Proof. Lord Malden will never believe me otherwise. Or Brother Trocend." Trocend might discover more than Mazael wished. But he had no other choice. If the San-keth infiltrated Knightcastle, if they plotted to kill Lord Malden and Rachel, then Mazael had to stop them.

Whatever the cost to himself.

"Let's go," said Mazael. Morebeth nodded and handed him the war hammer. "You're...quite good with that."

"Thank you." Morebeth plucked at her hair, adjusting her crown of braids. She almost smiled. "Sir Brandon, my husband...showed me. Before he died."

Mazael swallowed. "I'm sorry." Her remembered Romaria's skill with blade and bow and felt again the grief.

"The woman you loved," said Morebeth. "She was skilled with weapons, wasn't she?"

"She was," said Mazael.

"So was Brandon."

They stared at each other in silence.

Mazael looked away first. "No sense standing about all day."

A ghost of smile flickered across Morebeth's face. "Of course not."

###

"Mazael, my friend!" said Lord Malden. "Come, sit! I see you had a successful hunt."

"Of a sort," said Mazael.

They found Lord Malden and Sir Tobias encamped at the edge of the

Lords' Wood. Sir Tobias's party had claimed a half-dozen stags, while Lord Malden's hounds had run several foxes to bay. The huntsmen, pages, and squires busied themselves preparing the kills. Both Lord Malden and Sir Tobias seemed in excellent spirits.

"We had best go at once," said Mazael.

"Whatever for?" said Lord Malden, his full attention on Claretta, who sat besides him.

Mazael pulled free the changeling's head, the snake-eyes glazed and staring. A stunned silence fell over the hunters. Lord Malden blinked once.

"My lord Mazael," he said, "you certainly hunt exotic prey."

"There were about thirty of them," said Mazael, "led by Sir Roger Gravesend, who's been trying to kill Lady Rachel for weeks. I rode them down, scattered them, killed several, but Gravesend got away."

Lord Malden's eyes flicked to Morebeth. "And you did this all by yourself?"

Morebeth didn't blink. "It would be most unbecoming for a lady to take up arms." Her gray eyes sparkled with amusement. "And Mazael is the mightiest warrior I have yet met."

"They were planning to kill you," said Mazael. "And me, and Lady Rachel, and your sons." He left out Lord Richard. Lord Malden might approve, after all.

"Did they?" said Lord Malden, still gazing at the head. "We shall have to increase our guard."

Mazael nodded. "We ought to leave at once."

"No," murmured Lord Malden, "no, it's almost nightfall. No sense blundering about in the dark. We'll leave at daybreak."

Mazael had yet another sleepless night, though less pleasant than those he had spent with Morebeth. He spent all night on guard, watching, waiting for Sir Roger and the changelings to strike.

But no attack came, and they rode to Knightcastle the next morning.

Mazael found Brother Trocend in a forgotten corner of Knightcastle.

Trocend occupied a warren of mismatched rooms created by successive expansions to the castle. He sat a writing desk in a tower chamber, near a balcony overlooking the Riversteel. Shelves of enormous ledgers occupied one wall, and cages occupied the other wall, pigeons cooing and flapping their wings. Trocend used the birds as messengers, sending Lord Malden's commands throughout Knightrealm.

"Ah, Lord Mazael," said Trocend, clad in a voluminous monk's robe. He did not look up from the papers on his desk. "What brings you to the home of this humble clerk?"

"I need your help," said Mazael.

Trocend gave him a thin smile. "I am always eager to serve."

"You might not be." Mazael unwrapped the changeling head. The thing had begun to rot, and smelled quite unpleasant, but the black-slit eyes still glared.

"Damnation." Trocend sighed. "I rather doubted they would give up."

"A group of thirty, in the Lords' Wood," said Mazael, "they were plotting to kill Lord Malden. Sir Roger Gravesend was with them."

"You really should have killed him," said Trocend.

"A mistake I intend to rectify," said Mazael. "I'm sure there are San-keth changelings in the castle, somewhere. And Straganis might still be alive." He omitted Lucan's discoveries. "I want you to use your...special talents to find the San-keth changelings, if you can."

"I see," said Trocend. He folded his hands. "You brought your court wizard. Why not use him?"

"Timothy's talents do not lie in divination," said Mazael.

"And where do they lie?"

"In good sense."

Trocend smiled. "A rare commodity."

"The changelings will try to kill Lord Malden," said Mazael. "I realize you might prefer Gerald and Rachel to remain unwed..."

"Do you imply that I would stand by and let the San-keth murder them?" said Trocend. "Yes, I wish Lord Malden would turn his attention from the Grim Marches. But I am Lord Malden's servant, and I carry out his will. I serve the Lord of Knightcastle."

"And if the San-keth kill Lord Malden and his sons, there will be no Lord of Knightcastle," said Mazael. "I need your help. Lord Malden needs your help."

Trocend sighed. "As you wish, Lord Mazael. I will look. Bear in mind, however, that I do not promise success. Divination is not a precise science."

"I will," said Mazael.

"Leave the head," said Trocend. He smiled his thin smile. "I will require...components...for my spells."

Mazael nodded and tried not to shudder.

CHAPTER 14
HAMMER OF THE OLD KINGDOMS

Mazael awoke well before dawn.

He had not slept at all well. His nightmares conjured visions of the San-keth slaughtering Lord Malden's court, Roger Gravesend slamming a dagger into Rachel's back, yellow eyes staring at him from the darkness.

He yawned, turned his head, and almost screamed.

Morebeth's head lay in a pool of blood.

But it was only her hair spread out across the pillow. Mazael stared at her sleeping face, feeling both foolish and guilty. Suppose the San-keth killed her to get at him? Suppose she died just for having known him?

Mazael rolled out of bed, trying to push aside the dark thoughto.

He walked onto the room's small balcony. It had a splendid view of Castle Town and the Riversteel. Stars blazed overhead, the eastern sky beginning to brighten. The maze of tents and pavilions surrounding Castle Town had doubled.

Mazael stared at the tents. Lord Malden's tournament began tomorrow. Hundreds of minor lords, landless knights, and their followers had swarmed to Knightcastle, eager for wealth and glory. How many San-keth changelings hid amongst them? Or, for, that matter, how many hid in Knightcastle itself, waiting for a chance to strike?

The prospect of his own death did not faze him. He worried for too many other people.

"Cannot sleep?"

Morebeth walked naked on the balcony, the faint dawn turning her pale skin rosy. The sight sent a pleasant shock down Mazael's nerves, but only added to his burdened mind. He had spent almost every night with her since returning to Knightcastle. It had been nothing more than desire at first, nothing more than a yearning for her in his arms, but that had begun to change. He was not in love with her, not by any means, but he had begun thinking of her as an ally, and perhaps even as a friend.

Sometimes he wandered what she really thought of him. It was hard to read anything through her usual cold mask.

"Nothing to say?" she said, amused. "Or will you simply stand there and stare?"

"You're unclad," said Mazael.

"Observant. And so are you," said Morebeth.

"Someone will see us."

Morebeth yawned, hair sliding against her back and shoulders. "Let them. I care nothing for what they think. I was a proper lady all my life, and it has brought me nothing but misery."

Mazael thought of Rachel. "I think I understand."

Morebeth laughed. "You are a man, so you do not, but I forgive you." She wrapped her hands around the balcony's rail. "Will you ride in the tournament tomorrow?"

"I will," said Mazael. "Lord Malden would take it amiss if I do not."

"You worry a great deal about what he thinks," said Morebeth.

Mazael found himself staring at her and forced himself to look away. "I do. He could, if he chose, bring ruin and war to my people. I cannot let that happen."

"So you will instead carry war and ruin to the Dominiars?" said Morebeth. Her tone conveyed neither anger nor approval.

"If I must." Mazael watched her eyes. "Does that anger you?"

"It should." Morebeth looked at the valley, hair blowing across her face like a veil. "Yet it does not. I have lived in Mastaria all my life, yet I care nothing for the Dominiar Order."

"What do you care about, my lady?" said Mazael.

Morebeth's slim shoulders rippled. "I don't really know, any more." She pushed aside her hair and looked at him. "But what of you, my lord? What do you care about? You seem as if you know."

Mazael looked back at her. "I want to keep my sister safe. I want peace. I don't want my people, my lands, to suffer the horrors of war."

"Why not?" said Morebeth. "Do not knights glory in war?"

"Most do," said Mazael. "I did, once. But that was long ago." He stared at her, and almost told her everything. Only Lucan knew his secret, the truth of his nature, and he offered Mazael no comfort. "It...I..."

"Shh." She pressed up against him and put her fingers over his mouth. "You are nobler than most lords, I think. You will have peace. I think you are strong enough to make your own peace, force the others to follow you." She took his hand, drawing him back into bedchamber. "Come. I know what will drive these shadows from your mind."

151

"You always say that," said Mazael, letting her lead him.

She smiled and sat on the bed, legs curling beneath her. "And I am always right, am I not?"

And as it turned out, she was right yet again.

"Shall you carry my colors when you ride tomorrow?" she murmured into his chest, after they had finished

"Perhaps," said Mazael. "I wonder what they'll say."

"That Lord Mazael rides with his mistress's colors," said Morebeth. "What matter what they think? Even Lord Malden spends more time with his mistress than…"

Someone hammered at the door.

Mazael growled. "What?"

"Lord Mazael!" It was Adalar. "Lord Malden wants you at once."

"Why?" said Mazael.

There was a pause. "Is Lady Morebeth…with you?" His voice crackled with disapproval.

"I'll ask once more. Why?" said Mazael.

"A group of Dominiars are riding for Knightcastle's gates, flying a banner of parley" said Adalar. "Lord Malden's going to ride out and meet them himself, and he wants you with him. And…Sir Commander Amalric wants Lady Morebeth to join him."

"Damn him," muttered Morebeth. "I had best go. And so should you." She rolled from the bed in a lithe motion, scooped up her clothing, and vanished through the hidden door to the Trysting Ways.

Mazael walked to the door and unbarred it, letting Adalar inside. "Help me dress."

Adalar's mouth was a tight line of disapproval, but he nodded and helped Mazael don his formal clothes.

"You seem distressed," said Mazael.

Adalar adjusted Lion in its scabbard. "I am happy to serve my lord." He stepped back. "And his lady, should he have one."

"Not this again," said Mazael. "Don't you have any urges, boy?"

Adalar said nothing.

"Well?"

"My father would not approve of what you are doing," said Adalar.

"I've done a lot of things Sir Nathan would not approve," said Mazael. "Yes, I suspect this to be one of them. Your father is a great man, Adalar, but he's not always right. Lady Morebeth is willing, am I willing, she lost her husband, and I…I lost…" Mazael shook his head. "We comfort each other. Gods damn it, Adalar. I wouldn't tolerate these questions from anyone else. Well, maybe Sir Gerald, but he would know better than to ask. Listen to me. I don't want to talk about this again. Understand?"

Adalar nodded. Some of the rancor faded from his face. Yet…yet something in his eyes…

Adalar was afraid of him. Over Morebeth? That made no sense.

"Is there anything else?" said Mazael.

Adalar shook his head, too quickly. "No. Nothing."

"Are you certain?"

"Lord Malden said we should make haste," said Adalar.

"As you will," said Mazael. "But we will talk later."

He followed Adalar to the High Court, where Mantle stood saddled and waiting. Mazael swung up into the saddle. Adalar mounted and picked up a lance flying the Cravenlock banner.

"Lord Malden awaits us in the lower barbican," said Adalar.

Mazael nodded, adjusted his cloak, and kicked Mantle to a trot, riding through Knightcastle's maze of courtyards and ramps until he came to the great barbican. There Lord Malden sat atop his stallion, surrounded by his household knights. Sir Garain waited by Lord Malden's side, yawning, and Trocend sat sunk in his monk's robe. Mazael wondered if Trocend had found any trace of the San-keth.

On the far side of the barbican waited a group of Dominiar Knights, Sir Commander Amalric at their head. Morebeth sat at his side, in her mourning veil again. Near them stood the Justiciars with Sir Commander Galan at their head, scowling at the Dominiars, who scowled right back.

"Ah, Lord Mazael," said Lord Malden. He seemed indifferent to the tension. "I will be glad for your counsel."

"Have the Dominiars sent another embassy?" said Mazael.

"Not at all," said Lord Malden. "Grand Master Malleus is coming here himself."

"What?" said Mazael.

"I rather expect he has come to offer congratulations and gifts on the occasion of my son's wedding," said Lord Malden. "Or maybe he wishes to ride in the tournament. And, perhaps, to discuss the minor matter of Tumblestone, which has caused some petty quarrels in the past."

Mazael said nothing. Malleus would not come to Knightcastle to celebrate a wedding, or to ride in the tournament. Only one thing would bring the Grand Master of the Dominiar Knights to Lord Malden's castle.

Malleus had come to demand Tumblestone back.

And when Lord Malden refused, war would begin.

"No sense in keeping our illustrious guest waiting eh?" said Lord Malden. "Let us ride out and meet him. "

They rode out the gate and down the road towards Castle Town, the Justiciars and the Dominiars flanking Lord Malden's party. A group of black-armored horsemen waited below Castle Town's gates. They carried the banner of the Dominiars knights, a silver star on a black field, and the personal banner of Malleus, a golden hammer on black. Lord Malden raised his hand, and his party reined up.

One man rode out from the newcomers. He wore well-crafted black plate armor, the breastplate adorned with a relief of two crossed hammers. Above his breastplate, the man had a leonine mane of white hair and an enormous white mustache. Mazael had never seen the man before, but knew him at once.

Malleus, Grand Master of the Dominiar Order. The man who had led a triumphant crusade to distant lands, who had conquered the Old Kingdoms, who had almost defeated Lord Malden and conquered Knightcastle. Some believed him the greatest living commander of armies. Mazael believed it. If he had not defeated Aeternis outside Tumblestone, nothing could have stopped Malleus.

Lord Malden and Malleus stared at each other, waiting for the other to make the first move.

Sir Garain spurred forward, breaking the silence. "Grand Master Malleus, I am Sir Garain Roland. Permit me to welcome you to Knightcastle, and to introduce my illustrious father, Lord Malden Roland."

Malleus smiled beneath his mustache. "An honor, Sir Garain." He had a voice like a booming drum. "Your son is fairly spoken, Lord Malden. A worthy heir to the throne of Knightcastle."

"He does my house honor," said Lord Malden, with a smile that did not reach his eyes, "as do you, Grand Master. Knightcastle has not hosted such an illustrious guest for quite some time."

"Why, I wish to offer congratulations to your noble son and his fair bride," said Malleus, "on the upcoming joy of their marriage. And rumor of your most excellent tournament has spread far and wide. I am an old man, and though I cannot take part in such things anymore," he waved his hand, "my preceptors and commanders are eager for renown and glory. I'm sure you understand, eh?"

"But of course," said Lord Malden. "After all, my son Mandor won great glory in the conquest of Tumblestone, did he not?"

An uneasy rustle went through the Dominiar Knights.

"I'm sure," said Malleus, turning his head. "Ah! Sir Commander Amalric! There you are. Come here, my friend."

Amalric rode past Mazael, reined up before Malleus, and bowed deep from the saddle. "Grand Master. How might I serve you?"

His voice was quiet and calm, like a frozen sword.

"Amalric." A genuine smile spread across Malleus's face, and he gripped the younger man's arm. "How have matters proceeded?"

"Well, Grand Master," said Amalric. "All has gone as you wished."

"Good, good," said the old man. "We'll speak more later."

Amalric bowed again.

"Young Amalric has been a tremendous boon to the Dominiar

Order," said Malleus to Lord Malden, "my strong right arm. Once I am gone, I believe he will make a fine Grand Master."

"No doubt," said Lord Malden.

Malleus's eyes fell on Mazael. "And this is Lord Mazael, I take it? Ah…of course. I recognize that sword of Aeternis's. I suppose Malden has promised you vast lands in Mastaria?"

Mazael met the old man's sharp gaze. "Nothing of the sort. I want peace."

Malleus laughed. "Don't we all? Ah, Lord Malden…you must show me Knightcastle. I have heard so much about it, but never have had the opportunity to see it with my own eyes. Lord Mazael saw to that, did he not?"

"Of course," said Lord Malden. "Knightcastle is mine, but I have no qualms about letting others see its splendor."

"Then let us begin at once," said Malleus. "And mayhap we can discuss a few…trifling matters of mutual interest, no?"

Lord Malden's smile never wavered, not a bit, but his eyes had turned to ice. "Of course."

They rode to the castle in silence.

CHAPTER 15
TOURNAMENT

The day of Lord Malden's grand tournament dawned.

Armies of workmen descended on the fields outside Knightcastle, raising the lists, assembling benches, and building platforms for the ladies and the great lords. Throngs of peasants from the countryside and townsfolk from Castle Town surrounded the tournament field. Merchants sold food and ale, armor and weapons. Jongleurs wandered the crowd, singing ballads of heroic deeds. A few enterprising fellows set up betting pools, the good money riding on Tobias Roland and Amalric Galbraith.

Mazael watched the crowd from the walls of the High Court, wondering how many San-keth changelings hid among them. He had heard nothing from Trocend, and Lucan had disappeared yet again.

"Lord," grunted Adalar, "I'll never get this breastplate adjusted if you keep fidgeting."

"I'm not fidgeting," said Mazael.

"Fine. Then stop sighing. And complaining," said Adalar.

Mazael gave him a look.

Adalar grunted again. "You ought to get a new breastplate. This one looks like a peasant's cook pot."

"It suffices," said Mazael. He wore a mail coat, gauntlets, a helmet, and a cuirass, all of it well-used. "And it has saved my life on more than one occasion."

"It looks bad," said Adalar, buckling Mazael's sword belt.

"That's what the surcoat is for," said Mazael.

Adalar shook his head and helped Mazael don the surcoat.

"You're going to the squires' melee, I hope," said Mazael.

Adalar nodded.

"The prize is substantial," said Mazael. "A hundred gold pieces, three horses, a suit of plate. If you win, you'll be quite well equipped once you become a knight."

Adalar stepped back and scowled at Mazael's armor again.

"Once we return to the Grim Marches, I think it is time you were knighted," said Mazael.

Adalar's head jerked up in surprise.

"It's almost time," said Mazael. "By the time we return home, you'll be more than old enough. I hope you'll swear to my service then."

"I don't know," said Adalar. "I...was thinking about striking out my own..."

Mazael frowned. "Why? I..."

Adalar peered at the barbican. "They're lining up. My lord, we'd better go."

Mazael frowned, but followed his squire to the stables. Adalar already had Chariot saddled and waiting. The big destrier stamped his hoofs, eager for combat. Mazael grinned, patted Chariot on the neck, and clambered into the saddle.

"Eager devil," muttered Mazael. He remembered feeling that way about battle. Still, it was just a tournament. And he had used more lances in war than in sport. "Let's get on with it."

Mazael and Adalar rode to the barbican, the Cravenlock banner billowing from Adalar's lance. Hundreds of landless knights, minor lords, and a few greater lords eager for glory waited in the barbican. More than a few Justiciar and Dominiar knights traded barbed glances. Mazael had never seen so many knights gathered for a single tournament.

Sir Commander Amalric Galbraith sat atop his horse, watching the assembled knights like a wolf overlooking sheep. Sir Garain wove here and there through the knights, lining them up according to rank. Then Lord Malden's heralds rode to the gate, their banners billowing.

"The time has come," they boomed, "and Lord Malden summons you to the Field of Valor."

The knights galloped out in a long line, squires riding at their sides, banners flapping overhead. Garain, Tobias, and Gerald led the way, their Roland banners almost bluer than the sky itself. Mazael followed them, Chariot's hooves pounding the road. Amalric Galbraith rode at his side, eyes lost in thought, and made no effort to speak.

A dull roar reached Mazael's ears. He looked up, wondering if the weather had turned sour, and realized it was the cheering of the crowds gathered for the tournament.

Long wooden lists had been raised, and spare lances stood like a forest around the edge of the field. Beyond lay an empty field for the squires' melee, and another lined with archery butts. An army of grooms stood ready to manage the horses. A wooden platform overlooked the lists, and Lord Malden sat there, Grand Master Malleus at his side. The heralds thundered the names of the knights, and one by one they rode past Lord Malden's platform and saluted.

Mazael took Chariot past the platform, saluted, received Lord Malden's regal nod in return. Rachel sat in the front row, smiling at Mazael and Gerald. Behind her sat Morebeth, all in black, her cold eyes glinting over the top of her veil. Mazael smiled at her, and she parted the veil just long enough to smile back at him.

Amalric scowled at Mazael.

The heralds blew their trumpets, and one climbed the railing of Lord Malden's platform.

"Lords noble and ladies fair!" called the herald, his voice ringing, "knights-errant and Knights Justiciar and Dominiar, folk of Castle Town, merchants and travelers, and all the free folk of Knightrealm, my noble Lord Malden bids you welcome to this, his tournament!"

Lord Malden favored the crowds with a shallow nod.

The herald waited for the cheers to die. "Many knights have come to compete for glory and renown. Only the noblest, the most valiant, the most chivalrous, the most puissant at arms, the true knight, shall be crowned victor of this tournament!" He swung his fist over the fields. "The squires shall test their skills at the blade, and the archers shall contest their mastery of the bow!"

The Archbishop of Knightrealm, a timid old man too fearful to breathe without Lord Malden's express permission, tottered forward and said a prayer to the gods, calling on Joraviar the Sacred Knight to lend his strength to the combatants, for the Holy Lady Amater to lend womanly courage to the knights' wives and sisters and mothers, and for Amathcon, father of all, to bless the tournament.

"And now!" said the herald, "Lord Malden bids you to ride!"

The knights dispersed to their tents and pavilions, save for Sir Tobias and a young Dominiar preceptor, who took their places at either end of the lists. Mazael reined up next to Lord Malden's platform, slid from the saddle, and bought a goblet of wine from a peddler. Adalar stood stiff and formal at his side, watching the knights.

The heralds loosed a trumpet blast, and Sir Tobias and the Dominiar galloped at each other. Sir Tobias's lance caught the Dominiar square in the chest. The black-armored knight fell with a mighty clatter, and Tobias galloped past. A few Dominiar squires and a surgeon hastened the fallen knight from the field.

Mazael glanced at the platform. Lord Malden clapped and grinned, while Malleus sat still, his face a calm mask.

Adalar snorted. "That was quick."

"Sir Tobias is built like a brick wall," said Mazael. "That Dominiar could have hit him with a hammer and not made a dent."

He glanced back into a nearby tent. Timothy sat cross-legged on floor, eyes closed, hands clutching a wire-wrapped quartz crystal. The wizard kept watch over Lord Malden's platform with his magic, waiting for any Sanketh changelings to approach.

For the thousandth time, Mazael wondered what had happened to Lucan.

"It ought to be easy," muttered Mazael, "to find an old man selling cheese."

"Lord?" said Adalar.

"Nothing," said Mazael.

A Justiciar preceptor and a Dominiar preceptor rode against each other next, broke two lances, and succeeded in unhorsing each other on the third. The Justiciar broke his arm, the Dominiar a leg, and the squires carried both from the field.

"He was holding his lance wrong," muttered Adalar. "My father would have boxed his ears."

"No doubt," agreed Mazael. As a boy he had suffered many such punishments from Sir Nathan, and the lessons had served him well.

Next Gerald rode against Tobias. Gerald's armor gleamed like silver, his shield like a mirror, and an exhausted-looking Wesson stomped after him. A silken lady's scarf had been tied around Gerald's right arm, no doubt a favor from Rachel. Mazael leaned forward, watching with interest.

The trumpets sounded, and the brothers rode at each other.

They broke lances on the first ride, and the second, both men swaying in the saddle like drunkards. Rachel winced with every blow. On the third lance Gerald caught Tobias's thrust on his shield and sent the blunted tip of his own lance right into Tobias's chest. Tobias sailed from the saddle in a smooth arc. Gerald jumped from his horse, helped Tobias up, and the two brothers bowed to each other.

The crowds loved it. Mazael heard Grand Master Malleus complement Lord Malden on his courteous sons. Rachel's eyes almost shone with pride. Mazael laughed and bought another flagon of wine.

Despite his worries, Mazael began to enjoy himself.

The herald's called his name. Mazael drained his wine in one gulp and mounted Chariot. The big horse stamped and whinnied in eagerness. Mazael pulled on his helmet, took his shield and first lance from Adalar, and rode to the end of the lists.

Sir Commander Galan Hawking waited at the other end of the field, resplendent in his armor and blue Justiciar cloak. He lifted an eyebrow, saluted with his lance, and dropped his visor. Mazael saluted back and waited.

The trumpets sounded.

Chariot surged forward of his own volition. Mazael dropped the reins and readied his lance and shield, trusting Chariot's instincts. Sir Commander Galan thundered towards him, faceless in armor and helmet. Mazael set himself and gripped his shield tighter. Galan's lance exploded against his shield. The blow nearly dislocated Mazael's arm, but he kept his saddle, his lance skidding off Galan's breastplate.

They wheeled around at the end of the lists. Both men snatched up fresh lances. Mazael had Galan's measure now. The man kept his shield too low.

The trumpets blew again. Chariot leapt forward, Mazael shifting his balance. Galan came at him, lance high, and dropped the tip at the last minute. Mazael lowered his shield, caught the lance, and sent his own lance arcing over Galan's shield. It crashed into Galan's breastplate, just beneath his gorget, and sent the Justiciar tumbling. Mazael reined up and wheeled around. Galan lay supine for a moment, groaned, and then tottered back to his feet.

"Are you injured?" said Mazael.

"Nay," growled Galan, staggering. A Justiciar squire hurried forward and helped him along, while another took the reins of his horse. "Your family never seems to bring me anything but misfortune."

He tottered from the field, grumbling.

"I did save your life," Mazael pointed out, to nobody. He shrugged and rode back to Adalar, who took the reins.

"That was good, my lord," said Adalar, grinning. "You took him in two passes."

"He wasn't trying," said Mazael, swinging down. "The others will be harder."

"Mazael!" Rachel waved at him from the platform. "That was grand."

Mazael did a little bow. "Thank you, my lady."

"I can't decide if I want you or Gerald to win," said Rachel. "Wouldn't it be splendid if you unhorsed each other simultaneously in the final pass, and both won the tournament?"

"My back groans at the thought," said Mazael. He looked up and saw Morebeth smiling at him, felt the familiar jolt, and smiled back.

Sir Aulus went against Sir Commander Aeternis of the Dominiars next. Sir Aulus lasted for two passes, but went down on the third, and limped from the field with a rueful grin.

"Are you all right?" Mazael called.

Sir Aulus nodded. "This is still better than spending time with my wife."

More knights mounted, charged at each other, knocked each other from the saddle. The sun climbed higher, and the day began to grow warmer. Mazael wished he could remove his armor.

Sir Commander Amalric Galbraith rode twice, first against a Justiciar preceptor, the second-time against a hard-looking knight of Lord Malden's household. Amalric took both men from the saddle in the first pass and broke one of the Justiciar's legs. Mazael watched Amalric with cold interest. The man was very good. Morebeth sat rigid and unsmiling as Amalric rode.

Then Mazael had to ride again, this time against Sir Garain Roland. He stifled a wince as he mounted up. Sir Garain was Lord Malden's chancellor, the glue that kept Knightrealm together, but he was not a skilled fighter. That was Sir Tobias's task.

The trumpets sounded, and Mazael let Garain break two lances. On the third pass he knocked Garain from the saddle with the least force he could manage. Garain wobbled back to his feet and bowed to the crowd, which cheered him. Everyone respected Sir Garain. Mazael sighed in relief. Hurting Sir Garain would have not pleased Lord Malden.

The heralds blew another blast, and the jousting halted for the squires' melee.

"My lord, are you coming?" said Adalar.

"I am," said Mazael. He turned and saw Trocend standing behind Lord Malden's platform, beckoning to him. "In a moment. Go! They'll start without you."

Adalar dug through their piled equipment, snatched out his sword, and broke into a run. Mazael pushed past the milling spectators and made his way to Trocend's side.

"You've ridden well today, my lord," said Trocend. "The Justiciars are so feared that everyone expected Sir Commander Galan to unhorse you." He loosed a dry chuckle. "You ought to see the bet-makers scramble to rework their numbers."

"Have you found anything?" said Mazael.

Trocend smiled, reached into his robe, and produced a small glass jar filled with clear liquid. The yellow eye of a changeling floated within, rotating.

"A grisly trophy," said Mazael.

"A trophy?" said Trocend. "What use has a simple clerk for a trophy?" He shook his head. "It acts as a compass." He held the jar steady, and the eye rotated to point at Knightcastle. "It points at San-keth changelings."

"Then they're at Knightcastle?" said Mazael.

Trocend nodded. "Some, at any rate. I've had a busy night." He beckoned again, and walked to a drab tent. Mazael followed him, watching the spinning eye. Trocend lifted the flap of the tent and pointed.

Six dead changelings lay within.

"A busy night, indeed," said Mazael.

"Two were working in the kitchen," said Trocend. "One masqueraded as a beggar at the gates of Castle Town." He shook his head. "A fourth was a servant with the Dominiars."

"The Dominiars?" said Mazael. "Do they know?"

Trocend shook his head. "They'll assume the servant ran off."

"What of the other two?" said Mazael.

"I don't know." Trocend toed one of the corpses. "I found them."

"Where?" said Mazael.

"In the Trysting Ways," said Trocend. "Someone killed them by magical means." He shrugged. "A San-keth cleric, most likely. Perhaps there was dissension in the ranks."

"Perhaps," said Mazael. Or had Lucan killed them? "How did you get the bodies here? Did you move them yourself?"

Trocend gave him a thin smile. "Well…not entirely by myself. My spirit-servants brought the bodies here, and will dispose of them once we are finished."

Mazael suppressed a shudder. "How many changelings are left?"

Trocend shrugged. "Dozens, probably."

"Dozens?"

"Yes. I see you set Timothy to keep watch over Lord Malden," said Trocend. "An excellent idea; I taught him a better spell than the one he was using. Best to have him keep watch over Lord Malden at all times, until I can exterminate these changelings. I'll arrange a watch kept over the kitchens."

"No need," said Mazael, remembering how close Blackfang had come to killing Rachel. "The changelings kill with poisoned daggers, or with their bites, but not food."

Trocend nodded. "One less worry. Now, if you'll excuse me, I must continue. Best if we are not seen together more than necessary." He wrapped himself again in his cloak and vanished into the crowds. Mazael stared after him, scowling.

Where the devil had Lucan gone?

He shook aside the thought and jumped back into Chariot's saddle. Brooding achieved nothing, after all. Mazael walked Chariot through the crowds, who hastened to get out of the big horse's way, and came to the squires' melee.

The four hundred squires attending the tournament had been divided into four teams. A ring of Lord Malden's heralds surrounded their field, accompanied by archers. As the squires battled with wooden weapons, the heralds called out the names of those who had been eliminated, who then left the field. Failure to comply earned a blunted fowling arrow from the archers.

Mazael spotted Adalar, who fought side by side with Wesson. Adalar caught a descending slash, twisted around, and struck his attacker across the back of the legs. The bigger boy went down with a howl. Mazael grinned; he had taught Adalar that move. The defeated squire rose with a growl, stalking towards Adalar, and caught a blunted arrow in the rump for his efforts.

Wesson went down with a blow across the knee and shuffled from the field, muttering. Adalar remained fighting, wheeling, ducking, dodging slashing. Mazael watched with some pride. The boy was good, very good, and Mazael knew he would only become better. Adalar parried, took his wooden sword in both hands, and knocked another squire over.

The melee raged on. One by one, the squires walked from the field. In few cases the fallen squires had to be carried. Adalar remained in the melee. Sweat poured down his face, his chest heaved, and his face was locked in a grimace, but Adalar remained untouched.

Finally it came down to Adalar and another squire, a young man in Dominiar black. The two youths circled each other, feinting, wooden blades licking out. Both combatants were winded. The Dominiar squire lunged forward, feinted high, and swung low. Adalar caught the blow and hopped back, trying to circle around the Dominiar squire. The Dominiar rushed at him, slamming hard on Adalar's sword. Adalar stumbled back, fighting for balance, and the Dominiar sprang. Mazael winced, thinking it over.

But Adalar twisted in a feint even Mazael had not seen, and came up behind the Dominiar. His sword smacked across the Dominiar's back, the other squire fell, and Adalar stood victorious.

For a moment silence reined, and then the crowds cheered in delight, Mazael's voice raised with theirs. A herald came onto the field, lifted Adalar's arm, and proclaimed him the victor. Others came out leading three horses loaded with a full suit of plate and a hundred gold pieces. Some of the squires swarmed around Adalar, slapping him on the back and offering him congratulations, while some of the others stalked away, scowling. Adalar took the reins of the lead horse, wooden sword dangling from his free hand, and looked about in weary bewilderment.

"Well done, Adalar," said Mazael, riding to his squire's side, "well done."

Adalar wiped sweat from his brow and smiled. "Thank you, lord."

Wesson appeared, bearing a pitcher of mixed wine. "Here." He grunted. "You look thirsty."

Adalar grinned and drained off most of the pitcher in one gulp. "Thank you. Lord, we had best go, you'll need to ride again soon…"

"Rest," said Mazael. He glanced at the horses. "Take care of your loot first. Once you're ready, come help me. I can manage well enough until then."

"But…"

Mazael pointed. "Rest."

"You heard him," said Wesson.

Adalar nodded, sweaty hair falling across his eyes. "All right. If you command."

"I do," said Mazael. "Now rest."

"If you ride back to the lists now, so you're not late," said Adalar.

Mazael laughed. "As the champion commands."

He steered Chariot through the crowds and reined up besides Lord Malden's platform. The jousting had begun again some time earlier. Mazael arrived just in time to see Sir Commander Aeternis unhorse a young Dominiar Knight.

"By the gods!" roared Aeternis, shaking his head. "I taught you to ride when you were a boy! When did you start holding your shield so low?" The young Dominiar retreated under a hail of withering criticism.

Then it was Mazael's turn to ride against Aeternis. He rode to the end of the lists and snatched up a lance. Chariot bared his teeth, recognizing to the Dominiar commander.

"So we face each other again, eh?" called Aeternis.

"So we do," said Mazael.

"Let's hope it's not another Tumblestone," said Aeternis.

Mazael said nothing, Chariot pawing at the earth. The heralds blew the trumpets, and Mazael and Aeternis rode. Mazael caught Aeternis's blow on his shield, but the force of it nearly dislocated his arm. His own blow cracked into Aeternis's shield. The other man reeled, black armor clanking, but managed to keep his seat. One of Lord Malden's squires brought Mazael a fresh lance. The trumpets sounded again, and Chariot's hooves tore at the trampled grass.

Both lances exploded in a spray of splinters. Mazael grunted, threw the ruined lance down to one of the waiting squires, and flexed his aching hand. Aeternis was very good.

Then the trumpets sounded again, and Mazael had no time to think, only to do. Mazael's lance broke again against Aeternis's shield, and Aeternis's lance hit Mazael's shield and slid down to shatter against his breastplate. A roaring cheer went up from the spectators. No joust had yet lasted more than three passes. Mazael pulled off his helmet, wiped the sweat from his brow, saw Lord Malden and Malleus whispering to each other, saw Morebeth watching him with interest. Mazael set his helmet back on, his mind racing. Aeternis was strong and fast, but Mazael thought Chariot a little faster than Aeternis's destrier.

The trumpets rang for the fourth time. Aeternis came forward at a full gallop, lance angled for Mazael's chest, while Mazael only kicked Chariot to a rapid trot. Chariot whinnied in displeasure, but obeyed. Aeternis leaned ahead, aiming for Mazael's breastplate. At the last second, Mazael booted Chariot to a full gallop, and the big horse surged forward. Aeternis's lance caught the edge of Mazael's shield, nearly twisting it from his arm, but Mazael had just enough time to slam his lance into Aeternis's chest. For a moment the Dominiar commander teetered, but he fell with a clattering crash. An exulting cheer went up from the crowds, and Mazael saw Lord Malden applaud, Malleus's face settling into a calm mask. Aeternis grunted, wheezed, and marched off the field with a rueful shake of his head.

Mazael rode back to Lord Malden's platform and found Adalar waiting for him.

"I told you to get some rest," said Mazael, swinging down from the saddle.

Adalar handed him a flagon of mixed wine. "I did. And Wesson took care of the prize for me."

"If you insist," said Mazael, drinking the entire flagon in three gulps. "Gods, it's getting hot out."

"Mazael!"

He saw Rachel hurrying towards him, a wide smile on her face. "You missed it! Gerald defeated a Justiciar commander, unhorsed him on the second pass. And you were magnificent. I thought Aeternis had you on the third pass."

Mazael laughed and caught his sister in a rough hug. "Come, now! You think I'd let him unhorse me? I'd never hear the end of it."

"And young Adalar," she said. Adalar bowed. "I heard you won great honor in the squires' melee."

"My lady," said Adalar. "I was but fortunate."

"A squire like you makes his own fortune, I think," said Rachel. "Mazael, might I speak with you for a moment?"

Mazael frowned. "If you wish. Adalar, keep an eye on Chariot."

They walked off a small distance, found a quiet corner behind a tent where they could speak.

"What's wrong?" said Mazael.

"I had an interesting conversation this morning, while watching the tourney," said Rachel. "I made the acquaintance of Lady Morebeth Galbraith."

Mazael stifled a wince, bracing himself for the sermon on the evils of keeping a mistress.

"She seems a gentle lady," said Rachel. "Did you know her husband died while under her brother's command?"

"I...heard a rumor of that nature," said Mazael.

"She never said it," continued Rachel, "but I wonder if Sir Commander Amalric made sure that Lady Morebeth's husband died in the battle."

"Possibly," said Mazael, shaking his head. He remembered what Aeternis had told him about Amalric, tales of women and children dying atop stakes. "He…seems a hard man."

"He does," said Rachel, staring at the ground for a moment. "I think you ought to marry Lady Morebeth."

Mazael coughed. "I beg your pardon?"

"I think she would make you a good wife," said Rachel. "Mazael…you cannot stay unwed forever. I…I know Romaria's death was…hard…"

"It was."

"A man needs a wife," said Rachel. "You do. Else…otherwise why would you take up with so many mistresses?" Mazael said nothing. "You…should have a wife, Mazael. The Lord of Castle Cravenlock should have one."

"Since you're soon to be wed yourself, I assume you'll be playing the matchmaker of Castle Cravenlock for the rest of your days?" said Mazael.

Rachel grinned. "It would fill my time, would it not?" The smile faded, and she took his hand. "Mazael…I know you are not happy. You hide it well, but I can see that many things trouble you. I think…maybe Morebeth could make you happier."

"Lords wed for alliance and power," said Mazael. He stared at Rachel. What could he tell her? That he was Demonsouled, and feared falling to his heritage's corrosive power? That he suspected the Old Demon stood behind the coming war, controlling men like puppets? That the San-keth still plotted to kill her? Still, it cheered him to know that she worried for him. It was good to know somebody did. "I'll think it over."

"I can introduce you after the tournament, if you like," said Rachel.

"Oh," said Mazael. "We've met."

"You have?" said Rachel. "Did you like her?" Mazael tried to keep his face neutral. "You…" She peered at him, and Mazael felt a surge of alarm. He kept quite a few secrets from Rachel, but she sometimes had an uncanny ability to guess his thoughts.

Rachel's eyes widened.

"Oh, gods," mumbled Mazael.

"You didn't!" said Rachel.

"What of it?" said Mazael.

"She's a widow!"

"So she's not married," said Mazael. He sighed. "If she's willing, I'm willing…gods, I made this speech already to Adalar, I've made it to Gerald a hundred times in the last ten years, and now I'm making it to you."

"If you've bedded her, it is only honorable to marry her," said Rachel. "Suppose you got her with child?"

Mazael opened his mouth to say that wasn't possible, but fell silent. He would not betray Morebeth's trust that way.

"I'm mindful of the danger," he said, finally.

"Well, good," said Rachel. "It wouldn't do for you to have a bastard son. It wouldn't do at all."

"I agree," said Mazael, remembering his previous worries. "You have no idea how much I agree." He glanced up at the lists. "I have to ride soon."

Rachel's eyebrows lifted over her green eyes. "To your vast relief, I'm sure."

"Vast." Mazael laughed and kissed her on the cheek. "Wish me luck."

"I'm not sure I can," said Rachel. "You're riding against Gerald, after all."

"I am?" said Mazael. "This ought to be interesting."

He hurried back to Adalar, who stood speaking with Wesson.

"I'm sure," said Wesson, his voice cracking, "that Sir Gerald will unhorse Lord Mazael."

"Care to make a wager?" said Adalar.

"Boys!" Gerald strode up, armor gleaming, helmet under one arm. "Wagering is an uncouth practice, to be sure." He smiled at Mazael. "So we are to ride against each other, I suppose?"

"We are," said Mazael. "Remember what I told you when you were my squire?"

Gerald nodded. "Keep your shield up, hold the lance steady, and lean into it. I ought to remember it. You repeated it often enough."

"He does repeat things," said Adalar.

Mazael gave them both a look. "You both remembered it, didn't you?"

"Let's see how well I learned, shall we?" said Gerald, holding out his hand.

Mazael gripped it. "I guess we will."

They rode to either end of the lists. Mazael took yet another lance from Adalar, while Wesson handed one to Gerald. Rachel sat on the dais by Lord Malden, her eyes darting from Gerald, to Mazael, and then back again. The trumpet blast rang out, and Mazael and Gerald rode at each other. They broke lances on the first and second passes. On the third Mazael sent Gerald tumbling in a clean arc to the ground. He wheeled up and rode back as Wesson helped Gerald to rise.

"Are you all right?"

Gerald coughed, rubbing his arm. "Well enough. My pride is bruised, and perhaps my backside."

They shook hands, to the cheers of the crowd, and Gerald rode from the field and joined Rachel.

The day drew on. The afternoon passed, and the sun began to sink into the west. Mazael rode twice more, both times against skillful household knights, and knocked them both from the saddle. Sir Tobias rode thrice more, and won, to his father's obvious delight.

Amalric Galbraith won again and again, to the clear annoyance of

Morebeth, and the pleasure of Grand Master Mallcus.

Mazael wandered to the tables where the heralds toiled, keeping track of the victors and the defeated. To his astonishment, he realized he had a good chance of winning the tournament. He had not been defeated once, and neither had Sir Tobias or Sir Commander Amalric, though Mazael had unhorsed more knights. Consequently Sir Tobias and Amalric would face each other, and then Mazael would ride against the winner.

He found himself hoping Sir Tobias lost.

He very much wanted to ride against Amalric Galbraith.

The penultimate match came, and Sir Tobias and Amalric faced each other across the lists. Mazael watched as the trumpets blared, watched as the two destriers thundered as each other.

They came together with a crash. Amalric caught Tobias's lance on his shield, shoved down, and rammed his lance into Tobias's stomach. The blow knocked Tobias from the saddle, and his horse staggered to a halt, dragging Tobias from the right stirrup. The squires hastened out and helped Tobias up, who staggered to the platform, reeling.

Mazael watched Amalric. He had not seen anyone move so fast in quite some time, and no one had ever unhorsed Tobias in one pass.

Then the heralds called his name, and Mazael led Chariot to the lists for the last ride of the day.

CHAPTER 16
BLACK KNIGHTS

"Be careful," whispered Adalar, handing Mazael his lance and shield. "He's as fast as you."

Mazael stared at Amalric. The Dominiar commander wore fine black plate, his features hidden beneath a black helm crowned with sweeping eagle's wings. Dominiar squires swarmed around him, adjusting his armor, his horse's traces, his shield, lance, and black cloak with the Dominiars' silver star.

"I think he wants to kill you," said Adalar.

Mazael glanced at his squire. "It's a tournament. Sometimes knights get killed."

"Aye," said Adalar, "but accidents are one thing, and malice another. I think he wouldn't have minded killing Sir Tobias. And I don't think he'd mind killing you." He hesitated. "You did bed his sister."

"I told you," snapped Mazael, "I don't want to hear…"

The trumpets blasted, and Amalric surged forward. Mazael cursed, caught his balance, and kicked Chariot to a gallop. The Dominiar commander seemed like a statue of black iron atop his horse, immutable and invulnerable. Mazael gritted his teeth, set himself, and brought his lance around.

Amalric shifted his shield, caught Mazael's lance, and leaned forward. His lance slammed hard into Mazael's chest, skidding past his shield. It exploded in a spray of splinters, Mazael's breastplate ringing like a gong. The force knocked Mazael back, almost tearing him from Chariot's saddle. He flung aside the shattered lance, seized his saddle horn, and managed to keep his balance.

"Gods, that hurt," muttered Mazael, brushing splinters from his armor.

Adalar sprinted up. "Are you all right? I was sure he cracked your breastbone."

"No," said Mazael, trying not to cough. His chest hurt, and he wondered if Amalric's blow had in fact cracked something.

"I think he's faster than you," said Adalar.

"I know," said Mazael.

"You'll have to keep your shield up, try to hit him as he hits you," said Adalar, handing up another lance. "Otherwise he'll unhorse you before your lance even gets near him."

The trumpets blared again.

Chariot sprang forward. Mazael set himself, kept his shield up, and rode at Amalric. Their lances exploded against their shields, splinters flying in all directions. The blow slammed Mazael's shield back, his hand cracking hard against his chest, the rim smacking against his chin. Both men rocked in the saddles, flailing for balance, but neither one fell. Amalric reined up, black cloak billowing like a flock of ravens. Mazael let Chariot come to a halt, shaking his shield arm. It hurt like the devil, and the shield had splintered. Gods, Amalric hit hard! He tossed it aside, and Adalar provided him with a fresh shield and a fresh lance.

They rode again, breaking a third lance.

And then a fourth.

The cheers from the crowds rose to a roar. Mazael and Aeternis had broken three lances against each other, but Mazael had knocked Aeternis from the saddle on the fourth pass. No one had yet broken four lances.

Mazael pulled off his helmet, wiping the sweat from his brow, and glanced over the crowds. It seemed as if all of Knightrealm had arrived to watch the final ride of the tournament. Both Lord Malden and Malleus leaned forward, watching keenly. The Justiciar Knights and Lord Malden's vassals cheered for Mazael. The Dominiar Knights clustered around Amalric like a flock of black-armored ravens. The throngs of common folk looked enraptured.

Rachel and Morebeth stood behind Lord Malden's chair, watching.

"Gods," mumbled Mazael. He might start a war right here, if he wasn't careful. Amalric's squires signaled readiness. Mazael slammed his helmet back on, gripped his lance and shield, and readied himself. The trumpets rang like a thunderclap. Amalric's stallion whinnied, tossed its black mane, and rolled forward like a black flood. Chariot leapt forward, breathing hard. Mazael gritted his teeth and leaned forward in the saddle, lance reached for Amalric's chest. The point shattered against Amalric's left shoulder, knocking him back.

Yet despite the force of Mazael's blow, Amalric's lance still struck true, sliding past Mazael's shield. Mazael's breastplate clanged, splinters spraying across his legs, and the stump of Amalric's lance stabbed into his left calf. The blow nearly tore him from the saddle, and only by jamming his feet into the stirrups did he keep from falling.

The effort sent a stab of agony shooting up his left leg. He seized the saddle horn, grinding his teeth in pain.

A bit of rage stirred in his mind.

"My lord!" shouted Adalar, running to his side. "My lord, are you…"

Mazael growled, yanked the bloody shard from his leg, and flung it aside. Blood stained his boot and stirrup. Beneath the pain, he felt a deep itch as the torn flesh began knit itself together, but he didn't care.

"The tournament is over!" Grand Master Malleus stood up. "They have ridden five times, and Sir Commander Amalric Galbraith has wounded Lord Mazael. Amalric is the victor!" A cheer went up from the Dominiar Knights, but no one else.

"It most certainly is not!" said Lord Malden, rising. Amalric's black helm turned to face Lord Malden. "Lord Mazael has not yet been unhorsed!"

"They have ridden five times," said Grand Master Malleus. "It is customary for knights in tourney to only ride against each other five times."

Lord Malden's heralds began to confer in anxious voices.

"It is only customary because most knights are unhorsed in the first or second pass!" said Lord Malden. "Both Sir Commander Amalric and Lord Mazael are most skilled, and neither one has yet been victorious. Shall we cut this contest short? Shall we not see a rightful victor?"

"But Sir Commander Amalric is the rightful victor," said Malleus. "Lord Mazael was wounded in the leg. He cannot ride again, and so Amalric triumphs."

Mazael stood in his stirrups, ignoring the agony in his leg. "I can yet ride, Grand Master!" His knee only twitched a little.

"If Lord Mazael says he can ride, then let him ride!" shouted Gerald. "Will we deny Lord Mazael and Sir Commander Amalric the chance to strive honorably for the victor's title?"

"Aye!" A woman's voice rang over the field, commanding and full of fire. Mazael watched in surprise as Morebeth stood, adjusting her skirts. "Lord Malden and Sir Gerald are correct! The tournament must finish. And if Lord Malden awards the victory to Sir Commander Amalric," Amalric's black helmet swiveled to face her, "then all men will say he stole this triumph."

Amalric shifted, hand closing about the hilt of his sword, every gesture radiating hatred. Malleus's calm mask cracked, and for just an instant he glared at Morebeth. One of the heralds approached the platform and cleared his throat.

"My lords," he said, "while knights rarely ride after five broken lances, that is because very few men have the necessary skill at arms." He turned an admiring glance Mazael and Amalric's way. "If Lord Mazael is yet able to ride, then our consensus is that the joust should continue."

Mazael felt fine. The aches from Amalric's battering had failed, and the blood from the wound in his calf had slowed to a trickle. Adalar stared at the wound with a fixed expression, but Mazael paid him no heed.

He could not think through the growing anger.

Lord Malden sat back down, the pages lifting his cloak. "Then let them ride!"

"So be it!" said Malleus, seating himself once more.

Mazael turned Chariot, reaching for still another fresh lance. Adalar said something, but Mazael didn't hear it. The anger hammered in his head, louder and louder. He thought of what Aeternis had told him, how Amalric had ground the Old Kingdoms into the dust. Romaria would have hated Amalric for that. Perhaps she had even fought against his armies, before she came to the Grim Marches. And Mazael remembered the pain and hate in Morebeth's eyes whenever she spoke of her brother…

The heralds' trumpets sounded, and Chariot raced forward, sensing Mazael's eagerness. Amalric kicked his destrier to a gallop, lance leveled, shield raised. Mazael gritted his teeth and leveled his own lance.

The anger raged through him, and he flung aside his shield.

Astonished silence fell over the crowds.

Amalric hesitated, then leaned forward, all his strength and the speed of his horse behind the lance.

Everything happened very fast.

Mazael's left hand snapped up and caught the shaft of Amalric's lance just behind the head, shoving it aside. His own lance stabbed under Amalric's guard and exploded into the black breastplate. Amalric bellowed, rocking back, and the shaft of Mazael's lance smacked hard across his arms.

Amalric hit the ground with a clatter of armor. His helmet rolled away across the trampled grass. Mazael tore past and managed to rein up, his blood racing through his ears.

For a moment silence hung in the air.

Then the field exploded with cheers. Lord Malden stood, smiling. Grand Master Malleus remained sitting, and did not smile. Gerald and Tobias pumped their fists in the air, and Rachel had a wider smile than Mazael had seen in years. His anger drained away, replaced with weariness and faint nausea. The rage had almost mastered him again. Romaria had died to keep him from succumbing to his Demonsouled spirit, and yet he had almost gone mad to avenge a wrong that may or may not have been done to her.

If his weapon had not been a flimsy jousting lance, he might have killed Amalric Galbraith.

Amalric Galbraith stood, brushing the grass from his black hair. He looked to Mazael and made a small bow, but his black eyes burned with hatred. With that, Amalric turned and joined the waiting Dominiars, who walked from the field without a word.

"The winner of this tournament!" boomed one of the heralds, "Mazael, Lord of Castle Cravenlock!" The common folk screamed cheers, and the Justiciars saluted.

Chariot, to Mazael's annoyance, began to prance.

He reined up before Lord Malden's platform, dismounted, and knelt.

His leg did not hurt at all.

"Well done, Lord Mazael," said Lord Malden. Grand Master Malleus had departed with the other Dominiars. "Well done indeed."

"My lord," said Mazael, rising. "Thank you."

Lady Rhea came forward, winked at him, and wrapped the white victor's cloak around his shoulders. Mazael tried to ignore the invitation in her eyes. "You have brought great honor to our house this day, Lord Mazael." She held out her hand for him to kiss.

He did so, catching a glimpse of Morebeth over Lady Rhea's shoulder. She looked amused, damn her.

"My lord!" Timothy hastened up. "My lord, are you hurt? I saw that lance pierce your..." His eyes widened at the blood on Mazael's boot.

"It was but a glancing hit," said Mazael. "I'm fine..."

Gerald and Tobias and Garain and Aulus and dozens of other knights and lords swarmed around him then, offering congratulations. Rachel kissed him on the cheek.

"A feast, of course," said Lord Malden, "to celebrate the grand honor you have won for your sister and the house of Roland." A small smile flickered across his thin lips. "And for the house of Cravenlock, of course."

Mazael wondered if Lord Malden had planned that from the beginning. Squires came forward, bearing horses, and the knights and lords mounted up and began riding back to Knightcastle.

As Mazael turned, Morebeth stepped before him.

She bowed. "My lord has won great honor for himself this day."

Mazael kissed her hand with more enthusiasm than Lady Rhea's. "My lady."

"I am glad," she said. Her gray eyes glittered as she glanced at the dark mass of the Dominiar Knights. "I am very glad." The setting sun touched the braided red hair beneath her feathered hat, transforming it into a crown of bloody gold. "Would my lord accompany me to the feast?"

Mazael hesitated, and then took her arm. Let them gossip; he no longer gave a damn. "I would be honored."

He looked around and wondered what had happened to Adalar.

CHAPTER 17
THROWN GAUNTLETS

Adalar wandered towards Knightcastle, his mind whirling.

He had seen the lance shard sink deep into Mazael's leg. The wound ought to have left Mazael in crippling pain, left him unable to endure the jouncing gallop of the joust. Instead he had ripped the shard from his leg, knocked Amalric from his horse, and ridden to victory.

Adalar had seen that wound close, watched the torn flesh flow back together. It had been a raw, gaping pit of blood when Mazael tore the shard free. A few moments later it had been a gash.

When Mazael rode to Lord Malden's platform, the wound was gone.

Adalar raked shaking hands through his sweaty hair. He remembered Mazael lying on the pew in Tristgard's church, the shredded flesh of his chest writhing as it knitted back together.

"Holy gods," mumbled Adalar. What had happened to Lord Mazael? Adalar remembered Mazael's vow to defeat the San-keth cleric Skhath and the necromancer Simonian a year ago. Had Mazael sold himself to dark powers in exchange for battle prowess and unnatural health? Skhath had used his unholy arts to masquerade as a mortal man. Had some dark creature killed Mazael and taken his place?

Adalar walked alone through Knightcastle's gates. The armsmen congratulated him for his victory. Adalar nodded, his mind far away. He wandered past Knightcastle's looming towers, the statues of Roland lords long dead and forgotten, up the ramps and barbicans until he came to the stables. He crossed to a pile of hay, sat down, and buried his face in his hands. He did not know what to do. His father would have known, but Sir Nathan was far away in Castle Cravenlock. Adalar might have turned to Timothy, or Sir Gerald, or Sir Aulus, but they would not believe him. And suppose Adalar spoke to Mazael? If Mazael had truly sold himself to dark powers, or been replaced by a wicked creature, he would not hesitate to kill Adalar…

"What am I going to do?" he whispered.

A soft voice answered. "Do you not know?"

Adalar's head looked up. Sir Commander Amalric Galbraith stood before him.

He did not look at all tired from the tournament.

Adalar jerked to his feet and bowed. "Sir Commander." He remembered all the dark tales that hovered over Amalric Galbraith like ravens circling over a gallows, stories of slaughtered peasants and crucified women. "Are…are you well, Sir Commander?"

A thin smile split Amalric's pale face, black eyes glittering. "You are afraid, squire, are you not? You think, perhaps, that I have come to slay you, in vengeance for my defeat?"

Adalar stared at him. "The thought crossed my mind."

Amalric scoffed. "Did it? Your Lord Mazael won fairly. In truth, I was irritated when Grand Master Malleus declared premature victory." He shook his head, black hair brushing against his shoulders. "I wished to win, of course, but fairly."

"Noble," said Adalar.

Amalric nodded. "I saw you in the squires' melee. You fought most skillfully, most valiantly."

"Thank you, Sir Commander," said Adalar.

"I suppose Lord Mazael plans to knight you, once you return to Castle Cravenlock?"

Adalar nodded. "He said as much."

Amalric paced to one of Adalar's newly-won horses and rubbed the mane. "And then you will swear to his service?"

"I might," said Adalar. "I don't know yet."

"You might?" said Amalric. "The life of a landless knight is a hard one, and Lord Mazael would feed and clothe you. Why turn down such a generous offer?"

Adalar licked dry lips. "I don't know."

"I suppose not," said Amalric. "Young men often do not know their own hearts, or their minds." He turned to face Adalar. "You ought to consider joining the Dominiar Order."

"Sir Commander?" said Adalar.

"Consider, squire," said Amalric. "Suppose you take up the life of a wandering knight? You will spend your days scraping along, fighting in petty wars, guarding the caravans of greedy merchants. Your life will be little better than that of a common mercenary. Or suppose you do swear to Lord Mazael? How then will you spend your days? You will fight in his wars, for the glory of his name, to make his lands richer, and you will spill the blood of men for his power. What purpose in such a life? Meaningless and futile, a crass scrabbling for gold and power."

Adalar said nothing.

"But the Dominiar Knights, our Order…we have duty. Purpose and meaning," said Amalric. "It is our mission to spread the light of the Amathavian gods throughout the world, to defeat the forces of darkness and idolatry."

"My father said your Order slaughters innocents and rules as tyrants," said Adalar, shocked at his own boldness.

"Some of my brothers do," said Amalric. "Some are overzealous, and oppress godly folk in their determination to root out evil. Sometimes it has happened under my command, I am ashamed to admit, though I do not permit it any longer."

"I have seen real evil, Sir Commander," said Adalar. "I have seen San-keth clerics and walking corpses and a Demonsouled necromancer. Every Justiciar or Dominiar I have ever spoken to says that neither San-keth nor Demonsouled exist, that they are the superstitions of fearful peasants. At least," he added, thinking of Galan Hawking, "until they see the San-keth with their own eyes."

"The San-keth are very real, squire," said Amalric quietly. "I have killed them with my own blade. And the Demonsouled…the Demonsouled creep through the realms of men like a cancer, masquerading as mortal men. They could be anyone, anywhere." He glanced at Adalar. "Perhaps even your Lord Mazael."

The words struck Adalar like a hammer. Something clicked within his mind. He thought of Lord Mazael's rages, his speed and strength, his unnatural healing, and his apparently endless lust for mistresses.

"That's impossible," said Adalar, mouth dry.

"Is it?" said Amalric. "His mother Lady Arissa was a notorious adulteress. And Simonian the necromancer was rumored to be Demonsouled."

"Simonian was," said Adalar. "He told Mazael himself. But Simonian didn't come to Castle Cravenlock until after Lady Arissa had died…"

"And how do you know that?" said Amalric. "Were you there? Simonian could have visited Castle Cravenlock, and Lady Arissa, long before you were ever born."

"No," said Adalar. "Lord Mazael is not Demonsouled." Yet his voice held no sincerity.

"Perhaps not," said Amalric. "But suppose he is. The Demonsouled always go mad, always try to make themselves tyrants of men. And here Lord Mazael is surrounded by the great lords of Knightrealm, men he could overthrow with ease." He stepped towards the doorway. "Perhaps, squire, you should think on that."

He left, leaving Adalar in confused turmoil.

"Mazael."

Mazael opened his eyes. Pale dawn sunlight streamed through the windows. Morebeth lay against him, head on his shoulder, her hand tracing slow circles across his chest. She had a sleepy smile on her lips.

"The great champion awakes," she whispered. She had looked happy ever since Mazael had knocked Amalric from the saddle. The expression seemed alien on her cold face. It almost suited her.

Mazael titled her head up, kissed her. "You seemed pleased."

"The expression on his face," she said, eyes glinting, "when you unhorsed him."

"He looked calm enough," said Mazael.

"He was furious," said Morebeth. "I know. I've known him all my life, have I not? He was enraged." She laughed a little. "He would have killed you, if he could have gotten away with it."

Her glee unsettled Mazael, but only little. Amalric had led Morebeth's husband to his death, after all.

"A victory for you, my lady," he said, kissing her again.

"And a triumph for you, my lord," she answered. "We ought to go to court. I wonder what Malleus will do, now that his pet has lost the tournament."

Mazael sighed and dragged his mind to more serious matters. "Nothing good." Morebeth rolled away, got up, and began to dress. She never brought any of her maids with her through the Trysting Ways, though that failed to deter the gossip.

Mazael sighed again. "We don't have to go right away."

She gave him a wicked grin. "Eager man. You seemed so weary before."

"You have a way of waking me up."

Morebeth's eyes glittered. "Wait until tonight, my lord. You'll beg for sleep, before we're done."

Mazael grinned back. "As my lady commands." He climbed out of bed and began gathering his clothes.

"Where is your squire?" said Morebeth, fiddling with some hideously complex undergarment. "Should he not help you dress?"

"I don't know," said Mazael. "I haven't seen him since the tournament."

"Mayhap he took after his lord," said Morebeth, "and found some eager lass who wanted to celebrate his victory."

"You are in a good humor," said Mazael.

"Quite." She finished dressing and gave him a quick kiss. "I shall see you at court, then." With that she turned and vanished into the Trysting Ways. Mazael grunted, adjusted his cloak, and stepped into the corridor.

He still saw no sign of Adalar. Maybe Morebeth was right, and he had finally found some willing lass. Mazael hoped so. It would do Adalar some good.

He walked alone to the Hall of Triumphs. Morning court had already begun, and Lord Malden did not like interruptions of his stately rituals. Mazael slipped through the door, past a pillar, up a stairwell, and to one of the balconies. Squires, minor knights, and a few petty lords leaned against the railing, watching the great lords in the Hall below. Their eyes widened when they saw him, and a few congratulated him on winning Lord Malden's tournament. Mazael thanked them and moved away, leaning against the cold stone railing.

Morning sunlight illuminated Lord Malden on his ornate throne. He did not look pleased. Before him sat Sir Garain and Brother Trocend at the councilors' table, and they also looked displeased. Mazael followed their gazes, and saw a dozen Dominiar Knights marching up the Hall's length. At their head strode Grand Master Malleus, his black cloak flaring out behind him. Behind him came Sir Commander Amalric Galbraith, grim and silent. Morebeth walked on his arm, cold and rigid, inscrutable beneath her black veil.

Mazael turned his head and saw Adalar leaning against the rail. His squire looked tired and haggard, dark circles beneath his eyes.

"Adalar."

Adalar whirled, hand fumbling for the dagger at his belt.

"What is it?" said Mazael.

"Nothing," mumbled Adalar, shaking his head. "I was startled, that's all."

Mazael laughed. "Long night?"

"It was."

Mazael jerked his head at the Dominiars. "What's happening?"

"Malleus demanded to speak with Lord Malden in court this morning," said Adalar. "I don't know why."

Mazael scowled. "I think I do." His stomach clenched.

Lord Malden's war against the Dominiars might begin right now.

The Dominiars stopped before the stone dais. Amalric slipped his arm free from Morebeth's and stepped forward, raising his voice. "The Grand Master of the Dominiar Order, Malleus, greets his brother the Lord of Knightcastle, and asks to speak on matters of grave import."

One of Lord Malden's heralds stepped forward. "The wise and noble Lord Malden greets his brother, the Grand Master of the Dominiar Order, and bids him to speak at once."

Malleus stepped past Amalric and gave a slight bow. "Lord Malden, all men speak of your wisdom, your clemency, and your justice." His stentorian voice carried the formal phrases over the Hall. "Indeed, what wrongdoer does not fear your wrath, or what villain your swift sword? Yet, my Lord Malden, an injustice lurks in your realm, an injustice that has lingered for five long years."

"Tumblestone," whispered Mazael.

"Tell me, Grand Master," said Lord Malden. "Of what injustice do you speak?"

"Beyond the southern border of your lands," said Malleus, "there lies a fair city called Tumblestone, a thriving port, overthrowing with the riches of all the world. The Patriarch of the Holy Amathavian Church gave that city to the Dominiar Order, many long years ago. Our Order has guarded that city from all foes for centuries, shepherding its people in the ways of righteousness and godliness. Truly, the people of Tumblestone are the people of the Dominiar Order. And yet this city that has been guarded by the Grand Masters of our Order for centuries lies in the hands of another lord." Malleus spread black-gloved hands. "Lord Malden, you are a man of justice and wisdom, prudence and mercy. Will you not restore the people of Tumblestone to their rightful guardians?"

A dead silence reigned over the Hall for a moment, all eyes on Malleus and Lord Malden.

"You speak," said Lord Malden, "of justice and mercy. Yet is it not just to uphold a man's rights? What of my rights, Grand Master? For, you see, Tumblestone is mine by right. By right of conquest, by right of blood. For it was my vassal, now Lord Mazael of Castle Cravenlock, who defeated Sir Commander Aeternis, who rode through the gates of Tumblestone in my name. It was Sir Mandor Roland, my son, my blood, who fell in the battle for the city." Sir Mandor had actually been killed two weeks before Tumblestone, deep inside Mastaria, but Lord Malden had never let that inconvenient truth trouble him. "Sir Mandor spilled his blood to win Tumblestone for Knightcastle, for all the heirs of the great King Roland. Therefore Tumblestone is mine, noble Grand Master. Mine by right of conquest and right of blood." He leaned back in his throne, keen eyes narrowed. "I will not give up that which has been so dearly bought."

"You will not?" said Malleus, his tone just as cold as Lord Malden's. "I advise my Lord Malden to be wary. That which has been dearly bought can prove even more expensive to maintain." His eyes wandered over Garain, then to Tobias. "A price even more painful can yet be exacted."

"And a just lord does not tolerate thieves," said Lord Malden, almost snarling.

"Indeed not," said Malleus. "And a wise lord does not lay claim to stolen goods." He shrugged. "And if a lord was foolish enough to buy stolen goods at a dear price, well…that is not the concern of the rightful owner."

"A fascinating point," said Lord Malden. "Perhaps the sophists and the jurists can debate it at length in their dusty halls. But the point is meaningless. After all, Tumblestone is mine, now and forever, and I will not give it up."

"I urge wise Lord Malden to surrender Tumblestone," said Malleus. "As all men know, goods obtained by theft, murder, and treachery only bring ruin and woe in the end."

Lord Malden's eyes blazed, and he stood. "Has the Grand Master failed to hear me? I will not give up Tumblestone." He glared down at Malleus. "And if any thieves come to take it from me…I will mount their heads on pikes over Tumblestone's gates."

Malleus stiffened. His face remained calm, but his eyes narrowed to icy slits. "So be it."

He turned and marched from the Hall, the Dominiar Knights following.

CHAPTER 18
CHILDREN OF THE OLD DEMON

Lucan Mandragon was in a foul mood. He stalked through Castle Town's bustling market square, past the ornate doors of the town's church.

Things had not been going well.

That the changelings had infiltrated both Knightcastle and Castle Town to an alarming degree, Lucan had no doubt. Several of the Dominiars' servants were also changelings. Lucan wondered if any Dominiars served the San-keth faith in secret. Or perhaps the San-keth just manipulated the Dominiars from the shadows.

Either way, the San-keth planned to kill a great many lords, and Lucan had to stop them. Most of all, he had to find and kill Straganis. With Straganis dead, the changelings would have no leader, and Lucan could destroy them at his convenience.

Yet finding Straganis had proven difficult.

Three separate times, Lucan had captured and questioned changelings. After they failed to answer, he ripped into their minds with his spells, but to no avail. Straganis had laid magical protections over his minions' thoughts, protections Lucan could not break.

But that was no hindrance for one such as Lucan. He had killed the changelings, readied the appropriate necromantic incantations, and set out to summon their shades. Again, his efforts had been blocked. Somehow Straganis had bound the spirits of his minions, shielding them from any necromantic summons.

And that left the vexing problem of Harune Dustfoot.

One wandering cheese merchant ought to have been easy to find. Instead, Lucan had discovered no trace of the strange peddler. Even odder, no one remembered seeing him. In exasperation, Lucan worked spells, probing the thoughts of those he questioned, yet none of them remembered Harune Dustfoot. Yet their minds held a curious echo, almost as if…

Lucan muttered a curse.

It was almost as if someone had used a spell to erase all memories of Harune Dustfoot.

And that didn't take into account the problem of Brother Trocend. Lord Malden's pet wizard had awakened to the danger of the San-keth changelings. Trocend possessed both potent divinatory magic and a small army of spies, hired assassins, and enslaved spirit-creatures to carry out his will. San-keth changelings had started turning up with their throats cut. While Lucan found the assistance useful, Trocend's divinatory magic might discover his presence.

And Trocend would not appreciate Lucan's presence.

Something heavy and feathered landed on Lucan's shoulder.

"G'day, squire!" The tip of a beak brushed his ear. "Why, you look like a man in need of cheering up, so you do."

Lucan sighed. "I trust this is worth my time?"

Mocker-Of-Hope had proven useful. The malicious little wretch could see the auras, the souls, of mortal men, and had spotted several changelings Lucan might have missed. Yet Lucan did not even want to think about what havoc the creature might wreak, should it escape from him.

"Why, sir!" said the raven, speaking in the little-girl's voice, "I would never disappoint you! It would hurt me ever so much! I have found something wondrous and glamorous and magical." The voice giggled. "It's delightful."

"Then stop babbling and show me."

Mocker-Of-Hope obliged, hopped from Lucan's shoulder, and transformed into the shape of the tow-headed boy. "This way, squire, right this way."

They walked unnoticed and ignored through the crowds of Castle Town's market. Lucan remained wrapped in his mind-clouding. No one paid any attention to Mocker-Of-Hope.

"And once you've seen my wonder, squire," said Mocker-Of-Hope, a weird gleam coming into his eyes, "you ought to go speak with Lord Mazael again, eh?"

"Perhaps," said Lucan. "If this news of yours merits it."

"Oh, it does, it does!" said Mocker-Of-Hope. His voice lost its human aspect, became low and grating. "It would be grand to see Lord Mazael again…to see the black fires in his blood…"

Something about Mazael's Demonsouled nature held Mocker-Of-Hope rapt with awe. The creature often seemed to speak of little else.

"He could be so much stronger than he is," said Mocker-Of-Hope, doing a mad little jig. "Why, he only uses the tiniest bit of his power, so he does. He could be mighty, one of the great."

"It is better that he does not," said Lucan.

Mocker-Of-Hope glared up at him. "He could become the Great Demon. He could be a god, and break your will like glass." All humanity had fallen from his voice, and his eyes looked like ravenous mouths.

Lucan feigned indifference. "This wonder you have discovered...it must not be so wondrous after all."

Mocker-Of-Hope shuddered. "Why, squire, you do me wrong!" He sounded the affable boy-thief again. "This way, so it is!" He scampered off, Lucan trailing after him.

They stopped before a massive, three-story public house of dressed stone and wooden timbers. A wooden signboard showed a silver helm crowned with a golden diadem, painted in bright colors.

"The Inn of the Crowned Helm," said Lucan, scowling. Perhaps Lord Malden wished to become King Malden. Of course, Lucan's own father no doubt desired a royal circlet. "What is so interesting about this?"

Mocker-Of-Hope became a raven, settled on Lucan's shoulder, and cawed at the door. Lucan shrugged, strengthened his mind-clouding, and stepped into the inn's common room. The place looked like any other inn, albeit a bit more prosperous. Dozens of merchants sat around the tables, drinking, arguing, and haggling. Most spoke about the coming war between the Dominiar Order and Lord Malden. Such news would please Lucan's father to no end, but he doubted Mocker-Of-Hope found it interesting.

Lucan turned, and saw Harune Dustfoot. He sat alone in the corner, still in his dusty cloak and boots, frowning beneath his mop of dusty hair. Every now and again he took a long swig from his mug, still frowning.

"Well," muttered Lucan, "well, well."

"Peculiar, ain't it, squire?" croaked Mocker-Of-Hope. "Like he's not there, you know?"

"What do you mean?" said Lucan.

"I can see the souls of mortal blokes," said the creature on Lucan's shoulder. "Yours looks like a pile of ashes." He sniggered. "But...this fellow, it's like he's not here, you know?"

"I don't," said Lucan. He traced a sigil with his fingers, muttering an incantation, and worked the spell to sense magic. He sensed potent energies gathered within Mocker-Of-Hope, and some lesser magic on a few of the merchants, no doubt a petty enspelled trinket or two. Yet he sensed nothing from Harune Dustfoot.

Nothing at all...

Lucan frowned and tightened the focus of his spell.

In fact, he sensed so little that it was as if Harune...wasn't there at all.

Lucan released the spell and began another, one to sense the thoughts and emotions of those around him. He finished the incantation and a welter of curious sensations filled his mind. The grumbling thoughts of the merchants flickered through his skull. Some were jovial, some cranky, some lustful, some bored. Mocker-Of-Hope's mind felt like a black pit caked with dried blood. Lucan scowled, shook off the distractions, and focused his spell upon Harune Dustfoot.

He sensed nothing, nothing at all. Either Harune had no thoughts, which was unlikely, or…

Or he was encased in warding spells so powerful that Lucan's magic could not penetrate them.

Only a wizard of overmastering might, someone far stronger than Lucan, could have worked such spells. A powerful wizard, or perhaps…

"Straganis," whispered Lucan. Did the San-keth archpriest sit here disguised as a human, like a viper lying in wait? For a moment he contemplated striking, unleashing the full of his power at Harune.

He hesitated, mind racing. If Straganis was here, Lucan's power might prove insufficient. And he suspected something else was at play here. Why would a San-keth archpriest move disguised among Humans when changelings could spy for him?

Harune rose, drained off the rest of his ale, and marched upstairs. Lucan followed, and saw him disappear into a room on the third floor.

"Well," said Lucan. "It appears you'll get to see Lord Mazael again after all."

Mocker-Of-Hope cackled in delight.

"Nothing," said Timothy, shaking his head. He looked tired, his eyes bloodshot, his black coat rumpled. "There's…a few times, when I felt changelings approaching." He turned over the wire-wrapped crystal. "They're here, somewhere. But I could never focus on them, though. I'm sorry."

"No matter," said Mazael. "You might have deterred them from making an attempt on Lord Malden's life."

They stood on the balcony outside Mazael's rooms, watching the valley of the Riversteel. The tournament camp had vanished, only to have a new one rise in its place. Lordly banners flew over the tents, flapping in the wind.

Lord Malden's vassals gathered for war.

"Keep watching Lord Malden and Lady Rachel," said Mazael. "The changelings will try to kill them sooner or later." He stared at the gathering tents and scowled. If the San-keth and Straganis wanted to kill Lord Malden, no better time would present itself.

"My lord," said Timothy. "You…should watch yourself, as well. The San-keth will most surely try to kill you as well."

Mazael grimaced. "Let them try."

A large raven landed on the railing, flapping its wings. Mazael thought it looked familiar.

"What a remarkably ugly bird," said Timothy.

The raven somehow managed to give Timothy a dirty look.

A dry, mocking voice answered him. "You don't know the half of it."

Lucan Mandragon stepped onto the balcony, wrapped in his dark cloak.

Timothy gave a violent start. "Lucan! I thought you had stayed at Castle Cravenlock…"

"No," said Lucan. "I've been here…in disguise, you might say, the entire time. Lord Mazael thought a hidden spy might prove useful."

"I thought you were dead," said Mazael.

"Again?" said Lucan. "Your lack of faith wounds me, as ever."

"You've found something?" said Mazael.

"Yes," said Lucan. "Harune Dustfoot."

"It's taken you this long to find a peddler of cheese?" said Mazael.

"For a peddler of cheese," said Lucan with some asperity, "he possesses some remarkably potent wards against divination. I only stumbled upon him by…chance, of a sort."

"Do you think he's in league with the San-keth?" said Mazael.

"Possibly," said Lucan, shrugging. "I had no way to tell."

"If he's in league with the San-keth," said Timothy, "why would he have sold a weapon of magic power to a Dominiar commander?"

"You only have the word of Sir Commander Aeternis that he bought your sword from Harune," Lucan gestured at Lion. "Suppose he lied to you?"

"Aeternis isn't the sort to lie," said Mazael.

"You did try to kill him," said Timothy.

"And he tried to kill me," said Mazael. "That's the way war works. And suppose Aeternis didn't buy Lion from Harune Dustfoot? Then it's just an unlikely coincidence that, as the Dominiar Order and Lord Malden prepare to go to war, there's a merchant in Castle Town hiding beneath protective spells?"

"It does seem unlikely," said Timothy.

"Well put," said Lucan.

"Where is he?" said Mazael.

"The Inn of the Crowned Helm," said Lucan.

"Then let's pay him a visit," said Mazael. "Come with me, both of you."

"Both of us?" said Timothy.

"Yes, both," said Mazael. "If this Harune's a wizard, or a San-keth cleric, I'll need your help to deal with him. Don't tell anyone about Lucan, though."

"I daresay," said Timothy. "I doubt Lord Malden would welcome him."

"That," said Lucan, "is perhaps understating the case."

The raven hopped from the railing and landed on Lucan's shoulder.

"You know, I've been to the Inn of the Crowned Helm," said Timothy. "They have the most splendid beer."

Lucan lifted an eyebrow. "During your search for the San-keth, I suppose?"

"Of course," said Timothy. "The inn had to be searched, after all. And searching is thirsty work."

Mazael stalked across the square. The townsfolk hastened to get out of his way. "Splendid beer, you say? If this goes well, I'll buy you an entire barrel."

He threw open the door and stepped into the Inn of the Crowned Helm. The gathered merchants and townsmen looked up at him. The inn's master scurried over, bowing and scraping. He had wide, fearful eyes for Mazael, and even wider eyes for Timothy's black wizard's coat.

He failed to notice Lucan.

"Nothing, thank you," said Mazael, striding past. "I wish to speak with a merchant about a purchase. Harune Dustfoot? Is he upstairs?"

"Yes, lord," said the master, still bowing. "Do you wish to try my beer? I've even some wine..."

"Thank you," said Mazael again, climbing the stairs. Lucan pointed at one of the doors. Mazael nodded, drew Lion, and kicked open the door. The room was large and spacious, with windows looking over the square. It even had a table and a chair.

Harune Dustfoot sat in the chair, wrapped in his dusty cloak, holding a tankard of beer.

Lucan and Timothy stepped to either side of Mazael, hands raised for magic.

Harune did not look alarmed.

"Lord Mazael." Harune set the tankard on the table. "It is an honor to see you again. Have you come to kill me?"

"Who are you?" said Mazael. Lion hadn't burst into blue flame, as it did when confronting creatures of dark magic.

"I told you, my lord," said Harune. "I am Harune Dustfoot, a merchant of fine cheeses."

"Cheeses, you say?" said Mazael. He waved his sword over the furniture. "Quite a fine room, for a merchant of cheeses."

"My customers appreciate my cheeses," said Harune, "and my friendly charm."

"I'm sure," said Mazael. "And do they appreciate your protective spells, your wards against divinatory magic? I'm sure those are helpful indeed to a man in the cheese trade."

"Ah," said Harune. He nodded at Lucan. "I suppose young Lucan here told you about that?"

"You can see him?" said Mazael.

"Of course I can see him," said Harune. "He's standing there plain as the day, after all." He shrugged. "He's using a particularly potent mind-clouding spell, true, but he's still standing there."

"You're a wizard, then?" said Lucan.

"No," said Harune. "I haven't the spark." He smiled. "Or that particular madness, if you will."

"Then who are you," said Mazael, "in truth?"

Harune shrugged. "Does it matter? I am a simple wanderer, and nothing more."

"I'm sure," said Mazael.

"I think you came here to ask me something," said Harune. He spread his hands. "Why not just ask it?"

Mazael lifted Lion, the blade gleaming. "Do you recognize this?"

"Of course," said Harune. "Your sword. Quite distinctive. I saw you use it during the fight with the bandits. And you carried it in the tournament. A splendid victory, by the way."

"Thank you," said Mazael. "Ever met a Dominiar commander named Aeternis?"

"I did, some years ago," said Harune. "It was during the wars in the Old Kingdoms. He seemed a solid enough fellow."

"He told me that you sold him Lion," said Mazael.

"I did," said Harune.

"And did you know it was a sword of old Tristafel, a weapon of power?"

Harune stared at him, unblinking. Then he sighed. "I did."

"And where did you find it?" said Mazael.

"Have you ever heard," said Harune, "of the Cirstarcine Order of monks?"

"I have," said Mazael. "They helped me fight Skhath and Simonian."

"They fight the San-keth and the Demonsouled everywhere," said Harune. "As you have taken it upon yourself to do."

"How did you know Simonian was Demonsouled?" said Lucan, eyes narrowed.

"The Cirstarcians told me," said Harune. "And I tell them many things. I work for them, in a way. When I learn something they might wish to know, I tell them. And sometimes they tell me things in return."

"Like where to find Lion?" said Mazael.

"Yes," said Harune, closing his eyes. "It was…ten years ago. Yes. Ten years. In a ruined tower far south of the Old Kingdoms, overlooking the sea. Your sword had lain in a vault under that tower for centuries. Even millennia, for all I know. The Cirstarcians had hidden it there until it was needed. They told me to take the sword and sell it to someone in the Old Kingdoms or Mastaria."

"Why?" said Mazael.

Harune shrugged. "Because a powerful Demonsouled was in the Old Kingdoms."

Mazael felt a chill. Had the Cirstarcians known about his Demonsouled nature?

Harune kept talking. "They knew that Demonsouled would rise to power, and they wanted Lion ready to fight."

"That's…a foolish plan, if I may say so," said Timothy. "Suppose Lion wound up in the hands of a bandit? Such a man wouldn't oppose a Demonsouled. And suppose the sword was lost?"

"You underestimate Lion's magic," said Harune. "The spells used to create it are far stronger than anything used today. It was imbued with purpose, with power to fight the creatures of darkness. It will seek them out. The sword's magic will not permit it to be lost. Throw it into the sea and a passing wave will bring it back to shore. Fling into a pit and a man will explore that pit, seemingly by chance."

Mazael looked at Lion with a new, uneasy light.

"So I sold the sword to Sir Commander Aeternis," said Harune. "He seemed valiant enough, the sort of man to fight against evil without hesitation." He shrugged. "Then you defeated him and took Lion with you to the Grim Marches."

"Hardly a brilliant plan," said Lucan. "And mayhap you place too much faith in the magic of old Tristafel. They were mighty, but they were not gods."

"Perhaps you're right," said Harune. "Lion went to the Grim Marches, not to the Old Kingdoms." He smiled. "But there was a mighty Demonsouled in Castle Cravenlock, was there not? Lion was needed there. And now it comes back to Knightrealm and Mastaria, where it might be needed again."

"Sophistic rubbish," muttered Lucan.

"Needed again?" said Mazael. "What do you mean?"

"You don't know?" said Harune. "Surely you must by now." His face tightened. "The San-keth. They swarm over Knightcastle, their changelings disguised as servants and common folk."

"We know," said Lucan. "We've been working to stop them."

"With limited success," said Harune. "Kill one changeling and five more will take its place. Have you found their master yet? Have you found Straganis?"

"How do you know that name?" snapped Lucan. "Perhaps you are in league with him."

"I know the names of all seven San-keth archpriests," said Harune. "They are all mighty and utterly mad. For all their power and guile, all their rage, they gain nothing. They spend their lives in hopes of regaining their lost limbs, in restoring their people, yet reap nothing but torment. I pity them.."

"I do not pity them," said Mazael, finding his voice, "for they have tried to kill my sister far too many times for mercy." His hand tightened around Lion's hilt. "This sword was made to fight the powers of darkness, you say? Then fine. I will find Straganis and end this."

"That will not end it," said Harune. "Do you think this is just about you, Lord Mazael, about your sister? The San-keth wish you both dead, yes. But your deaths are a minor concern to them."

"Then they're here to kill Lord Malden," said Mazael, "are they not?"

"Of course," said Harune, "but why?"

Timothy shrugged. "Why not?"

"Lord Malden scarcely believes that the San-keth exist, despite what you've told him," said Harune. "Why would they kill Lord Malden?"

Mazael remembered the dream after his first night with Morebeth, remembered the Old Demon sitting in Lord Malden's throne, mocking him.

"Not why," whispered Mazael. Timothy and Lucan frowned at him. "Not why. But who. Who is Straganis's master?"

Harune nodded. "Yes."

"What do you mean?" said Timothy.

"I think," said Harune, "that the San-keth act under the direction of a powerful Demonsouled."

Mazael suppressed a shudder.

"It has always been thus," said Harune. "The San-keth are mad with hate, and so are most Demonsouled. Yet the Demonsouled are stronger, and can manipulate the San-keth, use them as weapons and pawns."

"Yes," said Timothy. He swallowed. "Simonian was Demonsouled, and he was in league with Skhath."

"He was," said Mazael. Timothy didn't know the half of it. The Old Demon had used Skhath and the San-keth, but they had meant nothing to him. The destruction of the Grim Marches had meant nothing to him. The Old Demon had only wanted to unlock Mazael's Demonsouled nature, and if that failed, to kill him.

"Yet the San-keth are always betrayed," continued Harune, shaking his head. He sighed. "They are foolish enough to view the Demonsouled as allies or pawns, and are too blind with their hatred to see that the Demonsouled are stronger."

Mazael said nothing.

"So, then, what do the Demonsouled want?" said Timothy.

Harune shrugged. "Power. Dominion. The throne of a tyrant, I suppose, for the greatest Demonsouled all have the soul of a tyrant." His eyes flicked over Mazael. "And the children of the Old Demon burn with the hottest madness of all."

"The children of the Old Demon?" said Mazael, his voice hoarse.

"Most Demonsouled have but a small part of their souls twisted by demon magic," said Harune. "Some never notice it, live their lives free of the curse. Some others become killers, even twist themselves into inhuman monsters. But they are rare, and can be killed, though with difficulty." He sighed and rubbed his face. "But the Old Demon was the son of the Great Demon itself. He is half a god. And the children of the Old Demon are all filled with demon power. They also have the power to lead others, to dominate them, to work their will over men until they become slaves." He paused. "Have you ever heard of the Destroyer?"

"It's a legend of old Tristafel," said Mazael, remembering what Lucan had told him. "One of the Old Demon's children will rise up, become stronger than his brothers, and crush the lands of men. He will rule with an iron fist and a bloody sword, and claim the Great Demon's empty throne." Was that Mazael's fate? To succumb to his demon blood and become a monstrous god, or to fall at the hands of another of the Old Demon's children?

"Yes," said Harune. "And that is what I think is happening. One of the Old Demon's children yearns to become the Destroyer. Perhaps he hides among the Justiciars, or the Dominiars, or Lord Malden's court. Either way, the San-keth work at his bidding."

Harune was more right than he knew. One of the Old Demon's children stood before him, after all. Yet Mazael wanted peace, wanted to stop this war. But what if another of the Old Demon's children stood in the shadows, pushing both Lord Malden and the Dominiars towards war? Could Mazael stop it?

Did he even have the strength to face another of his monstrous father's sons?

"You seem quite well informed," said Lucan, voice cold. "Did the Cirstarcians tell you all of this? Or have you another source of knowledge?"

"I have told you," said Harune, "all that I know. Doubtless you know things that I do not. I know you don't trust me. Indeed, I see no reason why you should. But I swear to you, on the names of Amatheon the father, Amater the lady, and Joraviar the knight, that I have spoken no false word." He leaned forward. "The Cirstarcine Order sent me to Knightcastle to help, however I could. You, Lord Mazael, you are the only one working to stop the San-keth." He spread his hands. "Therefore I will help you however I can."

"Then help me," said Mazael. "Find me as many changelings as you can. Help me to find Straganis, and kill him. And if you are right, if one of the Old Demon's children is our true enemy, then help me to kill him."

"I will," said Harune. "I swear it."

"And I'm sure your oath is precious," said Lucan.

"Yes," said Harune. "It is."

"I do not trust him," said Lucan.

Mazael walked from the Inn of the Crowned Helm, head bowed in thought. He had expected Harune Dustfoot to provide answers.

Instead, he had more questions.

"The Cirstarcians are secretive, yes," said Timothy. "But they move openly enough when they feel the need."

"I don't know," said Mazael, scowling. "Who cast those wards over Harune?"

"It's rumored that many senior Cirstarcians are powerful wizards," said Timothy. "They could have laid the spells over Harune."

"Many things are rumored," said Lucan, "but few things are true. I'm sure Straganis could cast spells of that nature."

"Spells," said Mazael. "You told me that you knew a spell to determine the nature of a creature from a drop of its blood. Could you work such a spell over Harune?"

"Unfortunately, no. His wards against divination are powerful enough to render my spell useless."

The fat raven dropped from the sky and landed on Lucan's shoulder.

"Why does that damned bird keep following you around?" said Mazael.

"Ravens posses just enough wit to be useful," said Lucan, "so I tamed the beast to act as a pair of eyes."

The raven loosed a derisive caw.

"So," said Mazael. "Magic will not give us an answer. We are left with our wits. Why do you distrust Harune so?"

"Harune did not tell us anything we did not already know," said Lucan. "We knew about the San-keth. We knew about Straganis, and Harune likely learned about Straganis at Tristgard, just as we did. And you already suspected a Demonsouled behind the San-keth. Harune but strung these facts together with a few vague warnings of impending doom. A common technique of tricksters and rogues. At best, he is a charlatan. At worst, he is an agent of the San-keth, or Straganis himself in disguise."

"Then why didn't he kill us all?" said Mazael.

Lucan grimaced. "You seem determined to trust this man."

"I don't want to trust him. I want to know the truth of him." Mazael glanced at Timothy, who still looked troubled. "You can often read people well. What do you think?"

"I think." The frown lines in Timothy's forehead deepened. "I think…Harune seems to be what he claims to be. He was telling us the truth. But I doubt he told us all of it. He wasn't telling us something…whether about himself, or the San-keth, I don't know."

"See?" said Lucan.

"And there was something else," said Timothy. "Something that bothered me…ahh!" He slammed his right fist into his left palm. "Something about him unsettles me, or reminds me of something, but I cannot think of what it is!"

"That's good enough for me," said Mazael. "Lucan, can you keep an eye on Harune?"

"Oh, I shall." Lucan scowled up at the Inn of the Crowned Helm. "Believe me, I shall."

CHAPTER 19
COURTSHIP

Mazael Cravenlock and Morebeth Galbraith walked together through the Arcade of Sorrows.

He had expected Sir Commander Amalric's embassy to depart after Malleus had left in a rage. Instead they remained, brooding in their guest quarters. Mazael wondered why. Lord Malden's vassals gathered outside Castle Town, both petty knights and mighty lords with hundreds of vassals at their command. And reports had come of the Dominiars riding north, bands of their footmen gathering near Tumblestone.

Yet Amalric's embassy lingered, and Mazael was glad, for Morebeth had remained with the embassy.

They walked together, arm in arm, yet Mazael cared not who might see. A lord had every right to take a lady on a walk around Knightcastle's walls. Besides, everyone already knew about them.

"I have to ask you something," said Morebeth, glancing at him.

"Ask," said Mazael.

"What do you think will happen?" said Morebeth.

"With what?" said Mazael.

"This war," said Morebeth, "that seems unavoidable."

Mazael sighed. "I don't know."

"All of Lord Malden's vassals are eager," said Morebeth.

"They are fools," said Mazael, "all of them. I saw them sitting around a map of Mastaria, choosing which lands to claim after the war is done. Never mind defeating the Dominiars first. There are knights who already think themselves lords of places they have never been, nor will ever see." He sighed again. "I wonder if half of them will live to see their new lands."

"So do you think the Dominiars will win?" said Morebeth.

"They might, or they might not," said Mazael. "Lord Malden is overconfident. He thinks he can smash the Dominiars with ease. One grand charge of knights and it's over." He shrugged. "Of course, the Dominiars are just as overconfident."

"My brother is an overconfident, prideful fool," said Morebeth, "so you are right about that, at least."

"I don't know who will win," said Mazael. "I do know we will see carnage and sorrow before this is done."

Morebeth looked at him, eyes glinting. "There's something else, isn't there?"

Mazael looked back at her, struggling for the words. "Do...you believe in Demonsouled?"

"You mean the Old Demon, the Destroyer, those stories?" said Morebeth. She shrugged. "I never gave it much thought. The priests prattle on about it, of course, but they'll say anything to exact their tithes. And men are malignant enough. They hardly need some dark force to spur them to evil deeds."

"Aye," said Mazael, "that's true enough. But...Morebeth, the Demonsouled are real." Again he felt tempted to tell her everything, but dismissed it as a dangerous idea. "I have seen one. A necromancer, Simonian, in league with the San-keth at Castle Cravenlock. He was Demonsouled, could wield arcane arts of awful power."

"If you have seen them," said Morebeth, "then I believe you."

"Simonian's still alive," said Mazael. Again he remembered the Old Demon's taunting dream. It seemed to be coming true, yet Mazael could think of nothing to stop it. "I wonder if this war is his doing, if we are dancing on his strings."

"I doubt that," said Morebeth. "You are no man's puppet."

"You cheer me."

Morebeth's cold smile glinted across her face. "I but tell the truth. If it cheers you, well and good."

They came to Audea's Garden and sat side by side on one of the marble benches. The garden looked had grown greener with the spring, and some of the flowers had even begun to bloom. Morebeth's slim fingers laced with Mazael's.

"Will you fight when the time comes?" she said.

"I will," said Mazael, staring at the grass. "I don't have any other choice. I told Lord Malden I would. It's the only way to keep the horrors of war from my lands." He shook his head. "So instead I will bring the horrors of war to another land."

"Shall I tell you what I think?" said Morebeth.

Mazael nodded.

"You don't have enough faith in yourself," said Morebeth. "You will win this war, I know. Not Lord Malden, not Sir Tobias, not the Justiciars. You will win it, not them. The Dominiars cannot stop you."

"Perhaps," said Mazael.

"And after this is done," said Morebeth, "we should wed."

Mazael looked at her in astonishment. "We should what?"

"I know why you haven't wed already," said Morebeth. Mazael felt a twinge of alarm. Did she know about his true nature? Had she learned his secret?

"Why?" said Mazael.

Morebeth's fingers tightened about his. "Because you want Castle Cravenlock to pass to your sister's children, do you not? Because then Castle Cravenlock will be bound to both Richard Mandragon and Malden Roland, and neither will be able to wage war against the other."

"Yes," said Mazael. "How did you know?"

"It is plain to see, if you care to look," said Morebeth. "Most men yearn for sons to carry on their names. That is a very noble sacrifice to make."

"It may not be as noble as you think," said Mazael.

"But why should you deny yourself the comfort and companionship of a wife?" said Morebeth. "The life of a monk was meant for some men, but not for you. I cannot bear children, and we can lie together without fear."

"I don't love you," said Mazael.

Morebeth lifted her eyebrows. "Of course you don't. Nor I you. But what has love to do with marriage? Nothing, we both know. And are we children, to sit here and prattle about love? No." Her gray eyes turned distant. "No, I know what love is. I felt it for my lord husband, when he lived. Sometimes it is like a fire that devours you completely. And sometimes it is a thing that grows slowly over time, like water wearing away a rock." She turned her eyes back to him. "When a lord and a lady marry, most times they have never even laid eyes on each other, let alone love each other." She leaned forward and gave him a light kiss. "We are already friends. Is that not enough?"

Mazael said nothing, his mind struggling.

"I know you have mistresses," said Morebeth.

Mazael jerked. "How did you know that?"

"Because I've known you long enough," said Morebeth. "You may sleep with peasant women, and they may give you a little comfort, for a little while. But you can never trust them, and they are not your companions. They are not your equals."

"But you are," said Mazael.

"You know that I am," said Morebeth. The familiar wicked glint came into her eyes. "You may even keep your mistresses, if you please, so long as you are always ready to satisfy me when I feel the need."

"Your brother will never approve," said Mazael.

"Of course he won't," said Morebeth. "But I don't care. I hold my lands in my own right, small as they are. He is not my guardian, and I am not his ward. He has no right to declare whom I will or will not wed." Her eyes glittered. "And what does his approval matter? What will he do, attack your lands? You are already going to war against him."

Mazael laughed. "I am, aren't I?" He sobered. "But will you leave your lands, your home, to live at Castle Cravenlock?"

"I will," said Morebeth. "Mastaria means nothing to me. The Dominiar Order means nothing to me, and my brother has long ceased to care anything for me."

Mazael nodded.

"So," said Morebeth, "I am asking you to marry me. I know it is unseemly, a woman asking a man, but that doesn't trouble me. Will you wed me, my lord? Shall I be your lady, and you my lord?"

Mazael stared at her. He didn't love her, not as he had loved Romaria. But Morebeth was right. That didn't matter. Amalric would fly into a rage, and Lord Richard might not even approve. But Mazael didn't care. He didn't love Morebeth, but thought he might learn to do so.

And he was so tired of facing his burdens alone.

"Yes," said Mazael, "we shall."

She gave him a lingering kiss, a kiss that somehow promised much more.

"I just hope," said Mazael, "that I can live long enough to wed."

"My lord," whispered Morebeth into his ear. "You need not fear. Amalric is not as strong as he looks. You are the stronger. The future belongs to you and I, not to him." She pushed away from him. "Now let us speak no more of wars, and just walk together."

Mazael took her hand, and allowed her to lead him from Audea's Garden.

###

Adalar hastened through the maze of Knightcastle's corridors.

He should have stayed in Mazael's rooms, waiting on his lord. But he could not, not without flinching. Every time he looked at Mazael, he saw again the wounds closing of their own accord. He thought of Mazael's rage and fury, his prowess in battle.

What if Mazael Cravenlock was Demonsouled?

And what about Mazael's mistresses? The mere fact that Mazael had mistresses grated on Adalar. Should not a true knight lie only with his wife?

But what if Mazael was truly Demonsouled? What if his mistresses became pregnant with demon spawn? Suppose Mazael sired monsters on his lovers, or went mad and killed everyone in Knightcastle? How many innocent people might die in the resultant bloodbath?

Yet if Adalar had the power to prevent it…

His resolve stiffened, he came to the corner turret that held the Dominiars' guest quarters. Two Dominiar knights stood before the tower's door, the afternoon sun glimmering off their gleaming black breastplates. One stepped to the side, pulling open the door.

"Young sir," said the Dominiar, "you are expected. The Sir Commander awaits you within."

Adalar managed an awkward bow and stepped inside.

He entered a large solarium, the sun glimmering through the high windows. The chamber had a splendid view of the Riversteel valley. In the center of the room a polished table reflected the sun, surrounded by comfortable chairs. A few clerks in Dominiar livery sat there, writing letters.

Sir Commander Amalric Galbraith stood by the windows, rimmed in the red sunlight. He wore a black tunic and a black cloak with a brooch shaped like the Dominiar silver star.

"Sir Commander," said Adalar, bowing. "You sent for me?"

Amalric turned. "I did." He beckoned. "Please, come with me."

They walked in silence past the clerks, up the spiral stairs, to the turret's roof. They stood alone on the battlements, the wind rising from the valley below. The banners of the Rolands billowed and snapped overhead.

"Have you," said Amalric, "given any more thought to my offer?"

"Sir Commander?" said Adalar.

Amalric turned dark eyes towards him. "On joining the Dominiars."

Adalar looked away. "I have. I don't know yet, Sir Commander. I have to think about it."

Amalric nodded. "Do that. It is a momentous decision, to join our noble Order, and not one that should be lightly made." He paused. "Though I think you would make an excellent Dominiar Knight."

"Thank you," said Adalar, who could think of nothing else to say.

"Your loyalty to Lord Mazael holds you back, does it not?" said Amalric.

"I am loyal to Lord Mazael," said Amalric. Despite everything that had happened, he had no wish to betray Mazael.

"Why?"

Adalar blinked, taken aback. "He is my lord. My father thinks well of him. Lord Mitor was a cruel and lawless lord. Lord Mazael defeated him, defeated the San-keth and Simonian, and brought justice back to Castle Cravenlock. I think he might bring even prosperity to the Grim Marches, some day."

"Perhaps he might," said Amalric, gazing down at the lower levels of the castle. "He is a courageous man. Assuming his mind and soul remained uncorrupted, of course."

"They will," said Adalar, hating the doubt in his voice.

"Did you know that he is bedding my sister?" said Amalric, voice flat.

"I did," said Adalar.

"And do you approve?"

"No," said Adalar. "No, I don't."

"Why not?"

"Because a knight, a true knight, only sleeps with his lady wife," said Adalar.

"Yes, quite right," said Amalric. "She's a widow, you know."

"I did," said Adalar. "Ah…the veil and the black gown made that quite clear."

"Do you know how her husband died? Sir Brandon Clemand. Or, rather, how they say he died?"

"Ah…he fell in battle," said Adalar. "During your campaign against the Old Kingdoms."

Amalric glanced at him. "A knight always speaks truly."

Adalar tensed. "They say you killed him." He felt Amalric's gaze. "I mean, that you…put him in the front line of battle, during a siege, and then pulled your men back. The archers focused on him and shot him from his horse." Amalric regarded him without expression.

Then a ghost of a smile touched Amalric's face. "Thank you. You were honest with me, and I shall be honest with you. Do you know how Sir Brandon really died?"

Adalar's mouth went dry. "How?"

"Exactly as you told me," said Amalric. "We had laid siege to a stronghold of the pagan sorcerers. Sir Brandon had command of the first wave. Yet I gave secret orders to his officers to pull back, orders I did not share with Sir Brandon. When the attack pulled back, the archers turned their fire on Sir Brandon, and he fell dead with a hundred arrows in him."

Adalar backed away from Amalric, backed away until he slammed into the battlements. "You killed your sister's husband."

"I did," said Amalric. "Do you know why?"

Adalar shook his head, wondering if he could make a run for the stairs.

"Because he was Demonsouled," said Amalric.

"What?" breathed Adalar.

"There were a hundred arrows in him because it took a hundred arrows to kill him," said Amalric. "After the first volley, he rose, roaring in rage, ripping the arrows from the wounds. It took eight volleys to bring him down."

"You mean the wounds healed?" said Adalar, clutching the rough stone.

"Before our very eyes," said Amalric. "It is one of the signs of Demonsouled blood. Along with rage and battle madness and an insatiable lust for women. Does it sound familiar, squire?"

Adalar said nothing.

"My sister is a troubled woman," said Amalric. "She has always been steeped in dark arts, obsessed with a desire for occult power. She knew Sir Brandon was Demonsouled when she wed him. She wanted to control him with her wiles and her body, and through him, to rule the kingdoms of men." He paused. "And now the same thing happens to Lord Mazael."

"Lord Mazael is not Demonsouled," said Adalar, his voice little more than a weak croak.

"Adalar," said Amalric. "You are loyal to your lord, and that is admirable. But do not lie to yourself."

"In Tristgard," whispered Adalar. "He took four crossbow bolts. It should have killed him. At first I though it was just good fortune, that it wasn't the gods' will that he fall there. But then I saw him in the church, and his wounds...it, they, they just closed before my eyes. And again, when you wounded him during the tournament. And his rage, and his...his..." Adalar raked shaking fingers through his hair. "Gods, gods, he is Demonsouled."

Amalric nodded. "I am glad you could see the truth."

Adalar flinched. "You're going to kill him, aren't you?"

"I may have to," said Amalric, shaking his head. "But I hope we are not yet too late."

"Too late for what?" said Adalar.

"Sir Brandon Clemand was once a good and loyal Dominiar Knight," said Amalric. "His Demonsouled nature was locked away within him, imprisoned by his faith and his duty." His black eyes turned flinty. "Lady Morebeth drew the darkness out of him. Morebeth corrupted him, ruined him, and drove him to his death. I had no choice but to kill him, squire, no choice at all! If he lived, think what he could have done. What he could have become."

"Why didn't you stop Morebeth?" said Adalar, seeing her in a new, darker light. He had been angered to see Lord Mazael seducing a widow still in mourning black. But had it been the other way around? Had Morebeth seduced Lord Mazael? "Why did you let her do it?"

"She is my sister," said Amalric. "I thought the best of her. I refused to believe my eyes, even when I saw the evidence before them." He sighed. "A good man became a monster and died because of my error. I regret that. And I will not let it happen again."

"What are you going to do?" said Adalar.

"I think," said Amalric, pacing, "I think Morebeth wants Mazael to kill

Lord Malden, to seize Knightcastle and Knightrealm for himself. With her ruling at his side, of course."

"Can you stop her?" said Adalar. "Couldn't...couldn't you simply kill her?"

Amalric scowled. "My sister, squire. A Dominiar Knight does not raise his hand against women. And I see her for what she is, along with a few of my trusted knights. But who else would, squire? You have, for you have seen Mazael's unnatural powers. But most folk believe the Demonsouled to be a story to frighten children. Who would believe us?"

Adalar clenched his fists. He remembered Mazael dancing with Lady Morebeth, walking with her along the walls of Knightcastle. Had she been a spider all along, weaving her poisoned web around him? "We have to do something."

Amalric nodded.

"But what?" said Adalar.

"We must set watch over Lord Mazael," said Amalric. "Sooner or later Morebeth will twist him, convince him to kill Lord Malden. We must be ready to stop him. If we can stop him, if we can keep him from killing Lord Malden...we can show him the truth, turn him from the darkness within."

"I will help you however I can," said Adalar, "if we can save Lord Mazael."

"Then this is what you must do," said Amalric. "Do you know of the Trysting Ways?"

"Aye," said Adalar, nodding, "the secret passages in Knightcastle. The lords and ladies use them to visit their lovers in secret."

"Have you explored them?" said Amalric.

"Somewhat," said Adalar. "I...I thought San-keth assassins might try to use the Trysting Ways to get at Lord Mazael, or Lady Rachel. So I explored them as best I could, when I had the time."

"If Lord Mazael meant of his own accord to murder Lord Malden," said Amalric, "he would challenge him openly. But Morebeth will make him into a puppet, if she can. She will trick him into creeping through the Trysting Ways to murder Lord Malden in his sleep."

"Lord Mazael would never do anything like that!" said Adalar.

"Neither would Sir Brandon, once," said Amalric.

Adalar said nothing.

"Show us the Trysting Ways, Adalar," said Amalric, "the secret doors, the passages, all of them. Then we can lie in wait for Mazael when Morebeth sends him to kill Lord Malden." He spread his hands. "If we do...we can yet turn him from his black path." His hands closed into fists. "And then with his help, we can stop Morebeth, keep her from ever corrupting another man."

"I will help you, Sir Commander," said Adalar, relieved that he had at last found someone who understood, someone who could help Lord Mazael.

"Good," said Amalric. "Come to our quarters at midnight, and we will map out the Trysting Ways. Now go, and do not tell anyone of this."

Adalar nodded, bowed, and departed.

He came back to the High Court just in time to hear the heralds proclaim the betrothal of Lord Mazael Cravenlock and Lady Morebeth Galbraith.

CHAPTER 20
HARUNE DUSTFOOT'S VEIL

Something bothered Timothy, had bothered him since the confrontation with Harune at the Inn of the Crowned Helm.

But what?

Timothy spent most of his time following Lord Malden at a distance, his divinatory spells focused on the Lord of Knightcastle. So far no threats had shown themselves. Every now and again Timothy caught a flicker at the edge of his senses, like dry scales brushing against stone. There were changelings in the castle, Timothy knew, but none had shown themselves.

He could wait as long as necessary. Lord Mazael wanted to stop this war, and Timothy would do everything in his power to help him. Timothy had seen too much war in his life. His homeland had been rent by civil war in his youth, and his parents and brothers burned to death as raiders looted their farm. He had seen the devastation Lord Mitor's mad war had brought to the Grim Marches.

And if Timothy could stop war by guarding Lord Malden, then he would guard Lord Malden.

Now if he could only figure out what troubled him about Harune Dustfoot.

He brooded as he lurked in an unobtrusive corner of the Hall of Triumphs, as Lord Malden pronounced his judgments and prepared for the campaign against the Dominiars. Harune reminded him of something, but what?

Lord Malden retired to his bedchamber, accompanied by his mistress Claretta. Timothy ensconced himself outside, wrapping himself in his cloak. His divinatory spell would awake him should anyone approach Lord Malden with hostile intent.

He dozed off.

A few hours later he sat bolt upright, heart racing. His fingers fumbled for the quartz crystal, and for a moment he thought someone had murdered Lord Malden. But the crystal remained cool, and Lord Malden was most likely asleep.

But Timothy found himself thinking about something else.

He remembered Skhath, the San-keth cleric that had nearly killed Lord Mazael a year ago. Skhath had masqueraded as a human knight for years, wrapped in a spell of illusion. When Timothy met him for the first time, he had sensed something vaguely wrong right away.

Later he had seen the illusion melt away, revealing the San-keth cleric riding a headless human skeleton.

And Timothy had sensed the same wrong note from Harune Dustfoot. The truth struck him like a blow, and he felt a fool for not seeing it earlier.

Harune Dustfoot wore a spell of illusion to mask his true appearance.

Timothy stood up, hesitating. He needed to find out the truth now, without delay. Yet someone had to stand guard over Lord Malden. But if Harune was a changeling, even Straganis himself in disguise, and Timothy managed to stop him…

He made up his mind. He went to the stables, borrowed a horse, bribed one of the guards, and rode for Castle Town with all speed. Another judicious bribe got the watchman to open the gate, and he galloped into Castle Town and reined up before the Inn of the Crowned Helm.

A few determined drinkers sat in the tables, a bored-looking barman gazing at them with indifference. Timothy hastened through the common room and up the stairs. His hand dipped into his coat, and he pulled free a copper tube, one end capped with a length of cork.

If Harune meant to fight, then Timothy would be ready.

He kicked open Harune's door and sprang inside.

Harune sat at the table, writing something. He jerked to his feet in alarm, scrabbling for the short sword at his side.

"Don't!" said Timothy, brandishing the copper tube. "Don't even move. Do you know what this is?"

Harune's eyes fixed on the tube. "Aye. A wizard's war-spell."

"I'll use it if I must," said Timothy.

Harune seemed amused. "If you use that, you'll blast away the inn's wall, and most likely perish yourself in the fire."

"Who are you?" said Timothy.

"I told you before, you and Lord Mazael and Lucan Mandragon," said Harune, "I'm just a merchant who works for the Cirstarcians from time to time…"

"Nonsense," said Timothy. "You wear warding spells…"

"As I've already said," said Harune.

"And one other spell," said Timothy. "I didn't recognize it at first, but I've seen such things before. A masking-spell, a spell of illusion. Harune Dustfoot is no more real than a wisp of fog. Who are you, really?" He gestured with the tube. "Tell me."

Harune sighed. "You would not wish to know."

"Tell me," repeated Timothy.

"Understand," said Harune, "that when I said I wished to help Lord Mazael, I spoke truly. I want to help him. If you…if he learns who I really am, I may not be able to help him."

"You will tell me," said Timothy.

Harune stared at him for a long moment, then sighed. "Perhaps it is the will of the gods." He shrugged. "As you wish."

Harune Dustfoot shimmered and disappeared.

In his place stood something else, something most definitely not human.

Harune Dustfoot was a San-keth cleric.

Timothy yelled and stepped back. He almost loosed the war-spell, almost blasted the San-keth to ashes. Yet something stayed his hand.

The San-keth had arms and legs. It looked, in fact, almost like a scaly man, albeit with a serpent's head and a dangling tail. Timothy had never seen a San-keth with limbs, save for Straganis's freakish carrier. In fact, the San-keth claimed to have been stripped of their limbs long ago.

"Are you going to kill me?" said the creature, its voice unlike Harune's.

"What are you?" said Timothy.

"I," it hissed, "am Ang-kath."

Timothy frowned. "What is that?"

The creature told him, at some length, and then said, "I think you should take me to see Lord Mazael at once."

Timothy lowered the copper tube. "I think you're right."

The air shimmered. The creature vanished, Harune Dustfoot reappeared, and followed Timothy from the Inn of the Crowned Helm.

CHAPTER 21
DAGGERS IN THE NIGHT

Mazael lay asleep and dreamed:

He stood in the High Court, before the bronze statue of the first King Roland. The statue's head had been hacked off, its sword shattered, and lay in jagged shards at Mazael's feet.

Atop of the statue's broken neck rested Lord Malden's severed head, the eyes bulging in shock and horror. Blood trickled down the stone, dripping to the ground. Rachel's head had been impaled on the broken sword, her features bruised and mutilated.

Mazael turned, his hands tightening into fists.

The sky burned like a dying fire, streaked with ashen clouds. Gutted corpses hung from Knightcastle's walls, staining the stones with blood. Vultures wobbled overhead, bloated with dead flesh. The air hung heavy with smoke and the stink of rotting flesh.

The Old Demon before the Hall of Triumph, glaring at him. Something red and bloody dangled from his left hand.

"You," snarled Mazael, drawing Lion and stalking forward.

The Old Demon laughed at him. "No words of greeting for your father, my son?" The bloody thing swung from his left hand. "No words at all?"

"I'll kill you," said Mazael, raising Lion.

The Old Demon's eyes flashed like coals. "Miserable little fool. You could no sooner kill me than you could extinguish the sun. Ten thousand years from now, your bones will have moldered to dust, but I will still live."

Mazael did not slow, did not lower his blade.

The Old Demon snarled, revealing jagged, filthy fangs.

"Then look!" snarled the Old Demon, lifting the bloody thing, "look at what your future holds!"

He flung the bloody sphere at Mazael. It bounced off Lion and rolled away, spinning in a veil of red hair, and came to a stop.

Morebeth's bloodshot, dead eyes gazed up at him.

"Do you see?" whispered the Old Demon, black robes scraping against the ground like dead skin against a coffin. "You remember the first one, do you not? Romaria, that was her name? She died for you. She died because of you. Your sins, my son, your fault. And your new betrothed," his face twisted into a grimace of hate, "she will die because of you. Every woman in your life will die because of you, and you will see them suffer before you die."

"Did you come here to talk," spat Mazael, tearing his eyes from Morebeth's tortured face, "or to fight?"

The Old Demon laughed. "Your defiance is futile. You betrayed me, my son. So I will see everyone you ever love die. And then, only then, when despair has crushed your feeble soul, when you beg me for the mercy of death, will I lift my hand to kill you."

"No," said Mazael. Lion burned in his fist, the blade writhing with white flames. "Not if I kill you first."

The Old Demon laughed. "Blind fool. Do you even see the death gathering around you?"

Mazael said nothing, Lion blazing.

The Old Demon grinned. "You don't, do you? Fool. Tell me, my son, since you are so much wiser than your father. Do you see the betrayals that surround you? The treachery? The lies, the deceit?" One hand cupped and closed like a noose wrapping around a neck. "Your death comes for you like a wolf in the night and you do not even see it. It will spring from the darkness and take you, and you will just have time to choke on bitter tears before you die."

"Every word you've even spoken has been false," said Mazael. "Why should I believe you now?"

The Old Demon's smile turned crooked. "Your arguments grow trite." His breath rasped through his flaring nostrils. "You don't believe me? Then go. Go and see, my son. You will see that I am right. And before you die, as they rip the heart from your chest, you'll hear me laughing."

qThe earth shook, and the towers of Knightcastle fell, dust and ash rising up in a colossal plume...

###

Mazael jerked awake, sweat oozing down his face and arms.

Besides him Morebeth sighed, hair sliding over the pillows.

It looked to be almost midnight. Mazael stared into the gloom, but saw nothing. He strained his ears, but heard only Morebeth's slow breathing.

He sat for a moment, fists clenched.

It had just been a dream.

But dreams of the Old Demon were never just dreams.

Mazael rolled out of bed and dressed. He bucked on his sword belt and took a pair of sheathed daggers. His armor sat on a stand in the corner. He began to don it, pulling on the gambeson and hauberk, fumbling with the bindings of his cuirass.

"Mazael?" Morebeth sat up, holding the blanket close. "It's the middle of the night. What are you doing?"

"Trouble's coming," said Mazael.

He felt Morebeth's stare.

"I don't know how," said Mazael. "I just do. Something's going to happen, and I need to be ready for it."

Morebeth stood, wrapped herself in a red gown, and lit a candle. "Then you had better be ready, hadn't you?" She glided to his side, pushed away his hands, and began doing the straps of his armor. "Put on your gauntlets while I do this."

"Thank you," said Mazael.

Morebeth said nothing, her slim fingers working the straps.

Adalar slipped through the night, his cloak wrapped tight.

He stopped before the door to the Dominiars' quarters, knocked, and waited. Nothing happened for a moment. Then the door opened a crack, and Adalar felt unfriendly eyes digging into him.

The door opened, revealing a scarred Dominiar Knight. He scowled and beckoned Adalar forward. They passed through the darkened corridors and came to a torchlit hall. A half-dozen Dominiars stood around a table, grim-faced and silent.

"Squire," said Sir Commander Amalric. He wore black plate and a black cloak with the silver star of the Dominiar Order. "Welcome. I am pleased you came."

"Sir Commander," said Adalar, bowing.

"These," said Amalric, gesturing with an armored hand, "are my most trusted knights." The men turned cold, flat eyes towards Adalar. They all looked like experienced killers. "They have served me well for many years. We will need to rely upon them during the troubled times ahead." He paused, fingering his sword hilt. "Have you heard the dark news?"

Adalar nodded. "Lord Mazael has betrothed himself to Lady Morebeth."

"He has," said Amalric.

"Can you not stop her?" said Adalar. "You're her brother, her only male kin. Can't you forbid her from marrying Lord Mazael?"

"I could," said Amalric, rubbing his sword hilt. The hilt, wrapped with worn leather, had seen much use. "But she wouldn't listen to me. She never has, after all." His dark eyes met Adalar's. "Our time grows short. If

Morebeth has convinced your Lord Mazael to marry her, then her hold over him is strong. Very soon, she will ask him to kill Lord Malden, and he will be deep enough in her thrall to obey. Perhaps even tonight. We must act at once. Show us the Trysting Ways, squire. Show us how we can save Lord Mazael from my wretched sister."

Adalar nodded and walked to the featureless stone wall. He examined it for a moment, then pushed a stone block. Something clicked, the floor shuddered, and a portion of the wall swung aside.

Amalric's knights looked startled.

"You can find the triggers like this," said Adalar, pointing at part of the wall. "In direct light, they don't look like anything. But if you look at it from the side, you can something that looks like a rose. That marks the door triggers."

"Cunning work," murmured one of the knights.

"Good," said Amalric, nodding. "Show us more."

Adalar nodded, and led the Dominiars into the Trysting Ways.

Sir Roger Gravesend squatted in the darkness, sharpening his sword. The rasps echoed off the damp walls of the stone vault.

"Soon!" shrieked Calibah, brandishing a torch, her reptilian eyes reflecting the fire. "Soon the hour will come! Soon we will slaughter the heretics and the apostates and the unbelievers in their beds! They shall know the stern justice of the San-keth, and we shall be the instruments of great Sepharivaim's wrath!"

Two dozen changelings stood around Calibah, cheering in bloodlust.

Roger felt a tense eagerness. For weeks they had skulked in the shadows, hiding in Castle Town's warehouses, in the labyrinth of forgotten passages riddling ancient Knightcastle, in the surrounding wilds and woods. Things had almost fallen apart when Lord Mazael caught them at the Lord's Wood, but they had managed to escape.

The hiding grated on Roger. Calibah's endless preaching wearied him, and he wanted to kill her. He wanted to kill all the changelings. Sometimes he wanted to fall on his sword and escape the misery of his life.

But, by Sepharivaim, he wanted to kill Mazael Cravenlock. And Calibah hinted that tonight, they might make their move.

The whetstone scraped against the sword blade.

"The blood of the unbelievers!" Calibah shrieked, slashing with the torch, "will stain Knightcastle's walls!"

Something moved in the darkness. A vile stench struck Sir Roger's nostrils. He gagged and scrambled to his feet.

A ghastly shape, a mixture of spider, human torso, and scorpion tail creaked into the light. Straganis's head swiveled back and forth, his body grafted to his unnatural, alchemy-spawned carrier.

Calibah fell to her knees, as did the other changelings. "We await your command, great one," she whispered.

Straganis's tongue flicked at the air, dulled eyes glistening. "The word has come from our ally, my servants. The time has come. Tonight, the unbelievers will perish!"

The changelings cheered, and Roger found himself grinning.

Morebeth tied off the last strap and stepped back. "Now what will you do?"

For a moment Mazael felt foolish. Lord Malden would never believe him. Maybe the entire thing was just a fancy of his imagination. But dreams of the Old Demon were never just dreams.

And Lucan would believe him, and Trocend, and Timothy, if Mazael could but find them. If the San-keth meant to strike tonight, then Mazael needed their spells to battle Straganis's arcane might.

"I have to find Brother Trocend," said Mazael, stepping towards the door. "And extra guards for Lord Malden, Sir Garain....everyone, I suppose." He paused, glancing back at her. "What will you do?"

Morebeth shrugged. "I may as well remain with you. I suppose I am as safe with you as anywhere else. And I doubt I am important enough to assassinate."

Mazael's jaw worked. "They... might kill you just to get to me, now that we are pledged." He could not bring himself to tell her everything, could not tell her that the Old Demon might kill her out of spite, and cursed himself for his cowardice.

Morebeth smirked, eyes glittering. "Let them try."

Someone knocked at the door.

"Answer it," whispered Morebeth, picking up a dagger.

Mazael nodded, loosened Lion in its scabbard, and threw open the door.

Timothy stood in the doorway, looking worried.

Behind him waited Harune Dustfoot.

"Timothy?" said Mazael. "What's going on?"

"Lord," said Timothy. He glanced at Morebeth. "Lady." Morebeth gave him a gracious nod.

"Lord Mazael," said Harune, bowing.

"My lord," said Timothy, "there's something I've learned that you should know at once." He hesitated. "It...it will probably anger you. But I only ask that you don't kill Harune until he's finished speaking."

Mazael frowned. "What? What's happening?" Was this the doom the Old Demon had planned?

"I must tell you something," said Harune.

Adalar pointed towards a narrow staircase that spiraled upwards into the gloom. "There. And that stairwell leads towards Lord Malden's room."

Amalric nodded. "Good. Very good. Lord Mazael will pass this way when the madness takes him." He beckoned. "This way. We must return to our guest quarters before anyone notices us here."

Adalar nodded and fell into line behind Amalric. The Dominiar Knights filed behind him, hands on their sword hilts. They walked in silence, save for the occasional creak of armor, a scabbard tapping against a wall.

"Quiet," hissed Amalric. Every now and again Adalar started to point out the path, but Amalric silenced him. He remembered everything Adalar had told him. It made Adalar uneasy. He had expected to show Amalric the door to Lord Malden's chambers.

Instead, he had shown Amalric half the Trysting Ways.

Why did Amalric need to know so much?

They turned left, filing down a narrow passage. The torches in the knights' hands flared and flickered.

"Wait," said Adalar. "Sir Commander. This isn't the way back to your chambers."

"I know," said Amalric. He glanced back. "Trust me, please."

Amalric led them into a portion of the Trysting Ways Adalar had never seen. Dust coated the floors, and mold stained the walls. The stale air smelled of decay and something foul.

Amalric stopped before a massive door bound with rusted iron. He knocked in a complex rhythm and stepped backward. The door swung outward with a squeal of rust. Amalric nodded to someone and stepped through the door.

Adalar followed and came to a shocked halt.

Dozens of San-keth changelings filled the vault. Sir Roger Gravesend, who had betrayed Lord Mazael, stood nearby, a bared sword in his hand. Something creaked in the shadows, a ghastly stench flooding Adalar's nostrils.

Straganis skittered out of the darkness, his spider-legs creaking, his human torso and arms the color of a dead fish.

"Well," hissed the San-keth archpriest, "you have come." His dull eyes swiveled to face Adalar. "And you have brought a guest."

"Sir Commander!" shouted Adalar. "Run!" He fumbled for his sword.

Strong hands closed about his arms, wrenching them behind his back. Adalar jerked and twisted, trying to tear free, and realized that two of Amalric's grim-faced knights had seized his arms.

"Sir Commander!" said Adalar, confused, "what…"

One of the knights struck Adalar across the face. "Silence."

Amalric walked across the room, the changelings parting before him. He stopped before Straganis and gave a curt nod.

Straganis bowed in return, his misshapen body creaking. "Welcome, Sir Commander."

"Archpriest," said Amalric. "Is everything ready?"

"All is ready," said Straganis. "We shall win great glory for Sepharivaim this night."

"That is no concern of mine," said Amalric, "but our purposes happen to coincide."

Adalar stared at Amalric and Straganis in horror.

"What of the wards?" said Amalric. "Knightcastle crackles with divinatory magic. Malden has at least one wizard hidden away someplace. He will know the minute we strike. Can you defeat him?"

"Fear not," said Straganis. "The arts of great Sepharivaim shall crush this interloper."

"Good," said Amalric. "Lord Malden and all three of his sons must die. Kill any Justiciar officers you can find. Knightcastle will be leaderless, and shall fall easily to Grand Master Malleus."

"And Mazael and Rachel Cravenlock must perish," said Straganis, his head swaying. "He has murdered the servants of great Sepharivaim, and she is an apostate. Both will die screaming for their crimes."

Amalric shrugged, indifferent. "As you will."

"You liar!" shouted Adalar, struggling against his captors. Another blow bounced off his jaw, but he ignored the pain. "You'd consort with the San-keth just to defeat Lord Malden. Are you insane? They'll kill you!"

Sir Roger strolled towards Adalar, grinning. "Well. Mazael's squire. Quite a present you've brought us, Sir Commander." He lifted his sword, tapping the edge against Adalar's throat. "Let's take his ears, or his eyes and nose, and send him back to that bastard Mazael as a warning."

"Don't be a fool," said Amalric. "Lord Mazael is formidable, and must die without warning." His cold face tightened. "Unless you'd prefer to face him yourself?"

Sir Roger stepped back. "Let me kill the boy."

"No," said Amalric. "He may prove useful later, I think. Perhaps as a hostage, should things go awry."

"You bloody-handed coward," said Adalar. "If Lord Mazael dishonored your sister, then challenge him to a duel like an honorable man…"

"My sister is an annoyance. Lord Mazael is an obstacle to be removed, and nothing more," said Amalric, voice cold. He looked to Straganis.

"Prepare yourselves," said Straganis.

The changelings stood. As Adalar watched, their features flowed and changed, rippling like clay beneath a potter's hands. The changelings, one and all, took the shape of dark-haired Mastarian men. They donned black mail and black tabards adorned with the silver Dominiar star.

"Make certain you are seen," said Amalric. "It is my wish that the survivors tell tales."

"My servants know their business, Dominiar," said Straganis, turning his baleful glare on Amalric.

Amalric looked back without flinching. "See that they do."

Straganis hissed and looked away first.

"I might have a use for the boy later. Make certain he doesn't cause trouble," said Amalric.

Adalar struggled against the knights' iron grip. Something hard smashed into the back of his head, pain exploded through him, and everything went dark.

###

"What is it?" said Mazael. "Speak."

Harune opened his mouth, then Timothy hissed and fumbled in his pocket. The wire-wrapped quartz crystal in his hand shimmered and pulsed.

"Lord!" said Timothy. "Changelings!"

"Are you sure?" said Harune.

"Absolutely," said Timothy. "They're nearby...they're moving towards Lord Malden's chambers." His eyes widened. "Gods, there are hundreds of them, they're everywhere..."

"We have to go now," said Mazael. He looked at Harune. "We can talk later. Are you armed? We'll need help."

Harune nodded and drew his short sword.

Mazael pushed past them, into the corridor, and almost ran into Trocend Castleson.

"Lord Mazael!" hissed Trocend. His hair was unkempt, his eyes wide and bloodshot. He held a glass jar clutched in one hand. Within the jar a changeling's eye spun like a child's top. "The changelings are coming! We must move at once!"

"I know," said Mazael, stepping past him. "For the gods' sake, let's..."

"Lord Mazael." Lucan Mandragon appeared out the shadows, raven perched atop his shoulder. "The changelings are moving. We had best get to..." He stopped, and then Trocend saw him.

"You!" said Trocend, raising his hands. "Did your father send you to work mischief? Or perhaps you were in league with the San-keth all along?"

"Don't be a fool, old man," said Lucan. "I've been here all along. You simply lacked the wit to notice." He lifted his hand, the fingers working. "And do you really think yourself strong enough to overcome me?"

Mazael shoved between them. "You damned fools! You can butcher each other after we stop the changelings. Now…"

Something clicked, quite loudly. Mazael turned just in time to see the door to the Trysting Ways swing open, and a dozen men in the tabards of Dominiar footmen swarm into his bedchamber.

For a moment they gaped in confusion. Mazael saw their eyes flicker, saw the black-slit serpent gaze of San-keth changelings.

Then they sprang forward, drawing their swords, and swarmed at Morebeth.

Mazael raced forward, shoving Trocend out of the way. Harune scrabbled for his short sword, and Lucan began an incantation. Mazael yanked Lion free, his heart racing. He couldn't reach them in time, couldn't keep them from killing Morebeth…

But Morebeth wheeled aside, cat-quick, her free hand seizing a changeling's hair. Her other hand brought up the dagger in a quick slash, and the changeling fell with blood bubbling from a slashed throat. Another changeling stabbed at her, but Morebeth dodged aside, ducking towards the bed.

Then Mazael crashed into the changelings, Lion a steely blur. He took the head from one, slashed the arm from another, and gutted a third. His Demonsouled rage boiled beneath his mind, but he kept a tight focus. A few sword points skidded off his cuirass, but he blocked most of the blows, driving deeper into the changelings.

But still more rushed out of the Trysting Ways. Mazael hacked at another, saw Harune slashing with his short sword. Another changeling dashed at Morebeth, and she seized his arm, using his momentum against him. The changeling shot past her, slammed into the wall, and Morebeth drove her dagger through the back of his neck. Despite the mayhem, Mazael felt a brief flash of admiration for Morebeth's cold-eyed calm.

Then Trocend stepped forward, purple witch-light flashing around his raised fingers, and thrust out his hand. The air shimmered, and a ghastly specter appeared, a gruesome cross between a misshapen ape and a vulture. The creature loosed a warbling cry and ripped a changeling in half, its fangs tearing out the throat of another. Lucan made a chopping motion with his hand, and an unseen force seized three changelings and slammed them against the wall with bone-shattering force.

Mazael parried a blow, raised his free hand, and knocked a changeling back with a ferocious punch. The changeling staggered back with a wail of pain, and Trocend's winged monster tore it to shreds.

The last changeling fell, the rest fleeing into the Trysting Ways. Blood covered the floor in a sticky coat. Mazael stepped towards the secret door, sword raised, but no further changelings appeared.

"Timothy, Harune," said Mazael, kicking the secret door shut. "Push the bed in front of the damned door." The two men hastened to comply. "We've got to rouse the castle. Come on, move!"

"But the lady," said Trocend, squinting at Morebeth, "we cannot leave her here!" The bed slammed against the door.

"I will stay with you," said Morebeth, wiping her dagger clean on a dead changeling's tabard.

"Go!" said Mazael. "Lord Malden could lie dying as we speak!" He felt a surge of twisting fear. Had they gotten to Gerald already? Had they murdered Rachel? "Timothy! Rouse the castle. Get to the barracks and ring the alarm bells. Go!" Timothy turned and sprinted away in a swirl of black cloak. "Come!"

They hastened into the corridors of Oliver's Keep, which stood dark and silent. Mazael saw nothing, and heard nothing but the raspy breathing of his companions.

"We must go to Lord Malden's rooms," said Trocend, "if the Dominiars have come to kill him. He is lodging in the Tower of Guard tonight, with Lady Claretta…"

"But what of my sister?" said Mazael. They clattered through the gates of Oliver's Keep and into the Court of Challengers. "Or Sir Gerald, or Sir Tobias? They're all in the Old Keep! We can't…"

"Trocend can warn Lord Malden," said Lucan. "Lord Mazael and I will see to Lord Malden's sons."

"I cannot go alone," said Trocend. "I am but an old man…"

"Don't play me for a fool," said Mazael, running for the ramp to the High Court. "You're hardly helpless. And get some of Lord Malden's armsmen, if you need aid. Now go!"

Trocend scowled at Mazael, but nonetheless ran off with surprising speed. Mazael raced through the barbican to the High Court. The armsmen standing guard at the gate stared at him.

"We are under attack!" said Mazael. "Get to the Old Keep and defend your lord, now!"

They gaped at him. Mazael didn't bother to see if they had obeyed. He cursed under his breath, wishing he had insisted that Rachel stay in Oliver's Keep. Lord Malden had lodged Rachel in the Old Keep, in the quarters of the Rolands' most honored guest, since she would soon become a Roland.

She might well die in comfortable luxury, if Mazael didn't get there in time.

Four household knights stood on guard before the gates of the Old Keep. They moved to block Mazael's approach.

"Move, you damned idiots," roared Mazael.

"Lord Mazael," said one the knights, "no one is permitted to enter the Old Keep without Lord Malden's…"

Mazael shoved aside the knight and kicked open the door.

The knights yelled, stepped forward, and came to a stunned halt when they saw the two dozen changelings or so standing in the keep's great hall.

Mazael bellowed and sprang at them, Harune a half-step behind him. Mazael took the arm from a changeling, wheeled, killed another. He heard Lucan chanting something, saw Harune chopping and stabbing.

Lord Malden's knights stared in shock.

"Fight, you cowards!" said Morebeth, her voice ringing. "Fight and defend your lord!"

The knights ran forward, drawing their swords, and the armsmen dashed through the opened doors. Mazael tore into the changelings with abandon, blood running down Lion's blade. Rachel and her maids had been lodged on the second floor of the Old Keep. If he could just cut his way through …

Two changelings came at Mazael, screaming, swords raised high. Mazael parried the first blow, twisted around the second, and sidestepped the third. His sword crashed through a gap in the changeling's armor, sent it sprawling to the ground.

He wheeled to face the second one, Lion arcing in a crimson blur, and Lucan cast a spell.

The air crackled with energy. A half-dozen glowing, translucent wolves appeared out of nothingness, ripped from the spirit world by the force of Lucan's magic, and pounced upon the changelings. Fangs and claws shredded changeling flesh, blood staining the ancient flagstones of the Old Keep. Mazael cut his way through the melee, his teeth clenched. Another few steps, a few more changelings, and he could race to the stairs…

A high keening sound sliced into his ears, and then something hard and invisible slammed into Mazael with a thunderclap. He went sprawling to the ground, as did a dozen changelings and most of Lord Malden's men. Mazael groaned and went to one knee, trying to shake off the ringing in his ears. Had Lucan lost control of his spell?

He looked up, and saw Straganis.

The San-keth archpriest skittered towards him, spider legs creaking, green fires crackling around his ghastly hands.

"For your crimes," hissed Straganis, hands lifting, "for your murder of the cleric Skhath, I sentence you to death!"

Mazael lurched to his feet, his trying to regain his balance. He heard Morebeth shout something, heard the groans of wounded men, Straganis's voice droning in a necromantic incantation. He took a staggering step towards Straganis, but he knew could not reach his enemy in time…

Then a rushing roar filled the air. Straganis lurched back, the fires around his hands winking out, his spidery legs buckling with stress. Mazael saw Lucan running towards the San-keth archpriest, hands out, lips twisting in a spell. Straganis snarled and thrust out his hands. Part of the wall exploded in a spray of debris, and the rushing sound ended.

"So!" said Straganis, straightening up, "you dare to face me again, maggot?"

"I defeated you once before, did I not?" said Lucan, circling Straganis.

"You escaped because of chance," said Straganis. "And you will not escape again."

He thrust out his hands, and a half-dozen wraith-like tigers appeared from nothingness and sprang at Lucan. Lucan gestured, and his translucent wolves leapt from the mauled corpses of the changelings and intercepted Straganis's tigers. Both Lucan and Straganis began new spells, gesturing like madmen, their voices thundering with arcane power.

Mazael raced for the stairs.

Adalar blinked awake.

He had a gag in his mouth and a blindfold over his eyes. Rough hands dug into his shoulders, half-dragging, half-pushing him forward.

"Ah," he heard Amalric say, "here we are."

The click of a secret door opening seemed very loud in Adalar's ears.

A ghostly beast, like a lion with kraken's tentacles, fell from the ceiling, jaws snapping for Lucan's head. One of his wolves leapt up and intercepted the creature. Another of Straganis's tigers seized the opportunity and charged at Lucan. Lucan cast another spell, the arcane energies thrumming through his bones, and banished the creature back to the spirit world.

Straganis hissed, venom dripping from his fangs, and began another spell. The hall of the Old Keep thundered with the opposing magic, echoing with screams of pain and the ring of steel as changelings and armsmen battled.

Lucan gritted his teeth, spread his fingers, and made a lifting motion. Three dropped swords floated off the floor. He made a slashing gesture and sent the weapons spinning at Straganis. One of Straganis's tigers jumped, caught a sword in the throat, and vanished. Straganis crossed his arms, a silvery mist shimmering around his misshapen form. The remaining swords crumbled into a cloud of orange rust.

Straganis struck again, with a spell that made the floor tremble and the air ring, and Lucan barely turned it aside. The effort made knives of pain dig into his head.

Once again, he was overmatched. He had enough power to turn Straganis's spells, and even to strike back, but he had nothing to pierce Straganis's protections. Their struggle would become a battle of attrition, and Straganis would outlast him.

But he had expected that.

Straganis sent a chunk of shattered masonry hurtling towards Lucan's head. He gathered his will and flung it into a changeling. Straganis's will struck at Lucan again, and again, and the third strike sent Lucan flying.

He smashed hard into the wall, his head ringing, blood splashing across his lips. Lucan spat a curse and rolled to one knee, saw his spirit-minions fleeing in all directions, Straganis's creatures overwhelming them.

Lucan had landed next to one of the doors into the Trysting Ways.

He scrambled to his feet, triggered the door, and slipped inside.

He heard the skittering clicks as Straganis followed in pursuit.

Mazael dashed up the stairs, the noise of the melee below ringing in his ears. He wanted to turn and fight, wanted to plunge into the battle below. How could he leave Lucan and the others to fight alone? But he could not stand against Straganis's magic. And if he stayed, if he fought, Rachel might die.

If she hadn't died already.

He raced around a corner and came to her door.

It was locked.

Mazael spat a curse and rammed his shoulder against the door, all his strength behind it. The wood shattered and Mazael half-jumped, half-fell through the door. Rachel lay sleeping in the great bed, dark hair fanned across the pillows. Her maids and ladies-in-waiting slept on cots around the bed.

Seven changelings in Dominiar guise glided towards them, swords in hand.

They froze in shock, staring at Mazael.

Mazael sprang forward, yelling, Lion raised high. He cut down one changeling and wounded another before they had a chance to react. The rest dashed at him, swords slashing and stabbing. Mazael fell backwards, tripped over a sleeping maid, and rolled back to his feet. He parried a thrust aimed for his face and spun, his blade ripping apart a changeling's throat.

The maids woke up and began to scream. A sword cut open the inside of Mazael's left arm. He bellowed and hacked the head from another changeling.

Rachel sat up, blinking. "Mazael..." Her eyes widened in terror.

"Get out!" said Mazael. "Now! Run!"

Rachel scrambled up, kicking free from the blankets. A changeling vaulted over the bedpost, sword angled for her back. Mazael blocked the stab, and suffered a wound in his leg as another changeling seized the opening. His leg jerked and trembled. The changeling drove hard at him, feinting and thrusting. Mazael blocked, grunted, and kicked out his good leg, shattering the changeling's knee. The creature wailed and topped, and Mazael's counterstroke made a bloody ruin of his face.

"Mazael!" shouted Rachel.

"I told you to run!" growled Mazael. His leg throbbed and ached, but he could manage. Three of the changelings still stood, watching him with wary eyes.

"They'll kill..."

Mazael feinted forward, ignoring the pain. The leftmost changeling fell for the feint, and Mazael took off its hand. He wheeled aside, a weak thrust clanging off his breastplate, and decapitated another changeling.

The survivors fled, vanishing back into the Trysting Ways.

Mazael coughed and lurched towards the door, wincing. Rachel and her maids stood in a tight clump. "Is anyone hurt?"

One of the maids said, "I think you broke my wrist when you tripped over me."

Mazael shoved past them and back into the hallway. "I weep for you. Now stay with me, for the gods' sake." He broke into a run for Tobias's rooms. "This isn't over yet."

Lucan raced down the narrow corridor, his cloak flapping. He tore through the cobwebbed passages with reckless speed. If he did not reach his destination before Straganis, he would likely die.

Behind him he heard the creak of Straganis's legs, the tap of his claws against the stone floors.

"Flee, if you will!" said Straganis, his raspy voice echoing off the stonework. "It will not save you."

Lucan whirled and began muttering a spell. Straganis hissed, skidded to a halt, and began casting. Lucan's magic summoned a spirit-creature, a beast of claws and fangs and spines that sprang at Straganis.

He did not wait to see what happened next, but turned and kept running. He heard Straganis snarl a spell, heard the shriek and crackle of magical force, and the spirit-creature's scream as Straganis's will hurtled it from the mortal world.

The clicking creak of Straganis's pursuit resumed.

###

Mazael heard someone shout, following by a gurgling scream of agony. Mazael didn't slow, but lowered his aching shoulder and slammed against the door. It burst from its frame, a torn hinge shrieking.

Sir Tobias stood in the corner, naked, his axe clutched in both hands. He bled from half a dozen wounds, and a band of changelings pressed at him, slashing. Three dead changelings lay on the floor. Sir Tobias's current mistress, the daughter of some minor lord, huddled beneath the blankets, screaming.

Tobias bellowed and hacked off a changeling's arm. A sword flicked out and marked his chest.

Mazael raced forward and plunged Lion through the back of a changeling. He kicked the corpse free, wheeled, and killed another. The survivors whirled to face Mazael, and Tobias took them from behind.

The battle ended very quickly.

"Gods damn these devils!" spat Tobias, wiping his forehead. "Do they ever give up?"

"No," said Mazael, grabbing Tobias's shoulder. "Can you still fight?"

Tobias's eyes blazed. "I'll dash the brains from their skulls!"

"Good," said Mazael. He gestured behind him, where Rachel and her maids hovered in the doorway. "Get dressed. Stay with the women. They're trying to kill Rachel, too."

"What of you?" said Tobias, grabbing for his armor.

Mazael didn't answer, but shoved past Rachel's maids and into the corridor. He had to get to Gerald and Sir Garain and Lord Malden before the San-keth did. He wondered why the changelings had taken the guise of Dominiar footmen. Did they think to provoke a war between Lord Malden and the Dominiars? It seemed foolish. Lord Malden and the Grand Master were going to war anyway, with or without the encouragement of the San-keth.

Then the need for action silenced Mazael's thoughts, and he raced forward, Lion trailing a fine mist of bloody droplets.

"Lord Mazael!"

He glanced over his shoulder. Harune and Morebeth and Timothy ran behind him. Harune looked bruised and bloodied, his short sword stained with gore. Morebeth was untouched, but she had traded her dagger for a sword, no doubt seized from a corpse. Her gray eyes shone with a keen light.

"It's over in the Hall," gasped Harune, panting. "The changelings are dead. Lady Morebeth sent the surviving knights and armsmen to Sir

Garain's chambers."

Morebeth did not seem winded. "These devils are here to kill Lord Malden and his kin, most likely." Her unbound hair streamed behind her like a bloody banner.

"We're with you, my lord," said Harune.

Mazael considered sending Morebeth to Tobias, but she would not listen, and seemed capable with the sword, besides. He'd never thought he would wind up fighting a battle side by side with Morebeth again, but needed all the aid he could find.

"Come with me," he said, "quickly."

Gerald occupied chambers in one of the Old Keep's turrets, with windows overlooking the lower tiers of Knightcastle and the Riversteel valley. The door was ancient oak, banded with iron, but posed no hindrance to Mazael's Demonsouled strength. The door shattered, and Mazael kicked his way over the debris.

The bed stood on the far side of the circular room, near the balcony. Gerald lay asleep, his squire Wesson snoring at the foot of the bed. Mazael saw no changelings, nor any sign of anything amiss.

A slight breeze blew through the doors.

Gerald sat up and blinked. "Mazael?" His frown deepened. "Lady Morebeth?" Wesson grunted, rubbing his eyes. "Is something wrong?"

"Get your sword," said Mazael. Wesson scrambled to his feet, drew Gerald's sword, and handed it over. Gerald rolled out of bed, nightshirt flapping around his ankles.

"But...what's going on?" said Gerald.

Mazael opened his mouth to answer.

A large part of the wall swung inward.

A dozen changelings rushed into the turret chamber, more racing after them. Mazael roared and wheeled to meet them, Lion blurring as he slashed. Wesson yelped and scooped up a mace from under the bed. Harune wielded his short sword like an axe, hewing heads and arms like wood. Morebeth thrust her sword like a rapier, fencing rather than fighting, but left numerous corpses in her wake.

Mazael wondered what had happened to Adalar.

More and more changelings poured out of the secret door, brandishing weapons. Mazael gutted one, beheaded another, and ducked beneath a looping blow. If he lived through this, he would make sure Lord Malden walled up every last one of those damned doors.

And still more changelings stormed into the room. Three dozen filled Gerald's bedchamber, crowding against the walls. Mazael had scarce enough room to swing, and yanked his dagger free, stabbing with his left hand while thrusting with his right. Blows clanged and skidded off his battered armor. He bellowed again and killed another changeling. Gods, how many changelings had Straganis smuggled into Knightcastle? Bit by bit, the sheer weight of the press drove Mazael and the others back towards the door. Gerald had been wounded thrice, blood soaking into his nightshirt, and his face had taken a waxen sheen.

"My lords, move!"

Timothy shoved past them, a foot-long copper tube in one hand. He began a rapid chant, his free hand tracing intricate gestures.

Mazael's eyes widened. "Get back! Get back!"

Timothy stood rigid, arm extended. Either the changelings had failed to recognize the danger of Timothy's magic, or they hadn't been at Tristgard. As one, they charged at him, swords raised.

Timothy finished his spell.

The end of the copper tube exploded in a raging gout of flame.

The blast of the spell hammered into the changelings, killing the first rank in an instant. The others went up in flames, clothes burning, flesh charring. They stumbled into the others, the flames spreading. Shrieks of agony rent the air, mingling with the roaring of the fires. The heat smote Mazael like a fist.

"Out!" coughed Timothy, flinging aside the copper tube. "Out!"

They stumbled out of the burning room. A few changelings chased them, screaming and wreathed in flames, and Mazael cut them down. Then the roof of the turret collapsed in a roar of smoke and embers, the heat washing out in waves. They ran back to the relative safety of the corridor, Mazael half-dragging both an exhausted Timothy and a wounded Gerald.

"I always forget how tiring that is," mumbled Timothy, shaking his head.

"You set fire to my bed," said Gerald, sounding dazed.

Armor clattered and swords rattled. Mazael turned and saw a dozen of Lord Malden's armsmen running up the hall, escorting Rachel and a half-dressed Sir Tobias.

"The castle is roused!" said Sir Tobias. "We'll hunt down every last one of those damned changelings!"

"Sir Gerald is wounded!" said Mazael. "See to him at once!" He stepped past Sir Gerald, making for the stairs.

"Where are you going?" said Morebeth.

"The Tower of Guard," said Mazael. If the changelings had waylaid Trocend, kept him from reaching Lord Malden...

"My lord!" Timothy ran to his side, reeling a bit. "You'll not make it to the Tower in time. Come with me, quickly." He beckoned, and Mazael scowled, but followed nonetheless.

They ran onto a balcony jutting from the side of the Old Keep, overlooking the second tier of Knightcastle's walls. Mazael saw the battlements of the Tower of Guard far below.

"Do you expect me to jump?" said Mazael. "It must be three hundred feet..."

"Yes, it is," said Timothy, fumbling through his pockets. "And yes, I do." He yanked free a bit of wire and an eagle's feather. "A spell I have. You can make the jump safely."

"You're exhausted," said Mazael.

Timothy nodded. "But I can still do this. My lord, you'll need this if you hope to save Lord Malden. Hold still." Mazael complied. Timothy muttered under his breath, waving the wire and the feather in patterns. Blue light flashed from Timothy's hands, and Mazael felt a curious lightness, a thunderous rushing filled his ears.

"Now, my lord!" said Timothy, his voice muffled in Mazael's ears, "jump!"

Mazael shrugged, rammed Lion into its scabbard, vaulted the railing, and jumped. He plunged down, his cloak billowing behind him, and felt an instant of terrible fear.

Then his boots hit the battlements of the Tower of Guard with a gentle tap. Mazael reeled for a moment, his head spinning, then regained his balance. He had fallen over three hundred feet without injury.

He ran for the stairs.

###

Rough hands pulled away Adalar's blindfold.

The point of a dagger pressed against his throat.

"Keep silent, boy," breathed a voice into his ear. "One word, one twitch, and you'll choke on your own blood. The Sir Commander wants you to see this."

Adalar's eyes twitched back and forth. Through the opened door he saw a vast, opulent bedchamber, dominated by a bed the seize of a large wagon. Lord Malden lay sleeping in the bed, alongside a naked young woman Adalar recognized as Lady Claretta.

Amalric walked towards the bed, sword sliding from his scabbard with a gentle hiss.

###

A necromantic spell slammed into Lucan, a haze of green flames that threatened to rip the life and warmth from his flesh. He managed a warding spell, but the force still sent him sprawling.

Straganis raced down the corridor, moving ever closer.

Challenging Straganis might not have been a good idea.

Lucan looked up, gazed at the groin-vaulted ceiling, and realized where he was.

The ghost of a smile flicked across his face, and he rose, setting himself to meet Straganis's attack.

###

Mazael sprinted into the Tower of Guard's uppermost levels, where Lady Claretta had her chambers, and where Lord Malden often spent his nights. Two of Lord Malden's household knights stood at guard before the door, yawning and heavy-eyed. They glared at Mazael.

"What is your business here?" they said, staring at the bloodstains on Mazael's armor.

"You damned fools!" said Mazael, drawing Lion. "They've come to murder Lord Malden and you're standing here gaping? Get out of my way!"

The knights moved to block Mazael. He shoved them out of the way and hammered the door open. The bedroom was opulent with silken hangings and rich tapestries, as Lord Malden usually lodged his favorite mistress here. The bed was large and soft, because Lord Malden occasionally wished to spend time with more than once mistress at once. At the moment, it just held Lord Malden and Lady Claretta, both asleep.

On the far side of the bed stood a handful of Dominiar Knights, a half-dozen changelings disguised as Dominiar footmen, and Sir Commander Amalric Galbraith, a sword in his hand.

"Oh, gods," mumbled one of Lord Malden's knights.

Amalric looked at Mazael, his eyes cold and sharp as the blade of his sword. "Lord Mazael."

"You damned murderous bastard," said Mazael, circling towards him. The Dominiar Knights and the changelings raised their weapons. "You're in league with the San-keth."

"Hardly," said Amalric, raising the sword. "We share a few common purposes, but nothing more."

"Did you send the San-keth to kill me at Castle Cravenlock?" said Mazael. "And at Tristgard?"

"Straganis does as he pleases," said Amalric. "If it amuses him to butcher a few enemies on the side, what is that to me? Your name meant nothing me until a few months past." His eyes glinted. "Lord Malden is doddering old hypocrite, and will be removed for the greater glory of the Dominiar Order."

"Villain," said Mazael.

Lord Malden stirred, yawned.

"You are a debauched lecher, seduced by my whore of a sister," said Amalric. "Speak to me of villainy, will you?"

"But I have not sent the San-keth to murder men in their beds!" said

223

Mazael, stepping toward Amalric.

"What is this?" said Lord Malden, sitting up, gray hair tangled. He glared at Mazael, at Amalric, and back at Mazael. "If you two are going to kill each other, do it in the morning like civilized..." His voice trailed off as he saw the Dominiars and the changelings.

"Be silent, you old fool," said Amalric. He stepped towards the bed.

Mazael raised his sword.

"Another step and I'll kill the boy," said Amalric.

"What boy?" said Mazael.

Amalric gestured. "That boy."

One of the Dominiars shoved Adalar forward, his hands bound, a gag in his mouth.

"You damned coward," spat Mazael.

"I am nothing of the sort," said Amalric, raising his sword. "I'll kill the old man first, then you."

Lord Malden's hand blurred, dipped under his pillow, and reappeared with a dagger. Amalric's free hand lashed out and sent the old man sprawling across the pillows, the dagger falling from his hand. Lady Claretta sat up, clutching the blankets, and screamed.

Amalric raised his sword for the blow.

Lord Malden's dagger clattered at Mazael's feet.

He snatched it up and flung it. It whirred past Amalric's ear and buried itself in the eye of the Dominiar holding Adalar. The Dominiar shrieked and stumbled back, clutching his face, and dropped Adalar. Amalric hesitated for just a second, and that was long enough for Mazael to block the thrust intended for Lord Malden's heart.

Lord Malden's household knights screamed and charged into the room.

"Impressive," said Amalric, pressing against Mazael's block. "We already know you're my superior with a lance. Let us see who is better with the blade."

He came at Mazael in a whirlwind of blows.

###

Straganis skittered into the vault, watching Lucan.

"You lack the strength to run?" he said.

"No," said Lucan. "I am not running from you." He backed away a bit more. If he could get Straganis a few more feet into the vault, just a few more feet...

"Fool," said Straganis. "They all hold you in such fear. You are little more than a neophyte, a child dabbling with petty spells. I shall teach you proper arcane arts, once I enslave your spirit."

"Such boastful words," said Lucan, still backing away, heart racing. "Yet I still live." His back bumped against the vault's wall.

Straganis cackled. "Not for long."

He came into the center of the vault, and Lucan felt a fierce surge of triumph.

A fat raven flapped up, circled over Lucan's head, and changed into the boy-thief shape. Mocker-Of-Hope seized a rope dangling from the ceiling, swinging like a monkey.

Straganis laughed. "A lesser spirit-creature? It will not save..."

He looked up, saw the dangling corpses, and fell silent.

A dozen dead changelings hung from the ceiling, nooses around their necks. Necromantic sigils covered their faces and chests, sigils Lucan had painted in their own blood.

"Now!" shouted Lucan, beginning an incantation.

Mocker-Of-Hope blurred, became a nightmarish shape of leathery skin and talons, and spun. His claws sheared through the ropes, and the corpses fell in a ring around Straganis. Lucan finished his spell, necromantic energy shimmering around his fingers.

The corpses rose to their feet with terrifying speed and grace. Lucan had spent days preparing them, laying spells of strength and speed over their rotting flesh, burning latent magic in their flesh.

They flung themselves at Straganis, tearing and biting. Straganis's first spell blasted steaming chunks of meat across the room, and the second reduced a corpse to crumbling ash. Yet the sheer weight of his undead attackers bore Straganis down, drove him to the floor.

An axe leaned in a corner. Lucan seized it and raced for Straganis, the weapon raised high. He knew Straganis had armored himself in wards to turn most spells, but he doubted the San-keth had raised spells against material weapons.

His theory was confirmed when the axe took off Straganis's arm. A yellowish ooze burst from the wound, and Straganis screamed, the corpses tearing at his flesh. Lucan brought the axe up again, intending to take Straganis's head.

Straganis tore his remaining arm free, gestured, and shouted an incantation. Mist swirled about his maimed form, and he vanished, pulled back into the spirit world. Lucan's axe clanged off the stone floor, numbing his arms. The animated corpses stood and began wandering around the room, seeking for their quarry.

"Damn it!" snarled Lucan. So much effort had gone into the preparations, and he had been forced to use, again, the necromantic arts he had inherited from Marstan, yet Straganis had still escaped. "Damn it, damn it, damn it!"

The outburst irritated him, and he throttled himself back. He ought to have learned greater self-control, by now. He couldn't afford to lose his temper and kill everyone who annoyed him.

Something tittered. Lucan turned and saw Mocker-Of-Hope, wearing the shape of the noble girl.

"Why, sir!" she said. "That was ever so funny."

"We failed," said Lucan.

Mocker-Of-Hope blurred, became the boy-thief, still chuckling. "But, squire! Why, the expression on that snaky devil's face. Course, he doesn't have a proper face, not really, if you follow me." He pointed. "But I bet he'll not be causing you trouble for some time, so he won't."

The severed arm of Straganis's carrier lay on the floor in a pool of yellow slime. It had already begun to rot, and the stench was terrible. Lucan sighed, waved his hand, and canceled the necromancy binding the dead changelings.

They fell to the ground in a chorus of meaty thumps.

"Come," said Lucan. "More blood will be spilled, before this night is done."

The fat raven gave a satisfied caw and settled on Lucan's shoulder.

Sparks flew, and Lion clanged in Mazael's hands.

Amalric was fast and strong, his blade everywhere at once. It took all of Mazael's skill and strength to keep from losing a limb, or even his head to Amalric's sword. He inflicted a half-dozen minor wounds, and Amalric gave the same back to him.

The Demonsouled rage began to rise, filling Mazael with fire, numbing the pain of his wounds.

They battled, hacking and stabbing. A half-dozen of Lord Malden's household knights charged into the room, rushing the Dominiars and the changelings. Corpses fell like leaves in an autumn forest. Mazael's foot tangled in the legs of a dead knight, and he almost lost his balance. Amalric's sword lashed out and skidded off Mazael's forearm, drawing blood. He snarled, kicked free of the corpse, and parried a vicious cut aimed at his head.

More changelings rushed from the Trysting Ways, weapons raised. More household knights and armsmen ran through the door, yelling. Amalric flew into a raging whirlwind of harsh blows, trying to cut down Mazael and get to Lord Malden. Mazael held his ground against Amalric's fury. Sooner or later the armsmen and knights would push back the changelings...

Someone howled in hate. Mazael glanced sidelong just in time to see Sir Roger Gravesend lunge at him, a Dominiar war hammer raised high.

The blow crashed into Mazael's left shoulder, crushing armor plates and shattering the bones. The pain plunged into him like a burning spear, and his arm went numb.

"You bastard!" shrieked Roger. His eyes were wide and wild, his beard unkempt, and he looked utterly mad. "I'll smash your damned head in! I'll..."

Mazael ducked under Amalric's next blow and kicked out. His boot slammed hard into Sir Roger's stomach, sent him reeling. Amalric's next slash skidded off the top of Mazael's helmet. Mazael staggered with the blow, snarled through the pain, and stabbed even as Amalric raised his sword for an overhand slash.

Lion's point plunged into Amalric's left armpit and burst through the top of his shoulder, scraping against the inside of his armor. Amalric roared in pain and fury and lurched backwards, almost tearing Lion from Mazael's grasp.

Sir Roger bellowed and swung the hammer in a loop. Mazael staggered away from the whirling blow and lashed out. Lion's bloodstained tip caught Sir Roger across the jaw. Sir Roger groaned and dropped the hammer, clutching his face.

"Damned traitor!" spat Mazael. Roger half-lurched, half-crawled away, and Mazael stalked after him. "You've gotten away three times before, but this time..."

Amalric's sword cracked into the side of Mazael's helmet. His head rang like a bell, and he almost toppled, Lion's point scraping against the floor. Amalric pressed forward, sword angled for a killing blow. Mazael ducked under the blow and struck back, Lion smacking into Amalric's wounded shoulder. The armor turned the edge, but Amalric snarled in pain and staggered back a step.

More armsmen poured into the room, yelling and attacking the changelings. Amalric looked around with furious eyes, backing towards the door.

"Fall back!" he yelled, gesturing with his bloody sword. "Fall back!" The changelings raced for the door into the Trysting Ways. Amalric turned one last murderous glance at Mazael, then disappeared through the hidden door. Mazael tried to chase after him, but his head ached and his stomach swam, and it was all he could do to stand. Instead he leaned on his sword and waited, the warmth of his unnatural healing abilities spreading through him.

Bit by bit the pain began to ease.

The door the Trysting Ways slammed shut. The armsmen rushed forward and began pounding at it, trying to pry it open. Amalric and his men must have blocked it somehow. Mazael waited until his head stopped spinning, then rushed forward to help rip the door open.

They swarmed into the Trysting Ways, but Amalric, the Dominiars, and the changelings had vanished from the Trysting Ways.

And they had taken Adalar with them

Someone slammed Adalar against a wall, the back of his head cracking against the stone. His vision blurred, and when it cleared, he saw one of the hard-faced Dominiar Knights scowling at him.

"Sir Commander!" said the Dominiar. "We should kill him and leave him behind."

Amalric appeared behind the Dominiar's shoulder. "No. Take him with us." His wounds seemed to trouble him at all.

"Sir Commander!" said the Dominiar. "Every man in Knightcastle will be on our trail! It will be half a miracle if we make it to Mastaria alive..."

"We will escape without difficulty," said Amalric, turning. "Now, come. And take the boy. He may prove useful as a hostage."

Adalar's eyes fell on Amalric's left shoulder, on the grisly wound beneath the torn cloth and broken armor.

The flesh writhed and twisted like clay. The edges of torn skin pulled back together.

The wound was healing.

Adalar's breath wheezed in a terrified gasp.

Amalric Galbraith, Sir Commander of the Dominiar Order, was Demonsouled.

Amalric caught Adalar's eye, smiled.

"You ought," he said, "to have paid better attention."

The Dominiar looked at Adalar, grinning. "The Sir Commander's going to rule the world someday."

Adalar screamed into his gag.

"Make sure he causes no trouble," said Amalric, turning away, black cloak swirling around him.

Something hard slammed into the back of his head, and everything went black.

At Lord Malden's command, Mazael and the others scoured the Trysting Ways from top to bottom. They found the corpses of dozens of dead changelings, some of their bodies mutilated and marked with arcane sigils. They also found an ancient vault in Knightrealm's depths, where the Dominiars and the changelings had hidden dozens of horses for their escape. The vault opened into a tunnel that led into the Riversteel valley.

They found no trace of Straganis, nor Amalric Galbraith, nor Sir Roger Gravesend.

And no sign at all of Adalar.

CHAPTER 22
THE FAITHFUL ONES

Dawn sent pale rays of sunlight through the balcony door.

"I have to go after him," said Mazael.

"Hush," said Morebeth, rubbing his back. The bones in his left shoulder had more or less healed, but he still sported a hideous greenish-purple bruise. Most of the cuts had dwindled to livid red streaks. Mazael had tried to stay out of Morebeth's sight, lest she notice his healing, but she insisted on tending him.

Either she hadn't noticed his healing ability, or she didn't care. Sometimes Mazael wondered just how much she knew about him.

"You are not riding after them," said Morebeth. "You might be able to take wounds that would kill a dozen lesser men, but you're exhausted. And you're not invincible. They'd kill you."

"They kidnapped my squire," said Mazael. "I have to go after them." Dear gods, what would he tell Adalar's father?

"You will," said Morebeth. "With Lord Malden, when he marches against Mastaria. You'll crush the Dominiars like bugs, and rescue Adalar." Her slender fingers kneaded his skin, coaxing away the pain. "Mayhap you'll become the first King of Mastaria?"

He looked at her. "And you my queen?" He felt a pang. Romaria had said much the same thing when he agonized over becoming Lord of Castle Cravenlock.

"Of course," said Morebeth. "I would make a grand queen. And you would make a fine king."

Mazael laughed. It made his injured ribs hurt. "How gracious."

"Go to sleep," she said, standing.

He caught her wrist. "Maybe I don't want to sleep."

"Maybe you don't," said Morebeth, "but I do." She smiled. "Later. Lord Malden is having his war council at noon. You had best be there."

Mazael sighed. "I know." There didn't seem any way to stop the war, now that a Dominiar officer had tried to murder Lord Malden in his bed. Mazael wondered if Amalric had acted on his own, or if he had just followed Malleus's orders.

Or maybe Straganis commanded them both. Mazael didn't know. But war was now inevitable.

He wondered if that was the Old Demon's wish.

"Rest." Morebeth gave him a soft kiss. "I'll see you at the war council." She went into the corridor, where her maids waited, and left.

Mazael closed his eyes.

"There's far too much work for us to sleep."

Mazael grabbed for his dagger.

Lucan Mandragon sat slumped in a chair, wrapped in his dark cloak. He looked battered, bruised, and very tired.

"You're alive," said Mazael.

"I don't feel it," said Lucan, "but I am."

"And Straganis is dead?" said Mazael.

Lucan scowled. "No. He did lose an arm. Though he can probably graft a new one onto that damned carrier of his." He started to rise, winced, and sat back down.

"Are you wounded?" said Mazael.

"I've been better." Lucan blinked bloodshot eyes. "I envy you. Another day and you'll not have a mark on you."

"It comes at a price," said Mazael.

"Yes." Lucan winced again and stood. "Perhaps. But it must be a useful power."

"Enough of this," said Mazael. "What do you think?"

Lucan sneered. "I have thoughts on many matters. Which ones would you like to hear?"

"Are the San-keth controlling Amalric Galbraith?" said Mazael. "Is Grand Master Malleus in league with the San-keth? Did he order these assassinations? Did he even know about it?"

Lucan thought about it. "I don't know."

Mazael grunted. "Helpful."

"It hardly matters," said Lucan, glancing at Mazael's bloodstained tunic, lying crumpled in the corner. "Amalric Galbraith just tried to assassinate Lord Malden. Not all those Dominiars were San-keth changelings. Perhaps the San-keth commanded Amalric, or perhaps he commanded the San-keth, or Malleus commanded them, or their orders all came from Straganis. It no longer matters. Either the Dominiars will destroy Knightcastle, or Lord Malden will destroy the Dominiars." He shrugged. "We can do nothing to stop it."

"It does matter," said Mazael. "Before the changelings came...I had another dream of the Old Demon. He told me that I was going to die."

"Yet you still live, do you not?"

"It was a close thing," said Mazael. "So we are going to war. Is that the will of Lord Malden, or Grand Master Malleus, or the Old Demon?"

Lucan grunted. "All three, most likely."

"Then how are we going to stop this?" said Mazael.

Someone knocked.

Mazael glared at the door and picked up Lion. "Enter."

The door swung open, and Timothy and Harune Dustfoot entered.

"My lord," said Timothy, bowing.

"You did well, Timothy," said Mazael. "You saved our lives in Gerald's room. Thank you."

Timothy still had soot on his forehead. "My lord. Thank you. But...ah, you may not be so pleased with what I have to tell you."

"Why?" said Mazael. "What is it?"

Lucan leaned forward in sudden interest, his eyes fixed on Harune.

"I just ask," said Timothy, "that you don't kill Harune...at least, give him a chance to speak."

Mazael frowned. "Why? What has he come to say?"

Timothy swallowed and stepped aside. "Perhaps I had best let him speak. I will wait outside, if you have need of me." He bowed against and vanished into the corridor, shutting the door behind him.

"Well?" said Mazael. "I appreciate your aid against the changelings. But what do you want?"

"Lord Mazael," said Harune, clearing his throat. "Everything I have told you is true."

"But?" said Mazael.

"I did not tell you everything."

Lucan smirked. "Such a surprise."

"I did not tell you the entire truth of who I am," said Harune. "Just as you did not tell me the entire truth."

"What do you mean?" said Mazael, his fingers tightening around Lion's hilt.

"I'll show you," said Harune.

He spread his hands, shimmered, and disappeared.

Mazael sprang up, raising his sword. Lucan surged forward, muttering an incantation.

In Harune Dustfoot's place stood a San-keth.

At least, it looked like a San-keth.

Its body was shaped like a human man's, but with scales, a serpent's head, and a long, thick tail. For a moment Mazael was reminded of

Straganis. But Straganis's limbs were hideous, an unnatural fusing of stolen flesh into a ghastly carrier. This creature stood on its own legs, gestured with its own hands.

It was a San-keth with arms and legs.

"What is this?" said Lucan. "Are you some new breed of San-keth?"

"I am not San-keth," said the creature with a marked sibilance.

"Then what are you?" said Mazael. "Speak!"

"I am the San-keth as they should be, as they once were," said Harune. "I am Ang-kath."

"The Ang-kath?" said Mazael. "What is an Ang-kath?"

"How did the San-keth come to be?" said Harune.

Mazael stared at the serpent man. "They...were once a race of serpent people, with arms and legs." He remembered Skhath hissing the story at him,. "But they sided with the Great Demon in the last days of Tristafel. And the Great Demon was destroyed and they were defeated. So as punishment, the gods stripped the San-keth of their limbs, condemning them to crawl in the dust, and imprisoned Sepharivaim in the form of a giant snake."

"Again, that is the truth," said Harune. His scales changed color as he spoke, shifting from dark green to pale red and back again. "But that is not the entire truth."

"Then what is the whole truth?" said Mazael.

"These primordial snake people," said Lucan, his eyes gleaming, "these ancestors of the San-keth...not all of them worshiped the Great Demon?"

Harune no longer had human expressions, but he seemed pleased. "Most did. Perhaps eight out of every ten. But a bare remnant did not follow Sepharivaim in his madness. And when the great cataclysm came, when the Great Demon was annihilated and Tristafel destroyed, my ancestors were spared the cruel fate of the San-keth." His scales turned a sorrowful purple. "On that terrible day our race was split in two. The faithless ones, the San-keth, became as you know them now. But some had remained faithful, and took on themselves a new name. The Ang-kath, the faithful ones."

"Your people," said Mazael.

"The San-keth are my people, too," said Harune. "Our lost brothers."

"Why are you telling me this?" said Mazael. "Why share your secret?"

"Because you, Lord Mazael, you have the power to aid my people in their task," said Harune.

"And what is that task?" said Lucan.

"Ever since that terrible day when our people were divided," said Harune, "the San-keth have sought revenge. They want to see the races of man destroyed and broken. They want to free mad Sepharivaim from his imprisonment. They wish to make themselves lords and masters of the earth, all other races their slaves." He paused, forked tongue lashing at the air. "And we, the Ang-kath, work to stop them."

"Tristafel perished three thousand years ago," said Mazael. "You have struggled for so long?"

"It has been a long war," said Harune, "and only rarely have mortal men learned of it. And now a great battle comes."

"The war between the Dominiars and Lord Malden," said Mazael.

"Hardly," said Harune. "That will bring suffering and death, doubt not. But it is just a mask, a cover for the real battle."

"Against Straganis," said Lucan. "If you wish to kill him, you have my wholehearted approval."

"Straganis is powerful," said Harune, "but even he is not our greatest enemy." He stared at Mazael with inhuman, reptilian eyes. "You know."

"The Demonsouled," said Mazael, his mouth try.

Harune nodded. The gesture looked odd, with his serpentine neck.

"And the greatest of the Demonsouled," said Mazael. "The Old Demon."

"Aye," said Harune. "The spirit of the Great Demon lay with mortal woman, and the Old Demon was born, and from him was spawned the race of Demonsouled. He survived the destruction of Tristafel. For three thousand years he has wandered the face of the earth, sowing hatred, reaping misery, ruining souls, moving the kingdoms of men as if they were pieces on a chessboard."

"But why?" said Mazael. "What does he want? Is he evil or mad? Does he just act out of malice?"

"He does," said Harune, "but he has a greater goal. He wishes to succeed his father, to claim the Great Demon's empty throne for himself. But to do so he needs power even greater than his own. So he sires children, permits them to wreak havoc for a time, and once they have grown strong, he devours them, adding their might to his own." Mazael shuddered, remembering the Old Demon's furious taunts. "The Old Demon has grown strong in this way. Do you know the legend of the Destroyer?"

"A child of the Old Demon will one day enslave the kingdoms of men," whispered Mazael, "make himself lord of over the earth, and claim the throne of the Great Demon."

"It will happen," said Harune, "and then the Old Demon will devour the Destroyer, claim the Great Demon's throne, and make himself king and god over the earth. Why am I telling you this, you asked?" He looked Mazael in the eye, scales reddening. "I know you are Demonsouled, Lord Mazael, a child of the Old Demon."

Mazael said nothing.

"But I also know that you have, somehow, gained the strength to deny your father, to deny your black heritage," said Harune. "Your soul and will are your own, and not the Old Demon's. We need your help, if the Old Demon is to be stopped."

"What do you ask of me?" said Mazael, his voice hoarse.

"Sir Commander Amalric Galbraith is Demonsouled, a child of the Old Demon, just as you are," said Harune.

Lucan swore.

"He knows what he is," said Harune, "and unlike you, he has embraced his heritage. He wishes to become the Destroyer, to take the Great Demon's throne, and to impose his vision of order and justice over the world. He does not know that he is but the Old Demon's puppet, that his father will betray and devour him. Amalric wants to remake the world, and he will begin with Mastaria and Knightcastle."

"Morebeth," said Mazael, licking his lips. "What of Morebeth? Is she...is she..."

"Fear not," said Harune. "She is not Demonsouled. Nor does she know the truth about her brother. She hates and fears him for his cruelty, and believes you can protect her from him. She is cold and fearful, but not Demonsouled."

"Splendid," said Lucan. "She's but coldly manipulative, not evil. So. What do you require of Lord Mazael?"

"You have to kill Amalric," said Harune.

Mazael said nothing.

"In all of history, only three children of the Old Demon have rejected him," said Harune. "That gives you power. Not so blatant as the power usually conferred by Demonsouled blood, but potent nonetheless. You are the only one strong enough to face Amalric and have a chance of..."

The door burst open. Harune whirled, and Timothy shouted something.

Trocend Castleson stalked into the room, robe swirling around him, eyes wide and hair wild.

Lucan swore again.

"So!" said Trocend, glaring at Harune and Lucan. "The Mandragon wizard is in league with the San-keth? I thought so. This treachery ends now!"

"Stop this!" said Mazael. "This isn't a San-keth!"

"Do you take me for a fool?" said Trocend, all trace of his calm demeanor gone. "How else did hundreds of those damned changelings get into the castle? It only remains to be seen, Lord Mazael, if you were merely duped, or an active heretic..."

"I know it is hard to live a lie," said Harune.

Trocend froze, his face twisting.

"All your life you have labored in the shadows," said Harune quietly, "working to protect your lord from arcane threats, to keep his people safe. And yet, if they knew what you were, if they learned you were a false monk, they would kill you without mercy. I understand that. So strike me down, if you wish. I have fought to protect your home from the San-keth, but you know nothing of that. So I expect no gratitude, only violence."

Trocend said nothing, his hands knotting.

"Do you really think I allied with the San-keth to kill Lord Malden?" said Lucan, standing.

Trocend's bloodshot eyes shifted to Lucan.

"I can give you proof that I did not," said Lucan.

Trocend's lip twisted. "Can you?"

"If I had tried to kill Lord Malden," said Lucan, "he would already be dead. And you would have never known who had done it."

Trocend sneered. "You are an arrogant pup."

"Perhaps," said Lucan. "But I'm right."

Trocend stared at them. Mazael adjusted his grip on Lion. If Trocend decided to fight...

"We have not been introduced," said Trocend, his eyes flicking to Harune. Some his calm returned. "Perhaps you should explain to me why a San-keth with arms and legs is standing in my lord's castle."

"I am not San-keth," said Harune, "but Ang-kath."

Harune told Trocend everything he had told Mazael. He did not, though, mention Mazael's Demonsouled heritage. Trocend listened with a scowl, his gray brows knit, eyes glinting.

"Do you," said Trocend, when Harune had finished, "really expect me to believe that?"

Harune shrugged, scales rippling. "It is the truth."

"Is it?" said Trocend, shaking his head. "A fantastical tale, no doubt." But his voice held no conviction.

"You have heard the tales of Amalric's cruelties, how he waded through rivers of blood," said Harune.

"And does that make him Demonsouled?" said Trocend. "Men are cruel enough without diabolical influence."

"Do you believe in the San-keth?" said Harune.

Trocend scoffed. "I have seen the changelings. Do you think me a fool?"

"So, then, if you believe in the San-keth, is it so hard to believe in Demonsouled?"

"No," said Trocend, sighing. "No, it is not."

"We need your help," said Mazael, "to stop Amalric. You helped us against the changelings. Help us against Amalric."

Trocend said nothing.

"Amalric must be stopped," said Harune. "Trocend Castleson, your oath and your loyalty is to your lord. If you wish to serve him, if you wish to keep Knightcastle safe, then you must stop Amalric. Otherwise he will destroy Knightrealm with fire and sword, stain the walls of Knightcastle with blood. Lucan Mandragon. You wish to stop the dark powers?"

"How could you know that?" said Lucan, face cold.

"It is written in everything you do," said Harune. "If you wish to stop the dark powers, if you wish for no one to ever again experience your torment, then you must help stop Amalric. Lord Mazael. You want to keep your people safe from war and harm. Amalric will raze the Grim Marches, if he grows strong enough to become the Destroyer. He will destroy your lands, if he can, slaughter your people, and your betrothed will never be free of his shadow while he lives."

"I will do what I can," said Mazael, thinking of Romaria, thinking of the Old Demon, standing atop that altar. "If there is a way to stop him, then I will find it."

"And I am with you, too," said Timothy, hands clenched into fists. "I saw enough of that Demonsouled fiend Simonian at Castle Cravenlock."

"Lord Malden must know nothing of this," said Trocend.

"He would neither believe nor understand," said Harune. "He thinks the Dominiars came to kill him. When he marches against the Dominiars, we must come with him."

"We'll stop him," said Timothy. "By the gods, we will."

"The gods," said Trocend, "have nothing to do with the Demonsouled."

Mazael shuddered.

Lucan watched the others make their pact.

He needed power.

He had come so close to defeating Straganis. A little more power, just a little more arcane strength, and he could have rid the world of the Sanketh archpriest once and for all. Even a few seconds of extra strength would have proved sufficient.

His eyes strayed to Mazael's bloodstained tunic, lying in the corner.

The blood of even a minor Demonsouled carried tremendous power. The blood of a child of the Old Demon held great might. If Lucan could distill the essence of the blood, work it into an elixir, he could use it to power his spells, if only for a few moments.

As they left for Lord Malden's war council, Lucan pulled his mind-clouding glamour tighter and took the tunic.

He needed the strength. He would face Straganis again, no doubt, but this time he would triumph.

CHAPTER 23
DESTROYER

Sir Commander Amalric Galbraith stood on the walls of Castle Caerglamm, watching the sea.

The ancient castle sat on the high bluffs of the Mastarian coastline, its strong walls battered by centuries of storms. The landward walls faced grassy moors, dotted with occasional hills and boulders. A sea of tents now filled the moors, campfires crackling, the black Dominiar banner flapping in the sea breeze. The castle had been a druid stronghold, centuries ago, a nest of pagan worship. But the Dominiar Order had come and purified the castle in an orgy of slaughter.

Amalric watched the sea crash and foam against fallen boulders. He imagined it as a sea of blood, corpses choking the beach.

The vision would become real, soon enough. He would make it real.

The thought thrilled him.

He turned from the battlements, walking along the ramparts. It had begun, and nothing could turn it back. Nothing could stop Lord Malden and Grand Master Malleus from waging war upon each other. Amalric had failed to assassinate Lord Malden, but that didn't matter. War would come, and swiftly. Castle Caerglamm lay but two days' march from Tumblestone. They would march, and take Tumblestone, and then Knightcastle, and then...

And then...

The dark fire in his Demonsouled blood blazed, making him stronger.

Amalric smiled, closing a gloved hand.

He looked forward to the war, to killing Lord Mazael. Then man had proved an annoyance. He still had Mazael's foolish squire, rotting in a cell beneath Caerglamm. Perhaps he would present Mazael with the squire's head. Or perhaps he would give the boy to Straganis...

Of course, Malleus knew nothing of Amalric's alliance with the San-keth, nor of the changelings. The old man believed the San-keth legendary, a lie told to keep the commoners loyal to the church.

Nor did Malleus believe in Demonsouled.

Amalric laughed. He looked forward to the expression on Malleus's face when the old man leanred the truth. He looked forward to killing his sister.

He looked forward to many things.

"Amalric."

Amalric turned, annoyed and angry. Who had dared sneak up on him? For that matter, who even had the ability...

A man in a black robe stood on the ramparts, smiling at him.

Amalric's blood roared within him like thunder, power calling to greater power.

The gray-eyed, hawk-nosed man in the black robe had many names. Sometimes he went by the name of Mattias Comorian, a wandering jongleur, and sang songs of woe and death. Sometimes he called himself Simonian of Briault, a feared necromancer, and took the guise of an iron-bearded old man with murky eyes.

He had visited Knightcastle, millennia past, under the name of Marugot the Warlock, and convinced the last Roland king to ride to his death.

The Elderborn of the forest called him sar'diskhar, the Hand of Chaos.

In ancient Tristafel, long ago, they had called him the Malevagr.

But most folk knew him as the Old Demon, the last child of the Great Demon.

"Amalric," repeated the Old Demon.

Amalric dropped to one knee, head bowed. "My father."

The Old Demon beckoned. "Rise, my son."

Amalric obeyed and joined his father. The Old Demon gazed down at the sea. Sometimes a hint of red light glimmered deep in his eyes. Amalric felt the power in his father, the utter irresistible force.

"My son," repeated the Old Demon. "Tell me of yourself."

"It is beginning," said Amalric. "I have convinced Malleus to retake Tumblestone at any cost. And Lord Malden will fight, now that I have tried to murder him and his sons."

"Did you kill them?" said the Old Demon, indifferent.

"No."

"It matters not," said the Old Demon. "All mortals die, soon enough."

"I will kill them all."

"Yes," whispered the Old Demon.

"The war cannot be stopped now," said Amalric. "We march for

Tumblestone very soon."

"You have done well," said the Old Demon. "You have proved yourself worthy. Of all my children, you are the strongest."

Amalric's face twisted with hate. "I am the strongest."

"The worthiest," said the Old Demon. "I have something for you."

He opened his cloak and pulled free a sheathed sword.

Amalric's lips parted in wonder, his hand twitching towards the weapon.

From a scabbard of dark wood rose a hilt and crosspiece of crimson gold. The pommel had been carved in the shape of a roaring demon's head, the ears and fangs sharp as knives. Looking at it made the hair on Amalric's neck stand up. He sensed the power woven into the blade, worked into the very metal.

It called to his Demonsouled blood like a siren's song.

"It's yours," said the Old Demon, the sword resting on his palms. "Take it."

Amalric drew the sword from its scabbard, the blade rasping against the leather. The hilt felt like an extension of his hand. Long lines of runes ran down the center of the crimson blade, flashing with ruby light. Power seemed to thrum and crackle within the weapon, woven into the very steel.

The sun glinted off the metal, the blade gleaming like fresh-spilled blood.

"It is marvelous," said Amalric.

"It is a sword worthy of you," said the Old Demon. "A sword worthy of the Destroyer."

Amalric looked up.

"The time has come," said the Old Demon. "Of all my children, you have are the strongest. The world is yours, my son. You are the only one worthy to become the Destroyer."

"I am yours to command," said Amalric.

"Go from this place," said the Old Demon, "and lead your armies from here. Take Tumblestone. Take Knightcastle. Slaughter anyone who dares oppose you. Every death will make you stronger, make the blood of the Great Demon burn ever hotter within you. You will become the Destroyer. And when you are strong enough, when you are great enough, you can claim the throne of the Great Demon for yourself."

"But what of you, my father?" said Amalric.

"Myself?" said the Old Demon, distractedly, as if it did not matter a great deal. "Why, I shall watch over you from afar, as I have always done. I would seize the throne of my father, if I could." He sighed. "But it is not my destiny to do so. And even I cannot change my destiny." He glanced at Amalric. "But it is the Destroyer's destiny, your destiny, to replace the Great Demon and rule over the mortal races as a god over crawling insects.

And once you have become the Destroyer...why, I shall remain at your side forevermore."

Amalric did not know, and the Old Demon did not mention, that destinies could be stolen.

"We will make this world anew, you and I," said Amalric.

"Go," said the Old Demon, holding out the scabbard. Amalric took it. "You know what to do."

Amalric bowed low, turned, and began walking away.

"Oh, my son?"

Amalric turned again.

The Old Demon smiled, the red glint in his eyes brightening. "There is one thing I wish to ask of you, just one small thing."

"Anything, my father," said Amalric.

"Do you know Lord Mazael Cravenlock?" said the Old Demon, his voice darkening.

"My sister seduced him with her whorish ways," said Amalric, his own voice hardening.

"He is your half-brother," said the Old Demon, "my son."

Amalric stepped back a step, eyes widening.

"I once thought he could embrace his blood, embrace his potential," said the Old Demon. "I thought to make him the Destroyer. Instead he rejected both me and the gifts of his blood. He has chosen to live as a mortal, as a tame wolf among sheep." The red gleam spread across the Old Demon's eyes like a bloody glaze. "Kill him."

"I shall lay his head at your feet," said Amalric, banging his fist against his breastplate.

"Good," said the Old Demon. "Now go. Take what is yours by right."

Amalric blinked, and the Old Demon was gone.

He drew his old sword from its scabbard with his left hand. Grand Master Malleus himself had given Amalric that sword, years ago. Amalric had slain a thousand foes with it, slaughtered pagans and druids alike, won great glory for the Dominiar Order.

He flung it over the rampart wall. It hurtled end over end towards the sea, struck a boulder, and vanished into the waves.

With the sword of the Destroyer in hand, Amalric strode into Castle Caerglamm.

The castle had been taken and retaken many times during the Dominiars' wars against the Old Kingdoms. Every conqueror had rebuilt the castle to suit their own whims, and added their own network of secret vaults and escape tunnels.

Only Amalric knew them all.

Deep below the earth, he opened a secret door and stepped into a torchlit vault.

Dozens of changelings huddled against the walls, muttering to themselves. Sir Roger Gravesend sat with the female changeling, rubbing his injured jaw. Straganis stood in the center of the vault, whispering spells to himself, the fingers of his good arm writhing. Bit by bit a new arm emerged from the bloody stump of the old one, wet and fish-pale.

"Archpriest!" called Amalric, striding closer.

"Sir Commander," said Straganis, hissing. "Have you something for me?"

"Yes," said Amalric. "I do."

Roger Gravesend would have complained, but it hurt to talk. The right side of his jaw was a half-healed gash, and he lived in terror of infection. The wound made it painful to talk, to drink, even to eat. Of course, the massive bruise across his stomach would have made painful to eat in any case.

He moaned again.

"Shut your damned mouth," said Calibah, pacing besides him. "I am sick to death of your whining."

Roger almost retorted, but she might have killed him. Besides, talking hurt too much.

He turned away, and saw Amalric Galbraith walking towards Straganis. Roger watched with both interest and dread. Interest, because he still wanted to kill Mazael Cravenlock. Dread, because he did not want to face Mazael Cravenlock again. It was only sheer luck that Mazael had not killed him. Roger was tired of fighting, tired of hiding, tired of pain. He wanted to flee, to never have anything to do with the San-keth or Mazael Cravenlock again.

Amalric said something, and lifted his sword.

Something about that sword sent a jolt of terror down Sir Roger's spine. It looked forged from red gold, its pommel carved in the shape of a raging demon's head. Somehow, the sword looked hungry, thirsty for blood.

And as Roger gazed fascinated at the weapon, the blade burst into raging red flames.

Amalric wheeled and took off Straganis's head with a single slash.

The sword of the Destroyer roared like an inferno

Straganis's head rolled across the floor. The tongue flicked once, poison drooling from the fangs. The monstrous, deformed body went into spasms.

Amalric felt strength pouring into him like a river of molten steel. His own Demonsouled blood roared in response, filling him with power, encasing him in invincible armor.

Straganis's body went still. The changelings gaped at him in stunned silence.

"Master! " shrieked the female changeling at Sir Roger's side. "Master! " With a scream of rage she flung herself at Amalric, daggers in either hand, moving like a striking serpent.

Yet to Amalric she seemed so terribly slow.

He sidestepped and brought the sword hammering down. The blade ripped through her left shoulder, tore through her chest, and exploded from her right hip. She did not even have time to scream.

Amalric laughed.

The changelings rushed at him, yelling their rage. Sir Roger backed away, eyes wide.

Amalric walked to meet them, laughing.

Roger's back thumped against the stone wall. He heard a voice gibbering in utter horror, and realized it was his own.

Amalric strode unhindered through the ranks of the changelings. His blazing sword struck right, left, right, left, and every blow sent a dead changeling sprawling to the ground. Sometimes the changelings managed to land a blow, but Amalric's wounds healed in heartbeats.

Amalric laughed in fury the entire time. It reminded Sir Roger of Mazael Cravenlock.

But a thousand times worse.

Mazael Cravenlock was but a man. Amalric had become something alien. The rage in his eyes blazed like molten iron.

Then the last changeling fell, and Roger was alone with Amalric.

Amalric strode across the dead, kicking aside Calibah's head, his boots slapping against pools of blood. His sword blazed with the very fires of hell.

Roger raised his sword with a shaking hand. Amalric swung in an almost lazy slash. Roger's sword shattered, the shards gashing his face and hands. He fell to his knees with a scream, blood dripping into his mouth.

"Please," he croaked, sobbing, "please, don't kill me, I'll serve you, I'll do anything. Just don't kill me..."

How had things ever come to this?

Amalric barely deigned to notice him.

The burning blade came down, and Roger Gravesend lived just long enough to feel it split his skull.

With nothing left to kill, the sword of the Destroyer went dim.

Amalric gazed at the ripped corpses littering the vault. How many had tried to kill him? Yet he had killed them all, destroyed every last one of them without trace of injury.

In fact, he had never felt better. The fires of his Demonsouled blood raged through him, filling him with rage and power.

His work was not yet done.

Amalric strode from the vault, leaving Straganis and his minions to rot. A short time later he pushed open a set of double doors and marched into Castle Caerglamm's great hall.

The officers of the Dominiar Order sat around a long table covered with maps. Grand Master Malleus himself sat at their head, pointing at one of the maps, and looked up when Amalric entered.

"Where have you been?" growled Sir Commander Aeternis. "The council started an hour past!"

"Peace! " said Malleus, raising a hand. "We are all brothers here, after all."

"No," said Amalric, "we are not."

Malleus's white eyebrows lifted in angry surprise. "I beg your pardon, Sir Commander?"

Amalric saw horrified shock flood into Malleus's eyes. Perhaps the bloodstains on Amalric's armor had warned the Grand Master. Or perhaps it was the fierce, exultant expression on Amalric's face, so different than his usual grim scowl. Whatever the reason, Malleus shot to his feet, fumbling for his sword, and so the blow that would have decapitated him plunged into his belly instead.

Malleus toppled to the floor, clutching his stomach, blood leaking from his fingers.

The sword of the Destroyer burst anew into raging flames.

The commanders and preceptors of the Dominiar Order jumped to their feet with cries of shock and rage, drawing their weapons, and came at Amalric.

"Traitor!" roared Aeternis. "You damned traitor!"

Amalric laughed and met their attack, the sword roaring in his hand. He killed two preceptors and a commander, sent their bodies crumpling to the floor in sprays of blood. Then the sheer number of his enemies caught him, slamming him against the wall. Hands grabbed at his throat and hair, and sword and dagger points plunged into him.

Aeternis's fingers dug into Amalric's throat.

Amalric seized Aeternis's forearm with his free hand. It was an utterly useless hold; he had no leverage, no grip.

Yet he snapped the bones of Aeternis's forearm. Aeternis fell back in pained shock, eyes bulging. Amalric heaved and pushed himself away from the wall.

The commanders and preceptors of the Dominiar Order went flying, chaff in the wind before his Demonsouled strength. The wounds inflicted by their swords and daggers vanished like smoke. Amalric howled with laughter, stepped forward, and the slaughter began.

He made it a point to kill Aeternis first. His boot slammed down, shattering Aeternis's sword hand. Aeternis rolled over with a groan, his useless arms held out before him. Amalric swung his blazing sword and reduced Aeternis's skull to bloody mush.

The commanders and preceptors were skilled, hard men, veterans of the campaigns against the Old Kingdoms, knights who had defeated dozens of foes in battle. Amalric had led most of them on campaign. None of them ran, and Amalric cut them all down, the sword of the Destroyer ripping through steel plate and chain mail like cloth.

The last Dominiar died with a gurgling scream, Silence fell over the bloodstained hall. Amalric turned a slow circle, surveying the carnage. He wondered if he ought to feel grief. After all, these men had been his colleagues for years, his comrades, and some had been his mentors. And he had just murdered them all without mercy. He ought to feel grief.

Instead, he felt nothing but a fierce joy, as if he had finally seized his destiny, as if he had finally become what he was meant to be.

A wire clicked, and something hard slammed into his back, a burst of pain rocketing through him. He looked down and saw a crossbow bolt jutting from his stomach, the head battered and bloody from its passage through his armor and innards.

Grand Master Malleus leaned against a chair, a crossbow clutched in his hands. His face was white and bloodless, his mouth twisted in a rictus of agony and rage. Amalric wondered how the dying old man had found the strength to aim the crossbow, let alone load it.

"You were a son to me!" said Malleus, his voice thick with pain. The crossbow fell from his trembling hands. "How could you do this? How? How?"

Amalric reached down and yanked the quarrel from his stomach. It ripped out a long gobbet of flesh. The wound burned like a hot coal, but pain no longer meant anything to Amalric. After all, the wound had already begun to close.

Malleus's eyes widened. "This...this can't..."

Amalric strode across the room and shattered Malleus's elbows and knees in quick succession. The old man's howl of pain drowned out the snap of breaking bones. Amalric seized Malleus's collar and dragged him onto the balcony behind the great hall, overlooking the ocean far below.

Amalric lifted Malleus high and flung the old man over the railing.

Grand Master Malleus, the conqueror of the Old Kingdoms, screamed all the way down. He bounced off the cliffs once or twice and disappeared into the sea. Amalric watched the churning waters for a few moments, smiling, and walked back into the great hall.

Some Dominiars and a few servants stood in the hall, gaping in horror at the slaughter. A few had fallen to their knees, weeping.

"Sir Commander!" said one of the Dominiars, gazing at Amalric. "We had thought all the commanders were dead!"

"Lord Malden sent the San-keth to murder the Grand Master and the commanders," said Amalric. "I barely escaped. You can find the bodies of the San-keth in the vaults below the castle."

They stared at him.

"Move! " he roared, gesturing with his sword. The fire of his Demonsouled blood entered his voice, filling his words with power. "Shall we let this grievous blow go unavenged?"

They ran.

Amalric laughed. It had been so easy.

"I will lead the armies of Knightrealm myself," announced Lord Malden to the assembled vassals, standing on the dais of the Hall of Triumph. The squires had fitted him in his splendid silver-plated armor. Mazael stood below him, half-listening to the speeches, his thoughts dark and heavy.

A flicker of movement caught his eye.

A ragged, bloody man staggered from behind the nearest pillar. Dried blood caked his clothes, and Mazael glimpsed half-healed wounds through the rags. Yet the man's hands remained sure and steady as they brought the crossbow up.

Mazael saw the yellow glint of a changeling's eyes.

Somehow, one of them had survived.

"My lord!" bellowed Mazael, springing at Lord Malden. "Down!"

A pair of armsmen plunged their swords into the changeling, even as the crossbow fired. The errant bolt shot past Lord Malden's ear and plunged into Sir Garain's throat. The stout man fell down the steps of the dais, his head cracking hard against the marble floor.

"Garain!" shouted Lord Malden.

Mazael rushed to Garain's side, ignoring the changeling's dying scream. It was too late. Garain, Lord Malden's eldest son, his chancellor and wisest counselor, had been dead even before he hit the floor.

Lord Malden fell to his knees, weeping. All the court of Knightcastle looked on, waiting for Lord Malden to rise in vengeful wrath, as he had when Belifane and Mandor had been killed.

Yet the old man did not rise, did not even look up as the priests and the physicians swarmed to his side.

"Oh gods." Mazael turned as Morebeth joined him. Her hands flew to her mouth, her gray eyes wide. "Oh gods. How…"

"A changeling," said Mazael, "the damned thing must have survived, must have hidden itself…"

"What will you do now?" said Morebeth, voice quiet.

Mazael looked at Lord Malden. Gerald and Tobias had joined their father, and Rachel was weeping. The Dominiars were coming with a child of the Old Demon, and the Lord of Knightcastle knelt broken and weeping by his dead son.

"I don't know," said Mazael. "I don't know."

An hour later the army of the Dominiars marched north, making for Tumblestone. Amalric's speech had filled them with madness and bloodlust, with a desire to put the lands of Knightrealm to fire and sword.

Grand Master Amalric Galbraith rode at their head, the sword of the Destroyer in hand.

CHAPTER 24
CHAMPION OF KNIGHTCASTLE

"You have to talk to him," said Sir Tobias. For the first time that Mazael could recall, Tobias looked anxious, even frightened.

Mazael did not blame him.

Knightcastle had fallen into fearful paralysis. Lord Malden had disappeared into the Kings' Chapel, the ancient chapel of the Roland kings, and had not emerged since Sir Garain's murder three days past. The gathered armies of Knightrealm and the Justiciar Order waited outside Knightcastle, disturbed and uneasy.

And dark rumors came from the south. Some whispers said that Malleus had marched, slaughtering every peasant in his path. Other rumors claimed that Malleus had already laid siege to Tumblestone. And the darkest rumor said Amalric Galbraith had murdered Malleus and seized command of the Dominiars, and now rode at their head with a sword of hellfire.

"You have to talk to him," said Tobias, again. His voice quavered. The realization that he was now the heir to Knightcastle had hit him hard.

"Why would he listen to me?" said Mazael.

He stood in the High Court with Morebeth, Tobias, Gerald, Trocend, and Rachel. All looked tired, and Trocend himself looked awful. Everyone had always assumed that one day Lord Malden would die, and Garain would become the new Lord of Knightcastle.

His death had been hard.

"He won't listen to us!" said Trocend. A slight tremor went through his blue-veined hands. "He sits in the chapel and broods over Sir Garain's body. Now is not the time for grief! The Dominiars are moving against us, and we can expect them to lay siege to Tumblestone any day. Yet Lord Malden does nothing." He began to pace, shaking his head. "The vassals grow restless. Some want to return to their lands, to defend their keeps against the Dominiars. If that happens, we will lose Tumblestone, and the Dominiars will conquer us one by one. We must ride out and defeat them, with Lord Malden at our head."

"I tried talking to him," said Tobias. "He wouldn't listen. He just sat there, staring at nothing. I don't think he even noticed me. After a while I gave up and left."

"Garain could have talked sense into him," said Gerald. Rachel squeezed his arm. "Garain always did, when our father was bent on doing something foolish. And now...and now..."

They stood in grim silence for a moment.

"He won't listen to me," said Mazael.

"He will," said Rachel, trying to smile. "You shouted at him until he agreed to let Gerald marry me, didn't you?"

"You were the only one who could ever argue with him," said Tobias.

Mazael lowered his head. He had tried to avoid this war, and now that the war had come, Lord Malden had lost the will to fight. It was a bitter irony. And if Lord Malden did not take command, did not lead his men to battle, the Dominiars would conquer Knightrealm

And Amalric Galbraith would become the Destroyer, and the Old Demon would triumph.

Mazael closed his fists. "I will talk to him."

He walked across the High Court, towards the Kings' Chapel, Morebeth following after him.

"They need you," said Morebeth.

Mazael stopped, looked at her.

"They need someone strong to lead them," said Morebeth. Her face twisted. "Otherwise they will simply bicker and panic until Amalric comes to kill us all."

Mazael stared at her. Did she know Amalric was Demonsouled? He thought about telling her. But then she might realize the truth about his own nature. He could not risk that.

"Amalric has to be stopped, whatever happens," said Mazael. "We've...both seen what he is like." Morebeth nodded, her gray eyes sad. "A man like him should not conquer a kingdom. He would become a tyrant."

"And you alone are strong enough to stop him," said Morebeth. "If Lord Malden will not lead...then you must."

Mazael flinched. "Me?"

"You," said Morebeth, taking his hands. "You must. Neither Sir Tobias nor Sir Gerald can. There is no one else. You were once one of Lord Malden's household knights, were you not? His men still remember you, still respect you. Even the Justiciars will follow you. You saved Sir

Commander Galan's life, after all."

"I'll do what I can," said Mazael. "Wait here."

Morebeth nodded. "I doubt Lord Malden would be pleased to see me."

Mazael walked to the Chapel, opened the doors, and walked into the gloomy nave. Rays of colored light slanted through stained-glass windows celebrating the triumph of Rolands long dead. A half-dozen monks shuffled around the altar, burning incense, muttering prayers for Garain's soul. Garain himself lay on a bier, covered with a shroud, surrounded by a ring of candles.

Lord Malden sat slumped in the pew before the bier, head bowed, face hidden beneath his unwashed gray hair. He had not even bothered to put on a hat.

Mazael walked to his side. "My lord."

Lord Malden did not move. For a fearful instant Mazael wondered if the old man had died of grief.

"My lord."

Lord Malden looked up, tears glittering on his cheeks. "I wish to speak with no one. Leave me."

"No," said Mazael.

"Leave me!"

"No," repeated Mazael.

Lord Malden's bloodshot eyes narrowed, and for a moment his old glare returned. Then looked away and slumped back into the pew. "Do as you wish. I care not."

"You have to hold court," said Mazael.

Lord Malden said nothing.

"The Dominiars have marched," said Mazael. "They're probably laying siege to Tumblestone as we speak. If Tumblestone falls, there will be nothing to stop them from marching into Knightrealm, maybe even to Knightcastle. You must act now."

Still Lord Malden said nothing.

"Are you listening to me?" said Mazael. For a moment he wanted to strike the other man. He fought the urge down, fearing that it came from his Demonsouled blood.

"You were right," said Lord Malden.

Mazael blinked.

Lord Malden looked up. He seemed to have aged twenty years in the last three days. Mazael had seen Lord Malden angry and sad, exultant and mournful. But never had Lord Malden looked so weary.

For the first time that Mazael could remember, Lord Malden looked genuinely old.

"You warned me, didn't you?" said Lord Malden. "I already lost both

Belifane and Mandor to my wars. You said that if I went to war again, more of my sons would die."

"I did," said Mazael. He had forgotten that.

"Now war comes," said Lord Malden. "And my son lies dead on this bier. He should have been the Lord of Knightcastle after me. He would have made a good Lord. A better Lord than I, I think. My folly has slain him. Now leave me."

"You yet have two sons," said Mazael. "Fight for them. And you have Knightcastle, and your lands, and your people. They need you to defend them."

"Power and lands?" snarled Lord Malden, his voice shaking. "Those things are empty and meaningless. I thought you knew that already. Well, you'll learn it soon enough."

"Are your oaths to your people meaningless?" said Mazael. "A lord swears to defend his people?"

"How many other fathers will see their sons die in the coming months?" said Lord Malden.

"And how many more will die if you do not act?" said Mazael.

"Leave me!" said Lord Malden. "I am weary of life. Go!"

"With or without Tumblestone, this war still would have come," said Mazael.

"Then should I have simply given up Tumblestone?" said Lord Malden. "Should I have made Mandor's sacrifice meaningless?" He laughed, his voice shrill and unsteady. "But it seems I have, haven't I? Garain is dead, for nothing, and once the Dominiars take Tumblestone, Mandor will have died for nothing, too."

"Even if you had given up Tumblestone, war still would have come, in the end," said Mazael. He hesitated. "Amalric Galbraith is Demonsouled."

"There's no such thing," said Lord Malden.

"Don't be a fool," said Mazael, his anger growing. Lord Malden flinched as if slapped. "I've seen San-keth and Demonsouled with my own eyes. And you have, too, at least the San-keth. Keep lying to yourself if you wish. It's Amalric who convinced Malleus to retake Tumblestone, Amalric who allied with the San-keth, and Amalric who is coming for your people. Perhaps it would mean nothing if Malleus conquered Knightcastle. Perhaps one lord is much the same as another, at least to the peasants. But a Demonsouled, Lord Malden...would you give your people over to his hands? You've heard the stories of what Amalric did the Old Kingdoms...will you let him do the same to Knightrealm?"

Lord Malden stared up at Mazael.

"You might," said Mazael, "but I will not. If you will not defend your people then I will." He turned to go.

"Wait."

Mazael looked back.

Lord Malden rose. "I will hold court."

A dusty, weary messenger knelt before Lord Malden.

Lord Malden sat on his throne in the Hall of Triumphs. The banners, the statues, the shields, the triumphs of long-forgotten wars, seemed to mock the grief-stricken man slumped on the throne. Mazael, standing by Lord Malden's side, wondered if he was paying attention.

"Rainier Agravain, Lord of Tumblestone, and your loyal vassal," said the messenger, "sends word to you, Lord Malden, begging for your aid."

Lord Malden stared down, his faced etched with despair.

"The host of the Dominiars has marched," said the messenger. "They have burned every village in their path, seized all the crops." He swallowed and made a sign to ward off evil. "They...slaughtered all the peasants in their path. Even the women and the children. The Dominiars...they impaled them. Mounted them on stakes ringed around the burning villages. I saw it with my own eyes, my lord. It was like a scene out of hell."

A muscle in Lord Malden's face twitched, but he did not speak.

"Who commands the Dominiars?" said Mazael. "Malleus?"

"No, Lord Mazael," said the messenger. "According to the rumors," he glanced at Lord Malden, "our lord Malden sent San-keth assassins to murder Malleus and most of the Dominiar commanders. The Dominiar heralds call out the name of Grand Master Amalric Galbraith."

Mazael saw Morebeth's lip curl into a sneer.

"They were marching up the coast," said the messenger, "destroying every village in their path. Lord Rainier has only two hundred knights and a thousand militia from the city. The Dominiars have at least ten thousand men, a great host. Perhaps fifteen thousand, and maybe even twenty thousand. Lord Rainier dared not stand against them. He withdrew behind the walls of Tumblestone, along with many peasants fleeing the Dominiar armies."

"Have they laid siege yet?" said Mazael.

"They had not when Lord Rainier sent me," said the messenger, "though they were preparing to do so." He shook his head. "Tumblestone will have fallen under siege by now. Lord Malden, you must not let the city fall. The Dominiars will slaughter everyone within the walls, if they can." His eyes darted to Mazael, then back to Lord Malden. "My lord, we must march at once, if we are to lift the siege."

"What hope is there?" said Lord Malden, his voice soft and cracked. "More death, more slaughter, more ruin...that is all that awaits us." He lapsed into a grim silence.

An uneasy rustle went through the assembled lords and knights. Mazael scowled. If they fled back to their castles, there would be no way to stop the Dominiars, no way to turn back Amalric.

"Lord," said Mazael. Lord Malden turned watery eyes towards him. "You must ride out. There is no else who can lead your vassals, your knights. Knightrealm will fall, unless you can find the will to defend it."

"I am an old man," whispered Lord Malden, "why will they not leave me in peace?"

"The Justiciar Order will ride to defeat the Dominiars," said Sir Commander Galan Hawking, stepping from the Justiciar Knights. "With or without Lord Malden's help. The Dominiars are our ancient enemies, and once they enter Knightrealm they will come for us. We have five hundred knights and a thousand footmen here with us. Our Grand Master at Swordor will send more, but they will not arrive for at least a week. The Dominiars are stronger than us. We will have a better chance of victory if Knightcastle and Swordor stand together against the Dominiars."

Lord Malden's mouth twitched.

"If you will not go yourself," said Mazael, "then appoint someone to lead your army. Give the command to Sir Tobias, or Sir Gerald, or one of your vassals." He scowled. "Even give it to the Justiciars. Someone must defend your lands."

"Tobias," said Lord Malden, his voice a thick rasp. "Come here."

Sir Tobias approached the dais, his jaw set.

"You are my eldest son now," said Lord Malden, "the heir to Knightcastle. I...cannot lead our host against the Dominiars. I no longer have strength or will. You must take command, my son, and defend our lands and people."

"Father," said Tobias, swallowing. "I cannot—"

"Why not?" said Lord Malden, scowling. "You have led men in battle before. You have ridden well in tournaments across the land. And more, you are a Roland. The right to command is in your blood."

"I have never led the whole host of Knightrealm," said Tobias. His face worked. "It...I am not ready. If I take command...we could very well be defeated. What would then become of our lands and people?"

Lord Malden snarled. "If you will not do your duty..."

"Give Lord Mazael the command," said Tobias.

Mazael flinched. Morebeth smiled.

"He defeated the Dominiars once before at Tumblestone," said Tobias. "We always claimed that Sir Mandor had won the victory...but he had been dead for days by then. It was Mazael who took command, Mazael who won Tumblestone for us. He defeated his brother and became Lord of Castle Cravenlock. And he won the great tournament, did he not? Give him the command."

"I will follow Lord Mazael," Sir Gerald, stepping forward. "It would be nothing new, after all."

"If Lord Mazael takes command," said Sir Commander Galan, "then I will follow his will. He is the best commander among us all."

"I know my brother," said Morebeth, her voice ringing like a trumpet. All eyes turned to face her. "He is a hard and ruthless man. He will not stop until the Dominiar banner flies over Knightcastle and the people of Knightrealm have been made his slaves. Lord Mazael is strong enough to defeat Amalric. You must give him this command, Lord Malden. It is your only hope."

Lord Malden bowed his head, chin almost touching his chest. For a long moment he sat that way. Mazael wondered if he would ever look up again, or if the despair and grief had crushed his heart.

He looked up.

"Go, Lord Mazael," Lord Malden said, his voice little more than a faint rasp. "I name you the Lord Champion of Knightcastle, and give you authority to lead my armies in battle and to defend Tumblestone from the Dominiars. Go and do as you will. It matters very little to me, any more."

"I will, my lord," said Mazael.

Lord Malden said nothing.

Mazael turned, saw the assembled court of Knightcastle staring at him. "We fight," he said.

###

The fields between Knightcastle and Castle Town rumbled with the clap of hooves, the tramp of boots, and the groan of cartwheels. Clouds of dust rose high, staining the blue sky. Mazael rode on Mantle, a squire leading Chariot by the reins.

He wondered if Adalar yet lived.

Behind him rode a gaggle of lords and knights.

"Lord Tancred," said Mazael. The stout lord rode up. "Sir Garain was in charge of the train and supplies. Take over for him. Have the wagons and the mules ready by midday."

Lord Tancred bowed and rode away.

"Gerald!" said Mazael. Gerald joined him, Wesson jogging after. "Take charge of the footmen. Get them ready to march. Again, I want to be gone by midday."

Gerald nodded, then sighed. "Off to war against the Dominiars again, Mazael. You'd think the last time would have settled it."

"You'd think," said Mazael. Of course, five years ago the Dominiars had not been led by a Demonsouled, nor had Mazael known of his own dark nature. Life had been simpler. "Get going. We'll have plenty of time to reminisce on the march." Gerald nodded again and rode off, Wesson racing after.

"Sir Tobias!" called Mazael. Tobias looked happier already, now that the burden of responsibility had been lifted from him. "Take charge of the household knights and the vassals. Terrorize the proud fools into obedience if you must, but get them ready." Lord Malden's household knights, reliant upon Lord Malden's goodwill, were reliable, well-trained, and obedient. Lord Malden's vassals, each proud, ruthless, and commanding a band of knights and armsmen, were not. In the face of the disciplined Dominiar footmen and knights, an ill-timed charge from a glory-hungry vassal might get them all killed. "Have them ready to ride..."

"By midday," said Tobias.

"Glad someone was listening," said Mazael. "Go. Amalric will not wait upon our convenience."

Tobias galloped away. Mazael put heels to Mantle and rode for Knightcastle's barbican. Sir Aulus rode before him, the Cravenlock and Roland banners streaming from his lance. Four other horsemen rode below the walls of Knightcastle, and Mazael saw Timothy, Lucan, Trocend, and Harune Dustfoot riding toward him.

"We are with you, my lord," said Timothy, closing his fist. "I've seen tyrants like this Amalric before, and I won't let another one rise."

"Yes," said Lucan. He had abandoned his glamour of mind-clouding, choosing instead to disguise himself as a common armsman. Perhaps he wished to conserve his power. "And if Straganis comes for you again, you will need me."

"Everything is at stake here," said Harune, again hidden in his magical disguise. While Trocend had accepted the Ang-kath, Mazael doubted that anyone else would have done so. "We cannot fail. The cost would be to great."

"Rather understating things, I daresay," said Trocend.

"Good," said Mazael, reining up. "Wait here. We'll join the rest of the host after I'm finished here." He slid from the saddle and walked to the great arch of the gate. Many noble ladies stood there, watching their husbands ride off to war.

Rachel came up, hugged him. Mazael wasn't worried for her safety. The San-keth had tried to kill her, but the San-keth had been tools of Amalric. And Amalric's attention was focused upon war.

"Be safe," she whispered. "Come back to us."

"I will," said Mazael. "And I'll bring Gerald back, too." He hoped to the gods he found a way to do it.

She smiled, blinking back tears. "I...should be worried about Gerald. But I know he'll come back. I just know it." She bit her lip. "It's you I'm worried about. I'm worried that you won't come back at all. Or that something terrible will happen to you."

"I will come back," said Mazael.

Rachel kissed him on the cheek. "Be careful." She smiled again, sadly, and walked away.

Mazael watched her go, then saw Morebeth standing in the shadow of the arch. She came to him and gave him a forceful kiss that lasted for a long time.

"I think," said Mazael, "that they can spare me for a few minutes."

"No," she said, eyes glinting, "they can't. But I'll be waiting for you when you come back. Make that bastard Amalric regret that he ever met you."

"I will," said Mazael, "if I can."

"Of course you can," said Morebeth. "You're stronger than he ever will be. You'll defeat him and the Dominiars." She gave him a crooked smile. "Perhaps we'll have our wedding in the great hall of Castle Dominus."

"Perhaps," said Mazael. He gave her one last kiss, then went to rejoin his army.

CHAPTER 25
THE BATTLE OF TUMBLESTONE

They left at midday, crossing the Riversteel at Castle Town's great bridge, and swung to the south. Lord Malden's household knights rode in the van, along with the vassals and their knights, followed by a long column of footmen. Behind the footmen came the rumbling chaos of the supply train, wagons with cursing drivers, mules burdened with supplies. The Justiciar Knights rode in their own columns, knights at the front, footmen marching behind.

Mazael rode back and forth along the host, watching the men. The knights were battle-ready and skilled with weapons, though lacking in necessary discipline. Most of the footmen were peasant conscripts, and Mazael saw some men who carried their weapons well, veterans of Lord Malden's last campaign against the Dominiars. He even recognized some.

But he saw far too many young men, little more than boys, too young to have marched against the Dominiars five years past. He doubted that any of them had ever seen a serious battle. How many knew how to use a spear?

For that matter, how many would lie dead in a week's time? How many more would lose a hand or an arm, maimed for life? But if Amalric conquered Knightcastle, if he became the Destroyer, all these men would die, and many more besides. Mazael steeled himself. Mazael had fought to stop this war, but if war was the only way to stop Amalric, then he would wage it.

The Justiciars, at least, were disciplined, their footmen well-drilled and well-trained, the Knights riding in lockstep. Mazael might have no choice but to rely on Galan Hawking's men. The Dominiars were at least as disciplined as the Justiciars, if not more so.

They managed ten miles and made camp by the banks of the Riversteel. Mazael gave orders for the men to dig ditches for defense and for latrines, forbidding them from relieving themselves into the river. He did not want the army dying of dysentery before they even reached Tumblestone. A few judicious whippings of offenders emphasized his point, and the Riversteel remained mostly clean. Mazael left watch duty to the Justiciars and the household knights and went to sleep, half-expecting to dream of the Old Demon.

But if Mazael dreamed, he did not remember it.

They resumed their southward march the next day, pulling away from the valley and into hillier country. The terrain, at least, did not hinder them. Generations of Roland lords had devoted themselves to road-building, reaping vast income from tolls, and Lord Malden had been no exception. The march remained smooth, despite the hills rising into the low mountain ridge that divided Knights' Bay and Tumblestone from the rest of Lord Malden's domain.

On the third day they saw standing-stones crowning some of the hills, ancient rings of weathered monoliths. The pagan druids of the Old Kingdoms had once worshiped in these hills, praying to their gods of earth and wind. The Rolands, the Dominiars, and the Justiciars had all set themselves to exterminating the druids, and now only their menhirs remained. Mazael gazed up at the ancient stones, lost in thought. Romaria would have hated the long-ago butchery, just as she would have hated Amalric's cruelty.

Shortly before midday, they came to the slaughtered village.

Only a few folk dwelt in the hills, miners and goat-herders, living in isolated villages of stone and timber. But stone walls had been knocked down, and most of the timbers burned. The remaining timbers had been set in a ring around the village.

And atop the jagged end of every timber dangled the impaled corpse of a villager, men, women, and children, their foreheads branded with the sign of the Dominiar Order.

"Find them," snarled Mazael, staring at a dead girl. "Find them now."

The outriders scoured the hills, and found no trace of any Dominiars. But Mazael had other resources at his disposal. Trocend and Timothy worked divinations, and found a band of a hundred Dominiar footmen lurking in a wooded ravine seven miles southward. Mazael marched the army south, sealed off the ravine, and sent in the men.

The battle was very short. The horror at the village had put a fire in every man, from the proudest vassal to the lowliest footmen. Lord Malden's justice was often harsh, and that of the Justiciars more so.

But no one did such things in Knightrealm and lived.

After the last Dominiar had been killed the army camped, and Mazael took counsel with his commanders.

"There are at least three more bands like this roving the hills," said Trocend, face feverish. Divination spells seemed taxing work, and necessity had forced Trocend and Timothy to work their spells constantly. "Pillaging, burning, and murdering, I doubt not. Sent ahead of the main Dominiar host, most likely."

Mazael scowled into the campfires. "That's not good."

"No, it's not," said Sir Commander Galan. "There's only one good pass through the mountains, and it leads straight to Tumblestone. If Amalric is confident enough to send parties ahead...that means Tumblestone has already fallen."

"Or," said Tobias, "Amalric is confident that Tumblestone will fall, and he can spare the men."

"That," said Gerald, "or that he has raised enough men that the absence of a few hundred does not trouble him at all."

"None of those possibilities are good," said Mazael. "But if Tumblestone had fallen, then Amalric and the main Dominiar host would be here already. He'd have left only a small garrison to defend Tumblestone. Trocend. Timothy. Are there any signs of the main Dominiar force coming through the pass?"

Trocend and Timothy shook their heads in unison. Mazael's eyes flicked over to a nearby tent, where Lucan leaned against a spear, disguised as a common footman, though that damned raven still perched on his shoulder. He gave a slow shake of his head.

"Though," added Trocend, "I think there may be men in the pass. At least a thousand."

"Damnation," said Mazael. "Amalric sent men to fortify the pass. These marauders are just raiding parties, nothing more. Damn him. A thousand men could hold that pass against even a large army for weeks, if they were well-provisioned."

"We don't have weeks," said Tobias. "Tumblestone is strong, and Lord Rainier is a grim fighter...but not even Tumblestone's walls could turn the whole might of the Dominiar Order."

"No," said Mazael, "we have no time. None at all." He thought for a moment, head bowed. "We will keep marching to the pass. We can do nothing until we see how matters stand there. If we have to force the pass, so be it."

"Tumblestone might fall while we tarry," said Gerald, his blue eyes flinty, "and its people fall into the hands of that butcher Amalric." The slaughter at the village had filled him an icy, merciless fury. If Tobias died young and if Gerald came to the lordship of Knightcastle, then the Dominiars would have an enemy more implacable than Lord Malden.

"It might," said Mazael, shaking his head. The thought filled him with disgust. "It might. Then we will face Amalric and the Dominiars in the pass or in the hills, and do what we can to avenge the folk of Tumblestone. But if we have the chance to save Tumblestone, then we must take it." He looked to Trocend and Timothy. "Keep working your spells. If we come across any more raiding parties, we will take them. And if you find any scouts, kill them. I want no survivors to warn the men at the pass, or even Amalric himself. If we can take them by surprise, all the better."

They carried out his orders.

The next day, the fourth from Knightcastle, they came to the pass.

The hills climbed sharply into craggy, weathered mountains. A single pass, little more than a steep-sided valley, cut through the mountains. After the conquest of Tumblestone, Lord Malden had built a broad road through the bottom of the valley.

Now the road had been dug up and piled into an earthwork across the narrowest part of the pass. Sharpened, fire-hardened stakes stood at angle before the earthworks. Behind the wall Mazael glimpsed the glint of armor, and the cold eyes of watching Dominiar footmen.

Mazael swore, at length, under his breath. He rode with his commanders towards the wall, stopping just out of bowshot.

"You were right, Mazael," said Gerald. "This isn't good."

"Not at all," agreed Mazael, watching the earthwork. It even had a sturdy wooden gate. "Not at all." He half-hoped for the gate to burst open, for the Dominiars to launch a sortie. Mazael might then have a chance to storm the fortification.

But the gate remained closed.

"They even have a pair of catapults back there," said Trocend, his left hand tracing spells, "and at least a half-dozen ballistas." He grunted, fingers twitching. "Probably more."

"Can we force it?" said Mazael.

"Probably," said Sir Commander Galan. He shook his head. "Perhaps. But it would be a dreadful bloody slaughter. We'd lose...oh, perhaps a third of the footmen."

"Gods," muttered Mazael. That would come to over four thousand men.

"And that assumes our men will not break," said Gerald. "In the face of such slaughter, they might turn and run."

Galan gave him a look. "My armsmen will not break."

"They won't," said Mazael, "but your footmen are professional fighters. Most of ours are peasant conscripts. Brave enough, aye, but if the battle turns against them, they'll run." He glanced back at their army. "And your thousand aren't enough to force the pass."

"So what do we do?" said Tobias.

Mazael didn't know.

"Might we lay siege?" said Lord Tancred, mopping his sweating brow. "If we cannot take it by storm?"

"We cannot," said Gerald. "If we delay much longer, Tumblestone will fall."

"We may have no choice but to let Tumblestone fall and face Amalric on a ground of our choosing," said Galan.

Gerald scowled. "Then shall we sell the people of Tumblestone over to that butcher?"

"We can't besiege that fortification in any case," snapped Mazael, cutting off Lord Tancred. "Sieges only succeed when you starve out your enemy. They can bring up as much provender as they need, I doubt not, and have ample supplies of water."

"Tumblestone may have already fallen," said Galan.

"No," said Mazael. "If it had, the main Dominiar host would already be here."

"I doubt we can save Tumblestone," said Galan. "Let us then fortify this end of the pass, preparing our own earthworks and defenses. When Amalric comes, let him spend his men to break into Knightrealm proper."

"We would fail," said Mazael. "This pass is the quickest path from Tumblestone to Knightcastle, but it's only a day and a half ride around the mountains to the south. Amalric has only to swing around the mountains to come upon our flanks. Then we'll be trapped between him and the force in the pass."

"Then let us march around the mountains ourselves!" said Tobias.

Mazael shook his head. "And a thousand men will watch us march away. They'll send warning to Amalric, and he'll be ready for us. Besides, it's a day and a half's ride, but a three days' march for an army of this size." He paused. "Tumblestone will fall by then."

"It might have fallen already," muttered Galan.

"We can't go through the pass," growled Tobias, "and we can't go around, and we can't wait for the Dominiars here. What are we going to do?"

It had been five years since Mazael had commanded this many men in battle, and he had not forgotten the weight, the fearful burden. If he made an error, if his judgment proved unsound, thousands would die. Of course, if he did nothing, then Amalric would kill tens of thousands anyway. He had to find a way to save Tumblestone, had to find a way to stop Amalric before he slaughtered more innocents. Mazael stared at the pass, eyes hard, mouth pulled into a grim line.

He saw a way to do both. It was a horrible risk, but Mazael saw no other choice. If he tried to force his way through the pass, his army might fall apart. If he tried to circle around the mountains, Amalric would meet him and destroy him. And if he sat here, thousands would die in Tumblestone.

"This is what we're going to do," said Mazael.

The others looked at him.

"We'll dig in, as if for a siege," said Mazael. "Arrange the footmen, facing the earthworks. Then the horsemen will slip away from the rear, and make their way south, around the mountains, and ride for Tumblestone."

"Is that wise?" said Galan, frowning. "Splitting our force in the face of a stronger enemy?"

"Even with our full strength," said Trocend, "we barely match the Dominiars for numbers. If just the knights reach Tumblestone, they will be badly outnumbered."

"But," said Tobias, "the Dominiars will be besieging the city." His eyes glinted. "The footmen do all the work in the siege. The Dominiar Knights will be unhorsed, resting among the tents. If we come on them unawares, we might sweep them away."

"Their scouts will see us long before we can surprise them," said Galan, shaking his head.

"Trocend's arts can find their scouts," said Mazael. "We can kill them before they warn Amalric. If we hit them hard and fast enough, we can throw them into flight, drive them off at our leisure."

"Risky," said Gerald and Galan, in near-unison.

"Oh, aye," said Mazael, "but can you think of anything better?"

No one did.

"What if the Dominiars holding the pass try to break out, attack our footmen?" said Gerald. "They might put our footmen to flight."

"We'll leave the Justiciar foot," said Mazael. "Can your men stand a Dominiar charge?"

Galan scoffed. "We have fought the corrupt Dominiar Order for centuries. My men can stand a charge, and will hold your footmen firm."

"So," said Mazael. "The footmen will remain here. If we do it properly, the Dominiars in the pass will think our entire army remains. The knights will ride around the mountains, and with the aid of Trocend's and Timothy's arts, we will take the Dominiars besieging Tumblestone unawares."

"What of supplies?" said Lord Tancred.

"Every man will take as much as he can carry," said Mazael, "but no more. We will need to ride light and fast."

"Suppose Amalric has foreseen this possibility?" said Galan, "and has more men lying in wait?"

Mazael shrugged. "Then we'll deal with them."

No one said anything for awhile.

"Gerald," said Mazael. "I want you to take command of the footmen."

Gerald frowned. "I would rather ride with you and the knights."

"I know," said Mazael, "but if we fail...you and Sir Tobias are the only sons of Lord Malden. Lord Malden will have no more legitimate sons." He looked at Gerald, at Tobias, and then back at Gerald. "One of you must come out of this alive."

"It is a bold plan. We will be victorious," said Tobias, banging his fist against his breastplate.

"Yes," said Mazael, envying the younger man his confidence, "I'm sure we will. Get moving. Much work lies before us."

"So," said Lucan, "once more you need my help?"

"Aye," said Mazael, swinging from Mantle's saddle. "I do."

Lucan lounged before a campfire, still disguised as a common armsman, though the raven perched on his shoulder.

"You know what I plan," said Mazael. "We must...we absolutely must...take Amalric unawares. Trocend and Timothy can find Amalric's scouts, rid ourselves of them. But if Amalric has the help of Straganis or another San-keth cleric with divinatory arts..."

"Then no matter how many scouts you kill," said Lucan, "Amalric will still know you're coming."

"He will," said Mazael. "Can you stop Straganis again?"

"He almost killed me twice," said Lucan, reaching into his ragged cloak. "He is my superior in both knowledge and power. I've defeated him twice, yes, but the first time was through mischance, the second through trickery. I'll not catch him off guard a third time. But I will face him again."

He pulled out a small glass vial. It was filled with a viscous, dark fluid the color of congealed blood. The fluid writhed and twisted within the vial, boiling of its own volition. Just looking at it made Mazael's head swim.

"Do you know what this is?" said Lucan.

"No," said Mazael.

Lucan smirked. "You don't recognize it?"

Mazael shook his head.

"Good," said Lucan, tucking the vial into his cloak. "You're better off not knowing. It will give me the strength to defeat Straganis."

"What is it?" said Mazael. "Something dark?"

"The darkest," said Lucan. "But, fear not, there's no danger. At least not for you."

"Don't do anything foolish," said Mazael.

Lucan lifted an eyebrow. "Since I came to Castle Cravenlock, I have done nothing but foolish things. Yet I am still alive."

Mazael shook his head and walked back to Mantle.

Lucan watched Mazael go, his fingers still wrapped around the glass vial.

It felt warm beneath his fingers, almost hot.

The distilled blood of Mazael Cravenlock, purified down to its essence, crackled with Demonsouled power. It would only give Lucan a few moments of strength, just a few heartbeats, but hopefully enough to crush Straganis once and for all.

"He's a mighty lord," croaked Mocker-Of-Hope in the thief's voice, "so he is."

"We will see," said Lucan, "just how strong he is. And how strong am I."

They left at once.

Mazael had the footmen encamp, digging trenches and piling earthwork walls. Soon a small city of tents rose before the Dominiar fortification. Mazael saw the Dominiar footmen climb to the top of their own wall, watching the work.

And as the Dominiars watched the footmen, Mazael and forty-five hundred horsemen slipped around the rear of the camp, riding fast through the rugged hills. They passed more villages ravaged by Amalric's raiders, villages ringed by impaled corpses.

Mazael felt his teeth grinding.

They rode as fast as they could while sparing the horses' strength. Trocend's spells found a band of Dominiar raiders, a hundred and fifty strong, marching north. Galan's Justiciars swept them away in one brief and bloody charge. Mazael left the bodies to rot, ordering the men to keep riding. The roads were poor and often overgrown, and they did not make the progress Mazael had hoped.

He drove them on after sunset, long after it had become too dark to see, and finally permitted the knights to stop and rest. They woke again before sunrise, and kept riding. A few hours later they came to the end of the mountain ridge, the country opening into the rocky hills and thin forests of Mastaria, the land of the Dominiar Order.

They rode into Mastaria, hooked around the southernmost crag of the mountains, and galloped north for Tumblestone. Soon they came upon an excellent road in good repair. Malleus must have rebuilt for his planned invasion of Knightcastle. The road showed signs of the recent passage of many thousands of men. They rode northward, passing many small Mastarian villages. The peasants watched with flinty, cold eyes. They looked hungry. Amalric had taken the last of their food to feed his men.

And so they sent no word, no runner or rider, to tell Amalric of Mazael's coming.

A few hours later Knights' Bay came into sight, a broad, hazy, blue expanse, a finger of the great western ocean. The sea breeze ruffled the banners dangling from Sir Aulus's lance. Mazael ordered the men to ride faster. He felt time slipping away. If Amalric took Tumblestone, Mazael and the knights might find themselves trapped between Tumblestone and the Dominiar force holding the pass.

Trocend and Timothy discovered a dozen scouts ranging through the country around them. Mazael dispatched bands of knights to hunt them down, and braced himself for the counterattack. Sooner or later, Straganis would sense Trocend's spells, and strike back.

But no arcane counterattack came. For that matter, no counterattack of any sort appeared. Asides from the scouts, they encountered no other Dominiars. For the first time since leaving Knightcastle, Mazael began to feel hope. Maybe Amalric had miscalculated, failing to anticipate an attack from behind. He had sealed off the pass, but left only scouts behind him. And maybe the full weight of Straganis's arcane strength had been unleashed upon Tumblestone, leaving him with no power to sense Trocend's divinations.

Or maybe Straganis and Amalric had fallen out.

Mazael shook his head. The Demonsouled dominated and destroyed. Straganis may have thought himself the stronger, but in the end, Amalric had become the master. Mazael looked over the long lines of armored horsemen behind him. He fought against his Demonsouled nature, Romaria had died to save him from his black soul, and yet he still had become a lord and a commander. Would he next become a tyrant?

Mazael shook aside his grim thoughts. He could not doubt himself now. If he failed, if he turned back, Amalric would become the Destroyer, and uncounted thousands would die.

Trocend and Timothy found another dozen scouts, who soon came to bloody ends. How long before Amalric noticed that his scouts were no longer returning?

They pushed far ahead, following the road alongside Knights' Bay. The sun dropped beneath the waters, turning the waves the color of blood. Mazael had seen such things in his dreams often enough, seas of real blood, and hoped it was not an omen. After darkness fell, they camped. It was only another few hours ride to Tumblestone, and Mazael wanted both the men and horses rested for the battle.

A faint red glow illuminated the sky to the north, shining even as the sun vanished. He wondered if Tumblestone had burned to ashes. Despite that grim thought, he managed to fall asleep for a few hours.

They woke again before the sun rose, and rode northward. The land opened into a broad, sandy plain between Knights' Bay and the mountain ridge. Small villages dotted the plain, home to fishing and farming folk who had once fed the townsmen of Tumblestone. Now plumes of smoke rose from burned timbers, stark against the dawn sky. Bloodstained stakes surrounded the ruins like grisly flowers, bloated corpses dangling from the jagged points.

Amalric had left no one alive.

Smoke filled the sky ahead. He heard the echoes of ringing swords, the groan of siege engines, and the throaty shouts of dying men. The land rose in a gentle swell, covered in patches of tough grasses. Mazael and his commanders reached the top of the hill, reined up, and looked down at Tumblestone.

The city sat on a small peninsula jutting into Knights' Bay, ringed by massive stone walls. South of the city lay a deep harbor, now filled with the smoldering husks of burned ships. A road led from the city's gates and into the mountain pass, past crumbling, weather-worn hills. The city took its name from the occasional rock slides that tumbled off the ridge and into Knights' Bay. Memories flooded through Mazael's mind. He had fought the Dominiars here, five years past, defeating Sir Commander Aeternis's army and trapping Grand Master Malleus on the wrong side of the mountains.

And now another Dominiar army filled the plain before Tumblestone.

Mazael stared at the sea of tents, at the siege towers, at the catapults, at the black-armored Dominiar footmen swarming towards Tumblestone like ants.

"Gods save us," said Lord Tancred. "There are at least twenty thousand of them."

Arrows shrieked from Tumblestone's battlements, raining down on the advancing Dominiar ranks. The Dominiar footmen locked their shields and kept coming. The siege towers groaned and rattled forward, pushed by straining soldiers. One of the catapults fired, flinging a ball of raging flame over Tumblestone's walls.

"They must have been fighting all night," said Galan, sweeping his gaze over the battlefield. He pointed. "Look. A wrecked tower there, and there. And corpses everywhere. Lord Rainier must have beaten off a dozen assaults." His frown deepened. "And there..."

Mazael followed his pointing finger, and glimpsed a figure carrying a sword that burned with crimson flames.

"But the Knights themselves!" said Tobias, waving his hand. "Look! The horses are tethered, the Knights lounging in their tents. Their footmen are pressing the siege. They're not prepared to fight horsemen! If we strike now, now, we can sweep them away!"

Mazael's hands tightened around Mantle's reins. His gamble had paid off. If they struck hard, they might drive the entire host of the Dominiar Order into the sea...

Or, of course, it might be a trap.

"Go to your commands," said Mazael, voice hoarse. If this was a trap, then he had no choice but to walk into it, sword in hand. Perhaps the Old Demon had indeed manipulated everything to bring Mazael here. But if he had, then Mazael intended to die fighting. "Sir Tobias, take the left wing. Sir Galan, take your Justiciar Knights to the right. I will command the center myself. Ride them down, push them back from the walls, drive them into the sea. Kill as many of the Knights themselves as possible; if they can mount up and rally, we're finished. Go." He wheeled Mantle around and galloped back to the lines. A squire hurried up, leading Chariot, while another carried Mazael's helmet, lance and shield. He pulled on the helmet and climbed up into Chariot's saddle, taking the shield and the lance. It was a heavy war lance, far stronger than the flimsy things used in tournaments. Chariot neighed and pawed the earth, sensing Mazael's worry and excitement. Mazael gave orders to the squires, who galloped off, carrying his orders to the men.

The army walked their horses to the top of the hill. The siege towers had moved closer to the walls. The catapults still flung balls of fire over the walls and into the smoldering city. At least most of the buildings inside the walls were stone. A battering ram crawled towards the gates, pulled by men safe beneath wooden panels.

Mazael waited as Lord Malden's household knights, vassals, and the Justiciar Knights formed up behind him. It was maybe a half-mile to Thimblestone, and they sat in clear view, yet the Dominiars were so focused on the falling city that they did not notice. More and more black-armored footmen marched towards the walls.

"Sir Aulus," said Mazael, "now."

Sir Aulus raised a trumpet and blew a long blast. The other standard-bearers blew their trumpets, the brassy notes ringing in Mazael's ears. Some of the footmen whirled, turned, staring up at the hill.

Mazael raised his lance and booted Chariot to a gallop, racing down the hill. Behind him the earth thundered as the knights spurred their own destriers forward, the air ringing with their shouts. A surge of panic went through the Dominiar army like a ripple through a pond. Mazael let Chariot's reins drop, balanced his shield in one hand and his lance in the other, and set himself.

An instant later the knights crashed into the ranks of the Dominiar footmen. The sound was like the heavens splitting asunder. Mazael's lance caught a Dominiar footman through the throat, and another died in a screaming red flash beneath Chariot's hooves.

Some Dominiar footmen turned and fled. Most perished, either struck down or trampled.

Mazael and his knights thundered through the Dominiar army.

CHAPTER 26
BROTHERS

Adalar drifted awake, his bloody chin brushing against his chest.

He sat inside one of the Dominiars' tents, his hands bound to a heavy wooden stake with thick rope. He had tried to break free, but the rope had rubbed his wrists raw. Then a Dominiar sergeant had entered and kicked him until he passed out.

Now Adalar felt awful, his head aching, his mouth drier than dust. He had vomited out his stomach hours ago, but his gut kept twisting. Adalar groaned and doubled over, then jerked upright as the rope grated against his bloody wrists.

He leaned back against the stake, drenched in sweat.

He wished Amalric would just kill him. But it amused the Demonsouled monster to keep him alive. He suspected that Amalric would kill him in front of Lord Mazael, just to satisfy his cruel nature.

Adalar sobbed into his shoulder. If only he hadn't believed Amalric's honeyed words. If only he had warned Lord Mazael.

It was all Adalar's fault.

He had seen terrible things, seen the Dominiars round up villagers, seen children impaled on stakes, screaming as the jagged wood tore through their flesh. He had watched Amalric ride through fields of bloody stakes, his laughter drowning out the screams. If only Adalar had warned Lord Mazael. None of this would have happened. The slaughtered villagers would yet live.

And Adalar would not sit in this tent, praying for death.

Someone shrieked in pain.

Adalar looked towards the tent's flap, blinking sweat from his eyes. A Dominiar footman staggered inside, face twisted with fury, blood frothing from his lips. He took a step towards Adalar, and then pitched over onto his face.

A broken war lance jutted from his back. A dagger rolled from his fingers, coming to a halt near Adalar's boot. Through the tent flap he saw horsemen galloping past, fleeing Dominiar footmen, the flash of a Cravenlock banner.

Adalar felt a stab of terrified hope. Lord Mazael had come!

The gleam of the fallen dagger called to Adalar.

He strained and stretched out with his boot, trying to drag the dagger towards him.

Mazael's war lance killed another Dominiar footman, Chariot trampling still another. Most of the footmen had fled, and those that stood and fought were trampled. Mazael rocked in the saddle with every blow, his bones thrumming with the thunder of the charge. Everywhere he looked he saw the Dominiars throwing down their weapons, running.

He felt a surge of wild exaltation. They were winning.

The speed of their charge took them through the Dominiar camp, past the gates of Tumblestone. Many of the household knights and Justiciars, no strangers to warfare, had equipped themselves with torches before leaving the camp. Now the siege towers, catapults, and tents began blazing, greasy black smoke staining the sky. The orderly lines of the Dominiar army had broken, some fleeing towards the hills, others sprinting for the mountain pass. Mazael watched them go, his mind spinning new plans. They had to hunt down the Dominiars, force them to surrender, or else they would regroup, he had to send word for Lord Rainier to sortie from Tumblestone...

A new rumble went through the ground, a counterpoint to the horses' stamping hooves, and Mazael saw a great mass of black-armored horsemen wheel around the burning tents. There were at least two thousand of them, the standard-bearers carrying black banners adorned with eight-pointed silver stars.

Amalric, it seemed, had formed up the Dominiar Knights faster than Mazael had thought possible. The Dominiars lined up for a charge, presenting a wall of horses and black-armored Knights.

"Sir Aulus!" roared Mazael, riding to his standard-bearer's side. "Sound a halt! Now! Now!"

Sir Aulus nodded, wiping sweat and blood from his face, and trumpeted the halt. The other standard-bearers followed the call, trumpets ringing. The charge slowed to a halt, the knights and vassals reining up. The Justiciars and household knights, seeing the danger, formed up, and the vassals and their followers hastened to follow suit.

A storm of horns rang out from the Dominiars, and their Knights thundered forward in a black wave, banners flapping.

"Sir Aulus!" said Mazael, wheeling Chariot around. "The charge! Now!"

Sir Aulus blew the trumpet. Mazael put spurs to Chariot, and the big horse leapt forward with an excited whinny. Behind him Lord Malden's knights roared forward, and the two masses of horseman surged at each other like hammer blows. Mazael set himself in the saddle, shield ready on his left arm, lance raised in his right.

The charges smashed together with a thunderous crash, clouds of dust swirling, men and horses screaming, blood spilling into the ground. Mazael caught a lance blow on his shield, his arm burning with pain, and unhorsed a Dominiar in the same motion. The Knight fell backwards with a scream and vanished beneath the pounding hooves. The two armies disintegrated into pure chaos, into duels and battles between small bands. Mazael roared, giving himself over to the mayhem. Generalship was now useless; the outcome of a thousand different fights would decide the battle. He struck down a Dominiar trying to kill Sir Commander Galan, killed another on the verge of taking one of the household knights.

The Mazael wheeled, and saw Amalric Galbraith on horseback, encased head-to-foot in black plate, a lance in one hand and shield in another. Their eyes locked over the raging chaos of the battlefield.

The force of Amalric's gaze struck Mazael like a physical blow. Amalric's black eyes had developed a glowing reddish gaze.

Just like the eyes of the Old Demon.

Amalric wheeled his horse around, lance leveled.

Mazael yelled and spurred Chariot forward

Adalar strained, every muscle groaning. The edge of his heel touched the dagger's edge. Adalar wrenched forward, almost yanking his arms from their sockets, and hooked his foot back.

His boot dragged the dagger a few inches closer. Adalar sank back, panting. If he could just drag the dagger to him, cut his bonds, and get out his this wretched tent...

He smelled something burning.

Adalar looked over and saw the tent catch on fire.

His fear burst into full-fledged panic. He kicked out, dragging the dagger closer. The fire spread to the tent's roof, billowing acrid smoke. Either Adalar would choke to death, or the tent would collapse and he would burn to death. He got the dagger to his knee and stared at it, wondering how he would get it to his bound hands.

The smoke sent Adalar into a coughing fit.

He twisted his hips, drawing back his legs, and clapped the dagger between his boots. Then Adalar rocked back, lifting his rigid legs. His knees and hips screamed with the strain, yet forced his legs back. His scrabbling fingers closed around the dagger's blade.

He dropped his legs, reversed the dagger, and began sawing at the rope, back and forth, back and forth. Adalar snarled in frustration and terror, still coughing. He was going to die here, the rope wouldn't break, the smoke would fill his lungs and choke him or the flaming canvas would fall...

The rope snapped. Adalar jerked to his feet, battered muscles cramping, and half-limped, half-fell from the burning tent. He flung himself to the ground, breathing great gulps of blessedly smoke-free air, his arms and legs twitching.

Some time later he managed to look up, saw the battle raging around him.

"Amalric," Adalar spat, voice raspy from the smoke. He lurched to his feet, snatched up a discarded battle-axe, and limped into the battle. "Amalric!"

The Demonsouled monster would kill him, no doubt. But at least Adalar would die fighting the evil, rather in thrall to its subtle lies. He was through listening to Amalric.

Adalar limped in search of his enemy.

Chariot galloped towards Amalric, hooves tearing at the ground, Mazael's hands tightening about shield and lance. Amalric thundered towards him like a storm, black cloak billowing out behind him.

They came together with a tremendous crash. The impact of Amalric's lance tore away the top of Mazael's shield, the lance's head scraping against Mazael's shoulder. But Mazael's lance slammed into Amalric's belly, the force of his charge sending the point through steel plate and chain. Amalric catapulted backwards out of the saddle and fell to the ground, armor clattering. His destrier panicked and bolted off into the melee. Chariot tore past, and Mazael reined up, wheeling his horse around, shifting his lance to an overhand grip. If he could strike before Amalric recovered, he could end this with one solid blow.

Amalric rose, cast aside his lance, and drew his sword. Red gold blazed in the sunlight.

Mazael kicked Chariot to a gallop. He had seen that sword before, in his dreams. The Old Demon had offered it to him, promising power and mastery of the world, if Mazael but murdered his brother and his sister.

Amalric's sword exploded into raging crimson flames, fingers of shadow crawling through the fire. The sense of power radiating from the weapon washed over Mazael, called to his Demonsouled blood. Chariot raced forward and Mazael raised his lance, preparing to pin Amalric to the ground. Amalric made no move to dodge, no move to run.

Then Amalric twisted to the side, moving so fast than Mazael only saw a blur of black steel and red fire. The sword of the Destroyer rose and fell in a screaming inferno, and tore through Chariot's neck in a single terrible blow. Chariot's body managed a few more strides of its own volition and then collapsed, flinging Mazael from the saddle. He tucked his shoulder, rolled, and came to one knee, stunned and sore.

He had never seen anyone strike off a horse's head with one blow.

"Lord Mazael," said Amalric, striding towards him. Mazael stood, drawing Lion. "My brother." He laughed, a hideous grin twisting his face. His red-glazed eyes blazed with madness, stark against his pale face and black hair. Mazael sensed the strength in him, power that blazed like the sword of the Destroyer.

He wondered if the full weight of Demonsouled power had broken Amalric's mind, as had almost happened to Mazael.

"I knew you would come," said Amalric. The battle raged around them like a storm. "I have been waiting for you, brother."

"The Old Demon gave you that, didn't he?" said Mazael.

"My father," said Amalric. "You betrayed him!" He spat, the red glaze in his eyes brightening. "I am the Destroyer! I will claim the throne of the Great Demon, and all the kingdoms of the earth shall be mine."

"You damned fool," said Mazael. "It's all lies. The Old Demon cares nothing for you. Listen to me! He'll let you wax strong, then murder you and harvest your strength for his own."

"What do you know of power?" said Amalric. "You rejected your very blood. You are a wolf, and yet choose to live as a sheep." He lifted his burning sword. "You are the fool, not I!"

"The Old Demon told me himself," said Mazael, "when he tried to kill me, after I denied him. He will betray you!"

Amalric laughed, face twisted with the murderous glee Mazael knew so well, and took his sword in both hands.

Lion jolted in Mazael's hand, the edges shimmering. The blade blazed with raging azure flames. Mazael felt a wave of eagerness rush into him from the sword as its ancient magic stirred to life.

Lion had been created to destroy the powers of darkness, and the sword yearned to fulfill its purpose.

Amalric hesitated, his eyes fixing on the sapphire flames, and then sprang forward with a roar. Mazael just got his damaged shield up in time.

The sword of the Destroyer tore through the wood as if it did not exist. The shield disintegrated in a spray of splinters, the blow knocking Mazael backwards. Amalric roared and struck again, the Destroyer's sword howling like an inferno. Mazael ducked under the blow, and the sword's edge clipped his helmet. Mazael lost his balance and fell backwards. Amalric sprang forward, sword raised for the kill, and Mazael just got Lion up to parry. For an instant he expected Amalric's sword to shatter Lion, for the blade to plunge deep into his skull...

Lion stopped the sword of the Destroyer with a clang, red flames and blue flames snarling at each other. Mazael heaved, shoving Amalric back, and leapt to his feet. He went on the attack, driving at Amalric, slashing and thrusting, Lion blazing in his fist. Amalric backed away, growling, the sword of the Destroyer blurring in his hands, seeming to shield him in a veil of flame and shadow.

He was too fast, too strong. Mazael could not land a blow. Amalric spun, twisting past Mazael's blade, and stabbed. The blow tore upon a wound on Mazael's forearm. Mazael staggered back, trying to parry. Amalric hacked again and again, Mazael trying to parry, his arms trembling with the effort. The flames of both swords snarled and howled. Amalric locked blades, strained, and shoved Mazael back. Before Mazael could regain his balance, Amalric struck his face with the pommel, opening a gash across his jaw.

Mazael stumbled back, spitting out blood. The wounds he had taken from the sword of the Destroyer burned like fire. Nor did they seem to be healing. Perhaps the sword's power prevented Mazael's Demonsouled blood from closing the cuts.

He had not even hit Amalric once.

"Fool," said Amalric, laughing. "Look at you. You could have become the Destroyer. You could have taken the Great Demon's throne for yourself. And look at you! You can barely hold that sword upright." He laughed, deep and mocking. "Why did Morebeth think you strong? You're nothing but another weakling mortal."

"Then stop talking," said Mazael, trying to hold Lion steady, "and strike me down already."

Amalric's laughter sounded like a chorus of agonized souls. "If you wish."

He sprang at Mazael, the sword of the Destroyer trailing a curtain of flame. Mazael charged him, their swords meeting with a scream. They flashed through a dozen blows in as many seconds, blue fire blazing, crimson flames snarling. Mazael stopped thinking, his hands moving faster than his mind. His teeth pulled back from his lips in a snarl, mirroring Amalric's grimace. The Demonsouled rage crept into his mind, bit by bit, filling his limbs with burning power. He dared not let it claim him, dared not let it dominate him.

Yet without it, he might not have the strength to defeat Amalric.

More fury burned it him. He parried, feinted, and slashed at Amalric's head. Amalric ducked, spinning away, and Lion clanged off Amalric's breastplate. Amalric growled and ducked back, launching a backhand at Mazael's face. Mazael parried again, sidestepped, and slashed, opening a gash across Amalric's left arm. Amalric roared in fury and stepped back, sword raised in guard, eyes on Mazael's face.

And even as Mazael watched, the wound on Amalric's arm disappeared. Mazael's own Demonsouled healing had never closed wounds with such speed.

"Do you think," rasped Amalric, the fires from his sword reflecting his eyes, "that you can kill me? I am the heir of the Great Demon! No mortal can strike me down."

"The Great Demon said the same," said Mazael, "and he is no more."

Amalric howled and sprang at Mazael, the sword of the Destroyer raised over his head. Mazael sprang aside, the sword plunging past his shoulder. Amalric spun, his blade whirling into a slash for Mazael's knees. Mazael caught the blow, and Amalric turned the parry, sword flying up, and slashed open Mazael's thigh.

Mazael snarled in pain, fresh fury flooding him, filling him with new strength. He regained his balance and launched a furious attack at Amalric. Amalric backpedaled, whipping his blade back and forth to stop Mazael's attacks. Mazael lost himself to the rage, driving Amalric back. They fought across the battlefield, past the warring knights, past the fleeing footmen and the burning siege engines. The footmen took one look at their burning swords and fled. Their duel took to the bluff overlooking the harbor, to the lines of smoke rising from the smoldering ships.

Amalric's mouth tightened into a rigid line of concentration, the red glare in his eyes brightening. He flung himself into the attack, slashing and stabbing like a madman. Mazael stood toe-to-toe with him, trading blow for blow, the swords ringing like bells. He saw nothing but Amalric, nothing but the raging flames of the swords. Mazael caught a descending blow, shoved, and sent Amalric stumbling back. Mazael spun and sent Lion slashing across Amalric's knee. Amalric bellowed, almost losing his balance. Mazael stabbed for Amalric's face. Amalric jerked back, Lion tearing a bloody gash across his forehead and jaw.

Amalric roared and seized the wrist of Mazael's sword arm. Mazael clawed at the hand, feeling the bones in his wrist strain. The sword of the Destroyer came up, moving for a killing slash. Mazael seized Amalric's sword wrist and shoved. They roared and grappled like fighting wolves, spinning like two mad dancers, tottering on the edge of the steep bluff. The sword of the Destroyer waved in Mazael's face, while he tried to break his sword hand free and stab Amalric. Amalric strained, bending Mazael's wrist backwards, the sheer strength of his arm pushing Mazael's hand back. Mazael felt his muscles straining, his bones groaning. He shoved forwards, his forehead slamming into Amalric's gashed face, his boot cracking against Amalric's knee.

Both men fell apart with a gasp of pain. Mazael fell to one knee, panting, sweat and blood sheeting down his face. Amalric reeled back a few steps, blood sliding down his black breastplate.

The gash on his face had healed.

"Fool," grated Amalric, wiping the blood from his eyes. "You miserable fool. You cannot kill me. Look at you! You can barely stand!"

Mazael staggered back to his feet, raising Lion. The sword of the Destroyer had inflicted innumerable small cuts and nicks during their fight. None of them had healed, and every last one burned like fire.

"Wretch!" screamed Amalric. "Throw yourself down and worship me, and I might spare your useless weak life!"

"I denied and rejected your father," said Mazael, raising Lion to guard, "and I deny and reject you!"

Amalric's roar could have shattered stone. He leapt forward like a tiger. Mazael beat aside the thrust and struck back, striking past Amalric's battered armor, opening a wound in his side.

Amalric ignored the blow, kept coming, kept attacking. Mazael gritted his teeth and tried to parry. The red-blazing sword of the Destroyer seemed everywhere, stabbing high, swinging low, slashing at Mazael's face.

Mazael stumbled back, to the edge of the bluff, and the loose earth beneath his boot crumbled away. He flailed for a moment, trying to keep from falling and rolling down the bluff. Amalric struck with a massive, two-handed swing, and opened Mazael's left leg from calf to thigh.

Mazael groaned, his leg exploding with agony. It buckled beneath him, and he fell hard on the knee, the jolt sending an explosion of pain from his toes to his teeth. Amalric's pommel caught him across the face, snapping his head back, blood flying from his face. The world spun around Mazael, and he could not stand, could not focus, could not even think.

"I am," spat Amalric through clenched teeth, "the true heir of the Great Demon. Not you, not matter what she said!"

He raised the sword of the Destroyer for the killing blow.

Adalar saw Mazael fall, his left leg a bloody ruin, his face bruised and battered.

He had seen the flames of the magical swords from across the battlefield, had run through the chaos and the carnage, bellowing Amalric's name. And now Lord Mazael was on one knee before Amalric, about to fall to Amalric's blade.

And it was all Adalar's fault.

He sprang forward with a scream of denial and rage, the axe in both hands, raised high over his head.

Amalric, his attention focused on Mazael, did not even begin to turn until Adalar brought the axe hammering down with all his momentum and fury behind it, the heavy metal head cracking through both cuirass and chain to bury itself in Amalric's spine.

Amalric howled, his back arching, his sword slashing at the air. Mazael blinked his cloudy eyes just in time to see Adalar plunge a bloody axe into Amalric's back. Amalric roared again and his fist sent Adalar flying. Adalar hit to the ground and did not move. Amalric staggered towards him, jerking and reeling, the sword of the Destroyer twitching in his hand.

The sight of Amalric stalking towards Adalar filled Mazael with fresh strength.

He sprang up, ignoring the agony in his left leg, taking Lion in both hands. With all his remaining strength he plunged Lion through the rent in Amalric's cuirass, into the wound Adalar had made. Lion plunged through Amalric's chest, the tip smashing against the inside of Amalric's breastplate.

Lion's azure fire exploded into Amalric's flesh.

Amalric wailed and wrenched free from Lion, reeling like a drunken man. Mazael lurched ahead, trying to land another telling blow. Lion clanged off Amalric's feeble parry, and Mazael overbalanced and tumbled into Amalric.

They toppled backwards, grappling at each other, and fell, rolling over and over each other down the bluff. Mazael kept his grip on Lion, his free hand clawing at Amalric's throat. They skidded to a stop at the bottom of the bluff, at the narrow beach before the lapping waves of the sea.

Amalric's cuirass clanged away, its leather straps torn, and Mazael had his last chance.

He stabbed at Amalric's chest, throwing all his weight behind the blow. He lost his balance and fell atop his sword, the lion's head pommel smashing against his ribs. But Lion's blade plunged into Amalric's chest, through his back, and into the sand. The azure flames blazed, streaming down the blade and into Amalric, like water pouring into a desert.

Amalric screamed, clawing at Mazael, shuddering up and down the length of the blade. Mazael sagged against the sword, partly to keep Amalric pinned, but mostly from exhaustion and pain. Amalric's right hand closed around the hilt of the sword of the Destroyer, trying to raise it. Mazael stomped down, his boot landing on Amalric's wrist and shattering the bones.

The crimson fires of the sword flickered madly, becoming more shadow than flame.

"Damn you!" howled Amalric, clawing at Mazael with his free hand. "Damn you!" His wounds glimmered with sapphire flame, blue sparks twisting through his blood.

Mazael stared down at Amalric, horrified. Lion had gone through Amalric's heart, the blade shining like a shaft of light. Yet Amalric still lived, still fought.

"Why won't you die?" croaked Mazael.

Amalric screamed again, blood frothing at his lips. The red glow in his eyes dimmed, replaced by a sharp blue glow, his arms and legs flailing.

Adalar came to Mazael's side, wiping blood from his face. He stared down at Amalric, expressionless.

"You'll pay for this," spat Amalric, his voice weakening. A wave came to shore, the water brushing his hair. "My father...my father will..."

"He cares nothing for you," said Mazael.

"She did this to me!" said Amalric, his eyes clouding. Blue flames danced in his mouth, writhing across his teeth. Lion's hilt trembled, shaking with Amalric's heartbeat. "That whore. That damned whore." His lips peeled back in a vicious snarl. "My dear precious sister. She'll turn on you...just as she turned on me."

Mazael shook his head. "You're raving."

"My sister," whispered Amalric. "Our sister."

Mazael went cold. "What?"

"Our sister," croaked Amalric. "She will destroy you as she has destroyed me. I...I....the child is mine! Mine!" He heaved against the sword once more. "I am the Destroyer! I will be the Destroyer...not...not her damned brat..."

Mazael stared at Amalric's face in shock.

"I am...the Destroyer..." said Amalric, groaning. Blue fire raged through him like a storm.

He shuddered once more, his eyes bulging as if in horror, and then went still, the madness and the life draining from his eyes.

Besides him the sword of the Destroyer shattered with a thunderclap, the red fire blazing once and then going out. The shards crumbled to smoking ash even as Mazael watched. He groaned, managed to stand, and wrenched Lion from Amalric's chest.

The sword's azure flames went out.

"My lord."

Mazael turned, wincing at the agony in his leg.

"My lord." Adalar was shaking, crying. "I'm sorry...it was all my fault. All of it."

It took some time for Mazael to remember how to speak. "What?"

"He told me you were Demonsouled," said Adalar, voice shaking. "I...I saw some of your wounds heal with uncanny speed. Amalric told me you were going to kill Lord Malden, take over Knightcastle for yourself. I believed him. I'm sorry, I'm so sorry. He was Demonsouled, not you. He...he must have put a witchery in my mind, made me see those things." He waved his hand at Mazael's torn leg. "I...you're...not healing now."

"No," said Mazael. The wounds the sword of the Destroyer had inflicted had not healed, but he felt the start of a tingle against the pain.

"I'm so sorry," said Adalar, voice broken.

"It doesn't matter," said Mazael, limping towards him. "It...a Demonsouled is full of guile. He deceived us." He looked back at Amalric's corpse. "We...all were deceived."

The implications, the terrible implications, of Amalric's words filled him with horror. But everything that had happened since Blackfang had attacked Castle Cravenlock made sense, terrible grim sense.

"It doesn't matter," said Mazael, tugging his shredded cloak over the wound in his leg. The tingling had intensified. "Come. Help me up the bluff. We've a battle to win yet."

Adalar hastened to his side.

Behind them the rising tide washed away the Demonsouled blood of Amalric Galbraith.

CHAPTER 27
QUEEN OF THE WORLD

But the battle was over when they reached the top of the bluff.

Footmen streamed from the pass, and for a moment Mazael thought that the Dominiars had counterattacked. But the front ranks wore Justiciar tabards and armor, and the rest had the ragged look of Lord Malden's levies. Gerald must have found a way to force the pass. The gates of Tumblestone stood open, and Mazael saw men in Lord Rainier's colors marching across the field.

Dead and dying men lay strewn across the field, the screams of the wounded piercing the air. Mazael limped across the bloodstained grasses, leaning on Adalar, Lion dangling from his fist. Justiciar footmen strolled along with long knives, finishing off the Dominiar wounded. Lord Malden's household knights rode stood guard over captured Dominiar footmen, watching as they threw down their pikes and stripped off their armor.

"I think we won," said Adalar. Mazael managed to nod.

A band of horsemen galloped towards them, flying Roland banners, and Mazael saw Sir Tobias and Sir Gerald riding at their head.

"Lord Mazael!" called Gerald. "You're alive."

"Barely," said Mazael. "Find me a damned horse. They killed Chariot."

Tobias barked an order, and one of the footmen found a horse, the saddle splashed with dried blood. Mazael swung up into the saddle with a wince, his torn leg twitching. His head spun and his stomach twisted, but he managed to keep his saddle.

"You're hurt," said Gerald, "you need to..."

Mazael waved his hand. "It'll keep. What the devil are you doing here? I thought you were on the other side of the pass."

"We were," said Gerald, "but the Dominiar watchmen had grown lax.

So some of the Justiciar footmen crept over the wall, murdered the watchmen, and opened the gate." He shook his head. "They've done that sort of thing before, evidently. We broke the Dominiars, hastened through the pass, and came to Tumblestone in the midst of the battle. Just in time, too."

"Where's Sir Commander Galan?" said Mazael.

"Dead," said Tobias, face filthy with dust and sweat. "He was knocked from his saddle, and his own men trampled him before they could stop."

"Damn it," said Mazael.

"When we came down from the pass," said Gerald, "the Dominiars had fled north, and we trapped them against the ridge. It was a sharp fight, but they threw down their weapons in the end."

"What of Amalric?" said Tobias.

"Dead," said Mazael, not wanting to speak of it.

"At Lord Mazael's hand," said Adalar, with some fierceness.

Gerald and Tobias looked at him in surprise.

"He escaped," said Mazael.

"What should we do with the prisoners?" said Gerald. "We have thousands."

"Kill them all, I say," said Tobias, his eyes flinty.

"No," said Mazael. "Take their armor and weapons, but let them go." He looked over the field of corpses. "There's been enough slaughter for one day."

"We have won a great victory!" said Tobias. "The Dominiars' Grand Master dead, most of their commanders and preceptors killed, their host broken. Tumblestone belongs to the Rolands now and forever. We should follow up, take as much as Mastaria as we can." His eyes glinted. "Perhaps we can even destroy the Dominiar Order entirely."

"And if Amalric Galbraith was indeed Demonsouled..." said Gerald.

"He was," said Adalar, "Sir Gerald, forgive me, but he was. Lord Mazael stabbed him through the heart, pinned him to the ground, but it still took him a long time to die."

"Then it was a great victory over the powers of darkness," said Gerald. "Though we never did find Straganis."

"No," murmured Mazael. "Straganis and the changelings were Amalric's tools, I think. Perhaps Straganis thought he was following the will of Sepharivaim, but he was doing Amalric's work the entire time. I'd wager Amalric killed Straganis and the changelings, once he had no further need of them."

He looked at the bloody field, shaking his head. Amalric had been stopped, yes. He would not become the Destroyer. But the Old Demon still waited in the shadows. And if what Amalric had said was true...

"What should we do now?" said Gerald.

"Take command," said Mazael, making up his mind.

"What?" said the brothers in unison.

"Take command," said Mazael, turning his borrowed horse around. "Both of you. You are both sons of Lord Malden, and you should take command."

"But this is your victory!" said Gerald

"I have to return to Knightcastle," said Mazael. "Amalric said something before he died. There might be another San-keth assassin lurking at Knightcastle, instructed to kill Lord Malden if the Dominiars lost the battle." The lie rolled easily off his tongue. "A...final revenge, you might say. I have to stop it."

"Let us come with you," said Gerald. "You might need our help."

"No!" said Mazael. "Sir Tobias is right. You must follow up on our victory. Secure Tumblestone and take the army further south. With the Dominiar command broken...you'll be able to claim most of Mastaria before they recover. I must go alone. Though I will take Trocend with me, and Harune Dustfoot, and..." He almost asked for Lucan and caught himself. "If they are still alive."

They were the only ones with the power to fight besides Mazael.

"They both are, so far as I know," said Gerald.

"Good. Have them meet me at the pass," said Mazael, turning the horse.

"Lord Mazael!" said Adalar, running to his side, "I will come with you."

"No!," said Mazael, stopping. Amalric had almost gotten the boy killed. Mazael looked at Adalar's weary, smoke-grimed face. Adalar did not look much like a boy, at least not any more. "You'll stay here, help Sir Gerald and Sir Tobias."

"They've squires already," said Adalar.

"I know," said Mazael, "but not as a squire." He rolled from the saddle, and pretended to wince in pain, even though his leg felt better. No sense in reawakening Adalar's old suspicions. "You saved my life, Adalar. Amalric would have killed me, if you hadn't struck him."

"But..." said Adalar.

"Be quiet and kneel," said Mazael, drawing Lion.

Adalar's eyes went wide, but he knelt. Mazael put the flat of the blade on one of Adalar's shoulders, and then the other, saying the ritual words as he did so.

"Now, rise," said Mazael, "Sir Adalar Greatheart."

"Thank you," said Adalar, "Lord Mazael, thank you. I don't deserve this. Not after..."

"We all make mistakes," said Mazael, climbing back into the saddle. He didn't need to fake a grunt of pain. And he had made far greater mistake than any Adalar would ever make. "Now, go."

He didn't look back, but booted the borrowed horse to a gallop.

Mazael found Lucan walking among the tents, clad again in his black cloak and coat, and no doubt wrapped in his mind-clouding glamour. Lucan turned and looked up at him.

"It's done, then?" said Lucan.

"Yes," said Mazael, "Amalric is dead."

"Straganis must be dead," said Lucan. "No one attempted any arcane attacks during the battle." He laughed, smirking. "Amalric must have killed him, once he ceased to serve any purpose. And to think I made such efforts to prepare for our battle!"

"I thought as much," said Mazael. "Lucan. I need your help again."

"Such a surprise," said Lucan.

"Are you with me or not?"

"Yes," said Lucan, "yes, I suppose I am."

"Then get a horse," said Mazael.

Mazael rode north with Lucan and Harune and Trocend, leaving the army in the hands of Gerald and Tobias. He hoped they did not lead the men to disaster. But with Amalric dead, and the Dominiar Order shattered, they ought to face no serious opposition.

And something far more dangerous awaited Mazael at Knightcastle.

"Sister," muttered Mazael to himself, over and over again, "sister."

Two and a half days later, they reined up before the barbican of Knightcastle.

"What news?" shouted the armsman at the gate, looking at them. "Have we been defeated? Are the Dominiars coming?"

"We are victorious," said Mazael. "Amalric Galbraith is slain, Tumblestone is safe, the Dominiars are broken, and Sir Gerald and Sir Tobias are leading the army into Mastaria." He hesitated. "Where is Lady Morebeth?"

"Praying for victory in the Kings' Chapel," said the guard. He grinned. "The gods must have heard her."

"The gods," said Mazael. "I'm sure." He pointed up at the Hall of Triumphs, where the Roland banners blew in the breeze. "Go tell Lord Malden the good news. I...will say prayers for thanksgiving for our victory in the Kings' Chapel, then go to Lord Malden myself. Make sure I am not disturbed."

"My lord," said the guard.

Mazael rode through the tiers of Knightcastle, past the high stone towers, the mighty walls, and into the High Court. They reined up before the Kings' Chapel and slid from the saddle. Mazael thrust open the chapel doors and strode inside, the others following. Shafts of multicolored light shone through the stained-glass windows, throwing pools of color across the floor. A blaze of candles surrounded the altar.

Morebeth Galbraith stood near the altar rail, still in widow's black, her red braids wrapped about her head like a crown. She turned to face him, keen gray eyes flicking over his companions, and then a brilliant smile cracked through her icy mask. It sent an electric jolt of desire through Mazael's nerves.

"My lord Mazael," said Morebeth, "you have returned to me."

"I have," said Mazael. "Amalric is dead."

"I knew you would defeat him," said Morebeth. "I knew you were the stronger." Her blood-red eyebrows creased. "Though why are you not with the army?"

"I know," said Mazael.

"Know what?" said Morebeth.

"I know," said Mazael, "that you are pregnant."

A flicker of something, perhaps anger, but certainly not fear, flashed across Morebeth's face. "I told you that I could not have children. Do you mean to drag my shame before these rogues?"

"Don't lie to me," said Mazael. "I know."

Trocend muttered, "You dragged me away from the field for this tawdry..."

Morebeth shifted, gray eyes narrowing, and Mazael glimpsed the slight curve of her stomach, even beneath the heavy black fabric of her gown. "Perhaps I am. But maybe you are the father, my lord."

Trocend kept muttering, and Lucan gave him a black look.

"No," said Mazael. "You were already with child when I met you."

"And," said Morebeth, her eyes cold and sharp as knives, "who is the father?"

"Amalric Galbraith," said Mazael. "Your brother."

Morebeth said nothing.

"What?" said Trocend. "What is this? Are you accusing Lady Morebeth of incest? Why should we do such a thing? Why..."

"Because," said Mazael, "Amalric Galbraith is...was...Demonsouled. And so is Lady Morebeth."

Mazael stared hard with her cold gray eyes, eyes that were mirror images of Mazael's own.

"What?" rasped Trocend.

"The Old Demon came to our mother," said Morebeth, her voice soft, "twenty-seven years ago. Nine months later Amalric and I were born. We were both children of the Old Demon." Her eyes glittered. "As are you, my lord Mazael, my lover...my brother."

Trocend rocked back, gray hair sliding across his waxy face. "Lord Mazael...you...you are Demonsouled?"

Mazael nodded, not turning around, not taking his eyes from Morebeth.

"I always knew I was different," said Morebeth, her voice deadly soft. "After I had my first moon's blood, the Old Demon came to us, told Amalric and I the truth. We were the grandchildren of the Great Demon, heirs to a dead god...and the world belonged to us. He told us of the Destroyer, how one of his children would claim the Great Demon's throne."

"And you believed him?" said Mazael. "He is a liar..."

"Of course he is!" snapped Morebeth. "Do you think me a fool?" She smirked. "Amalric believed every word, swore that he would prove himself, swore that he would become the Destroyer. He was always strong, but a fool." She glared at Mazael. "He always thought of me as his servant, his footstool. So I swore that even if he became the Destroyer, the world would still be mine."

"You are a madwoman," said Trocend, voice hoarse, "a servant of dark..."

"Be silent, old man," snapped Morebeth. There was such power in her tone, such dark iron, that Trocend flinched back. "You know nothing."

"The child," said Mazael. "Amalric's child."

"He thought the child his," said Morebeth, "but it is mine, now and always. A child of the Old Demon has power. You know it well. But...ah, if two children of the Old Demon lay together and had a child...what power would might child have? What strength? And if I guided that child from birth, ruled it all my life...it would become an extension of my will." Her eyes shone with a fevered light, a light Mazael knew well. He had seen it Amalric's eyes, and had felt that same madness himself. "My child would become the Destroyer, and rule the earth...and I would rule the child. Let Amalric prance and rave, lead his armies of deluded fools, slaughter a few cities. I would rule him in the end."

"But it's over," said Lucan, stepping past Trocend. "Amalric is dead, and we know what you are."

"It will never be done," said Morebeth. "I seduced Amalric, let him impregnate me...and then I heard of Lord Mazael." She turned her eyes on him, and they filled with such desire that Mazael felt his own tainted blood burn in response. "A child of the Old Demon who found the strength to defy our beloved father? I could not believe such a thing. I had to learn the truth of it."

"So," said Mazael, forcing out the words, "so you sent Blackfang and his San-keth changelings to kill me...to test me."

"Yes," said Morebeth. "Amalric thought the plan his own. But I said a few quiet words to him, just a few, and he sent Blackfang to kill you."

"A foolish attempt," said Lucan. "Blackfang was weak, and I crushed him."

"All the San-keth are weak," said Morebeth, "for their faith is in a god that failed them. My faith is in myself, and I am not weak." She stepped towards Mazael. "And nor are you, my brother. I sent Straganis to test you, and still you survived. And then you came to Knightcastle and I saw you with my own eyes, ah, how my blood burned for you." Her fingers brushed Mazael's face and lips, sending fire down his nerves. "You could have been the Destroyer...oh, there is such strength in you, Mazael. Such power."

"Hawks," whispered Mazael.

Morebeth lifted an eyebrow.

"You told me how much you loved falconry," said Mazael, "how you could shape a hawk into a weapon of your will. Amalric was your hawk, wasn't he?" Morebeth gave him a slow nod. "And now...and now you've made me into your new hawk."

"Yes," said Morebeth, brushing his lips again with her fingertips. "Does that trouble you so?"

"It enrages me!" said Mazael. "I rejected the Old Demon...I will not become your slave." And yet, and yet, she still made his blood race and his nerves crackle. She could make him king of the world, and she would be his queen...

"My poor hawk," breathed Morebeth. "Always at war with yourself, always fighting against the power of your soul. Is that what you want? Always to be split in half, never to be whole, at one with yourself?"

"I..." said Mazael. "I..."

"I can make you more than you are," said Morebeth, "help you to become what you should be. I can purge my womb of Amalric's spawn, and then you and I will have a child together. We can raise him to be the Destroyer, and then we will rule the earth, you and I."

"The half of my soul that I fight," said Mazael, "the half that you have embraced...it will make monsters of us. I know what it almost made of me. I have seen what it made of Amalric, what it made of you. Don't you understand?" His voice rose, pleading. "The Old Demon betrays his children. He makes us strong, then devours us in the end."

"Do you still think me a fool?" said Morebeth, her voice cracking like a whip. "Do you think I did not know? I read it in his eyes. It is not his destiny to become the Destroyer, though he yearns to take the Great Demon's throne for his own. So instead he waits until one of us becomes the Destroyer...so he can devour us and usurp our power." Her eyes gleamed like sword blades. "But I will become stronger first...and I will devour him. Come with me, Mazael. We can destroy the Old Demon, take the Great Demon's throne together, and rule over the earth as a god and a goddess."

"No," said Mazael. "What right do we have? And how many innocents will we slaughter? How many thousands, millions, will we kill? No. I rejected the Old Demon," and it took all his will to keep speaking, "and I reject you."

Morebeth stared at him for a long moment. "So you mean to kill me?"

Mazael drew Lion. "If I must."

Morebeth laughed at him, long and high and mocking. "You mean to kill me? Yes, four strong men to kill one lone, unarmed woman?" She sounded amused, not at all frightened.

"Demonsouled or not," said Trocend, his mouth in a grim line. "I think the four of us are more than strong enough to destroy you."

"Are you, old man?" said Morebeth. Her gaze swept over them. "Mazael could be a god, but he rejects his heritage, and cripples himself. And you, false monk? Will you stop me? I know what I am. But you have spent your life pretending to be something you are not. Can your lies stand against my truth?"

Trocend did not answer.

Her gaze shifted to Lucan. "And you, Dragon's Shadow. The son of Richard Mandragon, but he rejected you. The apprentice of Marstan, yet you were nothing to him but a means of immortality. You could be a necromancer of power, yet you reject what you are. You reject yourself. You think to stop me?"

"I swore," said Lucan, voice cold and dark as his eyes, "that what happened to me would happen to no other. I will not let you inflict on others what I have endured."

"And you," said Morebeth, looking at Harune Dustfoot. "You. Angkath. Oh, I know you. Do not think your shabby disguise can fool my eyes. Your kind has always fought to defend the mortal races. Yet do they honor you, or even know of your sacrifices? Those that do know of you fear and loathe you. When you fall here, will anyone know? Or care?"

"The path of justice and righteousness," said Harune, "is my path, whatever the cost."

"Fools all," said Morebeth. She turned from them and walked to the altar.

And then, to Mazael's astonishment, she began to undress.

She slipped off her shoes, kicking them across the floor. Her hands undid the back of her gown with quick, sure motions, and she slid out of the garment and flung it aside. The sight filled Mazael with desire, made his Demonsouled blood burn, even knowing what he now knew about her. She pulled off her undergarments and stood naked and pale before them. One of her red braids came lose, stark against her white shoulder.

"What is this?" said Trocend, half-laughing. "Harlot! Do you think to throw yourself at us in exchange for mercy?"

"Strange," murmured Morebeth. She showed no sign of shame, or even embarrassment. "How did Lord Malden become so powerful with a fool like you for an adviser?" Her eyes flicked to Mazael. "Tell me. Did our father try to devour you?"

"He did," said Mazael, his heart racing from a mixture of lust and sudden alarm.

"Yes," said Morebeth. "He changed...didn't he?"

"He became a monster," said Mazael, "his true form."

"It is a power only the greatest of Demonsouled possess," said Morebeth. Her eyes began to glimmer with red light, not the haze that Amalric's eyes had possessed, but a fierce, piercing glow deep in her pupils. "To shed their moral guise, to become something more than human...my dear Brother Trocend. Do you think I took off my gown to seduce you?" She laughed. "It is a fine gown. I don't want to get your blood on it."

She took a quick, gliding step forward, and then another.

Lion jolted in Mazael's hand, shimmering with azure flames.

And then Morebeth changed.

Her blood-red hair spread over her entire body, crimson bristles like iron spines rising from her pale flesh. Muscles writhed beneath the skin, her arms and legs bulging. Her flanks rippled, the flesh parting like clay, and four more spindly legs emerged from her belly, clawed and ridged, armored with spine-like hairs. Curving, pincer-like fangs burst from her mouth, her teeth sharpening into fangs. Her entire body bulged and rippled, swelling and growing larger.

The entire transformation took place in less that three heartbeats. Morebeth had become a monstrous, crimson spider, her body the size of a large horse, limbs like tree trunks, curved fangs gleaming with bubbling slime.

"A giant insect?" said Trocend, his voice shaking, his face ashen, "is that the best you could do..."

The spider moved like a storm.

Mazael did not even have time to get Lion up before a foreleg struck him like a falling boulder. The blow knocked him back into a pew, the wood shattering to kindling. Mazael groaned and clawed back to his feet, trying to ignore his groaning bones.

Harune gripped his sword, his human guise slipping away. His scales flared an angry red. Lucan and Trocend both began chanting, tracing arcane sigils with their fingers. The air rippled, and a half-dozen ghostly wolves appeared before Lucan, while Trocend summoned a pair of monstrosities that looked like winged squids. Mazael raced back towards Morebeth, while Lucan's and Trocend's spirit-creatures circled around her, keeping out of reach of her spined legs and poisoned fangs. Mazael quickened his pace, readying Lion for a decisive blow. If the spirit-creatures distracted her, Mazael could get close enough...

Then the spider jumped.

Morebeth blurred over the spirit-creatures in a red arc, landing behind Lucan and Trocend. They both whirled, chanting spells. Morebeth was faster. She lashed out with a foreleg, sent both Trocend and Lucan sprawling to the chapel floor. Harune leapt at her, moving with the speed of a striking serpent, his sword stabbing like a snake's forked tongue. Morebeth skittered and danced, claws clacking against the flagstones. She struck out, sent Harune flying into the wall, and then Trocend's and Lucan's spirit-creatures sprang upon her. The wolves scrambled over her bulbous back, biting and clawing, while the squid-things lashed at her fanged head. Morebeth bucked and heaved, ghastly snarls coming from her inhuman jaws, and for a moment Mazael thought she was finished.

But Morebeth sprang up in a single leap, smashing her back against the vaulted ceiling. The spirit-wolves fell from her back, sprawled across the floor, and vanished into mist. Morebeth flipped over and gripped the ceiling, racing along the ribbed vaulting. Her pincers closed about one of the squid-things, tearing it to shreds. She caught the other between a pair of legs and ripped it in half. Mazael circled under her, Lion raised for a stab. She would have to come down sooner or later, and maybe he could spear her upon Lion...

Morebeth raced along the ceiling, spun, and fell. Mazael expected her to pounce upon him, or to drop onto Lucan or Harune.

Instead, she landed before Trocend and Lucan, even as they struggled to rise. Mazael sprinted towards them, Lion blazing like a torch in his fist.

Trocend scrambled backwards, hands waving as he tried to cast a spell. Morebeth stalked after him, crouching, preparing to spring. Trocend picked up the speed of his incantation, lights blazing around his fingertips.

Morebeth jerked forward, just a little bit, and her pincers ripped off Trocend's hands. Trocend fell to his knees with an agonized scream, blood jetting from the frayed ruins of his arms. Morebeth speared him through the belly, lifted him close, and bit off his face.

Trocend's wails ended in thick gurgle. Morebeth flung aside his ruined carcass and wheeled towards Harune. Mazael yelled and sprang at Morebeth, Lion raised high, and struck a blow along her flank. Black blood, shimmering with red fire, oozed from the gash. Morebeth shrieked, the sound writhed into Mazael's ears, and struck back. A leg smote his chest like an iron rod and sent him to the floor.

Harune ran at Morebeth, shouting a battle cry in the Ang-kath tongue.

He slid past Morebeth's thrashing legs in a sinuous blur of scaled limbs, and stabbed his sword into her side again and again. She whirled, claws clacking, and slashed one of her pincers across Harune's chest, opening a shallow cut across his ribs. Harune staggered back a few steps, leaning hard on his thick tail. He hissed, sprang back up, sword ready.

Morebeth backed away, legs creaking. Mazael groaned and dragged himself back up, leaning on Lion like a cane.

Harune took a step forward, then stopped. His scales turned a deep purple, laced with writhing lines of pale green. His arms and legs began to jerk. Yellowish foam bubbled in his mouth, stained his fangs.

The gash on his chest frothed and bubbled with Morebeth's poison. Harune groaned and sank to his knees, sword clattering from his grasp.

Mazael roared and raced towards Morebeth, the Demonsouled rage flooding into him, blanketing the pain in a layer of strength. He threw himself at Morebeth, hacking and slashing, Lion a blur of azure flame in his hands. Lion's point slashed through Morebeth's leathery hide, black blood dripping across the ground. Morebeth backed away, stabbing with her legs, pincers clacking. She sprang backwards in a single mighty leap, climbed up the wall, and perched on the balcony ringing the nave. Mazael waited, preparing for her inevitable spring.

Instead she whirled, her rear legs lashing like whips, and struck the stone image of Joraviar. The statue shattered, chunks raining at Mazael. He leapt aside, but a stone arm crashed hard into his knee, and the statue's head smashed into his shoulder. He stumbled back, just keeping his balance. Morebeth whirled again, smashing another statue, the debris raining across Mazael. A shard raked across his jaw, sent him falling back. Morebeth tensed, legs creaking, ready to spring down upon him. Mazael tried to stand, tried to get his legs beneath him, but his head kept spinning...

Then a storm of rubble whirled into the air and slammed into Morebeth. She backed away, forelegs raised to ward off a barrage of broken statues. Mazael saw Lucan stalking across the chapel floor, arms raised, lips bared in a snarl of strain. He gestured, and a pew exploded, a barrage of wooden shards raining into Morebeth. Some stabbed themselves in her thorax, drawing trickles of black blood.

Mazael staggered back to his feet with a groan, the Demonsouled rage burning through him. He felt his battered bones strengthening, his bruises and cuts fading.

Lucan shouted a spell and thrust out his hand. A thunderous roar went through the air, and unseen force seized Morebeth and crushed her against the chapel wall. For an instant Mazael thought the Lucan had won, had broken her.

But Morebeth twisted over and caught the wall, raced along the balcony railing, and leaped. She landed before Lucan, legs couched to catch the impact of her fall. Lucan stepped back, beginning another spell.

Morebeth slapped him across the face with a foreleg. Lucan sputtered, losing the incantation. Morebeth surged forward and speared Lucan through the stomach. Lucan shrieked and went rigid, the tip of Morebeth's clawed leg bursting from his back. Mazael raced towards them, Lion trailing a long stream of sapphire fire. Morebeth flicked her leg, and Lucan crumpled into the pews and did not move.

She turned to face Mazael, Lion's fire reflecting in the black orbs of her eyes.

She had killed all three of his allies, leaving him to face her alone.

She had saved him for last.

Mazael took Lion in both hands and waited for her to spring.

Lucan wanted to howl like a dying dog, but could not scream, could not breathe through the blood filling his mouth.

He felt nothing below his waist. Morebeth's blow must have severed his spine. A small blessing, that. Everything else hurt.

The back of his head rested against the cold stone floor. A deathly chill filled his ruined body, and blackness flooded his vision. He could not die here! Damn it all, he had vowed to outlive both his brother and his father...

His twitching hand fell into his torn cloak and closed about something warm, a cylinder of hot glass.

The vial holding the distilled essence of Mazael Cravenlock's blood.

A sudden wild hope seized Lucan. He fumbled for the vial. His fingers felt stiff and cold. He pried the cork free, the vial trembling in his weak fingers. Gods, to spill it now! He lifted the vial to his lips, threw back his head, and swallowed Mazael's blood, along with a good quantity of his own.

For a moment nothing happened.

Then fire exploded within him, burning fingers tearing through his flesh. Lucan screamed, his arms shuddering, his legs kicking of their own volition. His head filled with flame, and for an instant Lucan thought he would burn into a pile of smoldering ashes.

Then the power hammered through him.

All at once Lucan felt better. He looked down and saw that the ghastly wound in his stomach had healed, that he could feel his legs again. He sprang to his feet with a single, easy movement. He had never felt so healthy, so strong, in his entire life.

The rage burned through him, mingled with the power. Lucan yearned to kill, to slaughter everyone who had ever opposed him. First he would kill Morebeth, then Mazael, and then he would return to Swordgrim and slaughter his father and his brother, make himself King of the Grim Marches!

The Demonsouled power thundered in his mind. Why had Mazael rejected this marvelous strength? The fool!

Lucan saw Mazael and Morebeth locked in a deadly duel. Mazael wielded Lion with powerful strokes, the sword blazing in his fist. Morebeth skittered back and forth, pincers snapping, claws rapping against the floor.

Lucan laughed and strode towards them, raising a hand. A spell, ancient and terrible, rose in his mind. Marstan had known it, and the knowledge had passed to Lucan, but neither man had possessed the power to cast it.

But with the Demonsouled power raging inside him, Lucan could do anything.

He gathered his will, using the Demonsouled fury to fuel the spell. A rune of fire appeared on his outstretched palm, blazing like a shard of the sun. Lucan focused his mind and power upon Morebeth, and thrust out his shining palm.

There was a thunderclap and a dazzling flash. The rune appeared across Morebeth's back, burning its way through her thick hide and deep into her flesh. The great spider keened and reared back, legs lashing at the air. Lucan strode forward, beginning another mighty spell.

Then, all at once, the power drained from him.

Lucan reeled, clutching a pew to keep from toppling. He felt ghastly, his very bones caked in filth. It was as if the power had burned all away, leaving only its madness, its corruption.

Gods, gods, how did Mazael live with this in his mind?

###

Burning light exploded across Morebeth's back, etched in a rune of fire the size of a man. She reared back, thrashing like a mad thing, claws tearing at the floors and walls.

It was Mazael's last chance. Reeling from the wounds she had inflicted, the slashes, the bruises, the cracked bones, he ran at her. She lashed at him with a massive leg, but Mazael ducked under the blow, his sword cutting another gash in her side.

Morebeth shuddered, legs buckling, and Mazael sprang upon her back. The bristly spines covering her hide tore at his legs and knees, but he ignored the pain. Morebeth slammed up and down, trying to dislodge him, but Mazael held on.

He raised Lion high over his head, both hands locked around the hilt, and brought the point down with all his strength. It plunged through the back of Morebeth's neck, the blue fire blazing down the blade and into her flesh.

Morebeth lurched once, shuddering, and flung Mazael from her back. He struck the floor, his right hand clenched around Lion's hilt, his left arm shattering with the impact. Mazael groaned and rolled over, expecting Morebeth to fall on him, rending and tearing.

Instead she thrashed and bucked, her form beginning to blur. Mazael levered himself up, and as he did, Morebeth shuddered back into human shape.

The back of her neck was a bloody pulp, and blood dripped from a gaping wound between her breasts. The strange rune had been burned into her right thigh and lower back, the flesh scorched down to the bone. She looked dazed, and stunned, and in mortal agony.

Then her eyes fell on him, and filled with such hatred that Mazael flinched. She staggered towards him, her lips peeled back in a snarl, her hands twisted into claws.

Then her eyes dimmed and she crumpled to the floor, dead.

Lion's flame dimmed and went out.

Mazael stared down at her, grief and exhaustion churning through him. She had been his half-sister, his lover. She had tried to kill Rachel, slaughtered thousands, and done her best to transform him into a monster. And yet...and yet...she had made his blood burn as it never had before. If she rose up now, offered to give herself to him again...he did not know if he had the strength to refuse.

A boot scraped against the stones.

Lucan hobbled towards him, face pasty, black hair plastered with sweat. He looked downright crazed. For an instant Mazael thought Lucan would attack him.

"You're alive," said Mazael.

"I..." said Lucan, his eyes wandering. His gaze settled on Morebeth's corpse. "Is...is it over?" He sounded younger than Mazael had ever heard him.

"Yes," said Mazael. "It's..."

Morebeth's corpse shuddered. Lucan gasped and raised his hand. Mazael's fingers tightened around Lion's hilt as Morebeth's belly bulged and distended

The child, the Demonsouled creature in her womb, was trying to claw its way free.

With a yell of horror and disgust Mazael slammed Lion down. The blade flamed to life once more, azure fire pouring into Morebeth's cooling flesh.

The child, the unborn Destroyer, went still. Mazael yanked Lion free.

"Now," he said, not bothering to blink back the tears, "now it is over."

CHAPTER 28
HALL OF TRIUMPHS

On the day of the wedding, Mazael walked alone through the Arcade of Sorrows, his heavy cloak rustling against the floor. His tunic itched, and his new boots did not grip his feet well. Mazael walked into Audea's Garden, past the grasses and the fresh-blooming flowers, and leaned against the stone rail. He watched the hazy dawn sunlight glimmer through the valley, the Riversteel glinting like a silver ribbon. A small cluster of tents stood near the barbican; Sir Tobias's and Sir Gerald's knights, back from the ongoing conquest of Mastaria.

Mazael was so tired. He was tired of Knightcastle, tired of the endless intrigue of the court, tired of the war.

Silk rustled whispered against the grass.

Mazael turned and saw Rachel standing, brilliant in her white bridal gown.

"Rachel," said Mazael.

She hiked the voluminous lengths of her skirts and crossed the grass to his side.

"I thought," Mazael said, "that the bride was supposed to remain in seclusion until the wedding."

"It is a tradition, aye," said Rachel, "but just a tradition. Besides, it's not as if I've crept out to see Gerald."

Mazael shook his head. "The poor fool's terrified. In the past month he's survived assassins, the second battle of Tumblestone, and half a hundred minor skirmishes. Now ask him to stand before the archbishop of Knightrealm and wed a woman, and his courage turns to mush. I'd get him drunk, if he didn't think it ungodly."

"Mazael," said Rachel, looking at the railing. "I'm...I'm sorry about

296

Lady Morebeth."

Mazael touched her shoulder. "I know."

Both Morebeth Galbraith and Trocend Castleson had been assassinated by a San-keth, or so everyone in Knightcastle believed. Mazael had discovered the assassin an instant too late, but avenged Morebeth's and Trocend's deaths.

No one wondered why the body of the San-keth assassin had arms and legs. Harune Dustfoot had been a loyal friend and ally, and Mazael regretted the need to lie about him, even in death. It pained Mazael to see Harune's body hanging from a pike over Knightcastle's gates.

But Harune, who had dedicated his life to the secret war against the San-keth, would have understood.

"It's not fair," said Rachel. "You loved Romaria and she died. And then you loved Morebeth and she was killed..."

"I didn't love her," said Mazael. What he felt for Morebeth had been something rawer than lust, more elemental than love. The mad power in her Demonsouled spirit had called to the same fire within him. But he could tell none of this to Rachel, and the that made him even wearier. Morebeth, despite her madness, had understood him very well.

But she was gone.

"I didn't love her," said Mazael quietly. "But it would have been a good marriage."

Rachel looked away. "Did Gerald tell you yet?"

Tell me what?" said Mazael.

"That we're...,that he's going to leave your service after the wedding, that we're going to stay at Knightcastle," said Rachel, the words tumbling out in a rush.

"Yes," said Mazael, "he told me." In fact, it had been partly Mazael's idea. With both Sir Garain and Trocend dead, Lord Malden needed new advisors. He needed Gerald. "It's time, I think, for Gerald to come home. And you should enjoy living at Knightcastle."

Rachel hesitated. "I wish I could come back home with you."

"No," said Mazael. "You don't, not really." Castle Cravenlock held nothing but black memories for Rachel. There she had been dominated by cruel Lord Mitor, there she had fallen into despair until she drifted into the serpent cult and pledged herself to a San-keth cleric. Perhaps at Knightcastle, she could begin anew, and be happy.

"No," said Rachel. "I suppose I don't. But I will miss you, Mazael."

"I know," said Mazael. "And I will miss you."

He looked down at her smiling face with its green eyes. He had wanted her to wed Gerald, wanted that marriage as a shield between Lord Richard and Lord Malden. How many had died to bring this day about? How many sons, husbands, and brothers lay dead on the fields outside Tumblestone, never to return to their mothers and wives and sisters?

But if Morebeth had worked her will, had made Mazael into her hawk, then uncounted millions would have perished. Things had been bad, but they could have been far worse.

And that, Mazael supposed, was the only comfort he could draw.

That, and seeing Rachel happier than he could ever remember.

Someone called out. Mazael saw a half-dozen women hurrying down the Arcade of Sorrows, skirts flapping around their legs.

"It seems," said Mazael, "that your maids have discovered your escape."

"Bother," said Rachel. "I'll see you at the wedding?"

"You will," said Mazael.

"I love you," said Rachel.

"And I love you," Mazael echoed.

The maids gathered around Rachel like a flock of clucking birds and led her away.

Rachel Cravenlock wed Gerald Roland in the Hall of Triumphs, before a throng of lords and knights.

Mazael walked down the length of the Hall, Rachel on his arm, a pair of noblewomen carrying the long train of her gown. He stopped before the altar, bowed, and placed Rachel's hand in Gerald's. The archbishop of Knightrealm began droning into the ceremony. Mazael walked to Lord Malden's side.

Lord Malden leaned heavily on his cane, his face haggard and his eyes bloodshot. In the last month he had lost both his eldest son and his closest advisor. Both losses had taken their toll on the once-vigorous old man. Mazael wondered if the old lord would live out the year, if Sir Tobias might become Lord Tobias within a few months.

Mazael's eyes wandered, and he saw the Old Demon.

His father stood beside one of the columns, wrapped in his black robes, his shape ghostly and translucent. No one else seemed to see him. He looked at Mazael, and the fury in his red-glazed eyes washed over Mazael like a wave of acid.

His voice hammered into Mazael's thoughts like a hammer of glass.

Do you think yourself triumphant?

The hellish red light in his eyes brightened. The archbishop kept droning. Gerald and Rachel smiled at each other, holding hands.

Do you think yourself victorious? The Old Demon stepped towards Mazael. *You have slain two of my children. There are others. There are many others. One of them will become the Destroyer, and I will seize his destiny for my own and destroy you. His lips pulled back, revealing fangs both jagged and yellowed. I have forces at my command that you can neither understand nor resist. Throw yourself down and die, foolish boy. Struggle as you will, but in the end, I will have you.*

For a moment Mazael saw the futility of his life, the endless succession of battles against Demonsouled and San-keth that would lead to nothing but death and ruin. Sooner or later one or another would take his life...

Then he laughed, quietly, drawing an annoyed glance from the archbishop.

That was what the Old Demon wanted him to think, was it not?

Mazael focused and found that he could speak to the Old Demon in the same way the Old Demon had spoken to him.

I don't care. The Old Demon's snarl tightened. *I denied you once before, and I deny you now.* Something like white fire, bright and pure, rose up in Mazael's mind. *So come here before me, and we'll settle this, once and for all!*

The Old Demon's eyes blazed like orbs of hellfire. *I will crush you!*

Mazael let his hand fall to Lion's hilt. *Then come and crush me, father.*

The Old Demon snarled once more. For a moment he loomed like a vast shadow, wings rising up against the vaulted arches, a mountain of darkness that would fall and crush Mazael.

Then he vanished and did not return.

Mazael stood, and watched Rachel leave his family and become Gerald's wife.

###

Days later, after the celebration and feasting had finished, Mazael walked at dawn to the stables near Oliver's Keep. Mantle waited for him there, along with three new destriers, gifts from Lord Malden. None of them were as good as Chariot, but perhaps they would grow better, in time.

Sir Adalar waited for him at the stables, leading out Mantle and the destriers. All four horses had been prepared for travel.

Adalar bowed. "Lord Mazael."

Mazael smiled. "Sir Adalar." He walked over, gripped the young knight's shoulder. "You're not my squire any more."

Adalar shrugged. "No one else would have done it properly."

Mazael laughed.

Adalar straightened up. "My lord...I'm not going back to Castle Cravenlock."

"I know," said Mazael.

"You did?"

Mazael nodded. "I heard Tobias and Gerald talking about it."

"Sir Gerald offered to let me ride with him when he returns to the Mastarian campaign," said Adalar. "We've already taken the northern third of the country and Castle Dominus itself." Adalar shook his head. "The Dominiar Order has collapsed. What's left of their commanders are warring amongst themselves. And the people are glad to see us. Lord Malden is not a lenient lord, but he's still kinder than the Dominiars." He shrugged. "Though the Mastarians do not like the Justiciars very much. Amalric Galbraith and the Dominiars betrayed me badly. I...would like to see this through to the end, my lord."

"Plus there are lands and castles a bold young man can claim for himself, eh?" said Mazael.

Adalar nodded.

"Good luck," said Mazael. "Find yourself a castle and a good woman."

Adalar sighed. "A good woman. I always thought a true knight slept only with his lady. And I thought Amalric a true knight. Maybe...you have the right of it, my lord. Maybe I was wrong."

"No," said Mazael, swinging up into Mantle's saddle. "No. Do not betray yourself, Adalar. You're going to be a lord yet, I think. And there are far too many corrupt lords and false knights."

"Thank you," said Adalar. Mazael nodded and urged Mantle to a walk, leading two of the destriers behind him.

"My lord!" said Adalar. "Your third horse?"

"My horse?" said Mazael, glancing back. "That's yours, sir knight. Ride him well."

"Thank you, my lord!" said Adalar, grinning.

Mazael grinned back and rode off.

###

His knights waited for him at the barbican. Sir Aulus sat at their head, the Cravenlock banner dangling from his lance. He looked distraught at the prospect of returning home to his wife. Timothy leaned back in his saddle, yawning. The rest of the knights seemed eager to be off.

A single horseman, wrapped in a dark cloak, turned to face Mazael. None of the others paid attention to him.

"You appear grieved," said Lucan. He looked to have aged ten years since the battle in the chapel, though his sardonic matter had reasserted itself. Mazael wondered what manner of dire spell had permitted him to survive Morebeth's killing blow.

"Perhaps I am," said Mazael. "Why should I not be? I came to Knightcastle with my sister, my armsmaster, and my squire. I expected to ride home in the company of my new wife. Now I am going home without any of them. I've every right to be grieved."

"You're alive, aren't you?" said Lucan.

Mazael nodded.

"And a dark power has been destroyed," said Lucan.

"One dark power," said Mazael. "And there are many, many more."

"Then you still need my help, do you not?" said Lucan.

"I would have died a dozen times in the last four months without your help," said Mazael. "I still need your aid."

They gripped hands briefly.

"A mad necromancer and a child of the Old Demon allied against the powers of darkness," murmured Lucan. "Who would have thought it?"

"Who indeed?" said Mazael, riding to the head of his men. He looked out the opened gate, towards the road home.

He had never thought he would look forward to seeing the grim towers of Castle Cravenlock.

"Let's go home," said Mazael, urging Mantle forward.

They rode out the gate and left Knightcastle behind.

THE END

Thank you for reading "Soul of Tyrants". Turn the page for the first chapter of Mazael's next adventure! To receive immediate notification of new releases, sign up for my newsletter at http://www.jonathanmoeller.com.

SOUL OF SERPENTS BONUS CHAPTER
CHAPTER 1 - WARBAND

Mazael Cravenlock awoke from a dream of a great black wolf.

For a moment the wolf's howls echoed in his ears.

He sat up in bed, blinking.

Yet the howls continued.

Those weren't howls, he realized, but a blast from the horns carried by the night guards upon the castle's walls.

Castle Cravenlock was under attack.

Mazael surged to his feet, and his bedroom door burst open. A boy of twelve years stood in the doorway, clad in the black-and-silvery livery of the Cravenlocks. Usually the boy wore an expression of chilly arrogance, but now his eyes bulged with fear.

"My lord," said Rufus Highgate, "my lord, the sentries..."

"I know," said Mazael. "Find one of the pages, send him to Sir Hagen. Tell Hagen to rouse the garrison. Then get back here and assist with my armor. Go!"

Rufus sprinted off. Mazael paced around his bed, bare feet sinking into the carpet. His rooms atop the King's Tower held only a bed, a desk for writing, a wardrobe for his clothing, and racks for his armor and weapons. A thick carpet to guard against the winter chill was the only concession to comfort.

That, and the rooms had a superb view of the castle and the surrounding countryside.

Mazael hurried onto the balcony, seventy feet above the courtyard. The night guards stood upon the curtain wall, crossbows in their hands. Torchlight blazed in the courtyard as men raced back and forth. Sergeants bellowed commands to armsmen, while knights ran for the stables, followed by their squires. Good - Sir Hagen had already roused the garrison. Yet where was the attack?

Beyond the curtain wall, light flashed in the darkness. Cravenlock Town, an overgrown village of four thousand people, stood a half-mile in that direction. Mazael saw firelight from the town, and heard the distant sound of steel on steel, the shouts and screams of men and women.

The town was under attack.

His hands curled into fists. These were his people, his lands. And someone dared to attack them? He would make these attackers pay, he would make them suffer...

Mazael closed his eyes, forced himself to calm.

Fury was not a luxury that a child of the Old Demon could afford.

For a moment he remembered a blue-eyed woman lying on a cold stone floor, black hair pooled around her head.

He knew where the rage of the Demonsouled ended.

Rufus sprinted into the room, breathing hard.

"My lord," he said, "I've sent the message..."

"Good," said. "Help me with my armor."

He'd worn the same armor for years, but it had been destroyed last year during the great battle below the walls of Tumblestone. So Lord Malden had made Mazael a gift of a new set. A chain mail hauberk with a steel cuirass, and gauntlets backed with steel plates and armored boots, all crafted by Knightcastle's finest smiths. Mazael pulled on the armor with Rufus's help. The boy was nervous, but he worked quickly and without error. That was good. He would make a capable knight.

Assuming he lived through this attack.

Mazael tugged on a black surcoat adored with the sigil of three crossed swords, the symbol of the Cravenlocks. Rufus fetched his sword belt, and Mazael buckled it around his waist. A dagger hung on his left hip, and a longsword on his right. The longsword's pommel was a golden's lion head, glittering rubies in its eyes. Lion, Mazael called the sword, and it was worth more than his castle and everything in it.

Older than his castle, too.

He took one last thing. A silver coin, the size of his thumb joint, threaded with a fine chain. Mazael tucked it into his belt.

"Come," said Mazael, and he left his rooms, Rufus following, and hurried from the King's Tower. Chaos still reined in the courtyard, but it was an ordered chaos. Mazael's knights sat atop their horses, lances and shields in hand, armor flashing in the torchlight. His armsmen had also been mounted, sword and mace ready at their belts.

Two hundred men. Mazael hoped it was enough.

"My lord!"

A grim-faced man with the shoulders and chest of an ox strode to

Mazael's side. He wore a Cravenlock surcoat and a mail hauberk, eyes glinting over a close-cropped black beard. One hand rested on his sword hilt, and the other bore a shield adorned with the sigil of a burning bridge.

"Sir Hagen," said Mazael. "What news?"

"Someone lit the alarm beacon in the town's church tower," said Sir Hagen Bridgebane, Mazael's armsmaster. "The night guards saw it and summoned me." He scowled, shaking his head. "It's too dark. We can't see anything. But I think the town militia is holding. For now."

"Who is attacking?" said Mazael. "Bandits?" It would indeed take a daring band of bandits to attack a walled town. But who else? The Elderborn tribes? One of Mazael's vassals? Some of Mazael's knights and vassals hated him, but none were bold enough to stage such a raid.

Lord Richard Mandragon, perhaps? Mazael remained in his liege lord's good graces. But Lord Richard the Dragonslayer was feared with reason. If he decided that Mazael was an enemy, he would not hesitate to strike.

"I don't know, my lord," said Hagen. "But they've no horses, I'm sure of that. We're ready to ride when you give the command." He grimaced. "But the wizards want to speak with you first."

"Good work," said Mazael. "We'll ride when I give the word. Leave the squires here. I don't want any of them killed fighting in the dark."

Hagen hurried to his horse, shouting commands.

Rufus brought out Mazael's war horse, a vicious-tempered destrier named Challenger. The huge horse looked as eager for blood as any knight. Mazael swung into the saddle and accepted a lance and a shield marked with the Cravenlock sigil from Rufus.

"I should accompany you, my lord," said Rufus. "It is only honorable."

"No," said Mazael. "Stay here with the other squires. I'll not explain to your father why I got you killed in a night battle."

Rufus scowled, but obeyed. Mazael urged Challenger to a walk, steering the beast with his knees. Sir Hagen waited near the barbican, along with three other men. The first was old and tough as an ancient oak tree, clad in mail and leather. The hilt of a greatsword jutted over his shoulder, and a mace and war axe waited at his belt. Sir Nathan Greatheart claimed to have retired, but the old knight still fought with the prowess of a much younger man.

The other two men wore black cloaks and long black coats adorned with metal badges. The older of the two was nearing forty, with tousled hair and a pointed brown beard. The second was barely over twenty, face shadowed beneath his cowl. A black metal staff rested across his saddle's pommel.

None of Mazael's men went close to the two wizards. Especially the younger one.

"Lord Mazael," said Timothy deBlanc, the older wizard. "My war spells are at your command."

The younger wizard looked up, black eyes glittering in the depths of his cowl.

"And you'll need them," said Lucan Mandragon. He was younger than Timothy, but far more powerful. Men called him the Dragon's Shadow, and dared not meet his eye as he passed. "My wards were triggered. At least one of the attackers is using magic. Possibly more."

"Can you take them?" said Mazael.

"We shall do our best, my lord," said Timothy.

Lucan's contemptuous sneer expressed more confidence than words.

"Good," said Mazael. "Sir Hagen!"

The armsmaster spurred his destrier forward, lance and shield ready. "My lord?"

"Tell the armsmen to keep watch," said Mazael. "They're to close the gate after we leave, and leave it closed until we return. The knights and mounted armsmen will stay in formation. Any fool rides off on his own, I'll have his hide." Hagen nodded and bellowed the orders to the sergeants. "Sir Nathan!"

The old knight turned his horse. "Lord?"

"Take command of the knights," said Mazael.

Nathan frowned. "I am no longer armsmaster of Castle Cravenlock, and I..."

"Yes, yes, I know," said Mazael. "Do it anyway."

A flicker of a smile went over Nathan's seamed face. "As you bid, my lord."

"Sir Hagen!" said Mazael. "We ride."

Hagen gave the orders. Chains rattled, and the portcullis slid open with a metallic groan. Mazael kicked Challenger to a trot and rode through the gate, the knights and armsmen falling in around him. Sir Aulus Hirdan, Mazael's herald, rose at his side, the Cravenlock banner fluttering from his lance. Though Mazael doubted anyone could see it in the dark.

The road to Cravenlock Town sloped alongside the side of the castle's crag. The sounds of fighting grew closer, accompanied by strange, bestial roars. Had the attackers brought war dogs? Timothy shifted in his saddle, fumbling with a fist-sized chunk of wired-wrapped crystal. Mazael had seen him use that spell before. It bestowed a sort of limited clairvoyance, letting Timothy sense the presence of enemies. Timothy held up his hand, and the crystal flashed with a pale white light.

"Timothy!" said Mazael. "How many?"

"I...I do not know, my lord," said Timothy, shouting over the drumming of the hooves. His eyes darted back and forth, tracking things unseen. "At least...two hundred. Probably three hundred. They're at the town gates for now. But...my lord..."

"What is it?" said Mazael. "Are they in the town already?" Gods, he hoped not. House to house fighting would negate the advantage of his horsemen.

"No," said Timothy. "But…I've never sensed anything like them before. It's as if…it's as if they're not human…"

Lucan gave Timothy a sharp look, hand tightening around his black staff.

"The San-keth?" said Mazael. "Or the changelings?"

"No," said Timothy. "No, I know how they feel to my arcane senses. This is…different. Darker, considerably."

Demonsouled, then? The thought of three hundred Demonsouled gathered made Mazael's blood run cold. But Mazael doubted that any number of Demonsouled could cooperate for any length of time.

He knew very well the sort of homicidal madness carried by Demonsouled blood.

"Whatever they are," said Mazael, "they're still flesh and blood, and we'll sweep them away. They're massed near the town gates?"

Timothy gave a sharp nod, eyes still twitching.

"Then we'll hit them there," said Mazael. "Sir Hagen! Get the men in line. Once the enemy is in sight, we'll charge and ride them down." With luck, the gate held the attackers' attention, and they would not spot Mazael's horsemen until it was too late.

Hagen and Nathan bellowed orders, the knights and armsmen forming a wide line. The horses moved forward at a trot, ready to leap into a gallop. Cravenlock Town came into sight, the rooftops rising above the thick stone wall surrounding the town. Lord Mitor, Mazael's predecessor and elder brother, had let the wall fall into disrepair. Mazael had ordered it rebuilt, despite the expense. He also insisted that the town men's form a militia, training regularly, despite their grumbling.

He doubted anyone would grumble after this.

Torches blazed atop the stone wall. Militiamen fought from the ramparts, wielding crossbows and spears. A dozen ladders rested against the wall, and Mazael saw dark-armored shapes scrambling up the rungs, spears and axes in hand.

The invaders.

Mazael took a look at them, a good look, and blinked in disbelief.

The invaders were not bandits. Nor were they were Mazael's vassals, or Lord Richard's men.

They weren't even human.

Mazael had never seen creatures like them before.

They looked almost like men, albeit men with leathery gray skin and long, pointed ears. Their eyes were colorless, milky white, yet they seemed to have no difficulty seeing. The creatures wore greasy leathers, ragged furs, and black chain mail. Dozens of them lay dead below the gate, covered in black blood. Yet the creatures showed neither fear nor pain, and flung themselves at the defenders with abandon, roaring and howling like beasts.

Lucan swore, very softly.

"What are they?" said Mazael.

"I had never thought to see them," said Lucan.

"Damn it, what are they?" said Mazael.

Lucan looked at Mazael, his eyes reflecting the firelight. "Malrags."

"Malrags?" said Mazael. "Malrags are a legend, like..."

"Like the Elderborn?" said Lucan. "Like the San-keth?"

Mazael growled. "Legend or not, they are still flesh and blood. Sir Hagen! Sir Aulus! Sound the charge..."

The air crackled, and a bolt of green lighting screamed out of the cloudless sky, so bright that it filled the plains with ghostly light. It struck the arch over the gates with terrific force, blasting stone and wood to glowing shreds. Smoking debris rained over the Malrags and the town militia alike, knocking them to the ground, and the horses whinnied and stamped in terror.

For a moment the battlefield remained motionless, the echoes from the lightning blast rumbling into silence.

Then the Malrags raced for the ruined gate.

"The charge!" said Mazael, raising his lance. "Now!"

Sir Aulus lifted a horn to his lips and loosed a long blast, a thunder of a different sort rolling over the plain. Mazael put his boots to Challenger's sides, and the big horse surged forward with an excited snort. Behind him the knights' and armsmen's horses exploded into motion, the earth rumbling beneath steel-shod hooves.

The Malrags near the gate turned, forming a line of spears, but it was too late. Mazael caught a brief glimpse of a Malrag at the forefront of the mob. The hands gripping the spear had six fingers, black veins throbbing and pulsing beneath the leathery gray skin. Then the Malrag disappeared beneath Challenger's hooves in a flash of black blood, even as Mazael drove his war lance through the face of another Malrag. He ripped the lance free and struck again as Challenger thundered forward, the horsemen crashing into the Malrags. Horses screamed and stamped, men shouted, and the Malrags bellowed their battle cries.

Mazael stabbed his lance into a Malrag, the heavy blade crunching past armor and sinking into the creature's neck. Yet the Malrag showed no fear, no sign of pain, even pulling itself up the shaft to claw at Mazael's arm. Mazael plunged the lance into the creature's chest again, and the Malrag toppled, wrenching the weapon from Mazael's hand.

Challenger galloped through the Malrag mob, breaking free on the other side. Mazael wheeled the big horse around, drawing Lion from its scabbard with a metallic hiss. The ancient steel blade glimmered in the torchlight, seeming to flash and flicker.

And then Lion jolted in Mazael's hand. Power flowed up Mazael's arm, and the light reflecting in the sword's blade turned blue. A halo of sapphire radiance crackled around the sword, and then the blade burst into raging azure flame. Lion had been forged long ago by the great wizard-smiths of ancient Tristafel, created to destroy things of dark magic.

It seemed that the Malrags, whatever else they were, were also creatures of dark magic.

Mazael shouted, kicked Challenger into motion, and rode back into the fray, striking right and left. The Malrags had shown no fear of steel weapons, even of wounds and death, yet they flinched away from Lion's raging blue flame. Mazael struck the arm from one Malrag, and the head from another, Lion blazing like an inferno in his fist. The Malrags reeled back, and Mazael's knights and armsmen fell upon them.

The enemy broke and ran. The creatures did care about pain or injury, but they feared Lion's flame, and Mazael's men were more numerous and better armed. Dozens of Malrags sprinted into the darkness around the town. But others raced through the ruined gate, vanishing into the streets of the town.

Damnation. They could go from house to house, killing. Or hide themselves in the cellars and attics to attack later. For that matter, the ones fleeing from the town could band together and raid some of the smaller villages.

"Sir Hagen!" said Mazael. Hagen rode to Mazael's side, his sword and armor splattered with black Malrag blood. "Take seventy men. Hunt down as many of those devils as you can. I'll deal with things here." Hagen nodded. "Sir Nathan!" The old knight turned, greatsword in one hand. How he managed to use such a massive sword so effectively from horseback, Mazael had no idea. "Get the rest of the men together. We'll have to go from street to street, finish off the Malrags."

Sir Nathan shouted the commands, and Lucan rode to Mazael's side, that strange black staff laid across his saddle.

"My lord," said Lucan. "Listen to me. I've read the ancient records. Every Malrag warband has two leaders. A shaman, a spell caster. Probably the one that cast that lightning bolt upon the gate. And a chieftain, a war leader...a 'balekhan', in the Malrag tongue. The Malrags will not give up until both of them are dead."

"Then we'll simply have to kill them both," said Mazael. "You and Timothy can deal with the shaman, I trust?"

Lucan sneered. "Please."

Mazael turned Challenger toward the ruined gates. He rode into the town, his men following after. Some of the militiamen hurried from the walls, while Mazael ordered others to stand guard over the ruined gates. Hooves rang against the cobblestones, but Mazael saw no sign of any Malrags. Where had they all gone? At least a hundred had made their way into the town.

He heard the sounds of fighting coming from the town square. The square held two large buildings. The Three Swords Inn, four stories of mortared stone and trimmed beams. And the town's church, a massive domed structure, dating from the old kingdom of Dracaryl. When the town was under attack, the women and children fled to the church...

The women and children.

The sounds of fighting grew louder.

Mazael cursed and kicked Challenger to a gallop, his knights and armsmen following.

ABOUT THE AUTHOR

Standing over six feet tall, Jonathan Moeller has the piercing blue eyes of a Conan of Cimmeria, the bronze-colored hair a Visigothic warrior-king, and the stern visage of a captain of men, none of which are useful in his career as a computer repairman, alas.He has written the DEMONSOULED series of sword-and-sorcery novels, the TOWER OF ENDLESS WORLDS urban fantasy series, THE GHOSTS series about assassin and spy Caina Amalas, the COMPUTER BEGINNER'S GUIDE sequence of computer books, and numerous other works. Visit his website at: http://www.jonathanmoeller.com

Printed in Great Britain
by Amazon